Speak The Ocean

Speak The Ocean, Volume 1

Rebecca Enzor

Published by Rebecca Enzor, 2024.

Also by Rebecca Enzor

Speak The Ocean
Speak The Ocean
See The Depths
Seek The Shore

Watch for more at rebeccaenzor.com.

For Tilikum
I hope you found peace
And for Tokitae
I hope you found home

<u>Oceanica Training Manual</u>
16: IN WATER RESCUE

16.1 It is imperative that all personnel remain at least three (3) feet from water at all times, with the exception of personnel responsible for certain duties (electroshocker use, veterinary diagnoses, net use, etc.). If personnel need to work near water with Mer inside (veterinary, euthanasia, etc.), at least four (4) employees approved to work with Mer must be present, water should be cooled to 65°F and appropriate sedatives added, if necessary.

16.2 In the event of an employee falling into water with a Mer, the following procedures should be enacted immediately:

16.2.1 One (1) person calls SAFETY at x5523

16.2.2 Person closest to electroshocker should place it in the water to get Mer's attention. If no reaction from Mer and victim's head is above water, employ shock for two (2) seconds. If victim's head is below water, employ shock for one (1) second.

16.2.3 One (1) person should keep Mer in direct line of vision at all times and report movements to others.

16.2.4 Two (2) personnel should try to position a net between Mer and victim.

16.2.5 Once net is in place, a responsive/unharmed victim can swim to closest edge. If victim is unresponsive or injured, shepherd's hook may be used to drag to edge of pool.

UNDER NO CIRCUMSTANCES SHOULD ANOTHER PERSON ENTER THE POOL.

16.2.6 If net cannot be placed between Mer and victim: use electroshocker liberally and start resuscitation procedures immediately following retrieval of victim. Cover with towels to prevent hypothermia.

Corporate tells the public the mermaids aren't dangerous, but that's a lie. They killed another trainer last night, and now it's my job to euthanize the offending mermaid—or in this case, merman.

I tap bubbles out of the pink euthanasia fluid, cap the syringe, and set it on the bench before changing into my wetsuit. Next to me, Sergio de la Cruz zips his wetsuit over his small frame and claps me on the shoulder. "Ready, Finn?"

Hooking the syringe to a loop on my wetsuit, I take a deep breath, then shake the tension from my shoulders. I don't want to do this again.

"You're looking a little nervous there, bro."

"Bismuth's a big boy." Science geeks to the core, we name the Mer after periodic table elements. "And he's got the twins in the tank with him. Plenty could go wrong."

Plenty is already wrong. There have been six trainer deaths since we opened, which means, I've euthanized six Mer in four years. We've only known the Mer existed for six years, and I've already killed one a year.

Serge bumps my locker door closed, and we make our way through the gray concrete halls of Oceanica to the practice tank that contains the three Mer. "They've been chilled. You'll be fine."

Reflected shadows quiver along the walls and condensation runs down the sides of the tank as we enter the practice room. Filters hidden in the walls hum, and water gurgles where it enters the tank. Madison and Natalie wait for us at the bottom of the stairs, wetsuits on, eyes red-rimmed from a sleepless night mourning a friend.

The four of us ascend the metal stairs to the platform around the tank. The practice tank isn't the largest at Oceanica, but it's big. Nearly a million gallons—one fifth the size of the tanks used for orcas. Bismuth floats near the bottom, dark green scales against the bleary gray surroundings. His indigo eyes are wider than normal, sharp and intelligent, not the dead-eyed expression I'm used to. He was in the tank the last time we euthanized a Mer for attacking a trainer. Watching deters some of them, but others get pissed and want to kill us. Like Bismuth.

Hopefully, watching Bismuth foam will discourage the twins. Fluorine and Chlorine are impossible to tell apart, with their ice-blue hair and eyes. They have the second most popular show at Oceanica, and after I finish with Bismuth, we'll have to go hunting for a new male to perform with them.

A net hangs over the side of the tank, a metal shepherd's hook nearby. I cringe as nausea creeps through my stomach. That's how they retrieved Craig's body. Serge got the call from Oceanica while we were at the bar. Craig was supposed to join us after his training session with Bismuth and the twins.

Madison stares at the hook like she's imagining what happened, and I squeeze her arm as I pass to grab the net. "Let's get this over with."

"Yeah," she says, voice hollow.

Euthanizing a Mer isn't as easy as, say, a dog. For one, they're huge. With his tail, Bismuth's got a good two feet on me. They're also the perfect predator. Sharp teeth, sharper claws, more agile than a shark. And then there's the regulations. The Animal Plant Health Inspection Service has a strict set of rules regarding Mer husbandry, including euthanization. The Occupational Safety and Health Administration has even stricter rules regarding trainer safety.

Sergio grabs a long pole with an aluminum loop on one end from the wall. The electroshocker will send a current into the water, stunning the Mer. Natalie and Madison help me get the crane ready for the net. It's almost too heavy for me to cast, which is why the electroshocker comes in handy. I couldn't catch a Mer if they were swimming.

"Hit 'em," I say when I'm ready.

Sergio presses the button and all three of the Mer freeze, muscles contracting as lactic acid floods their systems, making them float to the surface. The way it works is kind of cool, despite the seriousness of the situation. With an expert flick of my wrist, the net soars over the water and the weights drop around Bismuth. I yank on the line to close the bottom, then unwind it from my arm and hook it to the crane.

"Cut it."

Serge removes the shocker from the water. Natalie starts the crane and Bismuth thrashes, trying to get out. The twins swim in agitated circles, like sharks, as he's lifted from the water, and the crane brings him to the side where Madison and I stand. I wipe my sweaty hands on my wetsuit and grab a climbing hook attached to a rope. Bismuth's webbed fingers reach through the netting, trying to sink his sharp claws into us. With a deep breath, I dart in, clip the hook to the net, and duck away before he can grab me.

"Maddy!" I snap when she doesn't move with the hook. "Pay attention, or you'll end up like Craig."

"Sorry," she mumbles and hooks the net.

I tie my line around a dock cleat and check that Maddy's doing the same before I lift the syringe from the strap on my waist. I pull the cap off with my teeth and stab it in Bismuth's neck, below his gills. Ten CC's of pink juice floods his system.

The reaction starts in his gills, turning the tissue to foam. In a matter of seconds, his head boils away and foam moves down his chest, even as his tail twitches with muscle spasms. It's disturbing to watch the first couple of times, but the four of us are used to it now.

When Mer die, nothing remains. No scales, no hair, no skeleton. It all turns to seafoam. It's one of the reasons it took so long to find them—they don't leave bodies behind. The only thing to prove that Bismuth existed will be the video footage of his performances.

The hiss of a line unraveling grabs my attention from the net. Maddy jumps to grab the rope. "Shit!"

Bismuth's tail spasms and the net spins toward me. I try to move out of the way, slip on the puddle of foam he's created, and slam my knee on the metal platform. Pain roars through my leg. My hands fly into the air before I realize there's nothing to grab, and I fall headfirst into the tank.

Saltwater shoots up my nose. Bubbles burst from my mouth. When they clear, a pair of ice-blue, Area-51 eyes surrounded by bright green scales stare back. I try to kick for the surface, but one of the twin's claws sink into my leg, holding me under. Adrenaline rushes through my veins, hot in my stomach, as the other twin pierces my shoulders with her claws.

I'm going to die.

I grab the gills in her neck, the rakers cutting into my fingertips, and rip them. She screams in pain—the sound oddly clear in the water—and releases me as blood blooms around us. The twin with the claws in my leg yanks me further down. I gasp. Cold, coppery water rushes into my throat and lungs.

A thousand volts slam into my face, and the world goes dark.

• • • •

MY SHOULDERS STILL ache where Flo or Chlo—I'm not sure which—pierced them three days ago. I limp through the front door of the house Serge and I rent in Key West, and head straight for the kitchen to cut the hospital bracelet from my wrist. Mom wanted me to stay with her for a couple days, "just in case," but I can't stand her worried gaze. It's been ever-present since Dad disappeared, looking for proof of the Mer, and she hates that I work with the beasts. She must have shit a brick when the medical center called to say I was attacked.

I was comatose for two days from the blood loss and electrocution. The rubber-based wetsuit—and Sergio's quick thinking with the electroshocker—saved my life. I pull my shirt over my head and peel the tape from the top of one bandage to check on the wounds. A single, neat stitch is threaded through each of the punctures where the claws sank in.

Sergio walks out of his bedroom. "I thought you'd be staying at your mom's tonight."

"And let my little sister make fun of me for getting my ass kicked by a couple of girls?"

He eyes me. "Dude, don't joke about it."

"Calm down. I'm fine." I toss him a beer from the fridge and grab one for myself. "The stitches come out in a week. The claw marks will scar, but how badass is it to have mermaid scars?"

Sergio snorts. "'I survived a Mer attack' has to be an even better pickup line than 'I work with mermaids.' And that one never fails." He grins, then takes a swig of beer. "You up for hitting Duval?"

"Maybe tonight. I'm heading out to the reef for a few hours."

"The reef?" Sergio's eyes sharpen. "You nearly drowned three days ago."

"But I didn't." I take a pull of beer, using the motion to hide the slight shaking of my hands. "Nothing will hurt me at the reef. No Mer there. At least, not during the day." And I *need* to swim. I need to get into the ocean; let it wash away the memory of those ice-blue eyes, the shrill scream.

Serge shakes his head. "I'm coming with you."

I choke on the beer as it goes down the wrong pipe. "On a boat? In the ocean? You?"

"Your mom will never forgive me if I let you go out by yourself today." He chugs his beer. "Grab a few more for the trip."

Wow. The attack rattled Serge even more than me. I grab my gear, and the rest of the six-pack, and we head to the dock. The boat's my father's—a twenty-five foot saltwater fishing boat they found washed up on one of the mangrove islands after he disappeared. My mother refuses to set foot in it, but unlike her, I have more memories of heading out to the reef to snorkel with my dad than I do of sleepless nights waiting for him to come home.

As soon as the waves rock gently beneath me, the shaking in my hands stops. Serge, however, turns a little green. I pull out of the harbor and into the channel between Key West and the mangrove islands. "What happened to the twins?"

He gulps beer and focuses on the boat controls, as if even the sight of the water around us will send him over the edge, puking. "Foamed. You damaged Chlorine's gills so much she suffocated. Nat grabbed Fluorine with the metal hook while the shocker was on and electrocuted her." He runs a hand through his hair, making it stick up. "Christ, I'm glad it worked."

"Me too." If it hadn't, Flo could have pulled Nat in, too, and we'd both be dead. I try not to think about it, though, or the fact that I ripped a mermaid's throat out.

Or the fact that it's not the worst way I've ever killed a Mer.

I shudder. A whole act gone in a matter of minutes. We need to fish for at least two more Mer to replace Bismuth and the twins, and we'll need a new trainer to take over for Craig. I plan to be that trainer.

"Tell Aunt D I'll be back tomorrow." Sergio's Aunt Delmara is "Corporate." She was my father's teaching assistant before he disappeared, and I helped her document the existence of the first Mer when I was fifteen. I've been working with her ever since.

Serge's dark eyebrows pull together. "Aunt D will give you as much time as you need."

I gaze at the ocean as the boat jumps a swell. The salty wind blows my hair in my face, and the spray of the waves sprinkles my skin. This is all I need to recover.

As we pass Higg's Beach, I notice that the usual umbrellas and chairs have been replaced by flashing police lights and news vans. I slow as we pass to see what happened.

"Another drunk tourist," Sergio says, and takes a long drink. "All over the news this morning."

"Mer attack?"

"Yep. Last night."

No wonder Serge didn't want me going to the reef alone. But the Mer only attack at night. The locals know to stay out of the water after dark, but despite the yellow signs with their big red letters, the drunk tourists go skinny dipping anyway. Their bodies end up on the beach in the morning, torn to shreds.

I glance at Sergio, overwhelmed with gratitude again. If it weren't for him, I'd be as dead as that body on the beach. As dead as Craig.

Before long, the waves breaking over the reef come into view, and all of my jittery energy melts away. I drop anchor far enough out that I won't damage any corals, and pull on a wetsuit. The doctors said no swimming with stitches, but that's not going to keep me out of the ocean. When I first jump in and the water bubbles up around me, my heart races with panic, my electrocuted neurons expecting to see the ice-blue eyes of the twins. As I breathe the salty air through my snorkel—so different from the filtered air of Oceanica—my heart slows, and the panic abates.

The wind and waves and far-off boat motors disappear into the hum of something I can only describe as *ocean*. It's noisy with life. Unlike the brittle air above, the water fills my ears with the noise of being alive. If the folk stories were true, and humans could become Mer, I'd stay in the water forever. They're not, though, and becoming a trainer is the closest I can come to being a part of the ocean.

Chapter 2: Erie

Seashells march across the limestone floor in whirling designs that change daily. Black squid ink stains several of them, as if they've suffered an oil spill. My gaze darts between them, counting, organizing, and still I can't see the pattern.

When will the boats come next? Why are the landfolk hunting us?

The first black-stained shell is on the outer circle, close to being rotated out, though I doubt the king will let that happen. We'll be given a larger room before we're allowed to forget the queen's disappearance. He's certainly never forgotten. He refuses to look at me for the similarity of her features.

He'll never forgive the landfolk for taking my mother and leaving me behind.

I count the shells again, focusing on the spaces between the abductions. There must be an order to them. First Mother, then a long stretch—so long, we thought she'd been taken by a shark. Then another disappearance, just before the stormy season. A couple more in close succession. A lull—all shells devoid of ink for an entire stormy and calm season. Then several so close it looks like someone murdered a squid over one calm season's shells.

Now, they're so irregular that I can't discern a pattern.

I grab the last ink-stained shell and turn it over in my fingers. "Where are you, Clair? When will the landfolk hunt again?"

The shell that represents my sister's abduction remains silent. The boats could come today, or the next stormy season. I have no answers for the merfolk.

Water pressure shifts as someone enters the room, and a long tail tipped in bright blue winds around my own. A green-scaled arm wraps around my waist and blue hair mingles with my magenta as Huron's teeth nibble on the small scales below my gills.

A low chuckle escapes me. "How'd you get past Niku?"

"He's at the surface, breathing."

Every member of the royal family has a dolphin guard. Niku is mine.

"We could sneak out before he returns," Huron says. "Go hunting."

My stomach rumbles at the thought of fresh fish, even as my gaze picks out the darkened shells. Fear of the landfolk has kept us from hunting as much as we need to, and the fish we keep in the pens have been rationed.

"We should wait for Neek."

"You know he won't let you leave the Seadom. Besides"—Huron's tail caresses mine—"I plan to do more than hunt."

Hunting's safer, and easier, with Niku, but he won't turn a blind eye to my dalliances with Huron. If we want to have fun, we'll have to leave before my guard returns.

I try one last, pathetic excuse. "I'm working."

"The shells aren't going anywhere." Huron runs a finger down my dorsal fin and heat like a hydrothermal vent ignites at the base of my tail. All the worried thoughts about boats and ink-stained shells flee my mind, taking my voice with them. I swallow hard, then nod.

We swim through the back hallways to avoid Niku. Crustaceans and reef fish scuttle into their homes within the pocked limestone walls as we pass. It's illegal to eat the fish and crabs within the Seadom, but everyone's so hungry right now, it's best they hide.

Corals ring a little-used side door, soaking up the light that reaches these depths. The Seadom comes into view—a vast city of limestone and hard coral, with bridges over dense cold-water streams and towers of polyps reaching toward the surface. Beyond the city, a meadow of deep-water corals stretches, all pinks and purples and yellows. The bright colors stop abruptly at the dark shadow of the petrified forest. Dead, leafless trees surround the Seadom, protecting our haven from storms . . . and the landfolk.

At the outer edge of the forest, Huron inches out to check for dolphin guards, then grabs my hand. We swim as fast as we can into the dark blue of the deep water.

My senses fill with clear water and distant fish. The Seadom is cramped and busy, and Niku never leaves me alone, but out here, I can get lost in the expanse and watch my reflection in the surface when it's calm. My hair streams around me as I corkscrew through the water, feeling free for the first time since Clair was captured.

I stop as I think of her ink-stained shell and what must have happened to the missing 'folk. This is stupid, swimming in open water without Niku. Stupid and dangerous . . . but each kick of Huron's tailfin brushes my stomach, making it clench. I tug on his hand, stopping him.

His blue eyes, when he turns to me, are full of the same hunger that's burning in my core. My tail wraps around his. My hands slide down his back to caress his blue-tipped dorsal fin. He groans.

I run my nails through his hair—the bright blue of a juvenile emperor angelfish—and kiss him. He shudders and pulls me closer, his hands caressing the scales on my sides and stopping at my waist. His tongue slides between my lips, and I press against his lean body.

"Oh, Erie. It's been too long." One of his hands slides to my chest, and I lean back as he kisses my breasts.

It *has* been too long. I hum in contentment as his tail caresses mine. My stomach clenches again before I notice a change in the water. A low rumble has drowned out the constant noise of the ocean.

I unwind my tail and push away. "Do you hear that?"

"No." Huron reaches for me again, but I grab his hands.

"Listen."

The rumbling grows louder, until I can feel it in my scales. Huron's eyes widen. "That's a boat."

I can't tell which direction it's coming from—the sound envelops me with terror. I kick toward home, Huron right behind me. A shockwave crashes into us as a net hits the surface.

Huron screams. "Swim, Erie! Hurry!"

The edge of the net slams into the back of my tail, knocking the breath out of me and bearing me down to the ocean floor. The weights hit first and send a plume of sediment up, choking the water and raking across my gills.

"No," I gasp and dig my nails into the sand. My tailfin rips on the rough netting, but I manage to pull myself free.

"Erie!"

Huron's trapped. The bottom of the net drags across the sand, cinching together, destroying any chance of escape. I grab the rope and pull, but I can't stop its movement.

"Get help!" Huron says. His blue eyes are wide with fear.

I hesitate.

"Go! Before they throw another!"

That snaps me out of my panic. I flee. I'll find a guard. Or a merfolk with a coral knife. They'll cut Huron free before the landfolk can take him.

I know in my gut that we are too far out, but I have to try.

By the time the forest comes into view, too much time has passed to save Huron. The shadow of a dolphin guard appears from the gloom and relief rushes through my veins—until I see the familiar crisscross of white scars along his back. Niku. His eyes practically glow with fury.

Before he can say anything, I do. "They captured Huron."

"Where?" The word is clipped.

I glance behind me at the water that looks forebodingly dark and murky now. My answer is barely more than a whisper. "Halfway to the reef."

Niku's eyes narrow as he takes in my torn fins. "You must have been confident the boats wouldn't show up today."

I drop my gaze and try to straighten a stray piece of fin, then flinch at the pain that shoots up my tail. "I . . . no. I haven't discovered the pattern yet."

"Perhaps staining today's shell will enlighten you."

My shoulders sag as I imagine the new arrangement, counting the shells between Huron's abduction and Clair's. I don't bother telling Niku that it's still too random to guess the landfolk's movements.

When I don't reply, Niku nudges me, the hardness gone from his voice. Only the disappointment remains. "Back to the

Seadom, Princess. Before another boat arrives and someone else is given the duty of dyeing the shells."

. . . .

TWO DAYS LATER, INK stains my fingers black and I cannot tear my gaze away. I am marked—this abduction was my fault.

The shell that represents Huron sits in its place on the floor, exactly one hundred and twenty three spaces away from Clair's. The image is already burned into my mind, so I stare at my fingertips instead.

Why now?

Niku clears his throat in the doorway, alerting me to someone's presence. "Good afternoon, Dowager."

I drop my hands as my grandmother enters. Her hair turned silvery well before I was born. Her scales have lost their color as well, but she's still beautiful. The webbing between her fingers is so delicate, it's transparent, and her eyes are the color of the sky. She adorns her silver hair with brightly colored seaweed and shells, and wears long strings of sea glass around her neck to make up for the lack of color elsewhere.

Clair used to tease me that, as the youngest of seven daughters, I would never inherit any of Grandmother's priceless sea glass. I find the shell that represents my sister; now it's Clair who'll never own a piece of the precious stone.

Grandmother's gaze flows over the room, landing on the oldest blackened shell. The corners of her mouth turn down. "You're bound to stain another shell soon. The scouts report boats daily."

"They just took Huron—why are they still hunting?" The landfolk have only taken a single merfolk for the past eight seasons. Did something happen to Huron already, that they need another so soon?

Grandmother's shoulders lift in a graceful motion. "Your father's landfolk advisor suspects it's for 'research.'"

A shiver crawls up my spine like a tiny crab. Whatever this "research" is, no one returns from it. Being caught is as good as a death sentence. I glance at my fingertips again, damning them for remembering the feel of Huron's fins.

Grandmother combs her nails through my hair. "Have you heard the news?"

"No." My gaze remains on my stained fingers. Who was taken this time?

"The king has declared a hunt."

My head snaps up. "Now? While the landfolk are active?"

She nods. "The scouts have found an area with plenty of fish that the boats don't visit. It's a day's swim from the Seadom, but we need to restock the pens. Your father has commanded all able-bodied merfolk and the dolphin pod to join."

Able-bodied. My tail throbs where the net ripped it, but my empty stomach hurts more. "They're sure the boats won't be there?"

Grandmother braids the magenta strands caught in her nails, turning my hair into tiny waves. "You tell me."

"I . . . can't." It's hard to admit I've failed, but the scouts have a better idea of the landfolk movements than I do, despite my room full of carefully arranged shells. "What do you see?"

If anyone could know the schedule of the boats, it's Grandmother. She taught me the tides and seasons, how to monitor the position of the moon and sun, how to move the shells to keep track of what will happen. One glance, and we know when the coral will spawn, or the lobster will begin their long trek to the depths to mate, or the algae in the northern waters will bloom and drive the fish into our territory. We know when the whales are migrating and the stormy season will start. But so far, not even Grandmother can predict the boats.

Her gaze lands again on the first black shell. "It's impossible to say for sure, but the scouts have reported clear waters in that area since the landfolk began hunting us."

I grab a white shell from the floor and turn it over in my stained fingers.

She tugs a lock of my hair. "Do not worry, little minnow. Niku will keep you safe on the hunt."

My fingers curl around the shell and its edges bite into my palm. I *will* figure out the schedule of the boats before another of the 'folk can be taken. I will do whatever it takes to learn the landfolk's secret.

I knock on the office door that's half open before I stick my head inside. Delmara de la Cruz, aka Corporate, aka Aunt D, is sitting behind a large desk covered in research journals and employee folders. The Gulf of Mexico stretches out behind her, dotted with mangrove islands and gleaming in the early May sunshine. The light that streams through the wall-sized windows highlights the cinnamon tresses of the redhead in the chair before the desk. She turns as I enter, and I give her my best smile.

"Ah, Finnegan," Delmara says. "I'd like you to meet Jennifer Stevens."

The redhead sticks her hand out to shake mine. "Jen is fine." Her smile is reserved, her deep brown eyes sharp. "You must be the Finn I've heard so much about."

I mock-bow over her hand. "The one and only." Her lips twitch. My charms won't work on this one.

"Finnegan will show you around this week. If you have questions, he can answer them." Delmara closes the folder in front of her and looks at me. "Bismuth's tanks need to be cleaned—you can show her what to do."

All of my attention, which had been hovering on the redhead, snaps to Delmara. "Whoa—what? Clean the tanks? I'm training the new Mer." The fishermen caught a male yesterday while I was at the reef with Sergio.

"You aren't allowed to interact with the Mer until your one-week checkup."

I wrap my fingers around the back of the second chair and lean forward. "Last summer, you said I could train the next one. Who are you giving him to? Not Serge."

Delmara's eyebrows rise in annoyance. "I'm putting him with Potassium and Radon."

She can't be serious. Potassium—otherwise known as "K" for her periodic symbol—isn't known for playing nice with the other Mer. It took weeks with the electroshocker to get her to behave. Not to mention, "We've never had two males in the same show before."

"I think Potassium will be able to handle them both."

Of course she can handle them—I'm worried she'll kill the new one. "I can handle him, too. Give him to me."

"Doctor's orders." Delmara holds up a sheet of paper from the medical center.

I slam the top of the chair, ignoring the slight jump from the redhead. "Come on, Aunt D. Give me a chance."

"I'm sorry, Finnegan. I'm not risking it. Not with you." Her face softens. "The doctor wants to make sure you're suffering no ill effects from the electrocution."

My grip on the chair tightens until the corners of the wood cut into my skin. "I promise, I'm not. I went to the reef yesterday, and I was fine. Give me the new Mer."

"I'm giving you a chance to train the newest employee. You can have a Mer next summer, when you graduate."

"That wasn't the deal." I can't believe Corporate's doing this to me over a stupid doctor's note. "Make Maddy clean the tank—she's the one who caused the accident." I'd feel bad throwing Maddy under the bus like this if she hadn't nearly gotten me killed last week. She's the one who deserves to scrub tanks.

"Finnegan." A warning tints Delmara's voice. I can't believe she'd demote me to tank cleaning, even for a week. I've been cleaning tanks since I was fifteen—I should have become a trainer by now.

Delmara adds the doctor's note to my folder. "We're done here. Give Jennifer the tour, and get those tanks cleaned. I'm sending my boys out hunting as soon as they're ready."

I clench my teeth, but I know I'm not winning this one. We've been working together for the past six years. I know her moods. This is her "don't fuck with me—I'm not playing games" mood.

"Fine. New girl," I snap at her. "Follow me."

"My name's Jen." She sounds more than annoyed as she stands, her lips pressing into a thin line.

"Welcome to Oceanica, Jen. I hope you like cleaning fish shit."

She follows me down the stairs and through the hall, while I point out the break room and locker rooms. When we reach the restricted door that leads to the holding tank area, I swipe my ID badge and lead her in. There are four sets of double tanks—each one about thirty feet in diameter, connected by tubes. If you could see the whole thing without the walls blocking your view, it would resemble a giant hamster habitat. One tank of each pair leads to the big practice tank I nearly died in. The other connects to the arena—the outdoor tank where we hold the shows. It's bright and sunny and painted blue, with a view of the ocean from the top stands. The holding rooms, by contrast, are all damp concrete and fluorescent lights.

"These are the tanks we'll be cleaning." I can't help the bitterness in my voice. "We'll drain the water, scrub them with diluted bleach, fill them back up, and let them cycle over a few days. Then the new Mer go in." And I better become the trainer of whoever goes in this room. It'll take us a week to get both tanks cleaned and cycled, and Corporate won't be able to use the doctor's note as an excuse then.

Jen's eyes are unsettled as she glances around the room. "I thought the tanks would be bigger."

"These are three times the size of the original tanks. The Mer could barely stretch out in the old ones."

Her frown deepens, but she signed up for this. Everyone thinks working with the Mer is glamorous—until they see what it's really like. It's all dead fish and cleaning algae and trying not to get yourself killed. And nothing in the world could make me quit.

We walk further down the hall to the next set of tanks. "These are our current stars—Radon and Potassium, otherwise known as Ray and K."

They float in the middle of the closest tank, while the new male huddles on the far side of the second. Their trainers, Mia and Laz, check the water parameters with long poles so they won't step close enough to be pulled in.

The new boy will blend into the arena with his blue hair and fins. No wonder Delmara wants him in with the fiery couple—their bright red and orange will contrast nicely.

Jen's eyes widen, and she walks toward their tank like she's in a trance. "Look at that hair. It's just like *The Little Mermaid*."

"Stop." I grab her arm before she gets any closer. She needs a healthy dose of fear if she wants to work with the Mer. "You can't think of K as Ariel. She's a lethal predator."

Jen studies them. Radon's indifferent, but Potassium's creepy red eyes are sharp as she stares at the new male. I give him one night if they put him in with her.

"You know what K did the first night she was in that tank?" My voice is low and quiet at the memory of the footage. "She killed the other female. Ripped her gills out. I think she'll do the same to this new male, but I'm not the boss."

An appropriate amount of fear colors Jen's eyes now, but I continue, just to make sure she understands. "You can cage them, and shock them, and teach them to perform, but they're clever as shit. They will always look for a way out. A weakness."

I step up to the tank and study the pair. K stares back, running a finger over each of her claws, one by one. "Don't be their weakness."

• • • •

SERGIO, MADDY, NAT, and I suck down beers at our normal table in the Porch and bet on how long the new male will survive in K's tank. The Porch is just off Duval in the old Porter Mansion, and laid back compared to the tourist traps on the main strip.

We're on our second round when Jen shows up. She's changed out of her khakis and blue polo with "Oceanica" stitched across the breast, and her red hair's damp. She's put on a little bit of makeup, and a sea glass necklace with a dolphin charm. The only open chair is between Natalie and Serge, which puts her directly across from me.

I raise my glass. "Everyone, meet Jen Stevens. Jen, this is everyone." They introduce themselves while I finish my Bell's Two Hearted Ale. I need another, so I lean over the table to her. "What are you drinking?"

"What do they have?"

I stand and hold out my hand. "Let's go see."

Maddy scowls as Jen and I walk to the bar together. I don't know why—Maddy and I are friends with benefits. She's not my girlfriend.

I lean my elbows on the damp hardwood of the bar, but Jen stands back a bit, like she's uncomfortable getting too close to me. Which is funny, because we spent most of the day scrubbing a glorified fish tank together.

"Hey, Shaun," I call to my favorite bartender. "Got a new girl here who needs a drink. What do you have?"

Shaun flashes a big smile, and Jen moves a little closer to the bar. Of course. He's tan and blond and works on a boat when he's not at the Porch. Whereas I'm pale from spending too much time with the fish in Oceanica. And have big ears.

"What kind of beer do you like?" Shaun asks.

"Um." Jen glances at me briefly before blushing. "I don't know. I like margaritas."

"Then I have the perfect thing for you."

She's probably swooning over him as he pops the top on a Kvasir—I can't stand them, but he knows what he's doing. One sip and she smiles at Shaun like he's Dionysus.

"I need another, too," I interrupt. The goal is not to get Shaun laid tonight.

"You got it," he grabs my Bell's, still looking at Jen. "So, you're the newest trainer at Oceanica?"

Her eyes follow him the whole time. "Well, I'm not training a Mer yet—they have me scrubbing tanks with Finn."

Shaun chuckles as he hands over my beer. "Damn, man, they still got you scrubbing tanks? That's gotta hurt."

Thanks for the reminder. "Only for a week. The next Mer is mine."

"Well," Shaun says as patrons crowd the bar. "It was nice to meet you . . ."

"Jen," she says, too quickly.

He grins. "Nice to meet you, Jen. I'm sure I'll see you around if you're hanging with these drunks every night."

Jen fishes her card from her purse, but I pluck it from her hand. "Put her on my tab tonight."

A flush creeps up her neck. "Oh, no, you don't have to do that."

"It's your first night out with the crew. You drink free."

Her blush deepens. She's quiet and watchful, like the Mer. I get the sense that she's a predator hidden in sheep's clothing, storing everything away to use against us later.

She's also a lightweight. One beer later, and she loosens up.

The girls break into laughter as Maddy grabs Jen's phone from her hand. "Oh my god, you're right—Finn does look like Colin Morgan."

Who the hell is Colin Morgan? I lean over to see, but Maddy passes the phone to Nat. "Look at those ears!"

"You know what they say about big ears . . ." I start, but no one listens to me. They're all laughing at whoever Colin Morgan is. How is he famous if he has ears like mine? He must be on *Big Bang Theory*.

I grab the phone—there is nothing sexy about this picture. My hair is longer, to hide my ears, and this guy has a goofy smile.

"I don't look like this." I hit the back button to see the other photos. "Wait, you think I look like the guy who played Merlin?"

Maddy grabs the phone. "I didn't know you watched *Merlin*."

"My little sister watched it," I mumble and turn my back on her as she cackles. "Yo, Serge. I need you to talk to Aunt D for me. She won't let me train the new Mer."

"What's wrong?" Serge smirks. "You can't work your *Merlin* magic on her?"

"Ha ha," I say as the table bursts into laughter again. "I'm serious, man. You heard her say I'd get the next Mer, and now the doctors have her scared that I'll have an adverse reaction to being electrocuted."

Maddy snorts. "You mean, besides using it to sucker some poor tourist into having sex with you tonight?"

I put my arm over the back of her chair, trapping her curly brown hair. "I don't need to sucker a poor tourist into my bed tonight. Someone owes me."

Maddy grins right back. On the other side of the table, Jen blushes and looks away, and Natalie rolls her eyes. "You'll get used to them," she says. "These two pity-fuck each other any time they can't get laid."

"It's only a pity-fuck in one direction." Maddy winks, and the whole table laughs again at my expense.

When I was fifteen, I loved cleaning tanks. Anything to be worth Delmara's notice—to help with her research. If she said scrub, I made sure there wasn't a speck of algae left. If she said test, I studied my kit for pH, salinity, and nitrogen levels. If she said cut . . . I would open a Mer at her feet, the gurgling noises from their gills a bloody sacrifice to science. To understanding.

To proving my father right.

Now, we have more proof than we could ever need, and I wipe half-heartedly at the purple coralline algae in the twins' former tank. Honestly, I'm letting Jen do most of the work. Cleaning the tanks is our version of hazing, and no one will respect her until she's finished.

She's bent over, scrubbing a particularly tough spot of coralline algae with her tub brush—while I'm enjoying the view—when Sergio walks in.

"They're letting the new boy in with K. Wanna see the destruction? Get your money ready."

Sergio bet that K would kill the new boy within ten minutes. Maddy said it'd take at least half an hour. Nat guessed lunch break, when no one was around to stop her. Jen looked at us like we were all horrible people and didn't put money on the table. And I know K's smart enough to let him live until lights-out, when none of us will be around to see and shock her. My twenty bucks is riding on the fact that he'll be foam by morning.

"I hope you brought your wallet." I grin. "Come on, Jen. Let's go watch Serge and Maddy lose twenty bucks. It beats cleaning tanks."

Jen drops the brush and stretches, shoulders popping. "I won't argue with that."

We climb from the tank on a removable ladder, wipe our hands dry, and follow Serge to K's tanks. There's already a small crowd of trainers and interns—everyone except Maddy, who was put on concessions for the week, a fate even worse than cleaning tanks. Mia stands near the tube connecting the two tanks, while Laz is on the platform, electroshocker in hand. K stares at it, ignoring the new boy completely.

The new male paces, gaze darting between all the new faces in the room. Mia grabs the top of the glass door that separates his tank from the tube and looks at Laz. "Ready?"

He sticks the electroshocker in the water. "Ready."

Mia lifts the glass door, and the Mer stops pacing to glance at this new development. She opens the door on the opposite side of the tube, and K sinks to look through it at the blue boy.

"All right, Argon," Mia says. "Come on through." She waves at him, as if he'll know what that means. But he does inch closer to look through the tube.

I wouldn't exactly say Ray and K look threatening, but they aren't opening their arms wide to greet him, either. The new boy—Argon—visibly relaxes, fins drooping and eyes closing for just a moment. Then he glances around the room once more and cautiously swims through.

Argon makes a noise—if I didn't know better, I'd say he's asking a question—and Laz shocks them. The buzz of the electricity is clear from here, and Jen gasps a little. Argon looks around wildly, probably wondering what the fuck that was, but Ray and K just glare at the electroshocker.

Potassium swims a menacing circle around the new boy, not touching him—which is also not allowed, especially for her murderous claws—but close enough to strike. She makes a tiny noise, almost like she's shushing him, and glares at the loop of the electroshocker.

The shock Laz sends through the water is so brief, K doesn't even seem to feel it, but Argon winces.

"See?" I say to Jen. "She's showing him that a quiet sound gets a small shock. And a louder sound—"

Right on schedule, Argon makes a noise, just like they all do when they're learning this lesson. He's louder than K, and the shock is long enough to spread their limbs, but not to float them at the surface.

"Gets a longer shock," I finish.

"But . . ." Jen stares at the tank with wide, disturbed eyes. "He's probably just confused. Why do they have to be silent?"

Serge answers before I can. "Look at them—if they started making noise during a show, people would freak out. You haven't even heard some of the noises they can make."

"What if he's just asking her what's happening?"

I snort. "They're fish. They may make noise like a hogfish, but they don't have a language."

"How do you know, if you never let them speak?"

A sigh huffs out of both Serge and me. Usually, the new employees are too excited about the idea of working with mermaids to ask so many inane questions. "You're still seeing them as Ariel. They're not human."

"They look pretty human to me."

"Which part?" Serge asks. "The gills, the green scales, or the giant tail?"

Trying to be a bit more tactful, I take over. "Just because two animals have similar characteristics doesn't mean they're anything alike. Spiders and octopuses both have eight legs, sharp beaks or fangs, and a bulbous body, but no one would consider them cousins. And everyone's going to be more scared of a spider."

"Except for the Pacific blue ring octopus," Mia says with a laugh.

"I'd take the blue ring over a black widow any day," I call back.

"Finn," Laz says, laughing from the platform, never taking his gaze from the Mer in the tank. "I swear, something pretty is going to be the end of you someday."

"Guess it won't be you, then!"

He guffaws, and in that split second, K slams the new boy into the glass, baring her teeth in a display of dominance. Everyone yells, and Laz hits the button on the electroshocker until the three Mer float belly-up at the surface.

Mia is halfway up the ramp by then. "Everyone out. This isn't a tour."

I take a deep breath as my heartbeat settles and my muscles relax. My puncture wounds ache from the sudden tension.

"See?" My voice shakes a little as I speak softly to Jen. "They will always find your weakness." I grab her elbow and lead her back to the empty tanks to finish cleaning.

Several days after Huron was captured, I wake on the ocean floor and snap to alertness. Niku floats next to me, one eye open, but rouses at my jerky movement. The pulse of echolocation he sends out awakens my sister's guards, as well. For a moment, I'm in the middle of a bristling ring of angry dolphins, but they relax as the soundwaves continue into the ocean, unobstructed.

"Sorry," I murmur, and glance at my fingers. Ink still stains the nails, but the shark-like skin around them has finally scrubbed clean. I clench my fists so my guilt is visible only to me.

"It's nearly time to hunt," Niku says, though it's still too early for the sun to rise. The ocean hums with nocturnal predators—turtles, eels, lobster. Soon, the water will lighten with the first rays of sun, and we'll be able to see well enough to hunt.

The dolphin pod meets with the king and his advisors, and Niku returns with the plan. "There's a large area and several schools of fish, so the 'folk are breaking up into groups. The pod will create bubbles to corral the fish while the 'folk catch as many as they can as quickly as possible."

I've hunted with Niku before, and his bubbles are a great way to confuse the fish and make the school form a tight ball. Easy pickings.

"All the action will attract sharks, so keep your wits about you," he says. "I'll try to stay nearby, but I'll be surfacing a lot to make the bubbles, and it'll be confusing."

I take a deep breath as my nerves win out. "No sign of the boats?"

He shakes his head. "We're too far from land—the boats don't come this far out. Not the ones catching merfolk, at least."

I grab my bags and follow him to the group we'll be hunting with. As deep-sea merfolk, we have green scales, darker on the dorsal side, lighter on our stomachs. The hunters have darker hair and fins, perfect for sneaking up on fish. The rest of us have colors ranging across the spectrum of the reef. Some of them show surprise at my presence, but the only one who speaks is a merman I vaguely recognize as my father's landfolk advisor. He has hair so dark, it's nearly black, and a protrusion where his nostrils are.

"Princess." His voice holds a tinge of surprise as his gaze sweeps over my tailfin. "I thought you were staying in the Seadom?"

"And miss the chance to hunt?" My voice sounds more confident than I feel.

He bows his head, his hair shifting in the water to reveal odd fins around his earholes. "May the Tides be with you, then."

"And with you."

The hunt begins. The merfolk let the pod go first; they're faster and better at corralling the fish. Once the fish are in a tight school, we strike into it, grabbing what we can. I rip into the first fish I catch, starving and savoring the cold flesh. I don't have time to pick out my favorite parts, so I eat what I can quickly, suck the eyeballs out, and let it float to the surface where the gulls have already gathered.

Hunting makes me forget about Huron and Clair and boats. About Father's resentment, and Grandmother aging into foam.

Occasionally, Niku swims by to check on me, and my bags grow heavy as the school shrinks.

The ever-present popping of shrimp fades away into bloodlust—the sounds of the hunt engulf me instead. The click of the dolphins that disorient the fish, the smack of the sea birds hitting the surface in their own hunt, the whoops of the merfolk as they dive into the fray.

Some of the fish break away, and I spot a long, fat one with a glistening silver coat devoid of parasites. A healthy bonito trying to make a run for it.

"Oh no, you don't." I lunge. It slips just beyond my reach, and I swim after it as quick as I can. It's fast, and I'm still slow with my ripped tail and heavy bags. I cut across the water, but the advisor gets there first and sinks his nails into it.

I snap my tail in annoyance and he bows, holding it out. "Princess, forgive me."

He's interrupted by a loud smack, like a giant bird hitting the surface. A shockwave travels through the water, and the fish wriggles from the advisor's slack grip.

A boat.

I drop my heavy bags to flee, but the advisor freezes, as if his muscles refuse to work. I don't even know his name, but he's floating there like a stupid minnow too terrified to move. I can't dye another shell. I can't.

The image of the design on the floor flashes before me, yet another darkened shell added to the tally, and I lunge, ignoring the pain in my tail.

The advisor's eyes widen in terror a moment before I barrel into him, pushing him out of the net's circumference. He yells a word I don't recognize as a weight hits my wrist. Pain flares, and I cup it to my chest.

Niku's panicked voice rings through the water. "Erie, no!"

It snaps me from the pain. He always uses an honorific.

The net falls before me like a curtain. "No!" I yank it with my good hand, trying to stop its descent.

"Erie!" Niku kicks hard and slips under the edge just before it hits the ground.

We're trapped. Niku grabs the net and tries to lift it, but the thick rope is already closing in around us. The advisor grabs a coral knife from one of his bags and starts sawing. Fibers snap apart. One section unravels, and he grabs the next, knife moving quickly. Niku tries to do the same with his teeth, but they aren't sharp enough.

He releases the net as it cinches together. Sediment chokes the water. "Get below me when they start pulling us up. If they think they've caught a dolphin, they might let us go."

The black-haired merman isn't fast enough. Fear sharpens his dark eyes. "I'm sorry, Princess. I'm so sorry." The hole is only big enough to stick my head through.

Niku's voice hardens as the net moves. "Stay calm, Princess. Hold your breath. Cover your gills if you have to—don't let them dry out."

Bile rises in my stomach as the bottom of the net touches my tail. I gasp and wrap my arms around Niku.

"You have to let go," he says, calm. "If they see your arms, they won't release us. Stay below me. Try to be as small as possible."

I release him and wrap my tail around myself, then gather my hair in, holding it close so the bright magenta won't give me away. Niku swims to the top of the net, where the landfolk will see him first, and I huddle on the bottom. The advisor grabs my hand through the hole he made. My stained nails peek out from his fingers.

When Niku crests, the net stops moving and I sag in relief.

Until it pulls taut again. I scream and pound on the side of the boat.

"Calm down," Niku says.

I can't. *I can't.* I have to get out of this net before I become nothing but bubbles.

"Erie!" Niku smacks me with a flipper and I stop screaming. "Listen to me. The most important thing is that we aren't separated. Grab my dorsal fin, and hold your breath as long as you can."

I shake as the net presses us together. Niku rolls on his side so he won't crush me, and his flipper disappears into the air. I hug him tight, gasping as my fingers crest, then my arm. For the first time in my life, I feel air. It hurts.

The advisor squeezes my hand one last time. "Deep breath, Princess."

I do as he says, sucking in as much as my lungs will hold, and shudder as the water breaks away from my head, streaming down my face. A whimper escapes me as the wind rushes past, and I close my eyes against the air and sun. The wind is like the roar of the waves during a storm—never-ending agony. It burns my earholes, my scales, the webbing of my fingers where they claw into Niku's side. Small drops of blessed relief drip from the top of the net, cooling me before the wind and sun ravage me again.

The net stops, and I squint one eye open. Niku's next to me, the scars on his back bright white in the sunlight. I turn my head toward the boat and see two landfolk. They look like mermen, but they're brown instead of green. They have a bump in the middle of their faces like the advisor, and ear-fins, and strange legs that don't end in a tail. One grins and says something I can't make out. With a shudder, I turn back to Niku and close my eyes. I don't want to see what happens next.

The net jerks, and it's all I can do to keep myself from screaming and losing my last breath. My gills burn with the need for water—my entire body burns and cracks and bleeds. When the movement stops, we hang over a large hole in the boat, and then the net goes slack and we drop.

I can't help the scream that tears from my throat. Water gushes from my gills.

We land with a hard splash in the water held inside the boat. It's warm, and I gasp a few times, breathing in deep to stop the burning in my gills.

"Breathe shallow," Niku says. "There's something in the water."

Too late—a lightheaded buzz fills my body and my muscles slacken. My heartbeat, which was racing moments ago, becomes sluggish.

"Erie, whatever you do, don't let them separate us. Got it?"

My fins droop, heavy. I don't know how to fight the landfolk when I feel like this. All I can do is nod, and drift.

<u>Oceanica Training Manual</u>

9: MER ARRIVAL

9.1 Clean/Cycle holding tanks one (1) week previous to hunting for Mer. All tanks (holding, transporting) and cranes (portable, dockside) should be inspected before arrival and ready to use.

9.2 Mer will be drugged with quinaldine for transport. USE CAUTION, even drugged Mer are dangerous.

9.3 Transportation Procedure:

9.3.1 Net will be loosened for trip back to harbor. Tighten net and lift Mer from tank with dockside crane. Place in portable transfer tank with head/arms facing back. One (1) employee must keep visual on them at all times.

DO NOT LET MER SIT IN SUN – THEY WILL FOAM FROM SHOCK.

9.3.2 Call veterinarian to examine Mer. Do not place hands near tank! Upon completion of visual inspection, hook net to portable crane in holding tank room.

9.3.3 Slowly lower Mer into holding tank. Dropping Mer into colder water too fast can cause lethal shock to their system.

9.3.4 Remove net from tank once Mer are stable. Throw one or two fish into tank and dim lights to allow Mer to recover.

9.4 Quinaldine may take one (1) or two (2) days to wear off. Mer may not eat while drugged.

9.5 If Mer makes excessive noise or show aggression, use electroshocker until Mer is under control.

The dock behind Oceanica is crowded when the boat with the newest Mer arrives. The fishermen had to go way out to find this one, and the past twenty-four hours have been filled with preparations, mostly of the tanks Jen and I cleaned last week. As the net pulls taut and lifts the Mer from the ship, I see something else is in there with it.

"Holy shit," I breathe.

Jen stands next to me, her eyes wide, lips parted in amazement. "Is that a dolphin?"

It is. It's a bottlenose dolphin, and that little mermaid has her arms around him like he's her teddy bear. *Damn.* It basically proves the theory that there's a symbiotic relationship between dolphins and the Mer. The fishermen have been saying for years that the dolphins help the Mer steer clear of the boats, and—though this one obviously failed—it's presence in the net is the first real proof we have that their stories are true.

The net lowers the pair into a transport tank that's barely big enough for both of them. Corporate and the men argue in Spanish about price, so Jen and I step forward to take a closer look. Sunlight shines off the Mer's magenta hair, and I suck in a breath—it's the same color as the one Dad found. I know exactly how to make this one mine.

"She's a younger one," I say. "Probably the same age as the last."

"How can you tell?" Jen asks. She kneels next to me to see into the tank better.

"The coloration. See the tips of her fins?" They're shredded, but bright magenta like her hair. "The color fades as they age. She's still perfectly vibrant, even at the tip."

Jen straightens. "I thought she'd be more active. You know, trying to kill all of us."

"She's sedated. They pump that tank full of tranquilizer for the trip, so the Mer don't go into shock. It'll take a day or so for the drugs to wear off. She'll be fairly easy to deal with until then, but be careful. Even drugged, they're dangerous."

Corporate and the fishermen punch the air with their fingers. Delmara doesn't want the dolphin, but the men want money for catching it.

"Do we have to separate them?" Jen says. "We could have a Mer/dolphin show. People would love watching them together."

There's something calculating in her gaze, but she's right. Nobody wants to watch dolphins alone anymore, but having one perform with a Mer would draw in the crowds.

I dodge an angry finger and tap Delmara's shoulder.

"Not now, Finnegan," she says. "I'm trying to get these *pendejos* to understand that *I'm not paying for a dolphin.*" She directs the last part at them, as if saying it in English will make it any clearer.

The fishermen bristle when she calls them dumbasses, and I lean my head toward her short frame. She's like a Chihuahua: tiny, but someone you definitely don't want to piss off. "Why don't we keep the dolphin? They could perform together."

Delmara shakes her head, crossing her arms. "I'm not paying Mer prices for a jacked-up dolphin. I don't have a husbandry license for cetaceans."

"Get one. It should be easy. And you know every little girl in America would beg her parents to bring her here to watch a dolphin perform with a mermaid."

She turns her gaze on the pair. We have to get them out of the sun before the Mer foams with the heat, so Delmara doesn't have long to decide. We can't separate them out here, anyway. Whether the dolphin comes back out to the Gulf or not, we have to take them inside to get them out of that net.

"Trust me, Aunt D. I can make money with them, and you promised me the next Mer. Jen can help with the dolphin—she studied cetaceans in college." We've spent a lot of time scrubbing tanks this past week, and, among other things, I learned that Jen studied marine biology at the University of South Carolina. "Plus, someone needs to take over when I go back to school in August."

Delmara turns her back on me. "I told you, next summer."

I grab a folded piece of paper from my wallet. The edges are yellowed and falling apart from all the times I've taken it out. It's a color sketch of a mermaid I found in my dad's office after he disappeared. The mermaid no one believed he found. The one with magenta hair.

"Come on, Aunt D," I say softly and hand it to her. "This one is mine."

She swallows as she studies the sketch, and an expression I can't read passes through her eyes. It's gone in a moment, and she pats me on the shoulder. When she speaks, her voice cracks slightly. "You have until the end of summer to turn a profit."

Hell yes! After six years of scrubbing tanks and euthanizing Mer, I've finally been promoted to trainer. A giant grin explodes across my face. "You won't regret this. I'll turn these two into the biggest stars you have."

"Get them inside before she foams." Delmara runs her finger over the sketch before she hands it back.

When I return to Jen, I pick her up and swing her around in a happy circle. "How would you like to train a dolphin?"

"Really?" Her eyes shine and her mouth is wide as I set her back on the dock. "Delmara said I could train it?"

"Well, she said I have three months to make a profit with them, and you're the one who gave me the idea, so I'm making you my assistant."

"Assistant?" She scoffs. "I came up with the idea."

"Yep," I grin. "And I'm best friends with Corporate's nephew."

She puts her hands on her hips. "I see how this works."

I have a lot of responses to that, but most of them would get me smacked. Instead, I change the subject. "Let's get these two inside."

The transport tank is ten feet long and three feet wide—barely big enough to fit the dolphin—with a set of wheels in the front and the back. A button in a panel on the back gives it gas, and controls on the front panel turn the wheels. It takes two people to move, the damn thing is too unwieldy for a solo job.

Jen eyes me as I walk to the transport and motion her over. "You steer from the front. I'll power it from behind."

It's slow going, but we get the pair to the tanks, and I call the veterinarian to check on them. The Mer hasn't moved—she's buried her head in the dolphin's side. Usually, they scrutinize us, trying to figure out the best way to injure us and get free, but she cowers. That'll make her easy to work with.

The dolphin, on the other hand, thrashes when the vet nears. He even snaps his jaw like a guard dog. This is more than a symbiotic relationship—he's trying to protect her.

"Hold the dolphin down so I can get a good look," the vet says. I'm not sure that's a good idea, but I put my forearm just behind the dolphin's blow hole and push with all my weight, holding him against the glass of the tank. One good heave and I'm on my ass, a large cut on my forearm streaming blood.

"Dammit," I snap. "Just get them in the tank so we can separate them."

The vet hands me a cloth to stop the bleeding, and I call Serge on the walkie-talkie. "Get your lazy ass down here—we need your help in the holding tanks."

His voice travels back, dusted with static. "I just heard the news. Congratulations, man. I'll be right down."

I show Jen how to connect the net to the crane, and we crank it up. When the net goes taut, the Mer gasps so loud I can hear it.

We lift them out of the transport and swing them over one of the newly cleaned tanks before Sergio arrives. He enters as we lower them in. There's a delicate balance between keeping the Mer from suffocating and keeping her from going into shock by dumping her into the colder water. Shock will foam her just as surely as suffocation if we're not careful, but as soon as the water touches her, she claws the net, trying to get her gills into it.

"Wow," Serge says. "Look at that hair. You should name her Neon."

"It's not neon," Jen says. "It's magenta. She looks like a dottyback or royal gramma."

A girl who knows her reef fish as well as I do? I think I'm in nerd-love. "Dotty would be a good name, but we usually stick to periodic elements."

"Helium?" she suggests.

"Cadmium," Serge says.

"That's a male name," I say. "We'll call the dolphin Cadmium."

Jen claps her hands together. "What about Iodine? We can call her Io, for short."

"I still think Neon's a good name," Serge says, but Jen's my assistant, so I go with her suggestion.

"Iodine it is."

The net fully lowers into the tank, and the Mer—Iodine—has her arms wrapped around the dolphin again. "Let's separate these elements."

"I call dibs on the shocker." Serge bounds up the steps to the platform and the electroshocker hanging on the wall.

That's fine by me; I don't want to get anywhere near that thing ever again. Still, I can't let Serge think he can shock my mermaid whenever he wants. "She's not a jellyfish, man. You don't have to poke her with a stick while she's stranded on the beach."

"Jellyfish deserve it," he says. "All those stinging tentacles. God, I hate the ocean."

I climb the stairs. "We only need to separate them. You shock her just long enough that she lets go—Jen and I will get the net between them."

Jen hangs back, grimacing. "Do we have to separate them? If they're going to perform together, can't they stay in the same tank?"

"They'll be easier to work with separately," I say, corporate lines streaming from my mouth. I can't afford to screw up this chance. "Once they're performing, we can probably keep them together, but not yet. It'll be a good incentive to get them working. A treat for cooperating."

Her shoulders sink as she ascends the stairs, but she doesn't argue. Together, we unhook the net from the crane so we can reposition it between them.

My arms cling to Niku like octopus tentacles until the net around us goes slack and sinks to the ground. I lift my head, surprised, and find myself in a place with no color or sound of life. It's gray like the forest, but uniformly gray, and a constant, low hum settles in my scales.

The net gathers below us in a line, the ends creeping up to the surface. "What's happening?" I whisper.

"I don't know," Niku says. He injured one of the landfolk already—I tasted the blood. "Just stay calm. Don't give them a reason to hurt you."

I nod, then peer at the surface where a loop enters the water. Niku pulls me away from it, and the net shifts beneath us.

"Neek—"

A loud buzz fills my ears and my muscles contract, spreading me out like a starfish. Every inch of my body burns like I've touched a fire coral. I can't move, can't scream, can't breathe. The buzzing stops, my muscles release, and I float belly-up at the surface. Niku floats an arm's length away.

My muscles twitch and shake, as limp as a jellyfish, and my gills sting. Before I can recover, the net lifts between us.

"No!" I gasp. Niku flips over and sprays water, then paces the length of the net. I reach through and grab him. "Neek! Neek, don't leave me. Don't let them take you away."

My fingers dig into his skin, and he doesn't tell me to stay calm now. His muscles are tight—ready to attack. I'm worried he'll jump right out of the water, trying to reach the landfolk, and beach himself.

The net jerks, then circles me from the bottom. The panic I held back presses into my core. "No! No, no, no. No, please." I hug Niku as the net closes around me once again. It lifts me, and I hold on to him as tight as I can. I refuse to let go.

"Princess, I don't know what to do. I can't stop them."

Never has Niku sounded so lost. "No!" I scream. "Stop!" I take a deep breath before surfacing, and whimper as Niku slips from my fingers. He swims circles below me, huffing water every few seconds. Each time the blast hits me, the despair builds.

The net swings away, turning me so I can no longer see him. I grab the rope to hoist myself around, but the net lowers again into a different body of water. As soon as I'm under, I scream. "Niku!"

When the net releases, I swim toward him, hands out, but they hit something clear and solid. "Niku? Neek?" I can see him, so I pound on the obstruction. "Niku!"

He watches me, but I can't hear him if he speaks. His voice doesn't travel far in the water, and now, we aren't in the same water. At least I can see him.

Until one of the landfolk steps between us. I back up quickly and glance at the surface, fearing the loop that caused so much pain. When I turn back to the landfolk, he smiles, a possessive look in his eyes, hands pressed against the invisible barrier. I wrap my tail around my body.

He's a creature straight out of my nightmares. His skin is pale and fleshy, like a snail, and his fingers are web-less. He's different colors—like a fish—but has no scales or gills. His two tails are the color of sand, which switches abruptly at his waist to a blue that reminds me of Huron's hair. The blue covers his chest and part of his arms, but then stops to become snail-like again. His hair is black, his eyes tiny, and a large bump juts out of his face where his nostrils are. Just like the protrusion on my father's advisor.

The landfolk man says something in a language I don't understand, and I cringe away. I want him to move so I can see Niku again.

A splash at the surface makes my heart race all over again, but instead of the painful loop, a dead fish floats through the water. Why are they throwing dead fish into the water? What kind of torture is this?

The landfolk man says something else, pats the enclosure, and walks away. I wait until I can't see him anymore, then press my palms along the invisible barrier, searching it. It's smooth and uniform, all the way to the surface, though I can just make out where it ends above the water. There are only two anomalies to the obstruction: one under the platform the landfolk stood on, and another facing Niku. A large circle breaks the flat surface. It's as deep as my longest finger, but stops again at another invisible barrier. Something that resembles a clear tubeworm case connects my enclosure to the one Niku's trapped in, but I can't figure out how to get through.

I stare helplessly at Neek until the adrenaline fades and my muscles become weak again. Spent, exhausted with fear and worry, I sink to the bottom of the enclosure and curl up in a ball.

"Who's ready for a celebratory drink?" I clap Serge on the shoulder as we descend the platform. Aside from the noise the Mer made, the separation went much better than I expected. Most of the Mer fight more—some even try to jump out of the water—so that was a cake walk in comparison.

Sergio grins, but Jen stares at the tank like she just witnessed the brutal murder of her childhood. When she speaks, it's no more than a whisper. "I didn't know Mer screamed."

"They don't," Serge says. "It's just a noise they make—like a hawk screeching. She'll learn not to do it soon enough."

"But . . ." Jen wraps her arms around her waist. "We can't leave them right now. Not after that."

"Trust me." I drop my arm around her shoulders, giving her a reassuring squeeze. "The drugs are still in her system. Once we leave, she'll calm down. She'll have a chance to get used to her new surroundings, and sleep off the excitement of the day. Tomorrow, she'll be easier to work with."

Jen shrugs a little.

Maddy walks in, her gaze sliding to the tanks before landing on my arm, which still hangs around Jen's shoulders. "You already got them in? They let me off concessions so I could help."

I stick my hands in my pockets. "I take it you're back to scrubbing tanks and cleaning filters?"

She raises an eyebrow. "I'm helping you train the new Mer."

I grimace, because I knew she'd be pissed when I told her. "Actually, Jen has experience with cetaceans, so she's taking over the dolphin while I train the Mer."

"But . . . we talked about this," Maddy says. "Last summer, when Delmara promised you the next Mer. You said I could be your co-trainer."

"Things changed."

She shifts her weight, eyes narrowing. "I'm training the new Mer."

Why does she think repeating herself will work? "Sorry, Mads. Jen has experience, and I can't risk you not paying attention again. You can co-train with Jen when I go back to school."

"I'm going back to school in the fall, too."

The hurt shinning in her green eyes isn't enough to make me change my mind. "Just the community college. You'll be close enough to work at Oceanica."

Maddy's lips press together in a thin line as she looks from me to Jen, and back. "Fine."

I feel bad, but I can't trust her right now. Maybe my near-death experience scared her into paying more attention, but Jen hasn't been here long enough to develop the indifference toward the Mer that Maddy has. That I have. I need someone who'll freak out if I get too close to the edge of the platform.

"You up for a drink?" I ask, trying to make amends. "It's on me."

Maddy swallows hard, and her gaze shifts beyond me to the tanks. "No, I—I'll see you guys later." She walks away without another glance at us.

• • • •

THE NEXT MORNING, I get to work early and go straight to Iodine's tank. She's curled up in a tight ball on the side nearest the dolphin. He floats as close to her as he can get, too, but his eyes are open. He watches me.

I put myself between them and crouch down to examine Io. Her tail is in shreds, but the bright color is there—it should heal just fine. Long magenta hair floats around her green scales, not quite hiding an area on the back of her tail where several are damaged. No wonder she was caught—even with a dolphin, she was too injured to get away from the boat.

One hand hugs her tail. Her fingers end in sharp claws, but the webbing is delicate. The tips of her nails are dark, like she was hunting octopus and pierced the ink sac instead. I tap on the glass with my knuckle. Her head snaps up, eyes wide. They almost appear human, despite the fact that they're larger and the same magenta color as her hair—I've never seen eyes so infinite.

"Morning, beautiful."

She swims to the far side of the tank and curls up again before looking at the surface. The movement disturbs the fish we threw in last night, and it spins in the water. She glances at it, then back to me, wary.

"Hungry?"

She must be, if she hasn't eaten since they caught her. I grab the bucket next to the door and head down the hall to the cooler. When I return with fish, she's making noises at the dolphin. As soon as she sees me, she swims to the opposite side of the tank, keeping as much space between us as possible.

"Don't worry, darlin'—I won't hurt you unless you try to kill me. So don't try to kill me, 'kay? I've already lived through one Mer attack, and I don't want to use the shocker on you."

By the time I reach the platform, she's huddled in the far bottom of the tank. I grab a fish by the tail and hold it over the water, but she doesn't move. I kneel down—dangerous and stupid—and dunk half the fish in the water, but she remains.

"Come on, Io. You have to eat. I promised Corporate you'd make money, and that won't happen if you starve."

She's probably still too drugged to move much, so I let the fish float. As I walk back down the stairs, she keeps the tank between us, not even glancing at the fish. I go to the dolphin's tank instead. "Cadmium will show you how it's done."

Goddamn, this dolphin is creepy. He watches me like the older Mer do, trying to find a weakness to exploit. From the scars on his back, I'd say he's tangled with human nets before . . . and won. Maybe giving him to Jen—who hasn't even experienced the Mer yet—was a bad idea. Dolphins are still predators, despite their "dolphin grin."

I swear Cadmium is frowning. I've never seen a dolphin frown before.

"Wanna fish, Cad?" I dangle it over the water. It takes a minute for him to stop guarding Io and surface. He doesn't open his mouth, just watches me. Not the fish in my hands. Me.

"Ooookay." I toss the fish into the pool. Cad doesn't stop watching me. I'm seriously reconsidering letting Jen anywhere near him. I toss a few more fish in with him and walk back down the stairs.

Jen walks in several minutes later. "Morning."

"Morning." I stare at the dead fish both my charges are ignoring. "I can't get them to eat."

"Maybe they're still drugged?"

I drum my fingers on my arms. That could be the problem. "Be careful around that dolphin. I have a feeling he's going to try to kill us the first chance he gets."

Jen's eyebrows pull together. "I've never heard of a dolphin killing a person—at least, not in captivity."

"There's a first for everything."

She walks to Io's tank. I keep forgetting that Jen's never seen the Mer up close—not that Io will let her get close. I have a feeling Io's more scared of me, though, so I walk to the other side. She puts herself right in the middle of the tank.

"She looks so strange," Jen says. "I always thought mermaids would look more human."

"Imagine being the first person to see one." My father's face looms in my memory. The excitement and disappointment mixing in his eyes as he told us about his discovery—and his lack of proof. I believed him, of course, because why would he lie? But Mom thought he'd gone off the deep end, and they argued about it over the course of many nights.

Jen peers through thirty feet of water at me. "Delmara must have shit a brick."

The pain of Dad's disappearance resurfaces, and though I rarely speak of my father anymore, I want Jen to know who really discovered the Mer. It wasn't Corporate. "She was the first to document them, but she was still a student at Florida Keys Community College when her professor, Dr. Cale Jarvis, found the first one."

"Jarvis? Was he—?"

"My father. He lost his job, was laughed out of the scientific community, and went missing in his pursuit to prove they existed." I swallow the memory of those horrible months. "They found his boat, but he was gone."

"That's awful."

I study Io. My father was driven to what many people considered suicide trying to prove mermaids existed—now the Mer perform four times a day. "Delmara was the only one defending him, and she made it her life's mission to prove him right. It didn't take long."

I remember that day well. I was working with Sergio at his family's Cuban restaurant when Delmara bounded in, all manic jubilation, waving her camera phone around her head. "I caught one!" she yelled, and shoved the phone in Sergio's mother's face. "I told you Cale was right."

The family closed the restaurant early and followed her to the community college, where the strangest goddamn thing I'd ever seen was chillin' in a tank. I was entranced by the creature, even more so by the knowledge that she'd proven my father right. I've been helping Delmara with the Mer ever since.

Jen's still awestruck, seeing a Mer up close. "Will her fins grow back together, like a beta fish?"

"As long as we can get her to eat."

"I hope we can—she's beautiful."

I press my hands to the glass and grin at Io, who backs up toward Jen. "She'll be the biggest star we've ever had."

• • • •

BY THAT AFTERNOON, the quinaldine sedative has definitely had time to wear off, but neither the Mer nor the dolphin have eaten. They swim away every time we throw a fish in the tank, as if it's a grenade and not food. The dolphin stares at us, and the Mer curls up in the middle of the damn tank, as if she can hide.

I'm checking the water parameters to make sure there isn't something wrong with it, making the Mer so lethargic, when Delmara walks in.

"Hey, Aunt D. What brings you down here?"

She glances from one tank to the other. "I wanted to see how you were doing with your first Mer. Have you had to shock her much?"

I set the pole with the water collection tube against the wall. "Just to separate them yesterday. I think she's still sedated. All she does is curl up on the bottom like that. Neither of them has eaten yet, which is usually a side effect of the quin."

The dolphin stares at Delmara as she walks closer. "This one is definitely not sedated. Why isn't he eating?" She directs the question to Jen instead of me.

"I think he's more concerned with protecting the Mer right now. When she starts eating, he should, too."

Delmara frowns. "I paid a lot of money for this ugly beast, and if he starves to death, I'll lose it all. Make sure he eats."

"Yes, ma'am." Jen bows her head as Delmara moves to the Mer's tank.

"Hey." She knocks on the glass to get Iodine's attention, but the Mer doesn't move. "She shouldn't be this sedated anymore. Has the vet seen her?"

"Not since yesterday," I say. "The fishermen may have put more quin in the tank for the dolphin on the way back."

"Idiots. Quinaldine doesn't work on mammals," Delmara mumbles. "Give her a little shock, see if it wakes her up before we call the vet back in."

The electroshocker hangs on the wall behind me, but I hesitate, remembering the sharp pain of the electrocution. *Get it together, Finn. This thing saved your life.* I take a deep breath and grab the handle. Making sure not to stand too close to the edge, I lower the loop into the water.

I barely press the button—a brief buzz that K wouldn't even react to, but it should wake a new Mer. Iodine curls up tighter, which I didn't think was possible.

Delmara frowns again. "A bit longer. Don't float her, but spread her out."

As I hold the button down and lactic acid floods her muscles, the Mer unfolds like a magenta sea anemone. When I stop, and she's had a moment to recover, she swims a panicked circle around the tank before curling up near the tube to the dolphin's enclosure.

"Well," Delmara says, "She's healthy enough to swim. I'll send the vet down to check on her." Corporate takes a few steps, but stops and glances at Iodine again. "I want her performing by July. Good luck, Finnegan." She leaves.

July. That's a tight schedule for a completely new act—less than two months—but doable, as long as we can get the Mer to eat something.

. . . .

TWO DAYS LATER, THAT damn Mer still won't eat. She must be starving, but all she does is curl up at the bottom of the tank, as far away from us as possible, and watch the dolphin. I like the ones who fight. Iodine is boring.

I kick the tank, and she practically jumps through the glass on the other side, which makes the fish she refuses to eat slosh around the bottom. It's disgusting.

"Hey, apprentice," I bark, and Jen glares at me. We've been in worse and worse moods since the euphoria of becoming trainers wore off. "Can you clean that shit up?"

She toes the empty bucket at her feet. "I just got Cad to eat. Why can't you do it? She's yours."

"Because I've already done my time cleaning tanks. It's your turn, grasshopper."

"Fine." The scowl she gives me could turn gold to lead. "But if your Mer kills me, I'm suing."

"Whatever. Be careful. I'm going to go talk to Mia and Laz, see if they have any tips."

She clomps up the metal staircase and grabs the long pole with the net. I've just left the room when I hear her scream.

"Jen!" I run back to the tanks. Io's at the bottom, cupping something in her hands. I take the stairs two at a time and find Jen, face white, hands pressed to her neck.

I slide onto my knees. "Are you okay?" I grab her hands, but there's no blood. Not even a scratch, just a faint red line on the back of her neck. "What happened?"

She shakes so hard, she can't speak, so I wrap my arms around her and whisper, "You're okay. You're okay. I've got you. She didn't hurt you."

Oh god, if something had happened to Jen, I would have had to foam Iodine. I still might have to—any attack is taken seriously by APHIS and OSHA.

Hot tears soak into my shirt as Jen takes a few deep, shuddering breaths. I'm a dumbass. I kicked the tank and left a rookie alone with a Mer. What's wrong with me? "Shh." I rock Jen for a moment, then hold her away to make sure she's not bleeding. "Did she hurt you?"

Jen rubs the back of her neck with shaking hands. "I didn't know they were that fast. I thought . . . I thought she was trying to pull me in." She gazes at the magenta and green blob that is Io under the surface. "She took my necklace."

Every bit of me deflates. "Your necklace?"

"She ripped it off me when I bent down to scoop the fish."

I release her shoulders and descend the steps far enough to peer into the tank. Io holds the necklace like she's never seen a piece of sea glass before.

My girl is motivated by pretty things, not food. Good to know. "I'll get the dead fish out. You"—I turn to Jen, still bent over, trying to cope with her not-so-near-death experience—"bring me the freshest fish you can find at Eaton Street Seafood, and a few more cheap necklaces."

Jen takes another deep breath, then pushes herself up and clasps her hands together. As she walks past, she mumbles, "That necklace wasn't cheap."

I swim to the side of the enclosure closest to Niku and hold up the necklace. "Look, Neek—sea glass!" I'd be the envy of all my sisters if I was home right now.

The landfolk girl screamed, of course, but it was worth it to get the sea glass. It reminds me of home. The water doesn't feel right here. There's a dissonant hum rather than the normal sounds of waves and shrimp, and instead of a current pulling me toward home, a hole in the wall pushes out water, constantly bubbling. No tides, just bubbles. I pop them at night when I'm bored.

Something breaks the surface and I spin—it's a loop, but not the same painful loop as before. This one has a small net attached, where the other was open. Are they trying to take the necklace back? I press it to my chest, unwilling to return it.

Instead of coming near me, the net scoops up the dead fish. Thank the Tides—the water was beginning to taste of rot. I turn my back on it and speak to Niku. I don't know if he can hear me, but it's the only thing keeping me sane.

My hands animate the story of stealing the necklace, and I don't notice the landfolk man until he steps into the gap between us. I gasp and kick back to the middle of the enclosure, clutching the necklace to my chest so he can't take it from me.

He tips a container full of dead fish toward me. "You need to *eat*, Iodine."

I have no idea what the air words mean, but he keeps using two of them, specifically: "eat," and "Iodine." "Eat" must have something to do with the dead fish, although I'm not sure what.

He uses "Iodine," or "Io," all the time. It makes me feel as if I'm a pet seahorse, trying to learn my new name. Have I been brought here as a pet? Was Clair? Huron?

When he says the name again, my fingers wrap around the sea glass. "Erie," I snap at him.

He frowns, his gaze shifting to the platform where the painful loop waits.

"Er-ie," I draw out the syllables. "I'm a princess, not your pet. Take me home."

The man sighs and shakes his head as he begins walking to the platform, dead fish forgotten. "I'm sorry, Io. Time to learn the first lesson."

I swim in front of him and slam my fists on the glass. "Erie! Not Iodine." I jab my finger into my chest. "Erie!"

He stops, eyebrows pulling together as he frowns and points at me. "Iodine."

I jab my finger into my chest again. "Erie!"

He cocks his head to the side and points at me. "Erie?"

"Yes!" I exclaim, throwing my head back in relief. When I look at him, he steps back, hands splayed like he's trying to find something to hold on to, eyes widening like a squirrelfish. "Erie?" He says a few more air words, then repeats, "Erie?"

I touch my chest again. "Erie. My name is Erie."

His jaw goes slack, and he turns away from me, running his hands through his hair. When he turns back around, his tiny, dark eyes blaze with stunned excitement. He steps forward, points to himself, and says, "Finn."

His name is Finn. I press my hands against the cold barrier, which makes him jump back—is he scared of me, too? What could I possibly do to him, stuck in the water like this?

I look past him. "Neek! I know his name—it's Finn." I still don't know if Niku can hear me, but Finn obviously can. He glances between us, brow furrowed.

I point to the other enclosure. "Niku."

"Niku?"

I nod, and Finn turns to study him. Neek has a murderous expression, and I wonder if Finn can tell, or if dolphin body language is another he cannot speak.

If only I could speak the air, I could find out what the landfolk want with us. I used to wonder what happened to the merfolk who were caught, but now that I'm living the nightmare, I'm more confused than ever. I'm sure the landfolk aren't going to eat us, but so far, the only thing Finn and the girl have done is watch us, speak air words, and throw dead fish in the water. I really want to ask what the dead fish are for.

The landfolk girl returns, a bag in her hand, and Finn lights up. He grabs her in a hug and says something. The girl raises her eyebrow, incredulous, as he pulls her to the barrier. He points to her and says, "Jen."

"Jen," I try, rolling it around my mouth. It's a strange name, short and hard, like coral. I point to myself. "Erie." Then to Neek. "Niku." Then to the man. "Finn." I like his name. It feels like a fish swimming around my tongue.

Jen's jaw drops, and I smirk. The landfolk speak to each other; Jen shakes her head, while Finn's tiny eyes are nearly as wide as a merfolk's. He pulls a brown package out of the bag. When he opens it, I can see there's a fish inside. For the Tides, not another dead fish.

He holds it out like he's giving me a present. I cross my arms. He mimes biting it, and I shake my head. He wants me to eat a dead fish? Gross.

My stomach grumbles, betraying me. I haven't had a proper meal in days. The fish's scales are bright, and its eyes clear—it hasn't been dead long. Still, the thought of eating a fish that was caught in a net, like me, makes my stomach turn. I shake my head again and back away.

Instead of getting mad, Finn reaches into the bag and holds something up—sea glass! It's a single pendant on a chain, a pretty green color that reminds me of a button polyp. Will he give me the sea glass for eating the fish? He raises his eyebrows, questioning. My stomach rumbles again, and I bob my head reluctantly. He grins. His teeth are strangely flat.

I follow him to the platform. When he doesn't throw the fish in, I crest until my eyes are just out of the water. The air burns—I have to squint them halfway closed.

"Hello, Erie."

I don't know what the first word means, so I wait, silent. He says something else and holds the fish out. When I don't move, he crouches down and holds it right in front of me. I glance at his other hand, where the sea glass is hiding, sigh, and take the fish. He jumps back as if I was going to pull him in. If I eat this fish, and he doesn't give me the sea glass, I will.

I sink below the surface and sniff the fish, but it smells fine. Better than fine—it smells like the ocean. I close my eyes and sniff again—a big, deep breath of open ocean, and sunlight, and a school of fish to hunt. My stomach rumbles, and I bite into the flesh. It might be dead, but I tear into it, barely taking the time to chew before I swallow, bones and all. The head is last, and I suck the eyeballs out, closing my own to savor the taste before popping the rest into my mouth.

With a content hum, I float in the middle of the enclosure. That wasn't nearly as disgusting as I expected. I could eat another.

A smug smirk graces Finn's face when I surface. He holds the chain with the sea glass pendant dangling over the water, but I don't want that yet. I want another fish. The bag is by his feet, and I snatch that instead.

"Hey!" he yells.

I dive to the bottom and open the bag—it's full of jewelry. Pretty necklaces sparkle back at me, and I dig through them, finding one that's the same color as my hair and fins. I put it on, then swim to the surface. Jen makes a sound so similar to merfolk laughter, it takes me by surprise. Finn's snail-skin face flushes, and his mouth once again hangs open.

They didn't try to hurt me, and I don't know what that means. I need to learn to speak the air so I can find out why we're here.

I can't believe I was outsmarted by a fish. Even more than that, I can't believe she can talk. I've always swallowed Corporate's line that the noises the Mer make are just noises—they're fish. They may be clever, but they can't be intelligent enough to have a language. All those little noises she made at Cad—er, Niku—weren't just noises, though. She was talking to him.

Worse, she was screaming his name as we separated them that first day. Realizing that, I feel like the world's biggest asshole. She deserves all those necklaces.

"Fuuuuuuck." I draw the word out as I run my hand through my hair. I just broke rule number one at Oceanica: *Never Humanize the Mer.* When you stop thinking of them as predators and start thinking of them as Ariel, you become complacent. Every trainer I know who started thinking *their* Mer was different—*their* Mer was friendly—ended up dead or injured.

Io—Erie—stares at me with her bright eyes just out of the water. She smiles, and now that I know she can speak, I can't help but think of her as anything except Ariel. I'm going to end up dead in her ink-tipped claws.

Jen bumps me. "It's not that bad, Finn. We'll fish the necklaces out later."

Who cares about the necklaces now? "You were right." My voice trembles as the implications of this discovery hit me. "When we separated them, she was screaming. She was screaming her dolphin's name."

The smile melts off Jen's face. "Oh."

I've just condemned her, too.

"Maybe . . ." Whatever Jen's about to say is dangerous. I've only known her for a dozen days, but even I can tell she's not about to say: "*Who cares? She's just a fish.*"

"Maybe we can let them into the same tank? You know, just for a little while. We can get the bag out while she's over there."

"And how do you plan to get her back into this tank before someone sees her?"

Jen grabs my hand, shocking me, but she's looking for the necklace I'm holding. *Duh, Finn, Jen's not hitting on you.*

"Bribery?" she says, holding up the necklace.

"There's no way that will work."

"It got her to eat the fish."

I stare at the Mer—at Erie—the jewel glinting around her neck. It could work, I suppose. She definitely likes pretty things. I kneel down to be eye level with her. "Listen. I'll let you go see Niku, but you have to come back to your tank when I say. Deal?" What am I doing? She can't understand me.

"Niku?" Her voice is clear in the water, no air in the way, like a human's would be. It's higher pitched, making her sound younger than she appears. The glass of the tank muffles it a bit, but it sounds . . . shit, it sounds as clear as Chlorine's scream when I ripped her gills.

I swallow a shuddering breath at the memory and walk to the tube that connects the tanks. A glass door closes off both sides. Before I can second-guess myself, I open Erie's side, motioning for her to swim in. She hesitates, running her fingers over the groove in the glass, then smooths her palm along the wall beyond it. She peers at it skeptically—once inside, there's no room to turn around. She'll be trapped if I don't open the other end.

I point to the other side of the tube and say, "Niku." That's all it takes. With her hands on either wall, she swims inside. Jen closes the door behind her, and panic rises in her magenta eyes, so I open the door to Niku's tank as quick as I can. Erie jettisons in like a cannonball and wraps her arms around him, just like they were that first day. She makes Mer noises, and he closes his eyes, looking . . . as if a dolphin can feel relief.

Jen touches my shoulder and beams. I can't match her grin, though. There's only one thing running through my mind at the moment:

We are so fucked.

"Niku!" I hug him tight, burying my face into his side as he turns his head over my shoulder in a dolphin hug.

"Princess, thank the Tides you're safe."

I squeeze him harder and finally let my muscles relax as I pull away. "I'm fine. Hungry, but I didn't know they expected us to eat the dead fish."

His eyes narrow as they land on the necklace. "Where did you get that?"

I finger the jewel that matches my hair. The tips of my nails are still stained, and I wonder whose fingertips are marked with my loss. Then I shake my head, push away the thought that I'm nothing more than a blackened shell.

"Finn bribed me to eat a dead fish with it."

"Finn?"

"The landfolk man. The girl is Jen. Such a strange name, don't you think? Jen." I roll it around my mouth again. "They were calling me Io, so I told them my name, and yours."

Niku gapes at me, his face a mixture of disbelief and annoyance. Basically, a regular Niku look. "When did you learn to speak the air?"

I can't speak the air—I speak the ocean. "I pointed at myself and said my name until Finn repeated me. I will learn to speak the air, though, to ask why we're here."

Niku turns away and examines the landfolk. Finn and Jen watch us. Jen is all smiles; Finn is . . . decidedly not. His eyebrows are pulled together, his shoulders hunched.

"I don't think it's a good idea to speak to them," Niku says.

"If I hadn't, they wouldn't have let me in here."

"They won't let you stay."

"Of course they will. Why should we be separated?"

Niku sighs. "I don't like this. Why let you come here when they went to such lengths to separate us before? Why the jewelry? The names? What's changed since we arrived?"

I play with the jewel around my neck, trying not to think about where we are and why I have it. "Maybe they feel bad? Maybe they'll take us back to the ocean now?"

He shakes his head. "No, Princess. We're not going back to the ocean. Of that, I'm sure."

I wrap my arms around him again. I don't want to think of being trapped here forever, of eating dead fish and only being allowed to see Neek every few days. What kind of life is that? Why would Finn and Jen do that when they gave me jewelry?

The words barely reach my lips as I gather the courage to ask my question. "Do you think this is what happened to Clair and Huron . . . and Mother?"

Neek is quiet for a long time. "Yes," he says, so soft I can barely hear him. "This is exactly what happened to them. And before them, to the members of the pod that disappeared."

I trace the scars on his side like I did when I was young and Mother disappeared. Some nights, the only way I could fall asleep was to trace his scars and imagine they were a secret path that would lead me to her, if only I could read them. Now, they've led me to the same fate, and I recognize them for what they are.

"How did you return from the landfolk the first time?"

Niku stiffens. "What do you mean?"

I follow one scar as it intersects with others at regular intervals. "These are net scars—you've been caught before. How did you make it back?"

In all the time I've known Neek, he's never mentioned his scars, nor how he got them. I only recognize them now because the same pattern is etched into my own scales.

For a while, I don't think he'll answer. He surfaces before speaking, and I hold my breath until he sinks back into the water. Finn and Jen are gone.

"I came back by the grace of your mother, Queen Manistique."

I push away to look in his eyes. "My mother?" His nose dips, and I settle on his back, curled around his dorsal fin. No one speaks of Mother anymore, except to say she brought the landfolk and their nets. I want to hear a story about Mother when she was still revered as Queen.

"I was the oldest of three brothers," Niku begins. "One day, we were scouting together, racing, trying to be the first to find a school of fish and bring word back to the Seadom. There was a storm building on the horizon—we could feel it in the waves and hear it in the cry of the gulls. The whole ocean buzzed with it."

I swish my tattered fins against him when he pauses. I used to bat my fins at him all the time in the Seadom. He was always such a jellyfish, back when life was carefree, before the boats began hunting the merfolk.

"We found a school," he continues, "and I thought I'd earn my place as a guard by corralling them back to the Seadom for easy hunting. My brothers agreed, though it was an impossible plan. They pinned the fish in on the sides with bubbles while I chased them forward. We were so intent on what we were doing, we didn't see the net stretched out between two boats. It was large enough for most of the fish to swim through, but my brothers slammed into it."

I gasp and sit up. "The landfolk let the fish through?"

"They weren't there for the fish," Niku says. "As soon as my brothers hit the net, the boats began to circle us. I could have turned and made it out, but I was so stunned by what happened, I didn't move fast enough."

He takes me to the surface again, spraying an angry blast of water so he can take another deep breath. I run my hand over his side, trying to calm him. I know Niku's moods—know he blames himself for every ill that befalls those he cares about. I wish I could take back all the times I've snuck out on him, all the times I've made him worry, all the times I've called him a jellyfish.

When he finally sinks back into the water, he continues. "The boats capsized in the storm, dragging us down. We strained against the net, trying to get to the surface to breathe, but we were trapped. That's when I was scarred."

He surfaces again and paces the enclosure for so long, I have to let go and sink into the water to breathe. I don't want to say anything, but I want to know how Mother saved him. I brush his flipper as he swims past and he slows, then stops and sinks to face me.

"Are you okay?" I rub his nose.

"It was a long time ago." He dips his head underneath me, and I lay on his back again, brushing his side in long, calming strokes.

"My brothers died. Drowned."

It's such a matter-of-fact statement that I stop my hand. "I'm sorry."

He doesn't acknowledge it. "I passed out. When I came to, I was on the surface, free of the nets. The storm had ended, and the sea was calm. I was too weak to swim, but I tried anyway. A merwoman stopped me. It was your mother, Queen Manistique."

I suck in a breath at the shock of that. I never knew my mother saved someone's life, especially not Niku's. "How did she know you were there?" I whisper.

"A scout heard our screams. He told the king we needed help, but your father said it was too dangerous. Your mother snuck out and came to our rescue. It was too late for my brothers, but she cut me free and held me at the surface through the storm so I could breathe. She stayed with me until I was strong enough to swim, telling me stories of her children—hotheaded Clair with hair like fire coral; her only son, Eaton, green from head to fins like his father; and her newest little one, Erie, still a minnow, but already getting into trouble."

I wrap my arms around him and squeeze. Some of the tension leaves his body.

"I pledged my life to her, right then and there, before I knew I would survive. She promoted me to guard and asked me to safeguard the one thing that was most precious to her—you." Several bubbles escape as he huffs. "And I have failed."

My heart breaks. "You haven't failed, Neeky. I'm safe. I'll learn how to speak the air and figure out what the landfolk want with us."

"Don't trust them, Princess. The landfolk are evil, and none of the merfolk or pod have returned once they're taken."

I squeeze him, swallowing hard because I can't stand that thought. "*We* will. I promise. We'll find a way home." I trace his scars again. Niku survived the nets once, and Mother saved him. This time, I'll be the one to save him. I'll save both of us.

Chapter 12: Finn

As we walk away from the tank, I grab Jen's arm to stop her. The light in her eyes falters. "We won't get in trouble, will we?"

"If anyone sees them in the same tank, we will."

"Should we get her back in her own tank, then?"

I consider the pair. Erie's lying on Niku's back, tracing the scars on his side. I may be the world's biggest dick for separating them in the first place, and I may be the stupidest person in Oceanica for letting them back in together, but not even I have the heart to tear them apart right now.

My shoulders sink. "Leave them. We'll come in early."

Jen turns, but I touch her arm again. "Do you need a drink? I need a drink."

"Meet you at the Porch?"

I shake my head. "We need to talk without everyone else. The Irish pub on Flagler?"

She nods, and we go our separate ways to meet up there. By the time I arrive, she's sitting at a table with a beer. The waitress comes over when I sit; I order a beer and two shots of whiskey.

"I don't know about that," Jen says.

I look her straight in the eye. "You talked to a mermaid today, and she talked back."

"Good point."

The shots arrive. We clink them together, hit the bar, and down them. Despite her lack of beer knowledge, Jen can do shots like a pro. She drops her empty glass in mine and takes a sip of her beer. "So, what do we have to talk about without the rest of the interns overhearing?"

"First, we're trainers now, not interns. Second, we are so fucked."

Panic crosses her face. "You said we could go in early to separate them. No one has to know."

"And you better not tell anyone, because then we're fired as well as fucked." I take a drink of beer. I need another shot—the last one isn't working fast enough. "I'm not talking about getting in trouble with Corporate, although that will certainly happen if anyone finds out. I'm talking about being really, truly in trouble."

Jen lifts an eyebrow. "Is it against the law to keep a Mer and dolphin together?"

"That's not what I mean."

"Then spit it out."

Another big gulp, and I motion the waitress for another round. I drain my glass as I try to figure out how to tell Jen I've just condemned her to death at the hands of a Mer. "When you think of Io—Erie—whatever . . . what do you imagine?"

Jen peers at me like I've gone crazy. "I imagine a mermaid with magenta hair."

"Ariel or velociraptor?"

The look doesn't leave her face. "What kind of question is that?"

"A very important one. Do you think of her as a predator or a pet?"

"I don't know. I think of her as Io. Depressed, won't eat, Iodine."

"Depressed," I echo, and when the next round arrives, I take a big swig. "Predators don't get depressed."

"What's this about?" Jen covers my hand with hers. "What's wrong?"

Her eyes are such a deep shade of brown. I've never seen a redhead with eyes like hers. Maybe she dyes her hair? I don't know—I'm doing whatever I can to not think about how much trouble we're in. "There was this trainer at Oceanica, right at the beginning. Her name was Hannah Michaels. She had eyes like yours."

Jen sits back, suddenly cold. "Let me guess, you slept with her."

"What? No. I was seventeen. She was, like, thirty, or something. She'd been a trainer at Orca World. Years of training under her belt." I sip my beer and stare at the grain of the table wood as I recall Hannah's easy smile. Her fearless nature. The kind-hearted teasing because I was young and awkward and boss's pet. "She claimed her Mer was tame—that she'd made friends with it. Her Mer was more like a pet than a predator."

I take a deep drink as Jen runs her fingertip through a wet circle on the table.

"Hannah's 'pet' killed her during a show. Jumped right onto the platform and pulled her under. Ripped her fucking face off. She thought they were friends."

Jen's silent, her gaze lost in her beer for a full thirty seconds. I finish my drink. "You can't think of Erie as a friend, or a pet. As soon as you do, you're dead. She's a predator. A velociraptor. A killer."

Jen spins her glass, watching with eyes as dull as Radon's. She's trying to reconcile depressed, vain Erie with the idea of getting her face ripped off. "But—"

"No." I grab her hands, pressing them into the cold glass. "No. I almost died two weeks ago because Maddy forgot how dangerous the Mer are. If you're going to work with me, I need you to keep your wits about you. I don't want to end up unconscious in the hospital again, or worse. Got it?"

Her face pales, and she swallows. I've probably ruined the most exciting day of her life, but hopefully, it'll keep us both alive.

"Another shot?"

"Yeah." Her head dips forward, hair falling to cover her trembling lips. "Yeah, I could do another."

• • • •

WHEN I WALK INTO THE holding room the next morning, Erie's curled up around Niku's dorsal fin, sleeping. His eyes are closed, but when I get closer, they snap open and he bares his teeth at me. I swear he's more pit bull than dolphin.

I salute him and decide to fish the necklaces from Erie's tank before I separate them. I've just pulled the bag out when Jen enters. She glances once at the pair, and her shoulders sink as she turns away. She's not imagining a velociraptor.

"Here." I hold out her stolen necklace as I descend the stairs, and she takes it with a soft word of thanks. "You may not want to wear it around Erie again. And don't call her Erie with anyone else—as far as they know, she's still Iodine, and she doesn't speak."

Jen runs her fingers over the dolphin pendant without acknowledging me. I feel like I've deflated every bit of happiness she's ever had. Unfortunately, it's time to destroy any remaining threads, because I'm sure this separation will go as well as the first—only, this time, we'll know what Erie's screaming.

Before we can start, Jen grabs my shoulder. "How did no one know they could talk before now?"

"You saw Argon's introduction to Ray and K. Silence is one of the first things they learn."

A derisive huff leaves her. "So people won't think they're human."

"They *aren't* human."

"They have a language."

"So do dolphins. Do you think dolphins are human, too?"

Jen hugs her arms to her chest and gazes into the tank, sulking. I tap on the glass. "Morning, Erie. Niku." He swims to the other side as she groggily raises her head and peers around. When her magenta eyes land on me, she uncurls from her dolphin.

"Finn?" That otherworldly, soft-yet-high-pitched voice again, muffled slightly by the glass.

A wide smile pulls at my cheeks, because despite the fact I'm absolutely fucked, a mermaid just said my name. Hopefully, if I keep smiling, she'll do as I ask. "You ready for breakfast, beautiful?"

She points to herself. "Erie."

"I know, sweet."

She shakes her head and jabs herself in the chest. "Erie."

All I can do is chuckle. "I know, Erie. Let's get you back in your tank and get you some breakfast." I fish the green necklace that didn't fall into the tank out of my pocket, and her wide eyes follow it. "Open the tube, Jen."

The glass slides up, and Erie glances around, panicked, before swimming to Niku. She wraps her arms around him.

"Sorry, darlin'. Time to go back." I point at the tube, and she shakes her head. I hold up the necklace, and her arms tighten. Bribery won't work—time to use threats.

I pocket the necklace and climb the stairs to the platform. They watch me, probably wondering what I'm about to do. When I grab the electroshocker from the wall, Jen speaks.

"Finn, you can't."

"I will if I have to." As soon as the shocker's in the water, Erie starts yelling Mer words at me. I turn to Jen. "Tell her to get into the tube."

Jen knocks on the glass to get Erie's attention and points at the tube. "Please, Erie, just go in. Don't make him hurt you."

Erie says something to Niku. She waits a moment, as if listening to his reply, though he doesn't click, or whistle, or make any of the other noises associated with dolphins. Then she hangs her head and swims toward the tube.

"Attagirl," Jen says and motions her on. Erie glances at Niku before she hunches her shoulders and swims in. I relax and take my finger away from the button as I watch Jen close the door behind her, and Niku—angry pit bull Niku—rips the electroshocker from my hands and the wall. I stumble and nearly fall in the water.

"Shit!" That's an expensive piece of equipment. He beats it against the side of the tank like a toy. Goddamn dolphin.

"What happened?" Jen says, but Erie's about to panic in the tube, so I point to it.

"Get the other end open."

She scrambles to open the door while I scrutinize Niku and the ruined piece of equipment I'll have to fish out of his tank. Fuck. Corporate's gonna be pissed.

Niku's right—the landfolk are evil. I run a finger over my stained nails as Finn walks to my enclosure, and when he throws a dead fish in the water, I throw it back. I pace, following the landfolk, glaring at them, and telling Niku, very loudly, that I'll drown them when I get the chance. I wish they could speak the ocean, so they knew what I was saying.

By the end of the day, they're arguing, and by the scowl on Finn's face, Jen's won. Good. I hate Finn more than Jen—he's the one who tried to shock me.

"Erie." Finn motions me over to Niku's side of the enclosure. I cross my arms and glare at him. He speaks some nonsense air words, including Niku's name, and then opens the door to the tube.

My arms fall to my sides. Is he letting me back in? I cautiously swim forward and peer into the tube, then glance at Finn. He raises his eyebrows and points to the other side. "Niku."

What if it's a trick? What if I'm stuck in the tube? I decide to risk it.

Instead of rushing to Niku like I did the last time, I swim in slowly and turn to face the landfolk. "What are they doing, Neek?"

He swims next to me, and I put my hand over his scars. "I don't know, Princess. Why make you leave for the day, only to let you back in at night? It makes no sense."

Finn walks to the platform, and I dig my fingers into Niku's side, but the loop doesn't appear, just a few dead fish. A sharp pain lodges in my stomach, but I'm not eating a dead fish in front of Finn. Let him feel snubbed.

He pats the barrier. "Goodnight, Erie. Niku." He says other air words, and then leaves with Jen.

In the morning, they open the tube again. "I'll be back tonight, I hope." I kiss Neek on the end of his nose and swim through the tube without fighting.

When Finn throws me a fish, I let it sink, but I don't throw it back. They let me into Niku's enclosure again that night. What do they want? After they leave, I try to get my nails into the space around the door to the tube, but it's sealed so tight, all I manage is to break the blackened tips of my nails.

Two days of being ripped away from Niku. What's the point? Finn and Jen constantly fight, jabbing the air with their fingers and raising their voices, and it's Jen who finally changes the routine. She shoves something against the barrier. Finn tries to rip it away, but she pierces him with a stern look that would probably stop even the likes of Father.

The thing in her hand is all black angles, but in the middle, something alive and colorful moves. It takes a long while for me to focus on it—it's too fast. A flash of green and red in a blue so unnatural it's hard to watch. Whatever it is, it's noisy.

The moving thing slows, and I gasp. "Clair?" I press my hands to the barrier. "Clair! It's me!" Somehow, the landfolk put my sister in that tiny rectangle, but Clair can't hear me.

"Clair!" I pound on the enclosure, trying to get my sister's attention, and Jen jumps back, taking Clair with her.

"Um, oops," she says. I don't know what that means.

Finn touches a similar rectangle a few times with his fingers, then presses it against the barrier. "Clair?"

My sister has moved to Finn's rectangle. She's perfectly still in the water, and I wonder what's wrong. How can she float in one place without the tiny fin movements to keep her there? How is her hair so still?

Finn takes her away, touches the rectangle again, and a different merfolk is in the box. I don't know this one—it's a male with orange hair and fins. He's also still. Finn shows me a few others that I don't know, and then the bright blue of Huron's hair catches my eye.

"Huron!" I press my hands to the barrier and gape at him. "Huron, please, can you not hear me? Say something. Move." He's as still and silent as the others.

I draw my broken nails over the barrier, wishing that I could touch him, that I could wake him. Finn takes Huron away, and I sink to the floor. I'll end up in one of those boxes, still and silent. That's a fate worse than turning to foam. I swim to the closed tube that leads to Niku's enclosure and curl my tail around myself.

"This is so wrong," Jen whispers, face pale.

I can't help but agree. However dangerous Erie is—however alien—she knows two of our Mer. From the droop of her fins and the loss on her face, she cares about them. I didn't know fish even had the capacity to care about each other. Clair and Huron—we call them Potassium and Argon.

"I wish you hadn't done that," I say.

"I wish I hadn't, either. I was just trying to show her what she needs to do." Jen covers her mouth like she's about to be sick.

I rub my hand across her back. She looks like she'll cry, if she doesn't throw up first. "We can't do anything about it now."

She swallows hard. "We can let her see them."

My hand stops as I consider the ramifications of that. "No. You saw how she freaked out when we took her from Niku—it'll be worse trying to take her from her friends."

"But—"

I squeeze her shoulder. "No."

She deflates, wraps her arms around herself, and stares at Erie, curled up next to Niku's tube. "I hate this job."

If she tries to quit, I'll have to remind her that anyone else will be trigger-happy with the electroshocker and won't let Erie into Niku's tank at night. And I sure as hell won't pass Erie over to Maddy at the end of the summer. Jen has to stay and take over the pair when I go back to school.

"Don't worry," I say. "We'll find something to cheer her up again. Jewelry . . . or something." How much jewelry can one Mer own? What the heck else do they like? And why am I thinking this way about a fish?

I don't want to admit it, but there was something in her magenta eyes—something as she gazed at Argon's picture on my cell phone—that was more than fish. She may be covered in green scales, but there's something unavoidably human about Erie, and it's going to get us all in trouble.

· · · ·

WE'RE LETTING ERIE into Niku's tank that night when Sergio walks in. "What the hell do you think you're doing? They're supposed to be separated."

It's too late to get her back in her own tank, so I open the door and let her through. "It's fine. She sleeps with him, and then goes back to her own tank for the day. It makes her easy to work with."

Serge glances at the new electroshocker hanging on the wall. "Guess what else would make her easy to work with?"

I don't honor him with a response. Erie swims forward to get a better look at him. He takes a step back when she smiles, her sharp teeth glinting in the fluorescent light. She raises her hand and points to herself, and somehow, like an idiot, I don't realize what she's about to do until it's too late.

"Erie," she says, then points at Serge. He gapes at her, dumbfounded, so she does it again, then points to Niku, Jen, and me and says our names. When she's finished, she points at Sergio again, waiting for him to introduce himself.

"What the fuck is going on here?" He turns on me, eyes wide. "Did she just say your name?"

"Did it sound like someone else's name?"

The smile fades from Erie's face as Serge ignores her. "Did you teach her to do that?" he says.

"She did it herself a few days ago."

"And you didn't shock her?"

Erie knocks on the glass until we look at her, then points to Serge and raises her non-existent eyebrows. I elbow him in the ribs. "Tell her your name."

"They're not supposed to make noise."

"Just tell her your name."

He shakes his head before he answers. "Sergio."

"Sergio," she echoes, drawing out the *R*. "Sergio."

He clutches his chest like he's about to go into cardiac arrest. "This is . . ." He can't even form the words. I expect him to say "amazing," or "unprecedented," or something similar, but he doesn't. "This is completely against the rules."

The grin that had been forming tumbles headlong off my face. "Since when do you care about rules? You used to be the one egging me on to break them."

"Yeah, at school," Serge says. He turns his back on Erie, which makes her face fall, too. "This is my aunt's place—if it's shut down, I have to go back to working at the restaurant, and, in case you don't remember, that's shit pay."

"A fucking mermaid just asked for your name and you're worried about your paycheck?" I can't believe it, and I refuse to shock Erie into silence like the others. I know he's being the smart one, but I don't care. "Erie won't shut down Oceanica. I mean, look at her."

I sweep my hand toward her and realize I'm seeing Ariel, not a raptor. From the expression on Serge's face, he knows it, too.

He jabs his finger into my chest. "You do remember Hannah, right? You remember the blood when Carbon pulled her under? You remember how she used to talk about him, like he'd never hurt her?"

That show is forever burned in my memory, but I can't reconcile Erie smiling at me right now with the cloud of blood in the water. "I know." I drop my gaze to the damp cement floor and clench my teeth. "I know, but I'm not getting in the water with her. I . . ."

I let out a long breath, and Jen touches my shoulder in an unexpected display of solidarity. "Don't worry, Sergio. I won't let her hurt Finn. We'll get her out in the morning."

He peers between us, and when his shoulders sink, I know he won't tell. "Fine. Whatever. Are you coming to the Porch?"

"Of course," I say. "Let me feed them, and we'll meet you there."

Serge scowls at Erie, shakes his head at me, and leaves. I clench my hands at my sides. He's right, of course. I know he's right. What I'm doing, what I'm saying, what I'm *thinking*, is dangerous. I glance at Erie. Her brows are pulled together, confused, one hand pressed against the glass. She has no way of knowing why Serge is upset. Why we're all terrified of her. I think of Chlorine piercing my shoulders and know we're terrified for a very good reason.

My hand, which I was lifting to the glass to mirror hers, falls back to my side.

Jen touches my arm and steps closer. "What do we do now?"

Does she mean, what do we do about Erie talking? How do we get her to perform without showing her a video that upsets her? Or what do we do to keep ourselves from getting killed?

I squeeze her hand. "We feed them and get the hell out of here for the night."

I take the stairs two at a time to get away from Jen.

The warm colors of the Seadom fill my soul as I lounge in the coral garden with Huron. He runs his fingers through my hair, which is weird until I realize the webbing is missing.

"What happened?" I ask.

Instead of answering, he pushes me back on a mushroom coral and kisses me. His tail wraps around mine as he presses me down, and the bright, pillowy mushrooms wilt to gray, then become the hard wall of the landfolk enclosure. I try to push him away. "Huron, stop. Something's wrong."

His tail rips in two, and he wraps both fins around me, trapping me. "Huron!" I yell.

"Princess."

He never calls me princess. I try to push him away again.

"Princess, wake up."

I jerk and shove away before I realize that's Niku's voice. I rub my eyes. "Sorry."

Neek nudges me until I'm draped over him again. I trace his scars while my heartbeat slows. Soon after, Jen walks into the room.

"Morning, Erie. Morning, Niku."

She says that every morning. It must be a greeting. "Mor . . . ing, Jen," I say, then try again because it didn't sound right. "Mor . . . Ning. Mor-Ning."

Jen tilts her head to the side, eyebrows pulled together like she's trying to decide something. After a moment, she walks to the enclosure and knocks on it with her knuckles. "Tank," she says.

I slide off Niku's back. My head mirrors hers as I try to figure out what that word means. "Tank." The word snaps, like a mantis shrimp killing its prey. "Tank." What is *tank*?

She presses her hands on the barrier and repeats the word. Does she mean *hands*? I lift mine and consider them. "Tank?"

Jen shakes her head, wiggles her web-less fingers at me, and says, "Hands." Then she raps on the barrier again. "Tank."

I tap the barrier with my broken nails. "Tank?"

She nods. So the barrier is *tank*. I know the air word for the enclosure now. They're keeping Niku and me in *tank*.

"Where's Finn?" Jen asks next.

I don't know what that word means. A question about Finn, who isn't here. "Wherrrrre's," I echo, trying the word out. "Wherrre's Finn?"

Jen chuckles. If Finn doesn't show, will she let me stay with Neek for the day? Will she teach me air words? I hope so, but it doesn't matter, because Finn walks in. Before he can say anything, I do.

"Mor-Ning, Finn."

He pauses midstride and peers at me, eyebrows pulled together in a frown. He asks Jen a question, but she shakes her head.

"Finn." I tap on the tank. "Wherrre's? Wherrre's Finn?"

He speaks to Jen again, then turns to me, puts his finger to his lips, and says, "Shh."

It's the same motion my grandfather used on us girls when we were young and too noisy. Finn's shushing me. When he begins talking with Jen, I knock on the tank again and shush him in return. Jen winks at me, as if we're co-conspirators, but Finn turns his back on me.

I swim to Niku. "He shushed me."

"I don't think you're supposed to talk."

"Then why does he ask me questions?"

Niku snorts. "Because he's an idiot landfolk."

A knock disturbs the tank, and I shush him again, but Finn points to the tube. My shoulders sag as I pat Niku's side. "See you tonight."

"Don't make them angry."

I hug him and go back to my *tank*. Once inside, I try to remember some of the air-words they say often enough to recognize. I'll learn to speak the air whether Finn likes it or not. "MorNing, Finn. Time for . . . brekfass?"

He gapes at me in disbelief. Did I say it wrong? It's the same thing he says to me every morning before he gives me a fish. "Brekfass" must mean fish. Maybe I asked if he wanted a fish. How in the Tides would he eat a fish with those flat teeth? What do the landfolk eat? Not merfolk, or I'd be dead by now.

"You want breakfast?" he says.

"Brekfass." I nod.

"Okay." He climbs the stairs with the bucket, and for the first time since I learned his name, I crest the water to wait for the fish. Instead of holding it out like he did the last time, he holds it high over the water.

I glance at the fish, then at Finn. "Brekfass?" I lift my arm out of the water, but it's too high. Why won't he lower it?

"Jump," he says. I don't know that word. "Jump," he repeats, then bends his legs and lifts into the air before falling back to the platform with a loud *clang*.

I dip under to stop the burning in my eyes. I crest again, but Finn is still holding the fish up high. The only time I've been that far out of the water was in the net. Why does he want me to jump out of the water? Is it to put me in the net again? Panic rolls my stomach at the thought. I'm no longer hungry.

I'll kill him before I let him stick me in another net.

Ignoring "brekfass," I swim to the bottom of the tank and wrap my tail around myself. My heartbeat races like a tiny minnow running from a predator.

"Erie?" Jen says. More air words.

I cover my ears—I don't want to hear anymore air words. I hate the air. Why can't they learn to speak the ocean?

Jen says something else, and though I don't know the words, I know what she's asking. "What's wrong?" What's wrong is that I'm trapped in this *tank* while two sociopaths harass me with dead fish.

A loud *plunk* at the surface heralds a fish. When I don't move, a smaller *plink* accompanies it. Finn is bribing me with a necklace. I clench my teeth, grab the fish and the necklace, and turn my back on them to eat.

Finn's the first to walk into my field of vision. "Sorry, darlin.'"

"Erie," I say. Why can he never get my name right? "Darlin'" must be a nickname. At least he doesn't call me Io anymore.

He puts his hand on the tank. "Sorry, Erie." He says some other words, and then motions me forward. I eye him for a long time before unwinding my tail and swimming toward him. When I reach him, he spins in a circle.

I tilt my head—what's he doing? I glance at Jen, who also spins, then back to Finn, who repeats the movement. Why are they spinning? I spin when I'm happy—are they happy I ate?

Finn stops spinning, and twists his finger at me. He wants me to spin?

"Please?" he says. I don't know the word, but I understand the pleading tone of his voice. He's asking me to spin.

I turn a circle in the water and they cheer. Finn motions with his finger, so I spin again. Again, they cheer.

They're ridiculous.

Finn stops spinning his finger that direction, and spins it from top to bottom instead. I do a backflip, and they cheer.

They may be ridiculous, but they're fun.

He puts his hand on the tank, and I do the same. His hand is bigger than mine, with no webbing and blunt nails. It looks so strange outlining my hand. I giggle.

"Tag," Finn says and removes his hand. He points to Jen, who puts her hand on the tank like she did earlier. Warily, I swim to Jen and put my hand over hers, which is a little smaller than mine.

"Tag," Jen says, then runs around the tank and touches Finn's hand. "Tag," she says again.

Finn runs to the other side of the enclosure and smacks his hand on the tank. It's been a long time since I've played a game—a long time since the threat of the landfolk has allowed it. I miss playing games and having fun, and it isn't as if I have to fear the landfolk anymore.

A smile grows on my face as I put my hand over Finn's. "Tag!" I swim to Jen. "Tag," I say again as our hands meet.

Jen tags Finn again, and he runs up the platform and holds his hand out. I kick hard, crest so far that my shoulders leave the water, and touch his hand. It's warm and soft, and I gasp. Brittle air scorches my throat, and I fall into the water, holding my burning gills.

He tricked me. He tricked me into jumping out of the water. I swim to the middle of the tank and wrap my tail around myself, gulping water to soothe my air-torn gills.

I've really fucked up this time. I run down the stairs and press my hands into the glass. "Oh god, Erie, I'm sorry. I wasn't thinking."

That wasn't how it was supposed to happen. She was supposed to touch my hand and realize that jumping out of the water didn't hurt—now I've taught her that it does. How am I supposed to get her to jump now?

I sink to my knees. "Erie, please, I'm sorry."

She turns around with a shaking hand and shushes me, then curls up again. I rest my forehead against the cold glass and squeeze my eyes shut, pinching the bridge of my nose. I'll never get her to perform.

Jen puts her hands on my shoulders. Her hands are warm—so much warmer than Erie's hand when she touched mine. She was as cold as a fish.

She *is* a fish, but it still surprised me, just as much as my warmth obviously surprised her.

Jen squeezes my shoulders. "She was having fun."

I stay where I am, because I don't want Jen to take her hands away. We argue more often than not, but I appreciate her presence more than any of the other employees. She keeps me human.

"I don't know what to do," I say, and she squeezes my shoulders again. "If I can't make money, Delmara will give them to someone else." Not to mention, I'm terrified of becoming Hannah—the trainer who thought she was friends with her Mer.

Jen kneels and wraps her arms around my shoulders. I want to press her against the glass and kiss her until she gasps like Erie did. Instead, I press the bridge of my nose until I think I might break the cartilage.

"Why don't you take the rest of the day off?" she says. "Go do . . . whatever you do on your days off. I'll let Erie into Niku's tank tonight and get her back out in the morning."

I don't take days off. Now that I've been given a Mer to train, and only a couple of months to train her, I'm here every day. I don't trust anyone else to take care of Erie. Maybe I should—I'm not doing a good job.

"Come on." Jen pulls me up and pushes me toward the door. "Go relax. Do something fun. Don't worry about Erie for the rest of the day."

That won't happen. She's all I'll think about for the rest of the day, whether I'm here or not. I glance at the tank where she's still curled up. "Let her in now. I'll tell Serge to keep everyone out."

Jen's eyes darken. "What if someone comes in?"

"Tell them I told you to do it." I call Serge on the walkie-talkie as I leave the room and go topside.

The majority of Oceanica is open air, except for the old Eco-Discovery Center that we absorbed when we bought the land between Fort Zachary Taylor and the Truman Annex. It's full of fish tanks, like a normal aquarium, but it's deserted right now because of Potassium's show.

The fish in these tanks don't talk. They don't laugh or play games or wear jewelry. They don't try to kill people, either. Maybe I should be an aquarium caretaker instead of a trainer. It's quiet here, except for the faint thump of the bass coming from the arena.

I push the door open and a blast of hot, humid air and loud cheering smacks me in the face. It's weird to be outside in the middle of the day—I'm not used to the sunshine, or the screaming children. I weave my way through the crowds until I find the gift shop where my younger sister works.

"Finn." She brightens as she lifts her face from the register. Her hair is lighter than mine—more brown than black—and she has a sunburn across her nose from spending yesterday at Fort Zach.

"Hey, Munchkin." Her name is Heather, but I'm her older brother—it's my job to make fun of her. "How're sales?"

"Booming between shows. What brings you topside?"

I pick up a stuffed representation of K. She's our star performer right now because the little girls think she looks like Ariel. "Oh, you know, pissing off my Mer and completely failing at my job."

"What's new?" Heather grins, and I throw K at her. It bounces off the register's screen. "You break it, you buy it." She snickers, then grows serious. "So, what did you do to your fish this time?"

I grab K from the ground and toss her back onto the stack. If I'm successful, that red hair will be replaced by magenta in two months. Right now, I can't imagine that happening.

"She finally jumped, but she breathed air and hurt her gills." A cheer from outside means K just jumped and flipped. "Now it'll be near impossible to get her to jump again."

"Still don't want to use the shocker?"

"Hell no." I grimace. "That shit hurts."

"That's kind of the point."

"I don't care. I'm trying a different method. Positive reinforcement, like training a dog."

Heather snorts. "Since when are you the Dog Whisperer?" Another cheer sounds outside, and she tilts her head toward it, probably counting how much longer she has until the gift shop's flooded with sweaty tourists. "Why don't you have the dolphin teach her?"

This time, I'm the one who snorts. "Yeah, right. That dolphin's an even bigger pain in the ass than the Mer."

"Yeah, but dolphins jump naturally. Put him in the big tank, and I bet he'll do it."

I doubt that, but I'm running out of options. It's worth a try, at least. "Yeah. I might."

A big, final cheer rattles the building. "Just use what works," Heather says as I back away from the throng of kids pouring in. "And be careful!"

• • • •

MAYBE, JUST MAYBE, I can get Niku to cooperate and show Erie that jumping isn't so bad. I show up early the next morning to schedule a time in the practice tank; he's too big to jump in the holding tank. Hell, he might be too big to fit in the tubes that lead to the pool.

Jen already has Erie in her own tank by the time I return. "Morning, Erie," I say, like usual. "Time for breakfast?"

She shushes me and turns her back. "I'll take Niku for breakfast then."

Jen grabs a bucket of fish. "Did you have a good day off?"

"I saw my little sister and went snorkeling at Fort Zach."

"That sounds nice."

Snorkeling usually makes me feel better, but all I could think about was Erie. Does she know about reef fish, or only deep-water species? Does she know people like to watch fish, just for their colors? Do the Mer know humans can swim?

Jen interrupts my thoughts as she climbs the stairs to Erie's platform. "Are you close with your sister?" Despite the size of the tanks, both platforms are against the wall, so it's easy to talk between them.

I toss a fish to Niku, who lets it sink because I swear he hates me. Getting him to jump will be no easy feat. "As close as we can be, I suppose. I mean, I never watched *Merlin* with her, or anything." I wink at Jen, and she blushes. "I've always looked out for her." I think about what Munchkin said. "I guess she's always done the same."

I throw another fish to Niku. "Yeah, I guess we're close."

Jen stares at me just a little too long. "That's really nice that you protect each other like that." She throws a fish to Erie, and something static ripples through the air with whatever she left unsaid.

"Do you have any siblings?"

She turns back to the water so quickly, it's like I've shocked her. "No. I mean . . . I did, but she died."

"I'm sorry," I say. Jen's too good a person to have lost someone like that.

"It's not—" She presses her lips together, then glances at me again. "It's not your fault, Finn."

That's a little weird. Saying thanks would be awkward, so I throw Niku another fish, although I'd planned to starve him a bit to get him to cooperate. I don't think I can bribe him with necklaces.

"Were the two of you close?" I ask.

"No." She blushes again, as if she's admitted something terrible. "She was several years older than me. The golden child. We didn't have much in common. I loved her, though. Looked up to her." Jen stops and drops her fish in the bucket; Erie's still eating the last one. "Do you think the Mer are a family pod? Like dolphins?"

I've been pushing one thought to the back of my mind since Erie responded to some of the photos on my phone, but not others. If the Mer live in pods, then there are either a number of pods in the area, or they live in pods too big to know all of the other Mer. Considering we caught Erie so far out, I was thinking the former. Once she identified two Mer we caught fairly close to Key West, I started to think there might be more Mer than we ever imagined.

Which means, we've been ripping individual Mer from their giant pod for years—ever since the first one Dad found. I wonder if he ever considered how human they might be, or if the thrill of discovery blinded him to what it was he'd actually found? It's certainly blinded Delmara.

"Okay." I clap my hands together, because that thought will lead to me ending up like Hannah of the ripped-off face. "We have the big tank before the shows start and the other Mer need the warm up, so we better use it wisely."

Jen's shoulders sink. I toss Niku one last fish, hoping he'll be in the mood to cooperate if he knows I gave him extra. "Ready, buddy?" I open the door to the tube separating him and Erie. He does . . . nothing. He doesn't rush forward to see her, or even sniff the opening like a pit bull might. If he had an eyebrow, he'd probably raise it right now—that's how interested he is.

"No problem," I say, leaving his door open. I open the door on the opposite side of Erie's tank and step back. She hates me for tricking her, but this is something her clever mind should be drawn to: a possible escape.

She does . . . nothing.

"You've got to be kidding me," I say and punch the glass of Erie's tank. "Go open the door in the big tank," I tell Jen. When the other end opens, Erie peers through the tube. "Go on, darlin'. Jen's in there waiting for you. You'll like the bigger tank, and I'll try to get Niku in there with you."

"Niku?" She turns to him.

"You want him to go first?" I open the rest of his tube. "Come on, Niku. Dolphins first."

Erie swims toward him, but I put my hand out in a stop motion, then wave at Niku to swim through the tube. "Come on, buddy. This is your chance to see Erie during the day."

She says something, and he slowly moves forward and peers through the tube, like he's trying to decide if he'll fit. She says something else and he moves into the tube—he barely fits—and rushes through as fast as he can.

"Good boy," I say as Erie hugs him. "Now, for your next trick . . ." I walk around the tank to the opposite tube. "Let's see if we can replicate that experiment." I knock on the glass and point to the tube.

I swear they're conferring with each other, though I've never heard Niku make a noise. Erie speaks to him, pauses as if listening to his reply, and speaks again. I wish I knew Mer words so I could tell what she's saying.

In the end, Erie goes first. This tube is longer than the one between their tanks, and when I lose sight of her through the wall, I run to the room with the practice tank. Erie pokes her head out of the tube and peers around, cautious. When nothing happens, she slides the rest of the way out and turns a slow circle. Then her lips part, and she smiles.

When Niku enters the tank, she swims circles around him that get bigger and bigger until she circles the perimeter of the tank, laughing as she spins. The sound is infectious—Jen shines with delight next to me, and even Niku swims alongside, speeding through the tank. He has to jump soon, and when he does, Erie will see it's not so bad and do the same.

Niku surfaces to breathe, but he doesn't jump. "Come on," I say and point at a red ball that hangs from the ceiling. The goal is to get them to touch that—they'll have to clear the water to reach it. "Jump!" I yell.

They ignore me completely, swimming around like mindless idiots. I sigh, my gaze shifting to the electroshocker on the wall. "This will never work."

"Maybe . . ." Jen begins, then bites her lips together. When she looks at me, a little fear and a lot of hope tinge her expression. "Maybe one of the other Mer can teach her?"

The look I level at her is unamused, at best. "No. We already talked about this."

"But how's she supposed to learn—?"

"The first Mer learned just fine."

She crosses her arms. "And how long did that take?"

Fuck, she's got a point there.

Jen continues. "We have a month and a half. Most of the Mer learn from the others and perform within weeks. If we let the others teach her some basics, we'll be done by July . . ." She trails off, and I see this bullshit for what it is, but I'm also desperate. Niku isn't going to jump on his own.

Time to try something completely different.

"If I get fired for this, I'm blaming you," I say to Jen as I walk away.

"Where are you going?" she calls after me in a sing-song voice. I don't reply.

I swim quick circles around Niku, brushing him with my tail fin. He's faster than me in a straight line, but I'm more agile. We twist and play, and even he grins at the ability to move with less restriction. I don't notice Finn leave until the scrape of a tube opening rumbles through the water. I recognize the bright blue head that appears right away.

"Huron!" How'd he escape the black rectangle? How is he able to move again?

He stops halfway out of the tube, and his dull, unfocused eyes sharpen as his gaze snaps to me. He pushes himself the rest of the way out before I barrel into him, corkscrewing him through the water with a hug.

He scrambles away. "Erie, don't."

My heart drops into my tail. Huron has never pushed me away before, not even in front of Niku.

His gaze darts behind me, and I turn to find my sister, red eyes wide in shock and horror. "Erie?"

"Clair!" I grab her in a hug, but she pushes me away, too. My heart sinks even further. "What's wrong?"

They've lost weight, and their gazes dart around, quick as fish being hunted. "Shh," Clair whispers. "We're not supposed to talk."

"Or touch." Huron's so quiet, I can barely hear him.

"What? Of course we can." I grab Clair's hand and drag her to the other side of the tank, where Jen watches us with an indulgent smile. "Morning, Jen."

"Good morning, Erie."

Clair gasps and jerks back. "When did you learn to speak the air?"

"A few days ago. They kept saying the same thing every morning, so I said it back. Then Jen started teaching me words. I know the air word for hands, and that the enclosure is called *tank*. And I can ask for fish, say please, ask where they are, and say sorry—although I don't, because I don't do anything to be sorry for. I only know it because Finn keeps saying it to me."

Clair's eyes widen further, and Huron shakes his head. "Your landfolk let you speak?"

"Of course. Why wouldn't they?"

They glance at each other, and whatever they find in each other's gaze, they don't share it with me. What happened to them since they were captured?

Clair whispers, even though I already proved we could speak in front of Jen. "If we aren't silent around them, they shock us."

"You mean, with that loop?"

Clair bobs her head.

Niku swims to me, and I put my hand on his side. "They did that the first day to separate us, and once after, though I didn't make any noise then. Finn threatened to use it again, but he hasn't."

"Who's Finn?" Huron says.

I turn to the glass, where Finn has joined Jen. His arms are crossed, and he stares at us, stone-faced. I point to him. "Finn." I point to Jen and say her name, then do the same to Clair and Huron.

One corner of Finn's mouth turns up. "Hello, Clair, Huron." He nods to each as he says their names.

Clair grabs my hand. "Did he just use our real names?"

"Of course. What other names would he use?"

"The landfolk usually call me K, or Potassium."

"They call me Argon."

I think back to when I first arrived. "They used to call me Io, but then I told Finn my name. Now, he calls me that, or 'darlin', or 'beautiful,' though I don't know what those words mean."

"I can't believe they let you talk." Clair sighs wistfully. It's strange to see her as anything but overconfident and rebellious. "I'm sick of being silent until they leave."

"Well," I say, "we can't have a conversation. I still don't know enough air words to figure out why we're here."

Huron blinks in surprise. "You mean, you haven't performed yet? When did you arrive?"

"Um . . ." I look at Niku, who raises his flippers in a dolphin version of a shrug. "Several days after you. What do you mean, perform?"

"Jump. Swim. Do tricks," Huron says. "There's an enclosure that's bigger than this, and we perform while a bunch of landfolk watch and cheer."

That doesn't make any sense at all. "But . . . why?"

They glance at each other, and it's clear that they don't know any more than me.

"That's why Finn wants me to jump?" I turn to him and frown. I wish I could ask what the point of it is.

"What's wrong, darlin'?" he asks.

"Jump?"

He points to something as red as Clair's hair above the water. I swim close enough to the surface to see it—that's much too far away. I dive back to Clair and Huron. "I can't do that—I'll have to clear the water."

"Yep," Huron says.

I back away as a cold lump settles in my stomach. "No. Finn tricked me into jumping yesterday, and I burned my gills."

"You have to hold your breath," Clair says. "And you can't refuse—they'll shock you."

"And that'll burn your gills more than air," Huron says.

Finn taps on the glass. "Erie, jump."

I turn around and shush him. His lips press into a thin line.

"Erie!" Clair grabs my hand. "Just do it."

"No."

Finn taps on the glass again. "Clair," he says, and her hand tightens around mine. "Jump."

Clair jerks away from me as if Finn shocked her, swims to the bottom of the tank, and propels herself out of the water. She smacks the red thing with her hand and dives back in gracefully. "See?" she says. "Easy."

I fold my arms over my stomach and shake my head. "I can't believe you just did that."

"You'd do it too, if you'd been shocked as many times as I have. Trust me, jumping's not that bad." She sticks her hand out. "I'll show you."

Huron sticks his hand out, too. "Just do it. I don't want to be shocked again."

I turn to Finn and Jen. Finn's arms are once again crossed, but he points a finger at the red thing. Jen has her hands on the glass, eyes wide with hope.

"You're not a princess anymore, minnow." Clair twists a lock of my hair around her finger, like she did when we were home. "You're a prisoner. You have to do what they say."

Niku's nose bobs. "She's right. Finn and Jen have gone easy on us so far, but it's time to face the future, and ours is this. I'm sorry, Princess. We can't beat the landfolk."

I play with the jewel around my neck, trying to think of a way out until my shoulders sink, defeated. I don't understand why the landfolk want to watch us swim, but Niku's right—we can't beat them. "Fine." I take Clair's hand.

Clair and Huron lead me to the bottom of the tank, and she squeezes my hand. "A good kick, and hold your breath before you surface."

"Finn wouldn't have shocked me," I mumble.

"Too late," Huron says. "Go."

They yank my arms, and I kick hard as they pull me up. "Breathe!" Clair yells, and I take a deep breath before we surface. Cold, stinging air rushes past my face, forcing me to close my eyes, and the water melts away from my body as I leave its safety. I shudder as air rushes by the tip of my tail, and then Clair and Huron pull me back down. The water envelops me again, and I gasp, opening my eyes.

When they release me, I swim to Niku and trace his scars for comfort. His voice is serious when he speaks. "Are you hurt?"

I take a moment to collect myself, assessing the damage, but there's none. Even my gills feel fine. Finn and Jen cheer, but I turn my back on them. "I'm fine."

"Told you," Clair says as she swims over, followed by Huron.

He has a big grin on his face. "Kind of exhilarating, isn't it?" His tailfin brushes mine like he used to, and I flush, glancing at Niku in embarrassment.

"Terrifying, perhaps," I say.

"You wanna go again?"

Clair shoves him. "Stop hitting on my sister in front of the landfolk."

"They don't know."

"Niku does."

Huron runs his fingertips over my dorsal fin, and I turn quick enough that his fingers caress my stomach as well. My blush deepens and an ache lodges at the base of my tail.

"Who'll Neeky tell now?" Huron whispers.

Niku shoves himself between us. "Who'll save you from me now?"

A loud knock rings out on the glass. "Niku," Finn says. "Stop harassing the Mer."

Huron smirks as Niku backs down. I don't know what most of the air words mean, but I do know Finn took Huron's side. I shush Finn, and he points at the red thing. "Jump."

I don't want to jump—I want to take Huron to a corner of the tank and finish what we started the day he was captured. I swim a tight circle around him, my tailfin caressing the length of his. "I'll go again."

Clair rolls her eyes. "For the Tides."

I ignore her as Huron pulls me to the bottom of the tank. He faces me and holds both of my hands. "Ready? Open your eyes this time."

I take a deep breath. "Ready."

His tail kicks, and I kick back—we've swam this close dance before. We move as one, cresting the water and clearing it. I squint my eyes against the air, and he arches backward. Our tails kick the red thing before we dive back into the water.

"Show-offs," Clair mutters as Finn and Jen cheer.

My stomach clenches and my scales flush with warmth as I catch my breath. If they'd let me stay with Huron, I'd jump whenever they asked me to. We swim through the water, twisting, touching, forgetting all about the landfolk until Finn knocks on the glass.

"Niku, your turn. Jump."

Niku growls, and I stop to watch him. He doesn't bother swimming to the bottom of the tank, he just kicks hard where he is, clears the water, and twists, landing on his side. A wave crashes over the glass, soaking the landfolk. Jen screams in delight.

Finn's mouth gapes, and he holds his arms out for a moment before his jaw snaps shut and his eyes narrow. "Playtime's over."

I don't know what that means, but the tone of his voice mirrors the dark look on his face. "Erie, Niku, tube. Now."

I *do* know what that means and grab Huron's hand. "No."

"Erie." Finn's voice holds a warning that says I can't get away with disobedience this time.

"Please," I beg, hugging Huron's arm. "I'll jump again. Please don't make me leave."

"Tube. Now."

I slam my fists on the glass. "This isn't fair! I did what you wanted. You can't take them from me again!"

Finn climbs the stairs to the platform, and Huron pulls me toward the tube. "He'll shock us. Just go, Erie."

"No." I pull free of him and swim to Jen, press my hands against the glass, and speak the air. "Please, Jen. Please."

"I'm sorry, Erie." Jen looks like she wants to stop Finn, but won't. "Please, go to the tube."

Huron and Clair pull me to the tube as Finn lowers the loop into the water. They shove me inside headfirst; there isn't enough space to turn around. "Please," I say again as they back away and Niku takes their place, nudging my tail.

My hands curl into fists, broken nails pricking my palms, but I swim forward. A low, burning anger grows in my chest. "Someday, I'll pull Finn into the water and rip all his fingers off so he can never use the loop again."

"Good," Niku says as the glass door scrapes closed behind us. "I'll help you."

<u>Oceanica Training Manual</u>

3: ELECTROSHOCKER

3.1 All new employees, regardless of daily interaction with the Mer, are required to attend a four (4) hour class on the proper use of the electroshocker during initial training. All employees, regardless of daily interaction with the Mer, must display proficiency using the electroshocker on a quarterly basis. All employees must read and sign the ELECTROSHOCKER EMERGENCY ACTION PLAN at least once (1) per year.

3.2 There are two (2) models of electroshockers at Oceanica: a permanent wall unit and a backpack unit. Both models include a handheld component with action and safety buttons and power adjustment dials, a long pole to keep the user as far away from the water as possible, and a loop electrode to be placed in the water. Backpack models are strapped onto the back. Wall models are connected to a panel in the wall. Both models are present in all holding tank areas and the practice tank area. In the "arena," units are stored behind "reef barriers," so as not to be visible to the public. Backpack models are only acceptable in the arena during emergencies. Two (2) backpack units are stored on either side of audience sightlines.

3.3 How to use electroshocker units:

3.3.1 WALL UNIT is lifted from metal hooks embedded in wall. Make sure power cord is connected to panel before operation.

3.3.2 BACKPACK UNIT is placed on back. All straps must be secured before use.

BACKPACK UNITS ARE NOT PREFERED EXCEPT IN EMERGENCY SITUATIONS.

3.3.3 Locate large blue button—do not touch until ready to deploy shock.

3.3.4 Stick loop end into water. Most Mer should react in a submissive manner to the presence of the electroshocker. If Mer do not submit, depress blue button for one (1) second. If Mer still do not submit, depress blue button until subdued.

3.3.5 Replace unit. If backpack model, replace battery and put used battery in charging station.

3.4 EMERGENCY PROCEDURE

3.4.1 If unit malfunctions, or personnel fall into water during shocking procedure, hit red safety button to immediately discontinue shock.

Chapter 18: Finn

I leave Clair and Huron in the big tank and radio Mia and Laz that they're ready. They were so much easier to work with than Erie. I know I've been trying something different, but it's time to put the fear of the shocker into her heart. I've been too easy on her.

"Finn?" Jen's voice is hesitant as I brush past her.

I ignore her. I know what I'll find in her expression: sadness, compassion for the Mer, and an underlying condemnation of everything I do. I can feel it rolling off her skin.

She must feel my intent rolling off my skin, too, because she scurries after me, trying to calm me down as we drip a trail back to Erie's tank. As soon as we get there, I slam the glass door to the big tank closed.

Erie paces like a lion. Niku eyes me warily. "Niku, tube, now." I point, and to my surprise, he goes. As I slam that door shut, Erie smacks into the glass next to me so hard I'm surprised it doesn't crack. She starts pounding on it, screaming Mer words at me before switching to "wrong" over and over again. "Wrong!" Pound. "Wrong!" Pound. "Wrong!"

"Stop!" I pound back.

She glares at me, chest heaving, and yells in my face. "Finn wrong!"

"Fuck you." I climb the stairs to the platform.

"Finn?" Jen's voice is worried. "What are you doing?"

"Teaching her a lesson." My hands are still wet from Niku's prank, so I dry them on a spare towel we keep hanging on a nail in the wall before I grab the electroshocker. "She needs to learn to behave like the other Mer."

"She jumped, just like you told her to."

"Only after she shushed me, and she refused to come back to the tank. She doesn't listen to me, and I don't have time for this bullshit." Maybe I can trade with Mia and Laz, take over Clair's show. Maybe my sister's right, and I just need to use what works. "I only have two months to prove to Delmara that I can do this, or she'll give Erie to someone who'll shock her all the time."

"Don't do this."

I stick the loop in the water, and Erie starts screaming "Wrong! Finn wrong!" again.

"Finn, I'm serious, don't—"

I hit the button—just a quick zap. It won't even make Erie float. I can't tell if the gasp I hear is from Jen or Erie, but Jen puts her hands on the glass. "Oh no."

Oh no? What the fuck does "oh no" mean? It was one little shock, but Jen covers her mouth with a hand, eyes wide with horror. I drop the shocker on the platform and run down the stairs to look into the tank.

Oh no.

The necklace is metal.

Erie rips it off, but foam bubbles where it was in contact with her scales. I'm so used to seeing it, I forgot she had it on, and now, I've run an electric current through the tank while a piece of highly conductive metal lays around her neck.

Bile lurches in my stomach—I've just killed Erie. As soon as the foam hits her gills, she'll suffocate. Images of the first few Mer we captured swamp my vision. We tried to dissect one, but she foamed before we could. So, we drugged the next one and opened her up alive, but as soon as the air hit her internal organs, they began to foam as well. We did it again, and I videotaped as Delmara opened her up from gills to tail and the organs inside dissolved into bubbles.

I've just done the same thing to Erie.

She wipes frantically at the foam with her fingertips, panicked, but then slows. By some miracle, the foam stops, leaving behind a necklace-shaped wound instead.

My legs shake like they're about to give out. I'm never using the shocker again.

"Erie?" My voice is weak as I press my hand on the glass. "Are you okay?"

As far as we know, Mer can't cry, but Erie's face is screwed up as if she's holding tears in. "Finn wrong," she whispers.

"Yes, I was wrong. I'll never do that again. I promise."

She turns her back on me, wrapping up in her tail.

Jen punches my arm. "You *asshole*."

Pain radiates through my arm, and I wrap my hand around it. "I forgot she had the necklace on! I just meant to shock her a bit . . ."

Jen's livid, face red, fists clenched. "I told you not to do it!"

"What else was I supposed to do? I've tried so hard not to hurt her, and she just keeps acting like—"

"Like we ripped her away from her friends, her family, her home? Like we're forcing her to do unnatural things to entertain an audience?" Jen's face is a mix of anger and disbelief. "What do you expect her to act like? Like Clair and Huron, who are so scared of being shocked they jump on command?"

I open my mouth to argue, but then shut it again. Clair and Huron may have been easier to work with, but Jen's right. When

Erie beams at us with those big, bright eyes, it makes every cell inside of me light up. Knowing some other trainer would shock that out of her makes me want to protect it. I couldn't live with myself, knowing that someone else had hurt her worse than me.

I've never questioned Oceanica before, not even after Flo and Chlo nearly killed me. Working with the Mer has been my dream since Delmara ran into the restaurant, waving her phone around like a madwoman. Hell, half the shit she claimed in her book on the Mer was discovered *by me*. I know more about the Mer than even she does.

Now I know that they have their own language, they can learn English, they have a concept of right and wrong. They live in a pod so large they don't know all the other Mer. And foam doesn't always mean death.

I also know I don't want to do this anymore. I can't be part of this mistreatment.

"I'm sorry, Jen. I can't be Erie's trainer." I turn and walk away. "I'll have Corporate find someone else to work with you."

"What? No." She grabs my arm and blocks my path, anger still radiating through her. "You can't quit now—anyone else will shock her the first time she says hello."

"She'll learn not to say it."

"They won't let her see Niku."

"She'll see him when they perform together."

"Goddammit, Finn." Jen punches my arm again, and I wince. "You can't quit because you don't want to see her hurt. Just because you're not here to witness it doesn't mean they won't hurt her worse."

"I can't be the one who does it anymore."

"Please." Jen runs her fingers down my arms to my hands, and squeezes them. There's desperation in her eyes. "Please don't quit."

The look on her face guts me. I finally squeeze back. "I won't."

She pulls herself up and kisses me. Just a quick peck on the lips, but she looks so surprised at herself that I smile to put her at ease. "Especially if you keep asking like that."

* * * *

WE LET ERIE INTO NIKU'S tank early and head to the Porch. Sergio's been complaining that I never come out anymore, but that's because I've been waiting until everyone leaves to let Erie into Niku's tank. Now that they've practiced together in the big tank, I don't see how anyone can have a problem with it.

Three drinks in, and Jen forgets she was ignoring me after her kiss. She's all smiles and flirtation, and even my tense shoulders relax. When Sergio asks her a question, she leans over me to reply and puts a hand on my thigh. It's warm and tingly.

I'm seriously about to pull her into my lap and kiss her. But then Natalie says, "So, how'd the big tank go today? Heard you brought in K and Argon to give a lesson."

Jen's hand leaves my thigh as she sits up. It takes every bit of self-possession I have not to groan and pull her back over. Instead, I take a drink and reply, "E—er . . . Io learned how to jump."

"Oh yes," Jen says. "They both pulled her up the first time, but then she did this thing with the boy where he jumped backward, and she basically laid on top of him in the air." She demonstrates with her hands, then breaks into a grin. "It was the coolest thing I've ever seen. I think he was her boyfriend, or something. There was a lot of fin touching going on."

Everyone looks at her like she's crazy. Maddy leans across the table. "You're not supposed to let them touch each other."

Jen's brow furrows. "How were they supposed to teach her how to jump without touching?"

"They have eyes," Maddy says sarcastically.

"The touching rule is stupid," I say, brushing it off as such. "The rest of them are together every night—do you really think they're not all up on each other once we go home?"

"Gross," Natalie says. "You think they're having fish sex every night? I clean those filters, ugh."

Serge and I snicker. Maddy rolls her eyes. "They're not having sex. None of the females have ever gotten pregnant."

"Maybe the eggs and sperm get sucked into the filters until Nat cleans them," I suggest, and Natalie squeals in disgust.

"Grow up," Maddy sneers at me. "Whatever they do or don't do after we leave, they aren't supposed to touch while we're there."

"Guess what, Mads?" I flash a big, shit-eating grin. "If Jen and I want to let our Mer touch other Mer, we will."

"I'll tell Delmara you're breaking the rules."

I elbow Serge. "Hear that, bro? Maddy wants to tattle on me to Aunt D."

Sergio chuckles. "Save your breath, Madison. Aunt D will never fire Finn—he's been working with her since day one. Hell, his dad discovered the little shits."

Maddy huffs and leaves for another drink. Nat rolls her eyes at me. Jen leans over and says, "Did I get us in trouble?"

"Of course not." I put my arm across the back of her chair and take a drink. "Everything worked out—Maddy's just extra bitchy tonight."

Nat leaves to join Maddy at the bar. Good riddance. Jen watches them while she drinks her beer.

"So," Serge says. "You finally got your Mer to jump. How about that asshole dolphin?"

Jen giggles. "He jumped, too. Shamu-ed us."

"Shamu-ed you?"

"You know, soaked us with water. It was great until Finn freaked out."

"I didn't freak out," I say, while Serge snorts. "Time was up—we needed to give the tank to K and Argon for warm-ups."

"You freaked out."

"I tried a new tactic."

"You almost killed Erie."

"What?" Serge says.

"Who's Erie?" Natalie says as she returns to the table with a fresh beer.

Jen's eyes widen as she realizes her mistake. I grab her arm and stand, pulling her with me. "Excuse us for a moment while I remind my assistant of this afternoon's events."

I lead her out to the porch, for which the Porch is named. The side in front of the bar is packed with people, but the other side—in front of a law firm—is empty and shadowed.

"Sorry," Jen says, sheepish. "I'm so used to calling her Erie, I totally forgot."

"It's fine." I run my hand through my hair. "I almost did the same earlier, and Nat probably won't care either way."

"Then why'd you drag me out here?"

"Because Maddy was coming back, and she *would* care."

Jen's silent for a moment. "I think Maddy hates me. If you ever find me floating face down in a tank, it was probably her that did it, not the Mer."

I chuckle and brush a piece of hair from Jen's cheek. Her lips part as she sucks in a breath. Her eyes are wide, and in the shadows, they're as deep as Erie's. I can't stand it anymore—I lean down to kiss her. Before my lips touch hers, she puts her hand around my neck to draw me closer. She has the perfect lower lip for kissing, and as soon as my tongue touches it, she opens her mouth. She tastes like excruciatingly sweet beer.

I expect her to pull away and make things awkward, but she presses into me instead. I grab her hips and press back, then snake one hand up her side until I can feel her bra through her thin shirt. She has both hands in my hair.

"You've got to be kidding me," Maddy's voice interrupts, and Jen pulls away so fast, the only thing that keeps her from falling is my hand on her hip. "God, Finn, you're such a whore."

Jen steps to the side, breaking contact. Dammit. I finally kissed her, and Maddy ruins it, because it's not enough that she almost got me killed this summer. She's gotta ruin my chance with Jen, too.

Maddy's fists are balled up on her hips. "You can't take advantage of every girl you meet, you know. You're an emotional fucking piranha."

"Is that like a vampire that sucks on emotion? I've heard of people who believe in that."

"Fuck you." Maddy turns on her heel and storms back into the Porch.

Jen and I stand a foot apart, staring into the bar, until she says, "Thank you for not saying 'maybe later.'"

"Huh?" I glance at her, but she looks anywhere other than me.

"Usually, when she says 'fuck you,' you say 'maybe later' and wink at her."

"Yeah, well, she's not usually such a bitch."

Did I just admit that if Maddy wasn't being a bitch I'd fuck her tonight? *After* making out with Jen on the porch? Maybe I am a piranha. Maybe that's why I like the Mer so much.

"Jen." I reach for her, and she stumbles in her haste to get away.

"I should go home," she says, but doesn't move. "I left my purse inside."

"Wait here. I'll walk you home."

"You don't have to."

This time, when I reach for her, she has her head turned, so I wrap my fingers around her arm. "I want to." Before she can protest, I jog inside and wink at Maddy as I snatch Jen's purse.

When I bring it back to the porch, Jen frowns. "I didn't close out."

"Don't worry. I'll cover you tonight and bring your card to work in the morning."

She looks like she'll keep arguing, so I put my finger over her lips; they're still warm from our kiss. "Let me be the good guy for once, huh? After what I did to Erie today, I could desperately use some good guy points."

She studies my face as though she's searching for something to use against me, but then her shoulders sag. "Fine."

I motion to the stairs. "After you."

We're on Duval, weaving our way through drunken tourists, when Jen finally speaks. "You should be nicer to Maddy."

Whoa, that's not at all what I expected from this walk. I was kind of hoping we'd make out some more. On Jen's bed. With no clothes on.

"Maybe Maddy should be nicer to me."

"I'm serious, Finn. You've had sex with her at least three times since I started working with you, and sometimes you treat her like that's all she's good for."

"She's also good at scrubbing tanks."

Jen stops walking, and the people behind us run into her, making her stumble forward until I catch her. She pushes away like she can't stand my touch.

"She's right about you, you know. You use Maddy to make yourself feel important. You use Erie to make yourself feel in control. I'm not sure what you're using me for yet. Maybe I'm the same as Maddy to you."

"Hold on. That's not fair." I pull her out of the crowd to a dark storefront. "First, Maddy uses me just as much as I use her. If she didn't want to come home with me, she wouldn't. Second, I am *rarely* in control of Erie, if you haven't noticed—"

"But you *try* to be."

"Yeah. That's my job. It's your job, too, I might point out."

"What's that supposed to mean?"

"It's *supposed* to mean you help me, instead of standing around, watching me make a fool of myself and pleading with me to be nicer to the Mer."

"You should be nicer. Erie responds better when you are."

"You don't get it, Jen. She's not a pet. She's not our friend. She's a fucking predator." I pull the neck of my shirt down to reveal the scars from Chlorine. "You haven't been attacked. You haven't had to pull a body out of the pool. You have no idea how dangerous they are."

"I *know* how dangerous they are, but Erie—"

"*She's. A. Fish.*"

Jen smacks me so hard across the face I expect to taste blood. She points an accusing finger at me. "You keep saying that thinking of her as a friend will get you killed, but you know what? Treating her like a fish with a two-second memory is what will get you killed. You keep hurting her, and she'll remember it. She's going to turn on you, just like Carbon turned on Hannah."

Before I can form a reply, she walks down the street, elbowing drunk tourists out of the way. It's not until later, when I wake up at three a.m., that I realize I never told Jen the name of Hannah's Mer.

As soon as the landfolk let me into Niku's tank, I curl up around his dorsal fin and wrap my arms around him. He doesn't ask questions, just swims to the other side of the tank, as far away from Jen and Finn as possible.

At some point I sleep, but jerk awake from a nightmare that I'm turning to foam.

"Princess?" Niku's voice floats into my ear.

I trace his scars, then lift my finger to my own. The burst of pain makes me wince.

"Do you want to tell me what happened?" Neek says.

I don't know about that—I'm sure he saw what happened. "I thought Finn was nicer."

"Erie—"

"Clair and Huron kept saying their landfolk would shock them for misbehaving—even talking and touching—so I thought Finn was different . . ." My fingers find the wound around my neck again, and I swallow hard. What if wiping away the foam hadn't worked?

When Niku speaks, he sounds as angry as I've ever heard him. "The landfolk are all the same."

"No." It's my gut reaction, although Finn and Jen are the only landfolk I've met. "They can't all be the same. The merfolk aren't the same, nor the dolphins in the pod, so the landfolk must be different, too." I drape over Niku's side. "I just didn't think he'd do . . . that."

I touch my neck as Niku shakes his head. "I saw Finn stick the loop in the water, but how did you get that wound?"

I wince again as I trace the outline with my finger. "The loop made the necklace dangerous. I . . . I started to foam." My throat closes around the word.

Niku's silent, brooding. I trace his scars again, hoping it calms him as it always calms me. "What do we do now, Neek?"

His eye twitches in distaste. "The only thing we can: whatever they ask. If Finn says jump, we jump. If he says tube, we swim through. Whatever happens, I won't let you be hurt again."

"None of this is your fault."

"I'm the one who angered him. I told you to do as he asked, and then I purposefully disobeyed. I thought he'd take it out on me."

Niku deflates, and I slide off his back. "Neeky—"

"My purpose is to keep you safe, and instead, I nearly killed you. If I can't keep you safe, I might as well beach myself."

"No." I touch his scars, then swim in front of him and put my hands on either side of his face. "That was my fault. I screamed at him. I refused to do what he asked. I knew better."

"I should have never let you go on the hunt injured."

I wrap my arms around him and picture the pattern of ink-stained shells the morning of the hunt. I don't know how long we've been here, so I can't picture their new design. "I should have known the boats were coming, and I'll find a way to get us out. We'll behave, this will heal, and we'll find a way out. Jen's nice—maybe she'll help."

"I wouldn't put your faith in any of the landfolk."

We don't have a choice, though. The landfolk are the ones who put us here. They're the only ones who can save us. I crawl onto Niku's back and wind around his dorsal fin, then wrap my arms around him again. I don't try to sleep, because I don't want to have another nightmare. When Finn walks in, Neek takes me to the other side of the tank.

"Morning, Erie, Niku."

I keep my back to Finn, and he knocks on the glass. His voice sounds worried, though I don't know all the words. "Are you okay, sweet? Do I need to get the vet?"

When I don't reply, he sounds more worried. "Erie?" He walks around the tank, so I'm facing him, and Niku swims away again. "Come here," Finn says and motions me over. "I have a gift for you."

He pulls something from the skin at his hips and I sit up, wondering how he did that.

"Do you want it?" Finn dances it in his fingers, and I slide off Niku's back to swim over. Instead of studying the "gift," whatever that means, I gape at the skin he pulled it from. A flap hangs open at the top of his leg—how strange is that?

Finn chuckles. "It's a pocket." He sticks his hand into it and pulls it inside out. I gasp. How did he pull his skin *inside out*? Then he pushes it back into place.

"Just a pocket, darlin'. Look what I have." He holds the thing he pulled from his "pocket" in my face. It's a figurine, I think, of a . . . landfolk girl with a merfolk tail? Her top half is the same snail-skin that Finn has, with a landfolk nose, and hair like Clair's. Her bottom is green scales like normal, though her tail hasn't grown long yet, nor is it tipped with the color of her hair. At first, I think it's a child, but its breasts are quite obvious, covered with seashells. That would be uncomfortable.

I tilt my head and touch the glass. Why did Finn bring me a half-merfolk, half-landfolk, seashell-wearing *thing*?

"You want it?" he says, then walks to the platform. I shrink away and hide behind Niku. My heart races as I wait for the loop, but it doesn't enter the water. Instead, Finn's fingertips do, and he wiggles them. "Come on up. I won't hurt you. I promise."

Slowly, I surface on the far side of the tank and scrutinize him. He's crouched on the platform, holding the figurine over the water. The loop hangs on the wall behind him, out of reach. I dip back under the surface and swim closer. When I resurface, I'm right under the gift. Finn pinches it between two fingers like he's nervous.

"Please don't kill me," he whispers, but I have no idea what that means.

I lift my hand out of the water, palm up, and he drops the figurine into it before leaning back. It's small enough to fit in my hand, and I swim to Niku with it.

"What is it?" he says.

I turn it over in my hands, studying it, but I have no idea.

"It looks like what would happen if your sister and a landfolk mated, and the result was half and half."

"Ew, Neek. Clair wouldn't mate with a landfolk."

"I'm just saying, that's what it looks like."

I glance around the tank and find Finn back on the ground, staring at us. I swim to him and hold the figurine up. "Clair?"

Finn shakes his head. "Ariel."

"Ariel," I echo, feeling the word. It feels like waves—where the ocean meets the air. I point to the nose and hands, the most obvious landfolk parts, and say, "Finn." Then I point to the hair and tail, "Clair."

"Oh no, Clair and I had nothing to do with this." He sticks his hand in his other *pocket* and pulls out the black rectangle I first saw Clair and Huron in. He taps it a few times, then holds it up to the glass.

There, in the box, is Ariel. She's . . . underwater, surrounded by things I don't recognize. In a cave, maybe? And she's singing. Are those air words? I recognize a few of them, but how strange that Ariel sings air words underwater, with no gills, and still swims around like a merfolk. I can't tear my gaze away.

"You like that, darlin'?" Finn takes the rectangle away when the song ends.

I examine the figurine in my hands and grasp it tighter. Something in Ariel's song says that she isn't where she wants to be, either. She's trapped, just like I am.

"Ariel?" I say, wanting to see her again.

"Time for breakfast. Then more Ariel."

Finn lets me into my tank, and I eat as quickly as I can.

Jen comes in while Erie's eating. She ignores me, as I knew she would, and says good morning to Niku and Erie. Erie answers her with a full mouth, she's so eager to get back to watching *The Little Mermaid*.

"Someone's hungry this morning," Jen says. "And what's that you've got, Erie?"

I answer for her. "It's an 'I'm sorry' present."

"What is it?"

"Ariel, from my sister's fish tank."

Jen raises an eyebrow and purses her lips. At least she isn't ignoring me. "You gave her a fish tank decoration?"

"It looks like Clair—I thought she'd like it. And you were right—she responds better when I'm nice." So does Jen, I might point out. I don't feel like dealing with two angry women all day, every day.

Erie swims over, fish gone. "Ariel?"

"Let me set it up." I grab a folding chair and set it in front of the tank, then open my laptop and find the movie streaming On Demand. I hit play, and the familiar music starts. I know every piece of this movie—my sister and I watched it every day after school when we were little. She would do all of Ariel's parts, and I would be Ursula, because she's a badass.

Jen and I work with Niku while Erie watches her movie. I'm not sure if he knows what happened with the shocker yesterday, but he behaves better than normal. Maybe he just likes the music from the movie. The tank is too small for him to do much, but if we can get him to spin or wave or something, we can take him to the big tank later to practice jumping. Without a giant splash this time.

"Hey," Jen says after a while, though she continues to watch Niku. "I'm sorry about last night."

"Which part?"

A flush of red creeps up her neck into her cheeks and ears. "All of it." Her voice is soft, embarrassed even.

"There are definitely parts you don't have to be sorry for."

The blush deepens, and she's silent for a moment. "No. I shouldn't have gotten so drunk."

"Don't worry about it. I was drunk, too." Total lie. "And you were right about Erie." Not a lie.

Jen tries to get Niku to spin. He swims a circle around the tank instead.

"Can I ask you something?" I say, because honestly, things can't be any more awkward than they already are.

"Sure." Her shoulders tense, like I'm about to ask her to kiss me again.

"How'd you know Carbon's name?"

Jen finally looks at me, eyes wide. That definitely wasn't the question she was expecting. "What?"

"Last night, when you were yelling at me, you said something about Carbon and Hannah, but I never told you Carbon's name."

"You didn't?" She turns back to Niku. "Maybe it was Sergio."

When would Sergio have talked to Jen about that? I'm about to ask when she puts up a finger. "Wait, I remember. When Serge was yelling at you about Erie the other day, he said Carbon's name."

"And you remembered it? Drunk?"

"Brains are weird."

There's definitely something weird about Jen, and it's not her drunk ability to remember names she's only heard in passing. I let it go for now—it'd be nice to make it through an entire day without pissing off either Erie or Jen. Considering it's still morning, I have plenty of time to screw up.

Erie's movie ends. "Ariel? Ariel!" She knocks on the glass as I close the laptop. "No, Finn. Ariel."

"Sorry, darlin', movie's over—time to practice. If you're good, I'll put it back on tonight."

She pouts, her barely there, green lower lip sticking out just like a human girl's would, but she doesn't throw a fit. "Let's practice spinning," I say, and twirl my finger. Without an argument, she spins. I guess the shocker got through to her after all.

• • • •

I LEAVE THE LAPTOP on, streaming Disney all night long, and when I return the next morning, Erie says hello like normal.

"Morning, beautiful," I say, and she spins like we practiced yesterday. Her eyes are red-rimmed. "Did you sleep? Or did you watch movies all night?"

"Movies!" She does a backflip. "Finn, I'm a princess!"

"Of course you are," I say, and then pause. "Wait, did you just use a whole sentence?" Oh crap. If Disney taught her how to speak in full sentences, I'll never keep her quiet around the other trainers. How did *The Little Mermaid* teach her English? What else did she watch all night?

"Finn?" Erie says when I turn my back on her. "You okay?"

Fuck. I scroll through the view list. Most of it is shows designed to teach little kids how to speak, not movies. How did it switch to this? I had it on the movie channel. *The Little Mermaid, Beauty and the Beast, The Lion King* . . . how'd it change to the learn-to-speak channel? Did it somehow run out of movies and switch itself over?

I'm so screwed.

"Morning, Erie, Niku," Jen says as she walks in.

"Morning, Jen," Erie says brightly. "I'm a princess!"

"Aww," Jen pats my shoulder as she walks to the tank. "Did Finn tell you that?"

As much as I'd like the good guy points for that one, I'm too freaked out. "Disney taught her English. And gave her an ego."

Jen giggles, because she doesn't understand what this means. "So, you're a princess, huh?"

"Clair's princess, too."

"Of course she is," Jen says, delighted. All that childhood-killing I did at the beginning of her apprenticeship has just been reborn. "Every girl's a princess at heart."

"No. Daddy is king," Erie says, her bloodshot eyes as earnest as possible. "Like King Triton."

Jen's smile slowly fades. "Erie . . . is Clair your sister?"

Erie closes one eye and peers up with the other, thinking. Almost under her breath, she recites lines from the movie, then lights up again. "Sister! Yes! Clair is sister."

Jen covers her mouth with one hand and reaches for me with the other. Oh god, this is worse than I thought. When I grab her hand, she looks at me, desperation in her eyes. She wants to let Erie and Clair back in together.

"Jen?" Erie says. "You okay?"

What the fuck—*the fish* asked if Jen was okay before I did.

"Excuse me." Jen's face is pale, like she's about to puke, and she rushes out of the room. I can't blame her—if I knew someone was keeping my sister in a cage like this, I'd be livid.

"Jen okay?"

I face Erie and contemplate her in complete amazement. Not only can she speak English in full—if short—sentences, but she's worried about Jen. Erie's the one stuck in a cage, separated from her sister, who she knows is somewhere nearby, and she's worried that *Jen* is the one crying over the situation. In a matter of weeks, Erie's turned everything I thought I knew about the Mer on its head.

"Jen will be okay, sweet. She's just . . . surprised, I think."

Erie's hairless eyebrows are still creased, and I'm worried she'll ask if she can see her sister, so I divert the only way I know how. I plaster a big smile on my face and reopen the laptop. "How about breakfast and Ariel?"

"Yes, please." Erie grasps the figurine in her hand a little tighter.

I turn Disney back on, feed Erie and Niku in the same tank, and head in the direction of the locker rooms to find Jen. "Are you in here?" I call into the women's locker room. No one replies, but I hear sniffling. Jen's definitely in there.

She sits in the back corner on a bench, her arms around her knees and her face buried in the crook of her elbow. "Hey," I say as I near. I'm afraid she'll scream at me to leave her alone, but all she does is wipe her face.

"Sorry." She sniffles.

"You have nothing to be sorry for." I sit in front of her. "Are you okay?"

She doesn't reply.

"Listen," I say. "I'm the one who's sorry. I didn't know Erie would learn to speak so quickly by watching movies all night."

Jen shakes her head and lowers it back onto her arm. "That isn't the problem."

I touch her arms, but she doesn't move. If she had a tail, she'd wrap it around herself like Erie does.

"Maybe . . ." I hesitate, because I don't want to make a promise I can't keep. "Maybe we can let Erie and Clair see each other more often. We can say Clair's teaching Erie a routine or something."

Jen finally lifts her head, but rather than the hope I was expecting, her brown eyes are full of disgust. "My god, Finn, what's wrong with you?"

"What?" I drop my hands and sit back.

"This isn't even animal cruelty anymore. It's *slavery*." She drops her legs to the floor and leans forward. "Erie may not be human, but she's an intelligent being, and we're forcing her to work for us."

"It's not slavery." I scoff, then think about the electroshocker and the scar around Erie's neck. I did that to her, because she wouldn't do what I asked. "What do you want me to do, Jen?" Anguish tinges my voice. "She's here, she's not going back to the ocean, and we're the only ones who won't abuse her."

"I know. I know that, but . . ." Jen wipes her face again, and finally faces me. "You see how wrong this is, don't you? We have to do something. We have to save her. And Clair."

"And then what? They'll just catch two more Mer to replace them. Two more with family, and friends, and a home."

"Then . . ." Her eyes are wild and desperate. "Then we shut down Oceanica."

"Another place just like it will pop up somewhere. Hell, they're already building similar places in California and Asia."

"Then we make it illegal. Talk to Congress, the UN. Pass a law."

"Jen." I grab her arms again, and her whole body deflates. "There's nothing we can do. If it's not Oceanica, it'll be researchers. If it's not researchers, it'll be poachers. Now that the Mer have been discovered, we can't do anything to save them."

She takes a big, shuddering breath. "This isn't what I expected when I started working here."

"Me either," I say. "I liked it better when they were velociraptors."

The movies are the only thing that makes this dreary tank bearable, and it was almost worth being shocked to watch them. Ariel is my favorite. She was trapped, and she found a way to escape, and all she had to do was get a landfolk to fall in love with her. I can do that, too.

I hum along with the Ariel music, singing the air words I recognize, when someone walks into the room. It isn't Jen or Finn, but the other landfolk man I met. The one who didn't want to tell me his name: Sergio.

"Hey, Io," he says absently. "Where's Finn and Jen?"

I stop humming and swim to the glass. "Jen left, sad. Finn follow."

Sergio freezes, body tensing. A muscle in his jaw twitches. "What did you say?"

Did I say the words wrong? I'm positive I said them right. "Jen sad. Left. Finn follow."

He stumbles forward and puts his hands on the glass. "When did you learn to talk?"

I back away from the anger in his eyes. "I watch movies. Learn air words."

Sergio glances at the movie, then slams it shut.

"Hey!" I yell. "Ariel!"

Finn's voice interrupts us. "What's going on?"

I swim to him, relieved. "Sergio stop Ariel."

"You taught your fucking Mer to speak English?" Sergio yells. I only know what half of those words mean.

"Not on purpose," Finn says. "She picked it up on her own."

Sergio pulls on his short, black hair, so it sticks out in every direction. "What the fuck is wrong with you?" He peers from Finn, to me, and back. "This is too far, man. She can't be talking to people—they'll start thinking she's human, and then Oceanica is done for."

Start thinking I'm human? Don't they already think I'm human? "I human," I say. They stop arguing and face me, Finn with sadness, Sergio so angry and shocked that his face is nearly the color of Clair's hair.

"Erie." Finn's voice is soft, like he's speaking to a child. "You're not human. You're a mermaid. A fish."

He thinks I'm a fish? It's like a punch to the gut, coming from Finn. "No, human. I speak air, like you."

"No, darlin'," he says. "You have a tail and gills." He touches his smooth neck. "You're a fish."

"But . . ."

"It's not a bad thing," Finn says, but he glances around the tank with a grimace. "I can't breathe underwater like you can."

I wonder where he lives—if it's a gray room like this. Can he see outside? "You want to be fish?"

"Huh?" His eyes widen, but Sergio smiles ruefully.

"He absolutely would. Finn would drown himself to become a Mer if the old stories were true."

The old stories? A small smile tugs at my lips. We have similar stories: if a merfolk finds a landfolk drowning, they can transform them into one of us. Maybe it's not so bad to be a fish, if I can turn Finn into a fish, too. "You want to be fish, Sergio?"

"Hell no," he says, too quickly. "I hate the ocean."

My smile fades, and I glance at Finn. At least he likes fish, though I still don't think of myself as one. I'm merfolk—a sea-human. I'll prove it to them.

How can I prove I'm human, though? I need to know more about air-humans. "I watch movie?"

"Of course," Finn says. "Ariel?"

"Not fish movie, human movie."

"You got it." He opens the rectangle again and does something to make a different movie start.

"I can't believe you let her watch movies," Sergio mutters, so I shush him. "Whatever," he says, "Have fun with your fish girlfriend, man. I'll see you at the Porch."

Finn waits until he's gone, then starts the movie. "Erie?"

"Yes?"

"Don't talk to anyone except me and Jen, okay?"

My shoulders sink. "Okay."

• • • •

THIS MOVIE'S WEIRD. It's about a boy—but not a real boy—who has a nose that grows. Then his ear-fins grow. Then a whale eats him. I'm positive the inside of a whale's stomach doesn't resemble that. None of the whales I've met are that big.

I knock on the tank. "Finn?"

He glances over from where he wipes his handprints from the glass. "What's up?"

I look up and Finn chuckles. "Sorry, I meant, what do you need?"

"I need . . ." I think about the air-words, "to tell, whales . . ." That's such a funny word for them. Whales. I like it—it feels bigger than they are. "Whales not that big."

"Whales not that big?" He glances at the movie and chuckles. "You're right. Whales aren't that big, but movies aren't always true."

"What 'true'?"

He screws his face up, trying to figure out how to explain it to me. I know that expression well—it's the same thing I do when he doesn't understand me.

"Sometimes," he says, "movies are bigger than real life. Like with Ariel—Ursula grew bigger than real life at the end."

Movies are bigger than real life? Ursula grew bigger than real life? I glance at the movie, where the strange boy is becoming a real boy. A *real* boy. And Ariel became a *real* human.

"Erie?" Finn puts his hand on the glass. "Are you okay?"

I can't breathe. I thought the movies were "true," that I could become an air-human. I learned air-words, and how to jump, and I've done everything he's asked, but I still don't know the schedule of the boats, and Grandmother is probably turning to foam right now.

I sink to the ground, ignoring the movie. "I not fish," I whisper. "I sea-human. I am."

Finn sinks down next to me. "It's okay. Being human isn't that great, either."

I wrap my tail around myself, but put my hand under his. The glass steals his warmth. "Where's Finn? When gone? Where's Porch?"

"The Porch?" He sits up, then puts his hand back over mine. "It's close. It's a place to be with friends. I'm guessing mermaids don't drink."

I don't know what that means. "Jen and Sergio friends?"

"They are." Finn dips his chin. "Sergio has been my friend since we were children. I only met Jen a few weeks ago, but I like her." His mouth twitches up, and his gaze shifts so he looks past me for a moment.

I may not be an air-human, but I can see through that. Finn likes Jen more than he'll admit. "Have you kissed the girl?" I imitate Sebastian's accent.

The corner of his mouth twitches again. "Yes. It didn't go as well as I'd hoped."

I grin and flick the tip of my tail. I like Jen and Finn, despite everything, and I like that they like each other. "You kiss again."

Finn chuckles. "At this point, I think it would be sexual harassment."

I don't know what that means, but it doesn't matter, because he asks me a question. "Do the Mer kiss?"

"Mer?" I don't know that word.

"You know, like you and Clair and Huron. You're Mer. That's what humans call you."

I thought humans called us mermaids? Maybe that's another untrue thing from movies. "We kiss. Not Clair . . . Huron." I flush in embarrassment as I imagine wrapping my tail around Huron and kissing him.

"Is Huron your boyfriend?"

"Boyfriend?"

"A boy you kiss a lot," Finn winks.

"Yes. Huron boyfriend." My heart begins to ache as I think of how he acted in the big tank. "Was. Was boyfriend."

Finn's head droops as he studies his hands. "I'm sorry you can't see him more often. There are strict rules, and I'm already breaking most of them for you."

"You have boyfriend?"

That makes him chuckle. "No, Erie, I don't have a boyfriend. Or a girlfriend. There are girls that I kiss . . . a lot, but I wouldn't consider them my girlfriends."

"Jen?"

He shakes his head with a small, sad smile. "I don't kiss Jen a lot. Or at all. The one time was a drunk accident."

I don't know what that means. "Where's Jen?"

His entire body seems to pause for a moment as he considers that. "I don't know," he says. "I don't know anything about her outside of work."

"Porch?" I ask.

Finn touches the glass with his fingertips, staring at the prints they make. "I don't know where she goes when she leaves. I don't know if she has any other friends on the island."

We're silent for a while, watching the movie. When it ends, Finn says, "Where do you live?"

That's a weird question. "Here."

"I mean, when you aren't here. Do the Mer live in one place, or travel?"

I tuck into my tail, not sure I should tell him anything. What if I do and he finds the Seadom? Would the landfolk capture everyone?

"Sorry, darlin', I didn't mean to remind you of home."

"Finn?" I whisper. "I go back? No one go back yet."

His thumb rubs against the glass like he's caressing my cheek. "I hope so. I don't know how to make it happen, but I hope you can go back home someday."

Jen hasn't spoken to me since her explosion in the locker room three days ago, but by no means has it been silent in the holding room. Erie talks constantly, asking what different words and phrases mean, asking about the shows at Oceanica, asking about Jen and me outside of work. Where do we live? What do we do when we aren't here? When will we kiss again?

That one made Jen blush.

Anytime I try to ask about Erie's life before being captured, she clams up. I'm not sure if it's fear, or homesickness, or the inability to put her words into English that stops her constant chatter, but it's clear she won't talk about it. The most I know is that her father is king, and she was caught because her injured tail made her too slow to escape the boats a second time. Sometimes, when she thinks Jen and I are busy, I catch a pensive expression on Erie's face.

"You okay, darlin'?"

Her eyes brighten, and I wonder if this was a trick she had to learn as a princess—to always be on for an audience. If so, it'll make her a great performer.

"I'm okay." It may be a lie, but since she never answers my questions about home, I don't push it.

"Good. I've reserved the arena tomorrow morning at dawn, so no staying up all night watching movies, okay?"

She eyes me, her smile faltering. "What 'arena' and 'dawn'?"

"Dawn is when the sun rises, and the arena is the open-air tank the shows are held in. It's really big, and you can see the sun. We'll practice jumping in it."

The interest in her face dims. I've gotten her to jump several times in the practice tank, but she still doesn't like being told what to do. It's for her own good, I remind myself. If she doesn't jump for me, Delmara will give her to someone who shocks her until she does.

"Trust me, darlin', you'll like it." I turn to Jen, who pretends to clean so she can ignore me. "You'll have to put on a wetsuit when you get here. Arena rules—everyone on the platform must wear a wetsuit, just in case."

She finally looks at me, a mixture of trepidation and disgust in her eyes. "In case of what?"

I pause before I reply, because part of me wants her to keep my gaze a bit longer, and I'm sure that what I'm about to say will make her turn away. "Accidents, although a wetsuit isn't likely to save you." Mine saved me from being electrocuted to death, but Hannah's didn't save her.

Jen pales and drops her gaze. "Okay."

• • • •

SIX A.M. IS EARLIER than I've woken up in years, and I kinda wish I'd scheduled the arena for after work instead. But I promised Erie sunshine, and I'm really digging the fact that we're the only ones here. Oceanica doesn't open until ten, first show at eleven, and most of the trainers won't roll in until nine, at the earliest. We've got three hours to ourselves.

Jen's wetsuit hugs her in all the right places, and my wetsuit's about to show my appreciation for it, so I lead the way as we let Erie and Niku into the arena. As predicted, Erie loves the extra freedom to swim, and she actually jumps on her own.

She swims to where Jen and I stand, next to the tank, her face beaming. "Finn! We outside!"

I can't help but return her smile. "I told you, you'd like it, didn't I?"

"Yes, I love it!" She spins a circle. "It bright. We come more often?"

"Once you start performing, you'll be out here every day." Hopefully, that'll be a small condolence for everything else we've put her through. "Why don't we see how high you can jump? You and Niku can compete to see who can jump higher." Maybe if I make it a competition, she'll like it better.

"I tell Neek." She turns to swim to him, then turns back quickly. "I love this tank."

I silently laugh as she swims to Niku, but Jen broods next to me. "Come on," I say, "don't look like that. She's having fun."

Jen shakes her head and walks up the stairs to the platform. Guess I'm still getting the silent treatment.

Erie and Niku jump high enough that they clear the water, but it's not as impressive as I was hoping for. "Higher, darlin'. You can do it!" She tries again, and the water sparkles in the early morning sunshine as it streams from her fins. Her magenta hair wraps around her like a cape.

"Almost there. Try again."

She circles the tank, building up momentum, and when she jumps, she flies into the air, her eyes opened in slits so she can see where she'll land. She's gorgeous, but when she reaches the top of the arch, she gasps, her hands fly to her gills, and she falls ungracefully back into the water with a huge splash.

"Erie?" I yell, alarmed, and run down a few steps so I can see her through the glass. "What happened? Are you okay?"

She sucks in water, and her eyes dart around like she's desperately trying to find something. She speaks Mer words, voice panicked. I can't tell what she says, but she's freaking out. She bangs on the glass. I have to calm her down before she hurts herself, but she's not listening to me.

"Erie, calm down. Stop banging and listen to me. Erie!" Nothing. She's beyond listening, and I run back to the platform.

"What's wrong?" Jen says.

"I have no idea, but I have to get her to stop." I glance at the shocker on the wall, but the last time I tried that, I almost killed her. I promised I would never do it again. What the hell else can I do?

Even up here, I can hear her screaming and pounding on the glass, so, without thinking, I do the stupidest thing I've ever done.

I jump in the tank with an enraged Mer.

All of the air words flee my mind at the sight of the ocean, the blue water shining in the sunlight as far as I can see. It's so close. So close I can almost jump to it.

"It's the ocean, Neek!" I pound on the glass. Maybe if I can break through, the resulting wave would carry us to the water. "It's so close. Help me break this."

"Princess," Niku says, voice even. "It's impossible."

"No, it's not!" I slam my fists on the glass. "You didn't see it. The water's *right there*. We just have to break through."

I slam my shoulder into the glass, then grab it as pain shoots through the joint. "Neek! Help me!"

A loud splash makes me spin. I find a curtain of bubbles that reveal . . . Finn? He's changed his skin, so he's almost all black, but I'm positive it's Finn. What's he doing in the water?

"Perfect," Niku says, and Finn snaps his head around, like he doesn't know where the voice came from. "Now we can kill him."

"Niku, no!" I'm closer, but he's faster, and he's about to slam into Finn like he would a shark. Finn won't survive that.

I won't reach him in time, so I swim at Niku, shoving his nose with my hands. He has too much momentum to stop, though, and we barrel into Finn sideways. He explodes into bubbles.

"Erie," Niku's voice snaps with anger. I've never heard him that angry—not at me, at least.

Finn reaches the surface, and Niku lunges past me, grabs his ankle and yanks him under. Finn tries to kick his face, but Niku shakes him hard, snapping his body from one side to the other.

"Neek, stop!"

"This is our chance to kill him."

"I don't want to kill him!"

"You did a few days ago."

Finn struggles to get to the surface, and Niku yanks him further into the water. Above the surface, Jen's muffled voice screams. If we kill Finn, what will she do to us? She certainly won't help free us.

"Finn and Jen are our only chance out of here," I say.

"We'll find another way."

"Let him go." I puff out my chest to look as regal as possible. "That's an order."

Niku pauses. "You heard your sister—you're not a princess here."

I swallow hard. "But I'm still *your* princess, and you will release Finn right now, *guard*."

Hurt and anger flash through Niku's eyes as he opens his mouth. Before Finn can kick away, I grab him and pull him to the surface. He gasps as he crests, and Jen yells, "Are you okay? Should I get the shocker?"

"No," he gasps. "God, no."

"But . . . I saw blood," Jen says.

"Yeah"—Finn gulps air—"which means my wetsuit is broken, so don't you dare electrocute me again."

I don't know what most of those words mean, but I can taste the tang of blood in the water. I dip below the surface to survey Finn's leg. Several puncture wounds wrap around his ankle, and when I touch them, he jerks away.

When I surface, Finn stares at me in disbelief. "You saved me." His voice is soft, like the tiniest puff of air across the waves. "Why would you do that?"

With my mouth and gills underwater, I say, "Why you jump in?"

"You were going to hurt yourself, and I promised not to shock you. I didn't know what else to do."

I study him for a moment, not sure if I want to tell him why I freaked out. He must know the ocean is right there. He must know I want to get out. And still, he keeps me here. Maybe I *should* let Niku kill him, but Finn and Jen are our only chance of getting out of here alive.

I sink under the water and glance at Niku, but he paces the opposite end of the giant tank, ignoring me. There's a splash, and Finn puts something over his face. Something clear covers his eyes and nose when he sinks below the surface. It makes his eyes appear even smaller than normal, and I swim closer.

I touch the new skin on his arm. It doesn't feel like his hand did when he tricked me into jumping—it's stiff and cold. Finn sticks his hand up like when we played tag, and I do the same, touching my palm to his warm one. The corners of his mouth pull up as I wiggle the tips of my fingers through his web-less ones, and he runs his fingers over my scaled arm to my elbow.

I suck in a breath, then brush the tip of my tail against him. I swim a quick circle around him and run my hands through his hair. It feels like normal hair, but it's completely black, devoid of the bright colors I'm used to. He runs his fingers through my hair, too, and I flush.

Finn surfaces for a breath, then sinks below the water. When I study his legs, he wiggles his toes. When he speaks, his air words come out in bubbles. I try to catch them, wanting to keep his words with me, but they slip through my fingertips. He chuckles and rises again. I follow him, squinting my eyes against the air.

"Jen, throw me the Scuba. I want to try something."

Jen's scowl dives deeper. "What are you doing? Get out of the water, Finnegan. You're bleeding!"

"Just throw me the Scuba. I'll be fine."

She purses her lips, but grabs something from the wall and tosses it to him. Two black, arm-like things join to the sides of a box that Finn sticks in his mouth. When he lowers into the water, he takes a breath. Finn can breathe underwater, just like me. I suck in my own breath at the shock. "We swim?"

He nods and dives deeper, but he's awkward and slow. I giggle and hold out my hand. When he takes it, I kick hard, my tail brushing against him, and propel us through the water. It isn't as fast as I can swim, because of his dead weight, but it's faster than he was swimming. I twist and grab his other hand, too, then spin with him.

"I can't believe you're doing this," Niku says, but I don't care. I'm having fun, and from the sound Finn makes, so is he. Maybe if I keep swimming with him, he'll help me get back to the ocean.

My ankle throbs, but I don't care. I'm doing something no one has ever done before: I'm swimming with a mermaid.

Despite the Scuba, I can barely breathe. Erie swims too fast for the gill-like device to properly separate oxygen from the water. But I couldn't care less, because I'm swimming with a mermaid.

Have I mentioned I'm swimming with a mermaid? I'll probably have a heart attack before I bleed out or drown.

Erie's laughter fills the tank as she spins us through the water, faster than I can imagine. Her tail brushes my legs, while her long hair tickles my wrists. At this moment, I would do anything she asked.

She pulls me to the bottom, then shoots up toward the surface, and *Holy God* the pressure change is gonna kill me. We break the surface, but I'm too heavy for her to lift, and we end up crashing back into the water. She laughs harder than I've ever heard her.

I push back to the surface, spit out the Scuba, and suck in air. Erie's magenta hair rises, then her forehead, then her eyes. Her grin stays under the water, but I can still hear her mirth.

"Darlin', you are the best." I grab her shoulders, breathless.

She pulls me back under and hugs me, spinning us. I give her a quick squeeze, then swim back to the surface to breathe.

"Finn!" Jen yells. "Are you okay?"

"I'm fucking great!" I yell back. When Erie surfaces, I put my hands on either side of her face and kiss her forehead. It's cold, and I realize I just kissed a fish, but I don't care. "You're amazing.

I'll get you out of here, I swear to god. I'm not giving up until you're back home. I promise."

Her face lights up even more. "You mean it?"

I do. I know I told Jen it was impossible, but I *will* find a way to free Erie. "I mean it," I say and wipe my thumbs over her shark-skin cheek. "It may take a while, and we'll have to do what Corporate wants until then, but I'll find a way to get you out of here. I promise, Erie."

• • • •

AS SOON AS I HAUL MYSELF back onto the platform and take my first step, my ankle goes out and I fall to my knees.

"Finn!" Jen kneels next to me with her hands on my shoulders. She's so much warmer than Erie.

"I'm fine." I try to stand again, but she pushes me down.

"You're bleeding."

"Still?" A trickle of blood dilutes the water that streams from my wetsuit, turning it pink. We have to clean this up before anyone sees.

Jen's hands shake as she grabs the Scuba and mask from me. Her face is pale, eyes wide with fear. "I'll call an ambulance."

"Hell no." I grab her wrist, and she drops the mask. "You can't tell anyone about this. Not about me jumping in, or Niku's attack, or swimming with Erie. I'd be fired, and they'd be foamed."

Panic flashes through her face. "But . . . you're *bleeding*."

"Yeah, and it'll stop." Probably. Actually, I don't know what happens when you get bit by a dolphin, because who the hell gets bit by a dolphin?

"Finn." She puts her hands on either side of my face and looks me straight in the eye. "I thought you were about to die."

I sit on my hip, my injured ankle stuck out awkwardly, and take a deep breath. "So did I." The swim with Erie erased the immediate terror, but when Niku grabbed me and pulled me under, I thought I was dead. I don't know what Erie said to make him let go, but I will forever be grateful.

Apparently, so will Jen, because she pushes me to the ground with a kiss. It's not the drunken kind of kiss from the Porch—it's the "I thought I lost you" kind from war movies.

She pushes away faster than I would have liked; her warm lips were making me forget the pain in my ankle. "Sorry," she says.

"Don't be."

She helps me sit and frowns at my foot. "You really need to see a doctor."

I wink. "I'll let you play nurse."

Jen shifts her weight so she can reach my ankle. I wince as she rolls the ruined wetsuit up to examine it. The wounds are neat punctures—no tearing, despite the fact that Niku twisted and yanked it. Now that I'm out of the water, the blood is slowing. Jen's probably right that I should see a doctor for antibiotics or something, but that'll mean Erie's death. I promised I'd free her, but not that way. That's not what I meant.

"Don't worry," I say, like I didn't just nearly die for the second time in a month. "Some Neosporin and a few Band-Aids, and it'll be fine. We need to clean this blood up, though—if anyone sees it, they'll look at the safety footage." In general, no one watches the security camera footage after hours unless there's an accident. If they don't see the blood, they won't know to look.

Jen wraps a towel around my ankle, washes the blood into the pool, then helps me to the locker room. The clock says seven—we still have two hours before anyone arrives.

She lowers me onto a bench. "Where's a first aid kit? And your clothes?"

"Clothes are in my locker, third from the left there, and the first aid kit is on the wall next to the door."

She grabs the kit and clothes. "Please tell me you're wearing something under that wetsuit."

"Boxers don't fit." I wiggle my eyebrows at her as she blushes. "But don't worry, I've got a Speedo on."

Most of the wetsuit is no problem for me, but Jen has to help me get it over my ankle, which is already bruised and swelling. I grunt in pain as she flips the pant leg inside out and forces the bottom over my ankle. It bleeds more, and she wraps the towel around it while she opens the first aid kit. I grunt again and squeeze the bench as she pours iodine over the wounds. She wraps everything in gauze and tapes it, then helps me get my pants on over the bandage.

She wipes her hair from her face. "Is there ice anywhere?"

"There are a couple ice packs in the break room fridge. Stuff the towel and wetsuit in my locker—I'll take care of them later."

She shoulders me to a chair between Erie and Niku's tanks, props my foot up on a second chair, and covers my ankle in ice before letting Erie and Niku in.

Erie swims straight to me and puts her hands on the glass, glancing at my foot. "You okay?"

I smile, exhausted now that the excitement is over. "I'll be fine, darlin'. Why don't you teach Niku English so he'll understand when I yell at him."

She glances at him, eyes narrowing. "I yell at him myself."

I'd love to be around for that. "Teach him anyway. I want to be able to understand him the next time he threatens me."

Jen closes the door to the tube. "What are you talking about, teaching a dolphin English?"

"He can talk," I say, and Jen purses her lips like she's about to drive me to the psych ward instead of the ER. "You have to be in the water with him, and it's the same fucked up fish language Erie speaks, but I swear to god, he was talking."

"We speak the ocean," Erie says.

Jen raises an eyebrow and stares at us like Erie and I are trying to pull one over on her. "Bullshit. Dolphins don't talk—someone would have noticed by now."

"Yep." I grin. "And that someone is me."

"We would be able to hear it. We can hear Erie. It makes no sense."

I shrug, because she's absolutely right, but I know what I heard. I heard Niku's rough, male voice arguing with Erie while he had a death grip on my leg. "It must be something to do with echolocation, because my ankle was in his mouth while he did it. Erie, do you know how Niku talks?"

"He speaks the ocean."

"Do other fish speak the ocean?" Jen asks.

"Dolphins and whales. Fish have own language, and sharks. Fish that live in Seadom speak the ocean. Creepy to hunt fish if know what say, so don't eat ones in Seadom."

"What's the *Seadom*?" I've never heard her use that word before.

Her eyes widen as she smacks a hand over her mouth and glances at Niku. When she turns back to Jen and me, she presses her lips together, then whispers. "Seadom is home."

Home. It's the first time she's said anything about it. "Do all the Mer live in the Seadom?"

She looks away and shakes her head, and now I know it's fear that keeps her from speaking about home. Fear that we'll capture the others.

"It's okay, darlin'. We won't tell anyone where you live."

Her eyes are wide and full of fear when she turns to me again. "Promise?"

"I promise."

The corners of Erie's lips turn up, and I reach out to put my hand on the glass, but the chair isn't close enough.

Jen glances at my ankle. "I hope you learned your lesson. You're not ever doing that again."

"Fuck that," I say. "I most certainly am."

"Yeah," Erie echoes. "Fuck that!"

Aww, my little mermaid is all grown up and swearing like a big girl. I burst into laughter. Jen rolls her eyes.

I don't know why Finn's laughing, but I love the sound of it and never want it to stop. If I can keep him happy, he'll free me. "Watch movie?"

"Sure, darlin'," Finn says. "But I'm taking a nap. Jen'll have to put it on." He yawns, stretches, and winces. "Wake me when it's over."

I can't tell time in this tank, because I can't see the sun or feel the tides, so I don't know how long the movie is. When it's done, I knock on the glass. "Movie over." Finn doesn't move, and I knock harder. "Finn! Wake up—movie over."

Jen touches his arm, then his forehead as he groans and opens his eyes. "Jesus Christ, you're burning up."

"I'm fine," he croaks and sits up. The melted ice falls from his ankle, revealing blood-soaked skin. "Oh. That's not good."

Jen grabs the ice pack from the floor. "We're going to the hospital."

"We can't," he says. "Erie—"

"Will be fine. Tell them you went for an early morning swim and ran into a dolphin, I don't care. We're going."

She shoves her shoulder under his arm and helps him stand. I press my palms into the cold glass, wishing I could help. "Finn? You okay?"

"I'll be fine, darlin'." He flashes a brief smile that falls from his face with his first step.

Soon, they're gone, the next movie has started, and I turn to Niku. He's on the other side of the tank, his back to me. I ball my fists until my nails dig into my palms. "I'm trying to get us out of here, Neek. You have to trust me."

He doesn't bother to turn around. "Get us out by swimming with the landfolk? That's a stupid idea."

"It worked."

"Finn's the one keeping us here, Princess. *He's* the one who won't let us go home. *He's* the one forcing us to do stupid tricks, feeding us dead fish. *He's* the one who almost killed you the other day, and I will kill him for that."

I huff a breath through my gills. "He didn't mean to. He said he'd get us out." My arms fall to my sides. "Finn promised, Neek. He said it would take a while, but he'll find a way to get us home."

Niku finally faces me. "He lied."

"Don't say that."

"Is that an order, *Princess*?"

My lips part in surprise—Niku has never spoken to me with such disdain before. When I speak, my voice is tight. "Finn is our only way out of here, and if you kill him, I will relieve you from your service as my guard."

I turn my back on him and sink to the bottom of the tank, wrapping in my tail.

• • • •

JEN AND FINN ARE STILL gone when the second movie ends. It was another one where a non-human became human at the end. This time, it was a giant beast who was redeemed by the love of a human woman. At the very end, the beast died, and the woman cried a tear that turned him into a human and brought him back to life. For a moment, I wish desperately that I could cry and turn Finn into a sea-human, but this must be another untrue thing from movies.

I ignore the next movie when it starts, and am dozing off when a familiar voice speaks. "Finn? Jen?"

I sit to find Sergio. "Where are your trainers?" he says.

Finn told me not to talk to anyone except him and Jen, but he also said Sergio was his friend. If it was my friend, I'd want to know if he was hurt, so I decide to tell him. Maybe Sergio can help.

"Jen took to 'hospital' because he 'burning up.'"

"Burning up? Does he have the flu?"

"What 'flu'?"

"Sneezing, coughing, fever—"

I don't know what any of those things are. "Niku bit him."

"Niku?"

I point to the dolphin sulking in the back of the tank.

Red creeps up Sergio's neck to his face. "How did Niku bite Finn? Was he stupid enough to stick his hand in the water?"

No, he was stupid enough to stick his whole body in the water. "Niku bit ankle."

"His ankle?" Sergio yells, his hands falling to fists at his sides. "How the hell did Niku bite his *ankle*?"

I back up—maybe telling Sergio was a bad idea after all. When I speak again, my voice is soft. "In 'arena.' Finn jumped in, and Niku grabbed." Sergio's face reddens, and I hurry on. "It okay! I make Niku release and took Finn to surface."

Sergio's jaw hardens in anger, and I wish I hadn't said anything. I'm definitely not telling him about swimming with Finn.

"Sergio?"

He presses his finger against the glass. "You better hope they don't kill your dolphin for that. They'll kill you, too." He spins and walks out of the room.

Kill me, too? Why would they kill me when I saved Finn? I turn to Niku. "I hope you're happy—we're in a lot of trouble for what you did. Sergio says they might kill us."

"Death would be better than this life."

I turn my back on him and wrap up in my tail. I can't die in this gray cage with a friend who doesn't trust me. I have to get out. I have to tell Father what happened to Clair, and tell Huron's parents where he is. For some reason, Finn doesn't treat me like the other merfolk, which means, I'm the only one who has a chance at getting free, so long as Niku doesn't sabotage it by killing Finn.

Niku surfaces and blows an angry spray of water, but he doesn't apologize. He doesn't say anything at all. I really wish I could cry.

No one at the hospital questions my story about an early morning swim/dolphin attack. It's not their job, I guess, and it's not like anyone outside of Oceanica knows we have a dolphin. The nurse ushers me into a room and hooks me up to an IV of antibiotics while I wait for the doctor. All I can think of is what'll happen to Erie if anyone finds out the truth.

Jen paces the room, driving me crazy. "You should probably get back to work," I say. "Before someone notices we're both gone."

She turns to me, rubbing her face. "Erie will want to know you're okay first."

I hold out my hand, and when she takes it, I squeeze. "I'm fine—it's like a cat bite. Once the antibiotics kick in, the fever will go down and they'll let me go home. I bet it won't even be an overnight stay. I'll limp around for a week from the sprain, and then voilà—good as new."

"Good as new? Finn, you almost died."

"Nah. I almost died a month ago—today was nothing compared to that."

Tears glisten in her eyes. Tears. And to think, she wouldn't even look at me this morning. Jen takes a deep breath, so I squeeze her hand again. Before we can say anything else, Sergio appears in the doorway. Shit.

Jen releases me and steps back. Serge's hair sticks up like he pulled at it all the way across the island. "What the fuck were you thinking, jumping into the arena with a Mer?"

"Uh . . ." How did he find out? Was there blood we didn't clean? Did he find the ruined towel and wetsuit in my locker? Did he decide to watch the security footage for shits and giggles?

"He got it swimming off the dock," Jen says. At least she's willing to lie for me, though she doesn't bat an eye as she does it, like she spends more time lying than not. I realize, once again, that I have no idea who Jen is.

"Bullshit," Serge says. "Io told me her dolphin bit you when you jumped into the arena."

"Goddammit, Erie," I mutter. I told her not to talk to anyone, and what does she do? Tells the first person she sees something that could get her killed. "Jen, go make sure she doesn't talk to anyone else." She leaves, and I turn back to Serge. "She hasn't talked to anyone else, right?"

"How the fuck am I supposed to know? You're her babysitter."

"I'm her trainer," I say, although that no longer feels like enough.

"Then *train her* not to talk to people. In fact, train yourself not to be such a fucking dumbshit. When my aunt finds out about this—"

"You are *not* telling Aunt D." My heart monitor races, the beeps so fast I'm sure the nurse will return any minute. "If you tell her, she'll kill them both. Or give them to another trainer, which is the same as a death sentence."

Serge clenches his jaw and stares at me without speaking.

"I'm serious, Sergio. You can't tell anyone. Erie saved my life—we can't let them kill her for it."

"If you hadn't jumped in—"

"What's done is done, okay? I'll be fine, so please, not a word to Aunt D."

It's a long moment before his shoulders sink. "If you ever do anything like this again, I'm going straight to Aunt D. For your own good."

And so they don't close Oceanica, he leaves unsaid. I know that's his biggest concern—not me being mauled by a dolphin. He's my best friend, but Corporate is family.

The beeping of the heart monitor slows, and I take a deep breath. "Deal. If Niku attacks me, you can run to Aunt D and kill him, but not Erie."

Serge shakes his head, because I just wiggled out of a promise to not jump in the tank again. "Whatever, man, get yourself killed if you want. Just don't shut us down."

Us. The guy that hates the ocean calls Oceanica "us." I used to be the one who called Oceanica "us."

"I won't let anything happen to Oceanica, okay? I won't let anyone hurt Erie, either. She doesn't deserve that."

Serge throws up his hands and walks out.

• • • •

I WAIT AN HOUR BEFORE calling Jen. The entire time, I imagine Maddy and Nat suiting up, preparing the pink juice that will foam Erie. The phone rings three times before Jen picks up, and I don't know if that's good, or bad.

"Oceanica, this is Jen Stevens." She doesn't sound they-just-killed-Erie upset, so that's good.

"It's Finn. Is Erie okay?"

She sighs in relief, and now, all Jen sounds like is tired. "She's fine. She didn't tell anyone else, but she's worried they'll kill Niku, and worried that he still wants to kill you."

If I was him, I'd want to kill me, too. "Tell her not to worry. Serge won't say anything, and I won't let Niku kill me."

"Good." A moment of awkward silence stretches between us before she says, "Any word on when you'll be back?"

"Not yet. The nurse said the fever's going down, but no one else has come by to check on me."

Silence hangs on the other end, and I can imagine Jen nodding, a frown stretched deep across her face.

"In any case," I continue, "I only took four days off when I was electrocuted, so this should be a quick visit."

"This isn't a joke, Finn."

Now I'm the silent one. It's kind of hard to come to terms with the fact that I almost died this morning, and that it was the *Mer* who saved me. I still don't know why Erie freaked out, and I *really* don't know why she saved me. It would have been so easy for her to let Niku drag me under until I drowned, but instead, she turned her back on the only friend she has to save the guy who's keeping her captive. Can mermaids suffer from Stockholm syndrome?

"Finn?" Jen says, worried.

"I'm fine." My voice sounds rough even to me, and I hope Jen doesn't mention it. "Call me if anything happens with Erie."

"Let me know what the doctors say."

"Will do. Hold down the fort, grasshopper." I hang up before she can reply; I can't stand to hear the worry in her voice.

I try to figure out a way to free Erie while I wait for the doctors to release me. Breaking her out *Free Willy* style will land me in jail, but I don't know what else to do. If I had the money, I'd buy her from Delmara, but I don't think my salary will cover the cost. Maybe a Kickstarter? Who would donate money to free a Mer they've never met? I need to get her in front of an audience, need to make them fall in love with her.

Then again, the more popular she is, the less likely it will be that Delmara will sell her.

I sag against the bed and lean my head back. There's almost no chance I can free Erie, and no way to keep her safe from the nets once she's free. Frustrated, I close my eyes and listen to the steady beeping of the heart monitor until the doctor arrives.

I haven't seen Finn in two days, though Jen promises he's getting better, and I can't help but worry about him. Who cares about movies and breakfast when my one chance out of here might be dying, and I can't save him? I need to see Finn for myself, to know that he's okay.

It would be better if Niku would speak to me. He grunted in acknowledgment when I told him the landfolk wouldn't kill us, but he hasn't said a word. At first, I was content with the silence, but now I'm lonely, and terrified, and want nothing more than to wrap around his dorsal fin and trace his scars. I trace my own instead, wincing as my nail drags across the scab covering my neck.

"You shouldn't do that," Niku says.

I spin to face him, surprised. "What?"

"Pick at your scab. You'll make it worse."

My hand falls to my side. "What do you care? You're trying to get us killed. The scar won't last long against the foam."

Niku shakes his head. "I'm not trying to get us killed, but whatever game you're playing with that landfolk boy won't work."

"Finn is our only chance to get out of here. We don't have a choice—we have to trust him when he says he'll free us."

"Free you."

"Yeah, well, maybe if you hadn't tried to kill him—"

"Like he tried to kill you?"

An annoyed huff escapes me as I touch the scab again. Finn didn't try to kill me—his reaction proved that. The expression on his face was pure horror when he saw the foam.

Arguing with Niku won't help, so I turn my back on him and stare at the Ariel figurine amidst the necklaces in my own tank. I've had two days to figure out what I need to do if Finn survives. I need to make him fall in love with me. If he loves me, he'll do whatever it takes to get me out of here.

I have no idea how to get a landfolk to love me, though. I wouldn't even know how to get a merfolk to love me. Huron and I had fun, but we were never in love. The only one who loves me is Grandmother . . . and Niku, before I made him release Finn.

The water shifts around me, but I don't turn until Niku says my name. He's almost next to me, close enough to touch, and I squeeze my hands together in front of my stomach to resist the urge to do just that. "What?"

"Even though you're stupid and reckless . . . and wrong, I'll do my best not to hurt your landfolk boyfriend." Niku scowls. "Unless he hurts you again—then, I'll kill him."

I consider him for a moment, trying to decide if he's telling the truth, or if it's an empty lie so I'll let my guard down. There's no way I'll tell Niku my plan, not now. All he'll do is argue. "You mean it? You won't try to kill Finn again?"

"I promise, Princess. I'll play nice if he does."

I put my hand on his side and run my thumb over one of his scars. "Good. Then it's time for you to learn how to speak the air."

• • • •

BY THE TIME JEN ARRIVES, Niku can say "good morning," "please," "time for breakfast," and "fuck that" in air words. I'm pleased that he's trying, even if the landfolk can't hear him unless they're in the water.

"Morning, Erie, Niku," Jen says as she opens the door.

"Morning, Jen." I raise an eyebrow at Niku until he says it, too.

"I have a surprise for you," Jen says, still holding the door open.

Two long, crab-like legs appear, then something big swings between them. It takes me a moment to realize what I'm looking at. "Finn!" Relief rushes through me from head to tail as he makes his way into the room. I do a backflip and press my palms into the glass.

A grin covers his face from ear-fin to ear-fin. "Hey, beautiful."

"What did he say?" Niku asks.

"'Hey' means hello, and 'beautiful' is a nickname, like darlin'."

Finn does a weird crab-walk to the tank and puts his hands over mine, but he's shorter than normal. His new legs have made him shorter, hunched over. "I missed you," he says, and the sadness in his voice gives away the truth of his words. He really has missed me.

My heart constricts so hard in my chest I almost gasp. No one—not even Huron—has ever sounded so sincere. This may be easier than I thought. "I missed you," I say, voice tight. "Niku promised not to hurt you, so I teach him air words. 'English.'"

Finn's face softens. "Is that right?" He wipes his thumb over the glass, and I wish he was in the water with me. Swimming together made him promise to free me, and if that's what it takes, then I need to get him back in the water.

"Are you okay?" I ask, to make sure there's no lasting damage from Niku's attack.

"I'm fine. Nothing a few days of antibiotics and rest couldn't fix. Tell Niku he'll have to try harder than that to get rid of me."

That's one thing I definitely won't translate.

"Listen, darlin'." Finn drops his hands to rest on his crab-legs. "I did a lot of thinking while I was gone, and the only way we'll get you out of here is to make the public fall in love with you. There are tons of 'save the whales' bleeding hearts out there who'd be happy to jump on the bandwagon, but we need everyone else to see you as something more than a fish. Otherwise, no one will help. So, it's time to get you in front of an audience."

I frown, because I don't know what "public," or "bleeding hearts," or "bandwagon" is, and I don't need to make all the landfolk love me, just Finn. "What that mean?"

"That means, we need to get you performing."

Performing? My fins droop. The last thing I want to do is a bunch of tricks for the landfolk. Niku nudges me to translate, and when I do, his glower deepens. "I told you," he mumbles.

I turn back to Finn. "We don't want to perform."

Finn puts one of his hands back on the glass. "I know, but this is the only way we can free you. We need everyone to fall in love with you. It's time to come up with a routine—one where you aren't just another silent, dead-eyed Mer—we need to make you a household name, like Shamu."

Jen shakes her head. "For all the good it did Shamu."

The expression Finn turns on her is so lost that I wish I could pull him through the glass to swim with me. "It's the only choice we have. We need to make America love Erie just as much as we do."

The breath catches in my throat—Finn loves me? If that's true, then his plan really is a way to free us, not just a way to get us to perform. I need to swim with him again. To wrap my tail around him and hear him say the words in the water, where I can feel them vibrate in my scales.

I put my hand over his on the glass. "Can we swim?"

He smiles. "As soon as my ankle's better, sweet. Then we can swim as often as you want."

Jen and I spend the next few days coming up with a routine. My ankle scabs over, but I still can't put any weight on it. That won't stop me from getting in the water, though. I plan to swim with Erie the first chance I get.

"We have the arena tonight after the park closes," I tell Jen. "Be prepared for the most amazing experience of your life."

She narrows her eyes, suspicious. "What are you talking about?"

I grin. "Swimming with a mermaid."

The confusion plummets into a scowl, and Jen hugs her arms. "No. I'm not a reckless idiot, like you. I'm not getting in that tank with a Mer."

"Come on, it's Erie. She wants to swim with you, don't you, darlin'?"

Erie smiles. "I swim with you, Finn."

I chuckle. "We'll swim, too. I promise. But I have an idea, so tell Niku not to hurt us tonight. If we want people to see you as human, we need to show you interacting with humans."

"This is a really, really bad idea," Jen says. "OSHA—"

"Can suck it. Erie won't hurt us, and I'll prove it."

Jen shakes her head, throwing her hands up in surrender.

. . . .

LATER THAT NIGHT, ONCE everyone's gone home, we let Erie and Niku into the arena. Jen's pale, her hands folded into fists at her sides, like she's trying not to shake.

I put my hands on her shoulders and squeeze. "You'll be fine. I'll get in first, so if Niku feels like attacking something, he can attack me."

"That doesn't make me feel better," she says as I hand her one of the Scubas.

"You'll love it, trust me." I throw my crutches to the side and sit on the edge of the platform with my feet in the water. So far, so good. No crazy dolphin teeth are coming my way, and the cold water feels good on my sprain. I slip into the tank, letting the water cover me. Erie's bright face is there to welcome me.

She spins and swims around me, brushing me with her tailfin. It reminds me of the way she swam with Huron.

A quick scan of the tank reveals Niku nearby, watching with his pit bull stare. I point at him and raise my eyebrows at Erie.

"He behave," she says. "He only hurt you if you hurt me."

I hold my hand out, and squeeze hers when she takes it. When I surface, Jen's holding the Scuba in her slightly shaking hands.

"Come on in, the water's fine," I say, after spitting my Scuba into my free hand. "Niku won't hurt you."

"Niku's not the one I'm afraid of," Jen whispers.

She must be joking—she's scared of Erie? I mean, sure, if Erie wanted to hurt us, she could do so quicker than Niku, but there isn't an evil bone in her body. I lift her hand out of the water. "Don't worry. I've got her under control." I grin, because how can I not? I've been waiting all week to get back in the water with her.

Jen slowly lowers herself to the edge of the platform with her knees tucked up. Erie's head pops out of the water. She blinks, then says, "Come in, Jen. We swim."

Her voice is happy, but muted beneath the surface. Jen takes a deep breath, extends one leg, and dips her toes in.

"Back up, so she can jump in, Erie."

The magenta hair disappears and reappears in my peripheral vision. I dip under the water to check Niku's location, but he still bobs a short distance away. When I resurface, Jen's second foot is in the water. She adjusts her mask.

"Ready?" I say, and wrap my teeth around the mouth guard again. Her shoulders are tense, but she slips into the water. I hold my hand out so Erie won't rush over until Jen's ready.

Taking your first breath with the Scuba is a strange feeling. Snorkels and scuba tanks have tubes leading directly to the air, but the Scuba stops in the middle of the water. The air is salty and extremely humid, and it's kind of a mind-fuck to use it for the first time. Jen's about to hyperventilate, so I grab her hand and take a couple deep breaths with her until she's more comfortable breathing through it. Then I turn to Erie, and hold Jen's hand out to her.

In one powerful kick, Erie's beside us, her hair floating around us like sargassum. "We swim now?"

I squeeze Jen's hand and let go so Erie can take it—she won't be able to pull both of us through the water. Jen stiffens, but it doesn't last long, because, in a matter of seconds, Erie takes off. While she spins Jen around the tank, I turn to Niku.

"Your turn," I say and swim closer. He moves away. I motion him to come to me, and he freezes. I motion him to stay and swim to him, but he moves away again. I need Erie's help.

When I wave at her, she crosses the tank with Jen and pulls her to the surface. Jen and I spit the Scubas out. She laughs. "That was amazing!"

"I told you." The stars have come out, and they twinkle above our heads.

Erie blinks her eyes out of the water and gapes at them. "Never see stars from surface." Little points of light dance in her wide eyes.

Jen grabs my hand and squeezes it, and she might hate me for this later, but I pull her to me and kiss her. Her lips are salty. Instead of pulling away, she wraps her hand around my neck and her legs around my waist. We can't blame alcohol this time—the only thing we're drunk on is the thrill of swimming with a mermaid.

We kiss until Erie wraps her hands around my good ankle and yanks us under. Jen breaks away to surface, while I try desperately not to cough and drown. Adrenaline pulses through my veins, but Erie releases me, and I claw my way to the surface to suck in air, coughing as she crests to watch me.

"I think someone's jealous." Jen winks.

Erie's magenta gaze is intense, like I'm prey. My heart thunders as I hold my hand out. "No need to be jealous, darlin'. Let's swim."

I bite the Scuba and sink below the surface. She takes my hand, but instead of pulling me through the water, she wraps her tail around my legs, pinning them together. Her tail is much stronger than I thought, and I swallow as I realize how easy it would be for her to pluck the Scuba out of my mouth and hold me here until I drown.

Maybe Jen's right, and Erie is jealous. What if she's a vindictive bitch, like a normal girl? To my horror, she wraps her fingers around the Scuba. I have just enough time to take a deep breath before she removes it. *Fuck*. Jen may not even realize Erie's drowning me until I'm dead.

Erie cocks her head to the side, and I try to stay calm to conserve the oxygen I have. She doesn't look angry, just curious, and when I reach for the Scuba, she leans back and smiles. She thinks this is a game. A few bubbles escape my lips as I try to hold my breath, and she grabs at them, then runs her fingertips across my forehead, down my nose, and into my hair to find my ears. If I wasn't about to drown—and Erie was a regular girl—I'd be turned on. Maybe she realizes that, because she pulls my face close and puts her cold, hard lips over mine.

I've never felt anything as warm and soft as Finn's lips. My tail tightens involuntarily around his legs and bubbles escape his mouth, filling mine with warm air. I breathe him in, his breath tickling—just shy of stinging—my gills as it passes through. The feeling is so new and delicious that it takes the pain of his fingers digging into my arms for me to realize I'm drowning him.

"Oh!" Bubbles leave my mouth and gills with the word, like I'm landfolk. I unwind my tail and push him to the surface, where he coughs and gasps for air.

By the Tides, I almost killed Finn. I didn't even think about it—I just stole his breath because I wanted to kiss him. Jen's right to fear me.

"What happened?" She reaches for him. "Are you okay?"

Finn coughs once more before answering. "Erie kissed me." He doesn't sound angry—or pleased—about it. Have I screwed everything up by kissing him? I thought it would help him fall in love with me.

"Maybe we should go," Jen says. "Where's your Scuba?"

I hold it up, and she takes it with barely a glance at me. "Finn didn't swim."

"Another time, darlin.'" He sounds tired, or wary. "Right now, I need to catch my breath and rest my ankle. We'll swim again soon."

Soon. We'll swim soon. He'll get me out of here soon. I'm sick of soon. I'm tired of being patient, of waiting for his promises to come true. I lunge in front of him, and he stops short. He glances at Jen, then turns his nervous gaze back to me.

I know why he wants to leave. I scare him. When he's in the water, I'm in control, and both times, he's nearly drowned. Part of me wants to drag him under and keep him with me forever. If I can't leave, then neither can he.

"Erie?" His voice is quiet. Worried. I kissed him so he'd fall in love with me, but all I've done is scare him.

I dive to the bottom of the pool before I hurt him again, and wrap my tail around myself so I don't have to see when he leaves, the tank as empty as his promised *soon*.

My arms shake as I pull myself onto the platform and collapse onto my back, as far away from the edge as possible. Maybe swimming with Erie isn't a good idea, after all.

Jen touches my arm. "You okay?"

"Yeah. Just need to catch my breath." And get the predatory look in Erie's eyes out of my mind. I've been seeing her as Ariel for so long, I forgot she's also a velociraptor. "Do me a favor?"

"Of course," Jen says.

"Kiss me again."

That's obviously not the favor she was expecting. She sits back and raises an eyebrow. "Why?"

"I need to get the cold feeling of Erie's fish-lips out of my mind."

Jen chuckles. "You're the one who wanted to swim with her."

"Yeah, swim, not be mouth-molested by a fish." Thank god Erie didn't stick her tongue in my mouth. I would have gagged, and she probably would have been so offended she'd have killed me.

Jen leans over me, still giggling. "You know, all the old myths say mermaids lure men into the water, then kill them with a kiss. You fell for an age-old mermaid trick."

"Not funny." I grab her wrist, pulling her to me. Her hair drips salt water on my face. "And it's sirens who do that, not mermaids."

"It's both," she says. I run my hand into her hair and pull her the rest of the way. She comes willingly. The cold ghost of Erie's kiss dissolves under Jen's warm lips and tongue.

Eventually, though, she pulls away. "We should get out of these wetsuits."

"Right here?" I wink. "I didn't know you were that kind of girl."

A pink flush covers her neck and cheeks, and there's no chance of hiding my erection with the wetsuit on, so I don't want to let her go just yet. Holding her against me isn't exactly helping, though, and she pushes away from me, eyes rolling as if I've just used the world's worst pickup line on her. *Hey baby, did it hurt when you fell from Heaven?*

She retrieves my crutches. "If you can manage to be an adult for a whole twenty minutes, we could go get dinner. I'm starving."

Is Jen asking me on a date? It's been a long time since I've been on an actual date with a girl. "I bet I can manage to be an adult for a whole half hour, even."

"I'll take that bet." Jen helps me stand and hands over the crutches, then walks down the stairs ahead of me because I'm slow. She waits at the bottom, staring into the tank. Erie's wrapped up in her tail, and I'm not sure if it's because she almost killed me, or because I so obviously snubbed her. I put my hand on the glass, but she ignores me.

Without a word, Jen turns away. We both know what she would say, and how I would respond. All I can hear in my head is Erie saying Huron *was* her boyfriend.

"Jen," I say, and she turns to me, all the playfulness dissolved away into pity. "How early do you want to wake up in the morning?"

"Finn—" Her voice has a note of annoyance in it.

"'Cause if we got here early enough, we could let Huron back into his own tank without anyone knowing he spent the night in the arena."

Her mouth parts in surprise, then she glances at Erie. "I can set my alarm for extra-early."

I grin. "You let Huron in—I won't be able to lift the damn door with my crutches."

Jen leaves, and I knock on the glass, but Erie squeezes her tail tighter. "You'll like this surprise, darlin'. Have a good night."

I ignore Finn as he knocks and speaks. Sure, I'll have a "good night" in this dank prison, knowing that the ocean isn't far away, that Niku might be right and Finn will never save us—a certainty that grows with every passing day.

A scraping sound vibrates through the water as the door slides open, and I uncurl to go back to the tiny tank with Niku. Instead of the door I'm used to, a different one opens, and I recognize the shock of blue hair in the unnatural light of the tube. Finn's trying to bribe me with Huron. I don't know whether to be grateful or angry.

"Erie?" Huron says, voice full of trepidation. He's thinner than last time. His big blue eyes have sunken into his cheeks, and the color of his fins is fading prematurely. I know I said Huron and I were never in love, but I cared about him, and seeing him like this—knowing that it's my fault—chips away at my heart.

"It's okay." I swim to him, but he backs away. "The landfolk are gone for the night." I glance in Finn's direction, but he's walking away, his extra legs clicking against the floor.

Huron peers around the tank; he must be here every day in the sunshine, "performing" for the landfolk. Has he ever been here at night, able to see the stars? Does he know how close the ocean is?

"What's happening?" Huron whispers, and I glance at Niku, because I don't know.

Niku shakes his head. "Maybe Finn feels guilty? Or it's another way to hurt and control you."

Finn has plenty of reasons to feel guilty, but he hasn't tried to hurt me since the loop incident. My finger traces the scar of the necklace, and I know—from the horror on his face then, and the fear in his eyes today—that this time is supposed to be a gift. But as I scrutinize Huron—this thin, subservient creature—it's less a gift and more a reminder of what I'll become if I stay here too long. Finn may have meant this as a gift, but in reality, it's a warning. If I don't play nice, this will happen to me.

I wonder if they've broken Clair yet. I can't imagine her as pitiable as Huron, but a deep ache lodges in my chest at the memory of her jumping when Finn told her to. My oldest sister, a princess of the Seadom, bowing down to the landfolk. She never even bowed to Father.

The screech of a door being shut vibrates through the water, and Huron glances toward his tube. Panic crosses his features. "Wait," he says. "Clair!"

He swims to the door as every part of me that was left whole shatters. He doesn't want me; he wants my sister. He'd rather be stuck underground, in a tiny tank with humbled Clair, than be under the stars with me. I reach out a hand that's no longer stained with ink. Niku swims to it, letting me rest my fingers on his scars—the only thing in this place that won't change.

"Erie," Niku says softly. He doesn't say more; he doesn't have to. He's spent the past several seasons protecting me from Huron, a common boy. Now, my common boy doesn't care a whit about me. Huron's wandering hands are no longer a threat.

I swallow to make sure my voice is steady. "Is our door open?"

"I believe so."

"Let's go, then." I gaze at the stars one last time, then glance at Huron, whose hands are pressed against the glass of his door. He can follow if he wants, but I don't think he'll even notice we've gone.

The gray walls are oddly comforting as we swim through the tube to the tank we share. For the first time in days, I curl around Niku's dorsal fin and trace his scars. "I thought he loved me," I say after a long silence.

"Huron? Or Finn?"

I don't have an answer for that.

When Jen walks through the door from Huron's tank, I leer playfully at her. "Wanna help this cripple get his wetsuit off?"

"Are you sure it's the wetsuit you want me to get off?"

Oh, I like this version of Jen. Wherever she's been hiding, I wish she'd have come out to play sooner. I grab her around the waist and pull her close. "One thing at a time, darlin'."

"You're right," she says, her voice purring as she pulls away. "Dinner first. I'm starving."

Cockblocked by food. Damn. We part ways at the locker room, and by the time I've changed into my work clothes, Jen's waiting for me in the hall. "So," she says as she opens the door for me to get my crutches through. "You know this island. Where to?"

It's well after nine, but every restaurant on Duval will still be serving food. I don't feel like dealing with drunken tourists, though, or running into people I know. "How about frozen pizza and beer on the couch at Café de Jarvis, so I can prop my foot up?"

She smiles. "I'll do you one better: frozen pizza and beer at Café de Stevens, so you don't have to hobble around your own kitchen."

"Perfect."

Jen drives, since Niku bit my right ankle and I can't press the pedals yet. Turns out, she only lives two blocks away from me, in a rental house on Caroline Street. "My roommate works at

Schooner Wharf, so she won't be home 'til late," she says as she unlocks the door.

So that's why she wanted to come to her place instead—not to keep me off my feet, but so we wouldn't run into any roommates. Not that Sergio would care. He's probably wondering why it took so long.

The house is small, but open. To the left is a living room with a comfortable-looking couch, an overstuffed chair, and a giant ottoman. The kitchen is on the right, with a two-seater table in front of the window. It resembles the house Serge and I rent, except, you know, cleaner.

"Need some ice?" Jen asks as I make a beeline for the couch. It feels damn good to sit back after a day of crutches jutting into my armpits and being squeezed to near-drowning by a mermaid.

"Ice would be perfect." My ankle throbs as I prop it on the ottoman. "Beer would be even better."

Jen leans my crutches against the wall. After a trip to the kitchen, she hands me a beer and drapes a bag of ice over my ankle, then grabs the pizzas out of the freezer while the oven preheats. "Feel free to watch TV," she says.

I grab the remote and check out what's streaming. The list is heavy on science fiction and fantasy, plus the requisite true crime shows. I turn on *Rick and Morty*; you can never go wrong with *Rick and Morty*.

"So," I say. "Which of these shows are yours?"

"Just *Merlin*." Jen stops long enough to wink at me. "I have a thing for boys with big ears and bigger—"

"Shoes?" I wink back.

"Smiles."

I smirk and motion her over. When she reaches the couch, I pull her onto my lap and whisper in her ear. "I have other big things, too."

She giggles, and I tighten my hold on her waist, kissing her neck. With a pleased hum, she relaxes against me. I kiss up to her ear, then turn her face to mine. She's straddling me, her tongue in my mouth, when the stove beeps.

Jen pushes away, and I groan. "Leave it. We can make pizza later." My fingers lift the hem of her shirt to brush across her skin, and she sucks in a breath as she glances from the kitchen to the hallway.

"I don't have any condoms."

"I do."

An incredulous smile lifts the corners of her mouth, but her eyes remain half-lidded. "You carry around 'just in case' condoms?"

"Of course. I don't want to catch a disease from some skanky tourist on Duval."

Jen snickers a little and shakes her head. "You're horrible."

"Yep." I lift her shirt a little farther, so I can brush my palms against her waist. "Which bedroom is yours? Or we can stay on the couch. I don't mind."

Her cheeks flush, and I can barely stand it anymore. I press against her as she straddles my lap again, and the flush deepens. When I push her shirt up further, Jen puts her hands over mine.

"My bedroom's on the right." She stands and hands me the crutches, because nothing's sexier than hobbling to the bedroom. She leads the way, flipping down a frame on the dresser as she enters. Photos of an ex-boyfriend she hasn't quite gotten over? I'm more than happy to be her rebound.

The room is jammed with boxes she hasn't unpacked yet. They sit three high along the corners of the room, and block the closet door from fully closing. She must have started at Oceanica the day after she moved in. There's a small desk—also covered in boxes—and a nicely made bed with a comforter the exact shade of Erie's hair.

It makes me think of Erie's cold lips on mine, and I have to suppress a shudder as I sit on the bed, lean the crutches against the wall, and pull a condom out of my wallet. This is all turning out very awkward, until Jen straddles me again and I forget all about Erie's lips, throbbing ankle, and pretty much anything except the feel of her tongue in my mouth, her fingers in my hair.

I thought Jen would be shy in bed, but as my hands travel to her waist, she pulls her shirt over her head and tosses it onto a stack of boxes. Her skin is almost as pale as mine, with only a faint tan line from a sun she hasn't seen all summer. I pull her against me, my hands running up the smooth skin of her back to her bra. As soon as I unhook it, she wiggles out and throws it onto another stack of boxes. Her breasts are small and perky, and I kiss from her collarbone to her nipple as she leans back and runs her hands through my hair.

"Oh," she breathes as her fingers creep their way down to the hem of my shirt. I have to release her for a second as she pulls it over my head, but then I flip her onto her back to continue my exploration of her body with my tongue. Her skin's salty and smooth, and I want to taste every inch of it.

I kiss her breasts, her stomach, her thighs, grazing the skin between until she gasps and pulls me to her to claim my lips. Her hands travel my skin as well, leaving hot trails and nail scratches.

I suck in a deep breath when she pushes me back to remove my belt and unbutton my pants, and when her warm hand finally wraps around me, I groan. "Oh god, Jen. I want you so bad."

She arches against me in response. My mouth covers hers as I unbutton her pants, and she spreads her legs, wiggling as I push the khaki material out of the way. I've been waiting a month and a half to touch her. I hope she likes it quick and rough, because I won't be able to prolong this.

My fingers slip into her warmth and her hand pauses as she makes small, pleased noises beneath me. Oh fuck, she feels amazing. She grinds against my hand until she gasps with each thrust. I twist my fingers inside her until her nails dig into my shoulders and she shudders. She whimpers when I remove my hand, but I can't wait any longer.

I push off my pants and grab the condom. "You have to be on top," I say. "My ankle . . ."

Jen pushes me to the bed, grabs my covered cock, and eases herself onto me. We both suck in a sharp breath, and I run my hands from her breasts to her hips as she rides me hard. A groan escapes me as she starts to moan.

She buries her face into my shoulder and bites down, and my body spasms as I shove as deeply into her as I can. Her moans are louder now, muffled in my skin, and I grab her ass as I feel her whole body tighten around me. I grunt as I release, and she bears down on me, her nails digging into my skin.

We're both left panting and shuddering, peeling away from each other to recover.

"Oh god," she says. "I needed that."

"Glad I could help." I roll onto my side and wink at her. "Let me know whenever you need it."

Jen stands to gather her clothes. She yanks her shirt over her head, rolls her eyes, and leaves the room, pants in hand. That takes care of any romantic ideas she might have been forming. Don't get me wrong—I like Jen. I'd even date her if I wasn't moving back to Miami at the end of the summer, but I'm not looking to stay celibate during my senior year of college. She'll have to deal with casual sex for now.

And who doesn't like casual sex?

I take my time hobbling around her room, collecting my clothes, and by the time I'm dressed and making my slow way down the hall, she's sitting on the couch with a beer in hand.

"Did you get what you came for?" she says. "Or do you still want the pizza?"

I flop down next to her. "I came for pizza and beer. Did you get what you brought me here for?"

She clenches her jaw and narrows her eyes. "I didn't bring you here for sex."

"Bullshit."

Her cheeks flare red, and she turns away. "I didn't bring you here *just* for sex."

I lean over and mumble against her shoulder. "And I didn't come *just* for pizza and beer." I lean back with a smirk as her shoulders loosen a fraction. "I wasn't lying when I said to let me know whenever you need it, though. I'm here to please."

"You're so full of yourself." She stands as the oven beeps the one-minute mark.

"That's funny"—my grin grows—"because you were the one who was full of myself a few minutes ago."

She throws a pillow at me, but I can see the silent laughter in her shoulders as she walks to the kitchen. Crisis averted with a sex joke—works every time. Besides, Jen doesn't want me. Once she comes out of this post-sex haze, she'll realize she's way too good for me and will probably never let me touch her again.

I plan to get in all the touching I can before then.

In my dream, Finn is merfolk. He has a tail and gills, and his short dark hair is mirrored in the tips of his fins. His lips are still as warm and soft as they were in the arena, but we swim through the reef instead, caressing each other as brightly colored fish swim around us.

When I wrap my tail around him, he says, "Morning, beautiful."

I hum in contentment and say good morning back in ocean-speak.

"What was that?"

He jerks beneath me, and I wake to find my tail wrapped around Niku, the gray light around us more reminiscent of the forest than the reef. With a high-pitched "Eeep!" I slip away from Neek, while he looks the other way. For the Tides, I was dreaming about a landfolk while wrapped around my guard. How embarrassing.

"You okay, darlin'?" Finn stares at me like I've gone a little mad, but those soft lips of his twitch up as I swim to him. He peers around the tank, and his smile fades. "Where's Huron?"

The broken pieces inside of me rub together, sharp as shards of coral. My shoulders sink, and I pick at my healed tailfin. "Next to door of tank, where I leave him."

"What? Why would you leave him there?"

When I answer, it's a whisper. "Where he leave me."

Finn frowns. "What happened? Did you have a fight?"

I shake my head, my hair floating in front of my face so that I have to push it back to see him. "He want Clair. He . . ." It takes me some time to find the correct air word. "Broken."

"Of course he is, if he wants Clair over you," Finn says. "You're the most beautiful Mer I've ever seen."

My fins sink. He doesn't get it. "No . . ." I furrow my brow, because I can't translate it into air words. "Huron fearless, joke, touch. Now . . . broken." I put my hand over my chest, trying to convey the meaning of *being* in air words. Huron's become less substantial than the foam he'll turn into someday. I never want to be broken like that.

"Oh, Erie, I'm sorry."

Finn puts his hand on the glass. I cover it with my own, but what I really want is to touch him. His warm skin, so different from Huron's cold scales. I want to breathe Finn in again, to wrap my tail around him until his warmth seeps into my core. "We swim?"

Before he can answer, Jen walks in, and Finn drops his hand to face her. "Huron's back in his tank," she says. "He seemed oddly . . ." She stops when she sees me. "Never mind."

Relieved? Happy? Despondent? It doesn't matter. Huron wants Clair, and she's the one he lives with. He was just a common boy, anyway. Someone I should never have talked to, much less snuck around with. My hand slips from the glass.

"We swim?" I say again, if only to make Finn turn back to me. But he doesn't.

"Tonight."

Tonight. Later. Soon. I punch the glass and he jumps, turning on his extra legs to face me. I scrutinize his tiny eyes, but

I have no words, so I wrap myself around Niku, my back to Finn and Jen.

"Erie," Finn says. "We don't have time to swim right now. We'll swim tonight." He moves to the other side of the tank, where I can see him. "I promise."

I turn my head into Niku's side and finger the scar around my neck. "Neek?"

"Yes, Princess?"

I want to ask him to hide me, but the walls are glass. I want to ask him to take me home, but it's impossible. "Never mind," I say. "You can't do anything." The words will cut him, but right now, I need someone to hurt as much as me.

·····

SOMETHING'S DIFFERENT about Finn and Jen today. Where she used to cut her gaze away whenever he met it for too long, she now watches, a smile growing on her lips. Where he used to barely touch her, his fingers now linger, confident, like they know the feel of her skin as well as his own. Like they belong there. It's the way Huron used to touch me.

Before Finn swam with me, I liked the thought of them together; but now that I need him to love me, I want nothing more than to rip the smile off Jen's face whenever she finds him looking at her. I would give anything—*anything*—to switch places with her.

What would it be like to be landfolk? To have the harsh wind constantly blowing against my skin? My tail split in two so I was as slow and awkward as they are? The landfolk are all jerky movements and constant blinking. Their skin and hair is bland, not the vibrant colors of the ocean. Is the land that boring?

Maybe that's why they need us to entertain them. All that snail and sand and blah. Who wouldn't want the vibrancy of the reef after that?

Apparently Finn wouldn't, because he runs his hands into Jen's hair and pulls her in for a kiss—right in front of me. If he really knew anything about who I was, he'd be bowing down to my every whim, but, like Clair said, I'm not a princess here.

I interrupt them. "We swim?"

They pull away, but they're still in each other's eyes. I'll have Niku soak them if they don't stop.

"Two hours," Finn says, after a brief glance at his magical rectangle.

"What 'hours'?"

He finally pulls away from Jen to face me. "It's a measure of time. In one hour, the park will close and everyone will leave. In two, we'll be alone and can swim as much as we want."

As much as *we* want, or as much as *he* wants before he leaves?

Or as much as *I* want before I stop him from leaving?

The urge to pull him under is overwhelming, and part of me is glad it isn't "two hours" from now. I'm not sure I'd be able to stop myself from spearing him with my nails, dragging him under until all his air was mine. It would rush into my mouth, tickling the roof, and push through my throat into my gills, where the warm bubbles would caress the life-giving part of me, that I might breathe him in again and again. I close my eyes and take a deep breath, but it's sterile.

Sometime later, Finn leans into the glass. "One hour, darlin'. We're going to go change."

Change into what? The old Finn and Jen?

They return in the black skin they use in the arena, and part of me is excited that it's "tonight," and I finally get to swim with Finn like he promised. The other part of me wants to rip his eyes out for even looking at Jen.

"Two things," Finn says as he comes back to the tank. "You can't drown me, because they'll kill you, and I couldn't bear that." He puts his hand on the glass, and I cover it. "And I want to swim with Niku, as well."

I pull my hand away. "Niku? Why?" I don't need him to love Niku.

Finn leaves his hand on the glass. "Part of the show. If you want to free Niku, we'll have to humanize you both."

He glances at Jen, and I realize what's happening. Finn isn't swimming with me because he loves me, or even because he wants to—he's doing it because he promised to free me, and this is his way of doing that.

Fine. If it'll get Niku and me out of here, I'll play his game. "Let me tell Neek." I turn my back on Finn before he can reply.

"I heard my name," Niku says.

"Yes." I run my fingers over his scars. "Finn wants to swim with you. Without drowning."

Neek dips his nose, contemplative. "I've heard the landfolk like that."

"It's to get us out. Finn says that if you want to get out, too, he has to 'humanize' you."

"'Humanize.'" Niku bumps his nose under my chin. "Maybe we aren't the ones who need to be humanized."

He's right, but there isn't anything we can do about it. I run my hand over his nose. "Just . . . don't hurt him. Please."

Niku bows his head. "You have my word."

· · · ·

THAT FIRST MOMENT WHEN we enter the arena and finally have room to swim is my favorite moment of the day. The water rushing over my scales and through my hair almost makes me feel like I'm back in the ocean—if I close my eyes.

We do a few laps, warming our ill-used muscles in the cold water, before I swim to the glass where Finn and Jen stand much too close to each other. Jealousy bites at my core, and I shove it away. I'm not supposed to be jealous. I'm using Finn to get out. "We swim?"

Finn grins. "No removing the Scuba this time, okay?"

"Okay."

Jen's eyebrows pull together, worried, but I'll be more careful this time. Like Finn said—if I kill him, even on accident, they'll kill me right back, and I refuse to turn to foam before I get back to the ocean.

When Finn slips into the water, I swim a circle around him, brushing his skin with my fins and shivering at the warmth. I wrap my tail around him again because I can't help it, but I don't squeeze. His heart beats so hard, I can feel it in his legs and the water around us. I can taste his fear in the water, too. He's trying to hide it, but I know it's under the surface, putting me in control.

"You warm," I whisper.

He swallows, then nods.

"You kiss Jen?"

He nods.

"A lot?"

He nods again.

"You . . ." I don't want to hesitate, but I'm scared of his answer. "You love her?"

He jerks back, eyebrows pulling together, and shakes his head in an emphatic "no." I can't help it—my tail tightens for a brief moment, then I release him and swim back a kick. "You act like . . ." Like Huron used to act toward me. The crushed pieces of my heart rub together again.

Finn reaches his hand out to me, and all of the anger and jealousy flows out of my fins. I can't be mad at Finn for kissing Jen, not unless it keeps him from freeing me. I grab his hand, and we swim.

By July, my life's become practice with Erie and sex with Jen, and I can't complain at all. Erie and I swim every night after the park closes, as I run her and Niku through the routine over and over. I don't want them to remember the moves—I want them to move even if they forget how. It has to be as natural as breathing, otherwise, the first time they get in front of an audience, they'll freeze up.

When I think they're ready, we show the routine to Delmara—without the part I play. She'd flip out if I jumped in the tank right now, so I tell Erie and Niku to do it without me.

Corporate's pleased with the routine, so the madness of gearing up for the first show begins. There's a photo shoot, and once I figure out a way to make Erie understand what a photo *is*, she preens for the photographer like any celebrity would. When the first posters arrive, I tape one to her tank so she can stare at herself like the narcissistic fish she is.

Her face is plastered on every store window and tourist booth in town. The streets are littered with her magenta hair as tourists drop business cards with Oceanica's hours on them. I can't even watch TV without a clip of Erie and Niku jumping in a commercial. The boxes of merchandise arrive, and my sister steals one of each item for me before she stocks the shelves.

I don't think I sleep the night before the first show. I toss and turn, worried that something will go wrong: Niku will decide at showtime to kill me; Erie will freak out and accidentally kill me; I'll forget to hold my breath and kill me.

Yeah, I'm pretty sure I'm going to die today.

"Finn? Finn!" Jen snaps her fingers in my face as we stand on the platform for one last practice before the show. Erie's scheduled at eleven, so we need to warm up now.

"What?" I don't bother to hide the irritation in my voice.

"You missed your cue."

Goddammit. Erie and Niku can do the routine by muscle memory, but I depend on the music, and I just mistimed it. They jump without me, still going through the motions, and Jen rubs my shoulders, kisses my neck, and whispers in my ear: "Relax. They can do this in their sleep, and you'll be too jazzed up to miss it at showtime."

When they're done, we let Erie and Niku into the practice tank, so they can keep moving without the restriction of the holding tanks.

Erie puts both hands on the glass. Her eyes blaze with excitement and worry. "You didn't jump."

"Sorry, darlin', my mistake." I put my hands over hers and smile. After that one day of weird almost-jealousy, she seems to have let it go, and has worked steadily toward the goal of putting on the show. That doesn't mean she's less possessive, though—when I'm in the water, I'm hers. "It won't happen during the show. I promise."

Erie paces the tank. I wish there was some way to calm her nerves, but the best I can do is hold her hand. By the time I reach the platform, her hand is out of the water, waiting for me. Her cold shark-skin wraps around my fingers, and I squeeze. The next three hours will be the longest of my life.

"Can we swim?" she says.

I squeeze again. "Sorry, no can do. If Corporate caught me, there'd be hell to pay."

Her brows pull together, and she dips her eyes back underwater. "What's 'hell'?"

"A lot of trouble," I say. "I'm not supposed to touch you, or be in the water with you."

"Why?"

I pause for a moment. I don't want to give her any ideas, but at this point, I firmly believe that Erie would never do anything to hurt me. "Because most of the Mer try to kill their trainers."

She squeezes my hand so hard I grunt and almost pull away. "I would never hurt you, Finn."

"I know, darlin'." Her claw-like grip relaxes. "They're just scared because they don't know that yet. They will after today. Today, everyone will fall in love with you."

Her eyes surface, and she stares straight into mine without blinking. "Like you did?"

I draw a line across her forehead and down her cheek with my free hand. "Just like I did, beautiful."

Her smile is so big, I can see it clearly beneath the water.

"What the fuck are you doing?" Sergio's voice booms from the door. "Are you *touching* her?"

At least it's Serge, and not Delmara or Maddy. "Erie's nervous. I'm holding her hand to calm her down."

His face is as red as I've ever seen it. "You can't fucking touch her. What if she pulls you in? She could kill you!"

Erie faces him. "I would *never* hurt Finn!"

The note of indignation in her voice is clear, and brings Serge up short for a moment. When he speaks, his voice quavers for a brief second. "I told you I'd go to my aunt if I found you in the water again."

I wave Erie's hand around the air. "I'm not in the water."

"And you, Jen." Sergio turns his angry scowl and damning finger on her, where she sits on the platform. "Finn's a dumbshit, but you should know better than to let him do this."

She snorts. "You think I could stop him? I tried. He's right, though—Erie won't hurt him."

Serge stands there, silently fuming, directing his angry gaze at each of us before throwing up his arms. "God, you're all a bunch of idiots. You better not let my aunt catch you doing that."

I glance at the clock on the wall. "I've got two hours before Aunt D comes down to wish us luck. Don't worry about it."

"Your arrogance will get you in trouble someday," Serge says, then shakes his head and drops his arms. "Good luck with your show. Don't do anything massively stupid before then."

I grin. "Thanks. It'll be the most amazing show you've ever seen, I promise. See you after."

• • • •

BY THE TIME DELMARA arrives to wish me luck, my nerves are churning my stomach so much, I might just puke. I imagine all the things that could go wrong. Missed cues, bad jumps, calling them by their real names instead of their stage names. Carbon pulling Hannah under while she screamed. I *know* Erie won't hurt me, and still, I can't stop seeing the blood in the water.

Delmara strides in, tiny and confident, but she doesn't catch me breaking the rules. I left the platform half an hour ago; Erie's hand was chapping from the air, and it's easier to speak through the glass.

"Finnegan." She opens her arms, and when I step forward, she places her hands on my cheeks, every inch my aunt and not at all my boss. "I'm so proud of you. I didn't want you to take on such a responsibility until after you graduated, but damn, if you haven't proven yourself."

She squeezes my cheeks, and my face warms at her praise. I've been working for this day since Oceanica opened four years ago. Hell, I've been waiting for praise like this since I first started working with her and the Mer when I was fifteen.

"Thank you, Aunt D." My voice catches briefly, so I clear my throat. "I promise this will be the most profitable show you've ever had." The old dream is eclipsing the goal of freeing Erie for the moment. I want nothing more than to please Delmara, to make her proud of me, show her that I'm not just a stupid kid obsessed with fish. Today, I want to prove that the decision to let me shadow her in the early days at the community college has paid off.

Delmara has spent so much time and money on me—I want to prove I was worth it.

"You'll do great," Delmara says. She pulls my head down and plants a kiss on my forehead, and all of my anxiety drains away.

Before the landfolk woman leaves, she steps to the glass and stares at us. I stare right back. I don't speak—I've learned my lesson about speaking to anyone but Finn and Jen—but despite my silence, her eyes narrow. I don't know what I've done wrong.

I glance at Finn, but all his energy is focused on this woman, like a seahorse waiting for a treat. For some reason, everything changed when she walked into the room. I hope I never see her again.

She taps the glass with her fingernail. "This one stares back like K does. I don't like it."

Finn's smile fades. "It's okay, Aunt D. She's just curious."

"I don't like them curious; I like them cowed. You know how important this place is to me, Finnegan. Do something about it before the next show."

She turns her back on me, and I bare my teeth at her, but Jen—standing off to the side, giving me the impression she doesn't like this "Aunt D" much, either—shakes her head "no." Who is this woman, to declare that I can't look at anyone? And why is Jen listening to her? Jen doesn't even listen to Finn, who's basically groveling now.

"Don't worry, Delmara. I won't let Io hurt anyone. I promise."

I bristle at my stage name, at the fact that anyone thinks I would hurt Finn. Or any of the landfolk. I know what happens if I misbehave.

The woman wishes Finn luck again and leaves, and when he turns to me, it's clear that whoever she is, when she's around, Finn belongs to her. His full attention isn't even on me when he says, "No more staring, okay, Erie?"

I cross my arms and glare at him.

"I'm serious." He grimaces. "Remember when I told you about 'Corporate'? Well, Delmara is Corporate. We have to do what she says when she's around, so please don't stare at her."

So she's the one keeping Niku and me here. She's the reason for the blackened shells. She's the one who broke Huron and made Clair bow. Someday, I will make her pay for that.

"Fine," I say, though I keep staring at Finn, arms crossed.

He shakes his head, but before he can say anything more, Sergio walks back into the room. "Showtime. You ready?"

My stomach plummets into a pit of feather duster worms, the nerves making my hands and fins shake. Is this how Clair and Huron felt before their first show? Or had they been shocked into indifference already?

I glance at Niku, but his features are unfocused and bored. "Ready, Neek?"

"To make a fool of myself in front of a bunch of landfolk?" He bats the water with an annoyed flipper. "Don't really have a choice, do I?"

"I guess not." I turn to Finn and nod—might as well pop this bubble and get it over with.

He puts his hand on the tank, and his face radiates excitement. "Good luck, darlin'. They'll love you." Then he follows Sergio out of the room while Jen opens the tube door.

An overwhelming energy travels through the water as I enter the tube, and as soon as I'm out the other side, I freeze. Landfolk of every shape and size fill the space. Finn told me that five thousand landfolk could fit in the stands, but that number meant nothing before now. Wrapping around one whole side of the arena, and far up into the sky, is a sea of snail-skin, impossible to distinguish as individuals. The noise of them is deafening.

Niku bumps me to move out of the way so he can enter, but my tail refuses to work. Even he glances around, nervous, as the landfolk notice us. They cheer so loud, I cover my ears and squeeze my eyes shut.

The cacophony reverberates through the water and presses into my scales. *Don't scream, don't scream, don't scream.*

I need to make these landfolk love me. That's all I'm here for. They think I'm here to entertain them, but really, they're here to fall in love with me and help me get free. I'm using them. *I'm in control.*

"Erie?" Niku whispers. He's allowed to talk because Finn says the "microphones" can't hear his voice. "It's okay. They can't hurt you."

I take a deep breath and open my eyes. The landfolk can't hurt me—they can't come into the water, and if they do, I'm in control. I can do this.

Some of the smaller landfolk—the children, I guess—have their hands pressed against the glass. I swim toward them. A few shriek and step back, but the braver ones stay put. I need to make them love me, so I smile, mouth closed so my sharp teeth don't scare them, and put my hands on the glass, covering the palm of a brown-haired child. It screams in delight. My nerves are so on edge that I jump back, then wave sheepishly at another.

"Mama, Mama!" it squeals with a little girl's voice. "She waved at me!" Then it runs forward and smacks its hands on the glass.

I put my hands over hers and very quietly, hoping that the microphones won't hear, whisper, "Tag."

She squeals again, and other children run forward. I move down the glass, tagging and waving and flicking my tail at them until Finn's voice booms through the arena and the crowd grows quiet.

"Ladies and gentlemen, welcome to Oceanica, the world's only mermaid marine park! I'm Finn, and I'm here to introduce you to Oceanica's two newest performers. Please give a warm welcome to Iodine and Cadmium!"

We jump, and the crowd cheers. When the noise dies down, I swim to the middle of the tank and pop my head out of the water so I can see Finn. His small eyes are lit up with excitement and pride. I raise my hand and wave like we practiced. "Good morning, Finn!"

The audience laughs just like Finn said they would. No one's heard a mermaid speak before; they probably think it's a "recording."

"Good morning, Io. Do you want to say good morning to the audience?"

I turn and wave to them, and when I say "good morning," I swear every little girl in the audience screams "good morning" back. I wish I had known the audience would be this loud.

I do a small jump and get out of the way for Niku. "Good morning, Cad!" Finn says, and Niku makes a happy noise I don't think I've ever heard come out of him before we started practicing. "Why don't you greet the audience?" Finn says. Niku swims to the other side of the arena, jumps, and lands on his side, soaking the first row. It made Finn angry when he got wet, but the audience loves it.

I will never understand the landfolk.

So far, the show is going well. I couldn't see what Erie was doing with the kids, but whatever it was, they loved it. And the reception of her "speaking" has gone over well with the adults.

How many of them have never seen a Mer before? How many will be blown away? How many won't think of Erie as anything but entertainment?

We start with some simple tricks for the kids. Erie and Niku race from one end of the arena to the other—Niku wins—then do a couple back flips and summersaults to show the difference between Mer and dolphin abilities. They have a jumping "contest," which Erie squarely wins. I've never seen a Mer who can jump as high as she can. The kids count how many times she can summersault while she's in the air—three—and I talk about Mer physiology the whole time.

Once the learning part of the program is over, it's time to make them fall in love.

"Who's ready for a show?" The audience cheers, and the music starts. It's a high-energy song that builds near the end—perfect for a performance like this.

Erie and Niku are flawless in their routine—they jump high, spin fast, and completely captivate the audience. Jen nudges me when it's time to start counting the beats, but I'm already on it. This show will be perfect.

The crescendo builds, and I dive into the pool. Even underwater, I can hear the collective gasp of the audience as Erie grabs my right hand. Niku's dorsal fin hits my left palm, so I can hold on. I close my eyes and hold my breath—Niku swims too fast for the Scuba to work—as they build up speed. They jump at the crescendo, pulling me into the air with them. Ecstasy bursts through every cell as we fly above the water. I take a deep breath as we reach the top of the arc and they release me, and then dive back into the water on my own.

When I resurface, the crowd is going nuts. Erie and Niku jump over me as the music ends, then stop next to me.

"Ladies and gentlemen," I say. "Erie and Niku!" I realize my mistake right away, but I doubt anyone could hear me over the deafening cheer of the crowd. I pull Erie over and kiss her forehead. This is by far the best moment of my life.

• • • •

WHEN I CLIMB BACK ONTO the platform, I grab Jen and swing her around in a hug while she beams. "That was perfect!" she says, and kisses me when I put her back on the ground. Her voice is caught by the mics, so everyone in the crowd can hear what she says.

"That was stupid," Sergio says. His voice is also picked up by the mics, and I motion the tech guy to cut the feed.

"What are you doing up here?" I ask. Serge hates the arena platform—he's always worried a Mer will jump up and drag him in.

"I ran up here for the shocker when you jumped in, though I don't know why I bothered. Aunt D is going to kill you."

"Are you kidding? I just pulled off the most groundbreaking show in Oceanica's history. Everyone will want to see Erie perform now."

Serge replaces the shocker on the wall. I can't believe he's being such a pussy about this. Yeah, Corporate will be pissed I pulled such a stunt, but if it equals higher sales, she won't be pissed for long. And a Mer/dolphin/human show is guaranteed to sell.

"You have to admit," I say, "that was pretty fucking cool."

He rolls his eyes, but the corners of his mouth turn up. "Good luck with Aunt D." He claps my shoulder and leaves the platform.

When I turn to Jen, I catch a glimpse of Erie jumping for the crowd. She's so different from the other Mer, who pace the arena after shows, waiting to be let back into their holding tanks. Instead, Erie's showing off and, knowing her, is probably talking to the guests. I'll be yelled at for that, too.

Jen clasps her hands together and fidgets. "How much trouble are we about to get in?"

I squeeze her arms. "We'll be fine. Corporate will get over it when she sees the record-breaking sales. Trust me."

"Okay," she says, but her tone says she doesn't trust me at all.

"You let Erie back in. I'll meet you downstairs." I give her a quick kiss, then take the stairs two at a time, my blood buzzing in my ears—I haven't come down yet from the high of the show. Every employee I run into looks at me like I'm crazy, but I don't care. That was the best performance in Oceanica's history, and I know it.

When I walk through the door to the holding tanks, Delmara's already there, waiting for me with a scowl. "What the hell was that? You fucking *pendejo*—you could ruin us all."

Not the greeting I was expecting. "*That* was the most profitable show Oceanica has ever had."

"*That* broke every rule OSHA and APHIS have ever had." She throws a training manual on the floor.

"Relax, Aunt D. As soon as they see the video, they'll see that Erie would never hurt me."

Her arms fly into the air. "Who the fuck is Erie?"

Oops. Before I can answer, Erie swims into the tank, spinning around in glee. "Finn—that was so much fun! I can't wait to do it again." She stops spinning when I don't answer, and her eyes widen as her gaze lands on Delmara. Her webbed hands smack over her mouth.

Delmara turns on me, her eyes full of fire and brimstone. I'm pretty sure she's about to hit me. "You taught it to *speak*?"

"*She* taught *herself* to speak. She's extremely intelligent."

It's easy to see the family resemblance between Delmara and Sergio now—they both turn the same shade of red and pull at their short, dark hair when they're upset.

"What is the first rule of Oceanica?" She points to the poster on the wall.

"Don't humanize the Mer."

"Don't fucking humanize the Mer!" She bangs her fist on the tank, and Erie swims to Niku, staring at us over his scarred back. I kind of wish I could do the same, faced now with Delmara's wrath. "Do you know why we don't humanize the Mer? Do you *remember*?"

"Of course I remember. Hannah."

"I don't care about Hannah—those little shits killed your father." She jabs her finger in Erie's direction.

"What? Aunt D . . . he drowned."

"Looking for *them*!" She shakes her head. "If Cale were still around, everything would be different. You'd see . . ." She glances into the tank, and her eyes narrow. Erie cringes behind Niku.

I don't know what to say. I had no idea Delmara blamed the Mer for Dad's disappearance. No wonder she didn't have a problem dissecting them. Still, I can't let her take it out on Erie. "Trust me, Erie would never hurt anyone."

"It doesn't matter if *she* wouldn't—the others would." Delmara paces in front of the tank. "People see you jump into the tank with a Mer, and they think it's safe. Next thing you know, some *pendejo* fifteen-year-old climbs the barrier and jumps in. And what if it's not your fish girlfriend in the tank when he does? What if it's K? Not only would we have a dead kid and a lawsuit to deal with, we'd have to spend time and money finding a Mer to replace her."

I never thought of that. I never thought anyone else would try what my dumbass did. I watch the puddle I'm creating as the arena water drips off me and swallow. "I'm sorry. I didn't think—"

"Of course you didn't." She slices a hand through the air. "You're not paid to think. You're paid"—she jabs me in the chest with her finger—"to follow"—jab—"the rules." Jab.

I don't have an argument for that. "I won't do it during a show again."

Her finger is still pressed against my sternum. "Damn straight, you won't. I'm removing you as trainer. You're going topside for the rest of the summer."

The news is such a smack in the face that I actually take a step back. I've never worked topside, not even when I was too young to legally work with the Mer. Why was she willing to break the law then, but not now?

"But . . . you-you can't," I stammer. "Oceanica is mine, too. I know more about the Mer than anyone—even you." She opens her mouth to speak, but I don't let her, desperate to argue my way out of this. "I've been here since the beginning. All the failed experiments. All the foam. I gave you the fucking idea for the Mer shows! You can't fire me."

The fire in her eyes dims. "You gave me the idea, not the funds. I'm beholden to shareholders now." She touches my arm gently. "Your help has been invaluable, Finnegan—which is why I'm not firing you outright. Spend the year at school, and if you can prove to me that you will follow the rules, you can train another Mer next summer."

Another Mer. Not Erie. Even if I can prove I'm not a dumbass, I won't get Erie back. I glance at the tank—at her wide eyes staring at me. I never thought I'd lose her. "Please, Aunt D. Please don't take me away from Erie."

"Too late, Finn. You've cost me too much this summer. OSHA will fine us—at the very least—for this indiscretion, and I've already had to replace an entire act because of you."

My attention snaps back to Delmara. "Because of *me*?" I can't stop my voice from rising. "I was doing my job that day—*Maddy* wasn't paying attention. I almost fucking died because I was following the stupid fucking rules!"

Delmara doesn't flinch, despite my hands folding into fists. "You were the one in the water," she says, her voice biting and cold. "You were the one we spent the money on. You're the one the shareholders held responsible."

Her voice softens, and she points at Erie. "I gave you this Mer so you could prove yourself. I'm sorry, Finnegan. I want to see you succeed, but you have to stop acting like this whole place revolves around you."

When I don't respond, because I don't know what to say, she holds out her hand. It's not for comfort—it's for the badge that lets me into the restricted areas of Oceanica. I close my eyes as I hand it over.

"Get changed and meet me upstairs," Delmara says. "Jennifer?"

"Yes, ma'am?" I'd forgotten Jen was even in the room.

"You're in charge—I'll send Sergio down to help you. If I see you so much as look at the water longingly, you're fired."

"Yes, ma'am."

Delmara turns and walks out, leaving Jen, Erie, and me to stare after her in silence.

"What just happened?" Niku whispers as the woman Finn called "Corporate" leaves.

"I don't know," I whisper back. "I think Finn got in trouble for jumping in the tank with us." They were speaking too fast for me to follow, and I don't know many of the words they used. When I'm sure she's not coming back, I swim to the front of the tank. "Finn?"

He turns. His eyes are red, blinking more than normal, and he looks . . . lost.

"What's 'fired'?"

His shoulders, which had been so tight they were nearly up to his ears, sag. "It means—" He clears his throat as his voice breaks. "It means, I'm no longer your trainer."

I scrutinize him and whisper, "And what does that mean?"

"Goddammit," he says and punches the tank. I jump back, but he leaves his hand pressed against the glass. "It means you won't see me for a long time."

A long time? My stomach plummets into my tail at the thought. I want to ask how long, but I'm afraid he'll slam his hand into the glass again. Instead, I put my hand over his. "Because I asked you to swim with me?"

"Oh, Erie." He leans his forehead against the glass and closes his eyes. "This isn't your fault. I knew I was breaking the rules. I just didn't think Delmara would fire me for it."

Jen puts her hand on his shoulder. "Maybe she'll let you return once her temper cools."

A sharp pang of jealousy tightens my stomach, and my nails scrape the glass as if they can break through. I should be the one comforting Finn, not Jen. I should be the one touching him, consoling him. I've never hated my tail and gills more than in this moment.

"Yeah," Finn says, his voice hollow. "Next year. With a different Mer."

A different Mer?

"What about me?" I blurt out. I need Finn. I need him to get me out of here.

His hand pulls into a fist, and I have just enough time to yank my hand back before he punches the glass above it. His eyes are still squeezed shut, his forehead still pressed into the tank. "You're Jen and Sergio's now." He opens his eyes. "If he hurts you, I swear to god—"

Jen squeezes his shoulder to cut him off. "I won't let him."

Finn ignores her and studies me like he's memorizing every feature—like he'll never see me again. The nervous pit of feather duster worms in my stomach writhes as I spread my fingers over his fist and it opens.

"Don't give him any reason to hurt you, Erie. Be good for Jen, don't talk too much to Serge, and do the show without me. I'll watch every performance. I promise. You may not be able to see me, but I'll be there, watching."

I nod. My throat is too tight to speak.

"Don't forget to smile for the audience—we still need them to fall in love with you."

I swallow to recover my voice. "Will I see you again?"

His thumb rubs across the glass like he's caressing my face. "Of course you will. I'll see you the day I take you back to the ocean, if not before. I promise, Erie."

My heart clenches—he promised to save me. I have to hold on to his promise until I see him again.

Finn lets his hand fall and takes a step back, his eyes unfocused. "I'll be watching tomorrow. Don't forget."

I press both hands into the glass, wishing I could shove them through and grab him. "I won't."

His mouth twitches up briefly. Before he reaches the door, I yell, "Finn!" When he turns, I say the only thing I can think of to make him remember his promise: "I love you."

"I love you, too, Erie." He turns and walks through the door.

As soon as he's gone, I realize I didn't say it to make him free me. I said it because it's true.

• • • •

I'M GLAD THE WATER in the tank is so much colder than at home; it helps my body go numb as I stare at the doorway Finn disappeared through. I sink to the bottom of the tank and wrap my tail around myself.

Jen turns to me. "Are you okay?"

No. I am absolutely not okay. I have no idea when I'll see Finn again, I'm stuck in a tank with my guard, and I'm cold. Always cold.

Except when I swim with Finn.

Niku's nose bumps my arm, and I realize I've not been paying attention. I put my hand on him and look at Jen, about to say that I'll be fine, when I catch a glimpse of black hair in the doorway. My heart leaps.

I unwrap myself, because I don't want Finn to see me sulking, but the face that materializes is tan and shorter than I'm used to. Sergio.

"I saw Finn in the hallway," he says to Jen. "He told me what happened. Guess I'm helping you with Io."

Why does he insist on calling me by my stage name when he knows my real name? I slam my fists on the glass. "My name is Erie!"

All of my resolve to stay strong in front of the landfolk dissolves, and I start banging on the glass, screaming Finn's name. I know if he hears me, he'll come running.

"Erie," Jen yells. "Calm down!"

I can't. I refuse. Maybe if I scream for Finn long enough, they'll give him back. My eyes burn with a sensation I've never felt before as I scream. Sergio starts up the stairs, going for the loop. Finn told me not to piss him off, but I can't help it. I keep screaming.

Until Niku rams his nose into my side so hard, I'm left gasping from the pain. "Neek," I manage between gasps.

"I'm sorry, Princess. I can't let them shock you."

Sergio pauses on the platform, hand on the loop, but I couldn't scream now if I wanted to. All I can do is suck in water, trying to breathe. That's when I feel it—the pocket of air inside me expands, and I suck in water faster as I float against my will.

"Neek!"

"Calm down, Princess. You're hyperventilating." He swims above me, pressing me into the water.

Automatically, my fingers find his scars, and I remember the first time this happened. The first time I hyperventilated and

Niku had to hold me down. The first time I traced his scars. It was the day they told me my mother was gone.

My entire body shakes as I cling to Niku. I can hear Jen's voice, but she sounds so far away.

"What do we do?"

"Sedate her," Sergio says. "Once she calms down, her swim bladder will shrink back to normal."

"Yes," I croak, and then switch to air words. "Yes, please." I don't want to feel anything right now. I want to float in a haze of apathy until Finn frees me.

"Last time, it took two days for her to normalize after sedation—she needs to perform tomorrow," Jen says.

Sergio rummages through a box on the platform. "That was heavy sedation. She'll be fine for tomorrow. Trust me. She can't perform like this, anyway."

Perform tomorrow? As Finn would say: fuck that. It doesn't take long for the bitter taste of the sedative to coat my tongue, and I sigh as the pain in my side fades away with the rest of the world.

Walking away from Erie is the hardest thing I've ever done. I swear I hear her voice screaming my name as I shower, but it must be my imagination. I can't get back inside the holding rooms, regardless. By the time I leave the locker room, I can't hear anything.

My god, I can't believe I won't see her anymore. The thought stops me halfway up the stairs, and I grip the railing to keep myself upright. I will never hear her cheerful "Good morning, Finn!" again. Never fall into the depths of her eyes. Never feel her fins brush over me in the fish version of a caress. Not until the day I free her.

I'm more determined than ever to make that happen, especially when the HR manager tells me I'm working in the gift shop with my sister. I'd rather be fired outright, but at least this gives me a chance to tell guests about Erie—about how amazing she is. About how we need to free her. If Corporate sticks me in the gift shop, then I'll undermine that decision as much as I can.

The one o'clock show is starting when I make my way topside, and the gift shop is deserted except for my sister and the other girl that works there. "Hey, Munchkin," I say.

Heather slaps me in the face. "Finnegan Phillip Jarvis, don't you ever scare me like that again." I'm still in shock over being slapped when she throws her arms around my neck and hugs me hard.

I rub my stinging cheek. "Nice to see you, too."

She releases me, but her frown is still in place. "You better call Mom—she freaked out when you jumped in the water. She's probably left seven voicemails by now."

"Mom was here?"

"Of course. She's pissed she had to learn about your first show from me." Her eyes bore into me. "Last night."

"Oh, uh, I guess I've been so busy, I forgot to tell her." If I'd known Mom would be at the show, I would have warned her I was jumping in.

Scratch that—I wouldn't have said a damn thing, because Mom would have told Serge's mom, who would have told Delmara.

"So," Heather says, "you here to rub in how amazing your show was and how they're changing the name of the park to Finn-land?"

Finn-land, I wish I'd thought of that, and wish I was in any sort of a mood to joke about it. "I'm here to work. Corporate wasn't happy with the show, so I'm topside for the rest of the summer."

Heather's jaw actually drops open. "You've been *demoted*?"

The word makes me sick. "I was trying not to think of it like that, but yeah, I've been relieved as Erie's trainer. If I'm a good boy, I can have a new Mer next summer."

"Who's Erie?" the other girl says.

I glance around the shop—I'm surrounded by Erie here. Stuffed animals, figurines, clothes, magnets, you name it, all emblazoned with her magenta hair and fins. I don't feel like explaining, though. I don't feel like being here at all.

"I'll be back," I say and escape the magenta commercialism. I walk to the top of the stands and watch the rest of K, Radon, and Argon's show instead. *Clair and Huron.* Huron, the broken ex-boyfriend of my Mer. This is what Corporate wants: dead-behind-the-eyes, broken Mer who never smile and can't wait to kill their trainers. Delmara wants to break Erie's spirit, but I won't let her. I don't care what it takes—I will destroy my dream job to get Erie out.

• • • •

I LEAN ON THE PASSENGER side door of Jen's car as she walks out of the staff entrance. Her shoulders are slumped, and a crease that wasn't there yesterday—or this morning—mars her forehead.

"Hey."

She lifts her head. "Hey."

The car beeps that it's unlocked, and I climb in. Ever since Niku attacked me, I've been carpooling with Jen. First because I couldn't drive, and then because I was spending my nights at her place. Awkward silence permeates the car. "How's Erie?"

"Sedated."

"As in mellow? Or you dumped quinaldine in the tank?"

"Quinaldine." Jen's knuckles are white on the steering wheel as she stops for a group of tourists crossing the street. "She freaked out and started to float. Sergio gave her a sedative, but promised she'd be able to perform tomorrow."

I should be thankful Sergio didn't shock her when she freaked out, but I can't believe they drugged Erie. "But—"

"She asked us to." Jen's voice is strained, and my anger turns into guilt. They wouldn't have had to sedate her if I hadn't so royally fucked up. "Niku had to hold her down, and Serge said sedation would be the quickest way to stop her floating."

I stare blindly out the window as we cross Duval—I've seen Mer float before. After we shocked Carbon into releasing what was left of Hannah, he took one look at her and hyperventilated. He began to float and panicked, trying to swim to the depths of the arena, but unable to. I've always wondered if it was because he realized what he'd done, or if he knew what would happen to him for doing it.

When I don't answer, Jen keeps talking. "She balanced out after a while and curled up on Niku's back like normal."

I nod, imagining Erie's tail curled around his dorsal fin, while her hair hides her face from the gray concrete walls surrounding them.

Heavy silence wraps around Jen and me until she parks, turns the car off, and sits back. Neither of us moves.

"Where . . . ?" Her hands slide over the steering wheel. "Where did they . . . ?"

I'm glad she can't finish, because I don't want to hear her say the words. "Gift shop, with my sister."

Jen swallows. "Oh."

"She'll get a kick out of ordering me around, so at least someone's happy." That reminds me of what Heather said about Mom, and I fish my phone out of my pocket. Sure enough—several voicemails and a few texts. I rub my eyes with my fingers. "I hope you have something stronger than beer inside."

"Tequila."

Ugh. Tequila shots are the worst, but they're better than the feeling squeezing my chest right now. It's a fine mixture of guilt, denial, and pride that goes down even worse than tequila.

Two shots later, I sprawl on the couch with my arm around Jen, though she's stiff and I'm thinking of anything but sex. Or her.

She takes a deep breath and stiffens more. "Can I ask you something?"

"From the sound of your voice, I'll need more tequila for this." The bottle's on the floor next to us, and I take another shot before I tap her arm. "Go."

Another deep breath. "What did you mean when you said you gave Delmara the idea for the Mer shows?"

That was her question? I expected her to ask what was going on with Erie saying she loved me, or why I was so convinced Corporate would never fire me, though I guess this is kind of a roundabout way to the latter. "When she first documented the Mer, I mentioned that it would be cool to see them perform at Orca World."

Jen tilts her head back. "That sounds like something a twelve-year-old would say."

"I was fifteen." She turns her face into my arm as I talk. "We were still at the college then, and the tanks were barely big enough to hold the Mer—they were made for much smaller fish. We had one female that kept trying to escape by jumping out, but there wasn't enough room for her to get any momentum, so she mostly just splashed around a lot. That's when I made the comment."

"So Delmara just . . . built Oceanica for you?"

My laugh is more a derisive snort than anything. "She did nothing for *me*—the Mer needed bigger tanks, so she went to Orca World and offered to sell them, with the stipulation that she would be hired to do research." That's what Oceanica should be—a research facility. But no one wants to fund a multimillion dollar research facility if they aren't getting a return on their investment.

"Orca World said no. They were in the middle of a PR shit-storm and thought that bringing in an even more dangerous—and humanoid—creature was a bad move."

"And now your Mer shows have put them out of business." The laugh that escapes Jen is humorless.

"Their former owner holds at least a quarter of the shares in Oceanica. He knew it'd be bad business for Orca World, but great for us."

Jen deflates. "That's . . . disheartening."

I can't help but agree. Freeing Erie means we don't just go up against Corporate—we go up against *Corporate*. Savvy businesspeople who can wind legal documents around us until we choke on ink. Despite the protests against keeping orcas, the only thing that tanked Orca World was the Mer shows—what will we have to discover to make people forget about mermaids? A unicorn? Aliens?

My promise to free Erie feels impossible.

Jen's voice cuts through my thoughts. "Do the deaths ever bother you?"

"Of course." That deserves another shot of tequila, as an image of the failed dissections flashes through my mind. "I mean, at first watching them foam was kind of cool, but you never feel good about having to do it."

She sits up so fast I spill tequila as I set the bottle back on the floor. "I meant the human deaths. The trainers."

What? I thought we were worried about Erie? "Of course the trainer deaths bother me, but it's not like it's my fault. It sucks when my friends are attacked, but they *asked* to work with the Mer."

The expression in Jen's eyes tells me that I'm the most reprehensible human being on the planet. "What about the ones who came from Orca World—because you shut it down?"

Maybe it's the tequila, but I'm not following this conversation. "They had just as much of a chance of being attacked by a *killer whale*."

Jen punches the couch and stands, pacing. "My god, Finn. Your stupid comment when you were fifteen has cost people their lives! Trainers have died. Mer have died. Erie—"

I stand, too, knocking over the tequila without caring. "Erie won't die."

Jen swallows back tears, her hands moving like she wants to say something, then folding into fists at her side. "Maybe you should go."

"You're kicking me out?"

"I'm asking you to go home."

I throw up my arms. "I can't fucking believe this. First, I lose my job—and Erie—and now, my girlfriend is kicking me out of her house."

Jen gapes at me for a moment, mouth open, before she snaps it shut and points a finger in my face. "I am *not* your girlfriend. Get out of my house."

All of the anger sags out of me. "I didn't . . . I didn't mean girlfriend. I meant—"

"Get. The fuck. Out."

I close my eyes and take a deep breath before I punch something. "Fine. Tell Erie to smile tomorrow." I slam the door and begin the long walk home—to my mother's house. I don't want to deal with Sergio right now. And at least this way, Mom can yell at me in person, instead of over a voicemail.

My head aches when I wake, but at least I no longer wake disoriented, thinking I'm in the Seadom. The dim light of the tank is almost comforting now. The bed of Niku's scars. The knowledge that I'll see my favorite landfolk soon.

I'm floating in half-sleep when something bangs on the side of the tank. "Wake up. Breakfast time."

That isn't Finn's voice. I glance over Niku's back to find Sergio staring back at me. Yesterday's events wash over me in a rush. Finn isn't coming back. Not until he frees me.

Sergio bangs again. "I know you understand me. Get up."

I put one finger up in the same gesture I've seen Finn give Niku before.

"God-fucking-dam—" Sergio is cut off when Jen enters, looking almost as broken as Huron.

"Morning, Erie, Niku." Her voice is void of emotion, simply repeating the same morning mantra she always says. "How are you feeling, Erie?"

That's different. No one's asked me how I feel before. "My head hurts," I say, wondering why it matters.

Jen glances at Sergio. "Do you have any fish aspirin?"

"There's no such thing. Fish don't feel pain."

"Is that so?" She points at me. "Erie just said her head hurt."

"Why don't you call up Pfizer and let them know? I'm sure there's a huge market for fish aspirin."

"What's 'pfizer'?" I ask, mostly so they'll stop glaring at each other. And so they'll stop calling me a fish. I hated Finn and Jen's touchy-feely relationship, but this is worse.

"Don't worry about it, Erie," Jen says.

Sergio grabs the bucket of fish. "She'll be fine once she eats and starts moving."

Jen grabs the bucket from him, then scowls deeper. "What the hell—did you grab the oldest fish you could? Erie won't eat this."

"It's fish."

"She's picky."

"She'll eat it when she gets hungry enough."

"Trust me, she won't."

Tides, I hate it when they talk about me like I can't understand them. Sergio rolls his eyes when Jen leaves with the bucket, and when she returns, she walks past him without a word, climbing the stairs to the platform.

Neek and I eat, and they let us into the practice tank to warm up and run through the routine. Yesterday, I was worried the landfolk wouldn't like me, but today, I'm worried I won't be able to find Finn. I know he said he'd be watching even if I couldn't see him, but I *need* to see him. I *need* to know he hasn't abandoned me. My chest clenches at the thought.

As soon as Sergio lets me into the arena, I swim to the surface, searching the crowd for the sand-and-ocean combo of Finn's skin. There are several landfolk with similar skins—some even have black hair—but the only one who raises his arm in a wave is in the very back corner of the stands.

"Finn!" I wave back, and he cups his hands around his mouth and says something I cannot hear, but that I imagine as, "Good morning, darlin.'"

And I know everything will be okay.

. . . .

FINN IS IN THE SAME corner for the next few days. I wave
to him before every show, and actually enjoy performing for the
audience once I get used to the noise. At home, no one noticed
me, the youngest in a long line of daughters, stuck in the castle
with my little room of shells, but here, I'm the center of attention
and everyone loves me, including Finn. As long as he's in the
corner, I can smile wide, jump high, and get through the rest of
the day knowing that I'll see him again the next morning.

On the fifth day, I surface and beam at his corner, but he's
not there. My gaze slides across the audience, trying to find him,
but no one raises their hand in hello. No one says, "Good
morning, beautiful."

Finn said he'd watch every performance. He promised. Is he
hurt? Is someone keeping him from me? Did Corporate 'fired'
him for good? I swim from one side of the arena to the other
before turning to Jen. "Where's Finn?"

She puts a finger to her lips and bends down, speaking low.
"I'm sure he'll be here, but we need to start."

"We can't start yet—"

Jen shakes her head and stands, finger over her lips before
she drops it to smile at the audience and start the show. What's
wrong with her? We can't do the show without Finn.

Niku bumps my hand with his nose. "What's wrong?"

"Finn isn't here."

"It sounds like Jen's starting. We better go."

"I can't do the show without him." He has to show up.
Maybe when he hears Jen introduce us, he'll know it's time.
Maybe he forgot what time it was.

Niku bumps me, and I realize I've missed our cue. Jen repeats herself, "Ladies and gentlemen: Iodine and Cadmium!"

We jump, and I glance at the corner: no Finn. It's okay. He'll be there to say hello by the time I greet the audience. He has to be.

I swim to the middle of the tank and poke my head out, glancing at the empty corner before I say good morning to Jen.

"Good morning, Io. Do you want to say hello to the audience?"

Not if Finn's gone, but I turn and wave and still don't see him. "Good morning, everyone."

The audience is just as excited as ever, oblivious to the crucial missing piece of the show. Once they say hello back, I move out of the way for Niku to do his part. The entire time we race and jump, I glance at Finn's corner, but he never shows up.

When Jen says, "Who's ready for a show?" I almost reply with, "Fuck that." Even if I had, the cheers of the audience would have drowned me out.

The music starts, and I still can't see Finn. He's not coming. Despair burns inside my stomach, and I push myself to work it out of my system. I push so hard my tailfin brushes a wall before a turn. When I jump, I look for the ocean. The blue water winks back at me, tempting, so I jump higher and higher, trying to fill my sight with the ocean.

Ocean. Ocean. Ocean.

I don't realize I've jumped too far until I glance down and see the platform rising to meet me.

I swear to god, if this woman doesn't stop sending me into the back for a different size shirt for her hellion-child, I'll scream. It's not even an Erie shirt—it's Clair, which is why it's not on the floor in more than one or two sizes. No one's buying Clair stuff right now.

"The show's starting," I say as I hand over the shirt. "You definitely don't want to miss the new Mer."

"Who cares?" Hellion-child says. "I like Potassium. I don't care about the new one."

My hands fold into fists, and I glance at my sister and the other girl—Samantha—who are ringing up the last-minute purchases. Neither of them can take over.

Hellion wads the shirt up. "I don't like this one," she says and points to a different K shirt. "I want that one instead."

"Don't you think you should at least try it on?" her mother says. "See if that size fits?"

"No." Hellion stamps her foot. "I want that one."

The mother rolls her eyes, and I wonder why she doesn't smack the brat and say she can't have either if she acts that way. Her eyes are apologetic when she turns to me. "I'm sorry, can we get that one instead?"

Outside, the crowd cheers—Erie and Niku have started racing. "Sure," I say and walk back to the storage area, trying not to stomp like the brat. If Erie doesn't see me in the stands to say hello, she'll be pissed. I promised I'd watch every show, and so far, I've been able to leave the shop and hightail it to the bleachers before it starts.

I grab a shirt in every size, walk back to Hellion as the music is beginning, and dump them all at her feet. "Good luck, kid." Then I leave the shop with a salute at Sam and Munchkin—they'll have to deal with the repercussions of that.

By the time I reach the arena, the show is in full swing, and I can tell it isn't going well. I stop at the bottom of the stands, out of the way, where I have a good view of both the tank and the air above. Erie's pissed. She nearly runs into the wall and jumps higher than I've ever seen. Instead of concentrating on the audience or the arena below her, she stares straight out with a scowl. Can she see the ocean? She'll be doubly pissed, if so. Every time she jumps, she stares in that direction, and I'm sure she can.

And then, I see it—she jumps too wide, almost as if she's trying to jump into the ocean. When she looks down, she throws her arms up, but clips the edge of the platform with her forehead. A red cloud blooms in the water as she falls in on her side.

"Erie!" I scream and jump on top of the barrier without thinking. I kick off my boat shoes and dive in, to the collective gasp of the audience.

The cold water slaps some sense into me—I can't dive after her. She sinks to the bottom, a trail of pink following, and I can't do anything. "Niku!" I yell into the water as he reaches her. "Bring her up!" I point to the surface. He seems to understand, because he brings her to me.

When I surface, Jen yells my name, but I ignore her. I grab Erie's head, careful to keep her gills underwater. Niku helps hold her limp form up as I check her forehead. Blood streams from a gash that starts just above her eye and stretches into her hairline, but worse than that: foam is eating at the tissue. I wipe it away and press my palm against the wound to stop the bleeding.

"Please, darlin'." Even though I speak barely above a whisper, the mics pick it up. "Please don't foam." I hope Hellion and her mother are watching and feel like shit for keeping me away.

Erie's eyes flutter open and she squints against the air. I ease her head back into the water, my palm still pressed to her forehead. "Finn? I thought you weren't coming. I was looking at the ocean . . ."

I hug her closer. "Of course I was coming. I was held up. I'm so sorry."

Her claws dig into my skin as she hugs me. "I missed you."

I would give anything in this moment to pick her up, walk her to the dock, and let her back into the ocean she calls home. I'm about to ask how long she can hold her breath when Jen kneels and whispers harshly. "Delmara's coming."

Fuck. I'll be fired for this. I gaze into Erie's magenta eyes. They mirror mine, unblinking, just below the surface. "I'm sorry, darlin'. I won't be able to see your show for a while."

"Are you fired?"

"I'm about to be."

Corporate walks up the steps.

"You be good—don't give them any reason to hurt you. Smile, even if you don't want to." I have about two seconds left and an audience to enrapture, so I do the one thing I never thought I would.

I take a deep breath, stick my face in the water, and kiss Erie on her cold, hard lips. She wraps her tail around me and squeezes—in surprise or pleasure, I can't tell—but my air rushes into her mouth, and she sighs as bubbles float from her gills.

"Finnegan," Delmara barks as I lift my head from the water. She must have cut the mics, because her voice doesn't boom around the stands. God, I hope everyone heard Erie say she saw the ocean.

"Sorry, darlin'," I whisper. "Time for me to go."

Erie squeezes me once more before unwrapping her tail, and I remove my hand from her forehead. The blood and foam have stopped. "I love you," she says.

"Love you, too, beautiful." I run my finger down her cheek one last time before I turn my back on her and swim to the platform. If she dragged me under and stole all my air right now, I wouldn't blame her.

Delmara stares at me with all the warmth of a shark as I climb the stairs to the platform, where a splash of Erie's blood still stains one section red. In a desperate attempt to save my own skin, I say, "You're welcome for saving your star performer."

Doesn't work—her eyes harden more. "My office. Now."

"Can I change into dry clothes first?"

"No."

"Okay." I follow her down the stairs. "I'll drip all over your carpet, then."

She doesn't say anything, which is how I know I'm in fucking *trouble*.

As soon as the door shuts behind us and my soaked clothes are creating a wet spot on the blue carpet in her office, Delmara turns on me. "You fucking shit."

That wasn't even in Spanish. I swallow. "I saved—"

"Fuck you, Finnegan." She slams a file down on her desk. "You signed paperwork when you were hired saying that you would *never* have any contact with the Mer. I could have you arrested for what you did."

Arrested? Whoa—I didn't read that paperwork. I was barely sixteen when I signed it. The only thing I can do is repeat myself. "I saved your star performer from foaming."

"I don't fucking care!" Delmara yells. "I can buy another Mer. I cannot buy OSHA!"

I'm sick of hearing about OSHA and APHIS, but I keep my mouth shut. I'm in enough trouble as it is. Delmara paces, probably waiting for me to argue, and when I don't say anything, she grabs a sharpie and writes "TERMINATED" on the file she slammed onto the desk. My file. The first employee file in Oceanica's existence. I was prepared to lose my job for Erie, but it hurts to see those big, black, final letters marring the file that says "Jarvis, Finnegan."

"Get your shit and get out," Delmara says. "You're banned from the property. If I see you so much as step into the parking lot, I'll have you arrested."

The breath chokes out of me, as if she'd punched me in the gut. I don't know what to say. "I'm sorry, Aunt D. I never meant to break the rules or get Oceanica in trouble, but Erie—"

"Is a fucking fish!"

I bow my head, searching my wet feet for a reply, but Delmara will never understand. "Thank you for the opportunity to work with you," I mumble and leave the office. I drip a trail of saltwater to the locker room and change into clean clothes before grabbing a trash bag to dump all my shit into. I close my locker for the last time and lean my forehead against it. How did it come to this?

When I step barefoot out of the locker room, I glance at the locked door that leads to the holding tanks. I could bang on it until someone opens it, but by now, they'll all know I've been fired. The only thing I can do is start working toward Erie's freedom, even if it means closing this place down for good.

Of course, I run into Maddy on the way out, and I doubt if it's an accident. She's probably been lurking in the hallway, waiting for me. She grins from ear to ear. "Aunt D would *never* fire you, huh?"

I push past her without a response.

"I'll take real good care of your Mer."

My hands fold into fists, but I keep walking. Maddy can't touch Erie as long as Jen's in charge. And although Jen and I haven't spoken since our fight five days ago, she would never let anyone hurt Erie, especially not Maddy.

"Fucking bitch," I mumble as I slam the door open and squint into the midday sun. At least I've been driving myself to work and don't have to walk home barefoot with my trash bag of shame.

Chapter 41: Erie

My forehead throbs, and my eyes burn like I've held them open in the air for too long. Finn is gone for good. I watched him walk away, and I know he won't be back. He may not even be able to save me. All of my hopes just walked down the stairs and out the door.

Niku nudges my hand onto his back. "Are you okay?"

Numbness washes over my scales, like a jellyfish has stung me and the pain is so bad all my senses have been shut down. I don't know what to do without Finn—he taught me how to survive in this place, and now, I'm on my own. Jen and Niku might be here with me, but I feel empty inside.

Jen leans down. "Let's go, Erie."

I don't move until Niku pushes me toward the tube. The audience is still standing around, taking pictures, talking to each other in excited tones. I ignore them as they press against the glass and yell my stage name, trying to get my attention. I wish they'd disappear. The tube brings blessed silence when I swim into it.

Jen shuts the door to the tube behind us, and says, "Do you want me to call the vet to check your forehead?"

The words rush past me like I've forgotten how to speak the air. I prod the wound and wince—before long, I'll be just as scarred as Niku.

Sergio walks in, a magic rectangle in his hand. He scowls at my forehead. "I'll radio the vet."

"No," I finally say. I don't need to be stared at by any more landfolk today. "It's fine."

"It's policy."

"Fuck that." I curl up in my tail in the middle of the tank, hiding the cut with my hair. I don't want to see anyone right now, not even Niku. I don't want to do anything but sleep, and spend the rest of the day in my dreams, in the Seadom, with Finn.

As soon as I dump my trash bag in my room, my phone rings. It's Heather. I don't feel like explaining myself, so I hit ignore and let it go to voicemail. I grab my laptop from my desk and raid the fridge for beer—which is just about the only thing in the fridge.

A Google search brings up dozens of "Iodine Mer" hits, even though her first show was only six days ago. There are Facebook fan pages, a fake "Iodine" Twitter account (which makes it sound like being a Mer at Oceanica is some great celebrity life), and TikToks full of Erie videos. There are several Instagram communities, as well as one "Save the Mer" community, and a YouTube channel. I'll start there.

I haven't seen a video of the first show yet, and I'm amazed by how flawless it was. The guy shooting the video chuckles when Erie says hello, and gasps when I jump into the water. A woman next to him says, "Oh my god, I think the trainer just fell in!" And then, "Oh shit—she grabbed him!" It's clear the audience didn't realize what was happening until the jump. "Christ," the guy says, "it's part of the act. That's awesome!"

Their cheers drown out my flub with the stage names at the end.

Another video shows Erie post-show, jumping and smiling and, yes, talking to the audience. They adore her.

Videos from today's show are already popping up on the channel, and I click on one to see the beginning that I missed. As soon as Erie enters the arena, she looks for me, and you can hear her when she asks Jen where I am. After the first jump, she stares at the water. The audience doesn't notice anything wrong, but as someone who's studied her performance for the past month straight, I can see every flick of tail that's off.

Watching her hit the platform is even worse from this angle than it was from the bottom of the stands. It's easy to see the blood splatter the platform and to follow her as she flops, unconscious, into the water. There are gasps and questions as I jump in and swim to her, but once she comes to, you can very clearly hear her say: "I was looking at the ocean." *Bingo*. I download the video in case they decide to remove it.

I grab another beer and check out the "Save the Mer" communities. Would they listen to me, or would they write me off as part of Corporate? Probably best to prove myself first. The good news is that they already have a couple thousand followers each. That's a few thousand people who are already on my side, but it isn't near enough to how many I'll need.

Serge is so much better at web stuff than I am, but I can't ask him for help. I'd love a fancy website to catch people's attention, but settle for a Facebook page instead. It'll be easier to maintain, and I already know the platform.

"Save Erie," or "Save Iodine"? I choose the former, because I want people to know *her*, not her stage presence. And now, I'm lost—what do I share? Video of her shows might backfire and make people want to see the show instead. I wish I had video of her in the holding tank—why the hell didn't I think of that before I was fired? The audience sees her smiling in the arena, swimming in that giant tank, but they have no idea where she's kept between shows.

I do have one photo of her in her holding tank that I took when I was trying to teach her what photographs were, so I make that her profile picture. Her hands are pressed against the glass, her eyes wide in bewilderment. Behind her, the cement wall is a dirty gray, blurry through the water. It's not a great photo, but it's clear she's kept in a dingy room, not out in the sunshine like all the Corporate photos show. I find a photo on one of the fan pages of her jumping with Niku, the ocean behind them, the audience watching in the foreground. I bet the person who took it thinks she's treated like a celebrity, but all I see is the wall separating her from the ocean. I make it the cover photo.

Now what? No one knows who "Erie" is, so I guess I better start there. I type everything I know about her, starting with the day she arrived, how terrified and depressed she was, her love of jewelry, how and when she told me her name, and everything I've learned since. I even talk about Clair and Huron, and how he basically dumped Erie for her sister. By the time I finish, I have a small novella's worth of Erie factoids. No one will read this, though—it's too long. I write a CliffsNotes version, then break the rest into sections to post separately.

The last section is about to go up when a knock rattles the door. I glance up from the screen, surprised by how dark it is. A glance at the clock shows it's 8:15 p.m.—holy crap, how did it get so late?

The person knocks harder this time. It's probably Heather, coming to check on me since I haven't answered her call or texts. "It's open!" I yell.

I hit post as Jen opens the door. Not who I expected. She holds two large, fabric grocery bags and wears an expression that says she's sorry for intruding, but not that sorry.

She walks to the kitchen and deposits her bags. "You're less drunk than I expected."

"Ran out of beer."

She grabs a six-pack of Stella Artois from one bag, then a fifth of rum from another, a small, apologetic smile on her face.

"Oh my god, I love you right now." I make my way over to peer into the rest of the bags. That might have been the wrong thing to say, considering the last wrong thing I said to her, but I don't care. "What else do you have?"

"Tortilla chips, queso, and salsa." She steps aside to make room for me. "All the makings for 'I'm sorry' nachos."

I finally look her in the eye, but she drops her face, hiding behind her hair.

"You don't have anything to be sorry for—I'm the dumbass who jumped in the tank and got myself fired."

"Yeah." She starts grabbing things out of the bags. "But I'm sorry for freaking out the other day. I was tired, and stressed out, and—"

I grab her hands so she'll stop doing anything she can to avoid me, and kiss her. Just a quick, soft peck on the lips. "It was a bad day. I'm sorry for what I said, too."

Jen drops her hands to her sides. "I just . . . I mean . . ."

"Don't worry about it." I grab a couple of shot glasses and open the rum. "How's Erie?"

Who knew Jen's shoulders could sink even further?

"Curled up in a ball in the middle of the tank, hiding. She won't even let Niku touch her."

That deserves a shot. I hand one to Jen and down mine. "She won't eat tomorrow."

Jen takes her shot. "We already canceled the show. Clair's performing instead."

"Is her forehead okay?"

"She wouldn't let the vet check it. Says it's fine."

Stubborn fish. Jen turns her back on me again and starts opening cupboards, presumably to find something suitable to make the nachos in. When she stares blankly into a cupboard for entirely too long, it's clear something else is wrong. I don't know what to do—should I touch her? Get as far away as possible? Is this cupboard-staring about Erie, or me?

"Um." I squeeze past her and open a different cupboard, where we store a square glass pan. "I think this will work."

Her shoulders jerk with a hitch. *Fuck.* They hitch again, and she presses her fist to her mouth. *Double fuck.* I set the glass pan on the counter and touch her shoulder. "Is everything okay?"

That was the wrong option—the waterworks start, and all Jen can do is say "I'm sorry" over and over again while I pull her into a hug. "It's fine. You're fine," I say every time she apologizes, and when she finally pulls away and wipes her eyes, I still don't have any idea what's wrong.

"Goddammit, Finn. I want to hate you so much." Jen huffs out of the kitchen to the couch, bumping the laptop as she sits. The screensaver disappears, showing the Facebook page I've been working on. "What's this?"

"Step two of Operation Save Erie. Step one was to make people love her—and they do, trust me. Step two is to tell them who she really is."

"Step three?"

I rub the back of my neck where a crick has settled from staring at the computer too long. "Not sure yet. Ask Corporate how much it would cost to buy her?"

Jen scrolls through the page. "It can't be cheap to buy a Mer."

"I'm guessing a couple million for their star performer, plus more for Niku, transportation costs, etc."

Her lips part again. "A couple *million*? How will you get a couple million dollars?"

"Step four." I pop the nachos in the microwave. "Beg for donations."

Jen's shoulders sink again. "Do you really think you'll be able to raise enough money to free her?"

"I promised Erie I'd get her out." That's the simple truth—the hard truth is that something will probably go wrong before I can raise the money. She'll starve to death, or attack someone and be foamed.

The microwave beeps, and I take the nachos back to the couch with the six-pack. "Actually, I need you to do something, but you'll be fired if you're caught."

Jen eyes me. "It's not illegal, is it?"

"No, but Corporate won't like it. I need you to get video of Erie in the holding tank. The more depressing, the better."

Her shoulders sag, and she grabs a beer. "That shouldn't be difficult—everything about that room is depressing."

I clink the neck of my beer against hers. "To freeing Erie."

"To freeing Erie," she echoes and drinks.

"Welcome to Oceanica." Jen's voice drifts in from the hallway. I'm curious who she's talking to, but not curious enough to unwrap myself and check. She continues speaking to the unknown person. "These are our holding rooms, where the Mer are kept between shows. Morning, Erie, Niku."

"Good morning, Jen," Niku says, though she can't hear him. He nudges me, and I curl tighter in my tail.

"How's your forehead, Erie?" So far, the other person has been silent. I touch the wound and wince at the pain. "Come on," Jen says. "Let's see it."

I unwrap my tail and face her, fins sagging. No one else is here, but her magic rectangle is out, pointed at me. What does that mean? I narrow my eyes and swim to the glass. "Who are you talking to?"

"Everyone." She watches the rectangle instead of me. "It's a video, like when the people videotaped you jumping for the commercial. Do you remember Finn showing you the commercial?"

"Finn will see this?" My chest constricts, and my fingers cover the wound on my forehead. I know he's seen it already, but I don't want him to worry.

The corners of Jen's mouth curl up. "He'll be the first to see it."

For the Tides—I have a chance to talk to Finn, even if he can't talk back. What do I say? I want to blurt out so many things, but other landfolk will see this, too.

"Is there anything you want to tell him?" Jen prompts.

Everything. I want to tell him everything. How much I miss him. How much I want to steal his air so he'll be with me forever. That I don't know how to survive without him. But there's one thing I want to tell him more than anything else.

"I can see the ocean when I jump." I swallow and glance around the dank room. "Does . . . does he know the ocean is *right there*?"

Jen's smile fades, and my heart clenches. Finn knows. He knows how close the ocean is, and he's never taken me home. If he ever jumps into my tank again, I *will* steal his air, because he stole my ocean.

"Yes," Jen finally says, her voice sad. "Finn knows."

My hands fold into fists, because he's not the only one who knows. "And you know. And the audience knows. And you all watch me jump, and you know the ocean is *right there*, and you don't care!" I slam my hands on the glass.

"Finn and I care," Jen says. "We're doing everything we can to get you out, but we need help."

Lies! They aren't doing anything to get me out. They're playing with their magic rectangles, and making me do a stupid routine. I'm sick of it. "If that was true, I'd be home by now."

Jen shakes her head. "It's not as simple as carrying you to the ocean and dumping you in. For one, the shock would kill you. Two, we'd be arrested. And three, even if you survived the shock, anyone could fish you back out again or follow you home."

Lies and lies and more lies. "They can't follow me home—I'd be underwater. How would they see me?"

"Trust me—they have the technology to do it. They found you before."

I don't know what "technology" means, and I don't know if I can trust Jen, but if she *is* telling the truth, then I can't take the chance of putting the entire Seadom in danger. They'd hunt down everyone—my sisters, my brother and father . . . Grandmother. Bile rises in my throat at the thought. I can't take that chance. I can't let them hunt any more merfolk.

When I reply, I look straight at the magic rectangle and speak to Finn, not to Jen or the rest of the landfolk. "I hope someday, someone takes you from everything you love, puts you in a tiny cage, and makes you do tricks to amuse them." Then I turn my back on Jen and curl up in the middle of the tank again.

My phone buzzes on the nightstand and I grab it, squinting against the light. It's an email from Jen, and all it says is "sorry" with a huge attachment—must be the video. She left early this morning to record it before anyone arrived at work.

I hold the phone above my head and open the file. When I see the realization on Erie's face that I knew about the ocean, my heart drops into my stomach. I can't blame her for being pissed, and I know she's talking to me when she storms off to hide. No one else will know that was meant for me, though, making it the perfect video to shame people into helping. I call Jen.

She picks up after two rings. "Hey."

"Put the phone against the glass and put me on speaker."

"Hold on." A couple seconds later, I hear the phone clink against the glass, and Jen says, "Go."

"Erie?" I wait a moment, hoping to hear her voice. "Erie, it's Finn. Answer me, darlin.'"

Nothing. I can see her in my mind's eye, curled up in a ball, hugging herself tighter against my voice. "Erie, love . . ."

Jen interrupts as she takes me off speaker and brings the phone back to her ear. "She's ignoring you."

"Last chance, Jen. I won't post the video if you want to stay out of this."

"If I wanted to stay out of this, I wouldn't have made the video. I hate this job. And I don't think Serge will hurt her."

That makes me nervous. I don't want to leave Erie with only Serge, or Serge plus whoever they put with him. But Erie staring into the camera with a big "Fuck you, humans"? That's *perfect*.

"Cool. I'll talk to you later," I say. "Come over tonight?"

"Sooner, if I'm fired."

I upload the video to YouTube and the Facebook page. I throw it up on the 'Save the Mer' communities, as well—it makes *me* look like an ass, but they'll be all over it.

Two hours later, I get a call from an unknown number. "Hello?"

"Is this Mr. Finnegan Jarvis?"

What kind of trouble did I get myself in this time? "It is," I manage to say, in my best professional voice.

"This is Juliana Kaes from News 6 Miami. Are you the same Mr. Jarvis who jumped into the tank at Oceanica yesterday?"

Holy shit. I squeeze the phone so hard, the plastic protests in my grip. "I am."

"Glad to hear it. I'd like to interview you about the Mer this afternoon. Do you have time?"

"Can I ask what you'd like to know? I'll need to dig out my notes."

"We don't require notes."

Yeah, no. I'm not jumping into this booby trap. What if they're doing a piece from Oceanica's perspective? "I'll need to reference my notes for specific questions about Mer physiology and behavior."

"That's not what we're looking for. We want a human interest story about a trainer and his Mer."

"I'm not a trainer anymore." Every time I say those words, it rips out a piece of my soul.

"But you're the only one who's ever willingly jumped into a tank with a Mer. I'd like to know why."

"Type 'Save Erie' into Google and scroll to the page that isn't about one of the Great Lakes. You'll find a video that says why."

"I saw it. That's why I want to talk to you. I can give you a Miami audience—maybe national, if they like what they see."

Challenge accepted. "You saw today's video? I put it up two hours ago."

"I've kept a close eye on the Mer since the first trainer died a few years back. They sent me to cover the story, and I've been watching the Mer communities online ever since. Your video popped up this morning."

I remember this chick—I'm pretty sure she interviewed me when Hannah died, but didn't use any of the footage in her report. "What do you want to know?"

"Why didn't she kill you?"

Hell, *I* haven't even been able to figure that one out yet. If I was her, I would have let Niku drown me the first time I jumped in. "Maybe you should interview Erie, instead of me."

"Ms. de la Cruz won't return my phone calls."

"I see. I'm your second choice."

"Right now, you're my only choice, assuming you're willing to talk."

Why not? I can't really fuck things up more than I already have. "Sure, I'll talk."

"Great. Is three o'clock good? I'd like to get Oceanica in the shot."

"I'm no longer allowed on the grounds. Not even the parking lot."

"That's fine—we'll stay off the property."

"Sounds good to me." We make plans to meet at three, just off the property. During the call, several more people "liked"

Erie's Facebook page and shared the video. Good. Maybe after the interview, Erie will go viral.

• • • •

I BIKE TO THE INTERVIEW site, and when I arrive, the van's already there. Juliana Kaes looks exactly the way I remember her—long brown hair, chunky black glasses, shorter than me by a foot, even in heels. I lean my bike against the van and shake her hand.

"Mr. Jarvis, thank you for meeting me."

"Thank you for helping me get the word out about Erie."

She introduces me to the crew, who mic me and set up the shot. When they're ready, the little red light pops on, and she begins with the fake "Thank you" to the anchor. "I'm here with Finnegan Jarvis, the young man who jumped into the tank at Oceanica yesterday when a Mer started bleeding."

I smile a little at the camera, because I'm not sure what else to do. Ms. Kaes turns to face me. "Tell me, Mr. Jarvis, why would you risk your life like that?"

I can't help it—I chuckle. "That wasn't life-threatening. Erie would never hurt me."

"When you say Erie, you mean the mermaid known as Iodine?"

"Her real name is Erie. The dolphin is Niku—he's her guard."

"Guard?"

I wrote all this on the website, but I guess I'll have to rehash it now. I explain what I know about Erie's life before she was captured. Ms. Kaes asks how I met Erie, so I give her the short version of our time together.

"So this wasn't your first time in the tank with her?"

"Not at all—I've swam with her a few dozen times by now."

Juliana Kaes frowns. "And can you tell us why you're the only trainer who has gotten in the water and not been killed by the Mer?"

I shrug. "I have no idea why Erie hasn't tried to kill me yet."

"What sort of relationship would you say you share with the Mer?"

"All of them, or just Erie?"

"Both. How is your relationship with Erie different?"

She doesn't try to kill me—that's the biggest difference, but I don't want to sound like an idiot, so I think about it for a moment. "Well, I've been working with the Mer for as long as Ms. de la Cruz has, and I've always believed the Corporate line of 'Mer are fish.'" I pause as I think back on those early days with Erie, when she was still just a fish to me. "Erie was different, right from the beginning."

"How so?"

"Most Mer come in fighting—they want nothing more than to attack us for capturing them. Erie was terrified, though. She hid behind Niku, she hid in her tail, she curled up in the center of the tank, as far away from us as she could get. Niku was the one I was scared of, actually—I never knew dolphins could scowl before now."

A chuckle escapes me as I remember Niku's anger. "She also learned English. 'Air words,' she calls them. She did that on her own and told me her name without me asking. I think she was mad that I kept calling her by the wrong name."

A small smile graces Juliana Kaes's face. "Is that when everything changed?"

"Yes, and no. At that point, she was still just a fish to me—a talking fish, sure, but . . ." I stop and swallow. At that point, Erie was still a means to an end: proving myself to Delmara. "Everything changed the first time we swam together."

"When was that?"

It feels like months, but it hasn't been that long. "A month and a half ago. She freaked out, and I didn't know what to do. I had already promised not to shock her, so I jumped in the tank."

"What happened?"

"Niku tried to drown me, and Erie stopped him with a word." I glance at the bright blue side of Oceanica behind me and swallow again. "She saved my life."

"Is that why you jumped in the tank when she hit her head?"

Hit her head—Ms. Kaes says it like it was a little bump, not a massive gash across Erie's forehead that almost killed her. "A bad injury like that will cause the tissue to foam—if you don't stop it and it gets to the gills, the Mer drown."

"So you repaid a debt."

Not by a long shot—I still owe Erie so much.

Juliana Kaes keeps talking. "And, in the video, right before you leave the water, you appear to kiss her?"

Heat creeps up my neck, because I certainly didn't kiss her out of desire, but I can't tell everyone watching the news that. "She likes the feeling of my breath in her gills." Ms. Kaes makes a face, so I try to salvage what I just said. "I know, it sounds gross, but we keep the water much colder than what the Mer are used to in the wild, and she likes the warmth. And you saw what she said in the video—if I can give her even a little happiness in there, I'll do it."

I'm talking like I'm heading back to work tomorrow. Like I'm still a part of Oceanica, but Juliana Kaes doesn't seem to notice. She goes right for the most awkward question. "Do you love her?"

"Of course I love her. It's impossible to meet Erie and not love her. She's intelligent and compassionate and strong . . ." I falter, because my heart clenches at how true it is. So far, Erie's the only Mer who hasn't been broken. Maybe it's Niku, or the fact that we didn't shock her, but I think it's her spirit. She simply won't allow anyone to break her.

"Yeah," I say, my voice softer. "I love her, and I'll do anything I can to get her out of there."

"**M**orning, Erie, Niku."

I ignore Jen and stay wrapped in my tail in the middle of the tank. I hate Jen right now. I hate all the landfolk. I'd kill them, but I'm determined to get back to the ocean first.

"Finn sent a reply," Jen says.

I curl up tighter in my tail.

After a moment, the magic rectangle is pressed against the tank glass, echoing some woman's voice—and then Finn's. I listen, but I don't unwind until he says, "I have no idea why Erie hasn't tried to kill me yet."

My chest clenches—does he know how hard it was to hold myself back? I can think of so many times it would have been so easy to kill him. I don't know why I didn't.

They keep talking, and I'm drawn to his image like a guppy to an angler fish. By the end of it, my eyes burn and my nails scratch the glass with the need to touch him. To feel his warmth. To let his air—freely given—caress my gills. I have never wanted anything so bad in my life.

I would stay in this tank until I foamed if it meant I could swim with Finn one more time. Just once.

Jen interrupts my thoughts. "I can record a reply—just to him—if you like."

For the Tides, what would I say? I'd be such a jellyfish. "Just tell him I believe him."

"Jennifer!"

Jen and I both jump as Corporate walks in with Sergio and a girl I don't know. Sergio's face is grim, and he won't look at either

Jen or me. The girl smiles like my sisters used to when Father believed them over me in an argument. And Delmara looks like the wrath of a hurricane in human form.

"Yes, ma'am." Jen takes a step back.

"What the fuck is this?" Delmara holds up a magic rectangle, and I see my face, hear my voice telling Finn that I hope someone traps him someday.

Jen swallows so hard the muscles in her throat visibly contract. "It's a video I made for Finn."

"Bullshit. Why do you mention the holding tanks?"

Jen squares her shoulders. "Because he wanted to show people the conditions the Mer are kept in. Because people think they're treated like rockstars, but this is hell. Because maybe, if you treated them better, they wouldn't keep trying to kill everyone."

Delmara's lips press into a hard line. The other girl says, "They're dangerous predators."

Jen's eyes narrow in a hateful expression I've never seen on her before. "Yeah, they're also compassionate in the right conditions."

The girl squares her shoulders. "Maybe you should lecture your boyfriend about compassion."

"Maybe you should shut your mouth, because you have no idea what's going on."

Sergio grabs Jen's arms when she steps forward, hands folded into fists at her sides. The other girl puts her hands on her hips and grins, haughty. Delmara interrupts the almost-fight.

"I don't care what the fuck's been going on." She points at Jen. "You're fired. Madison is taking your place."

Jen's eyes plead with the tiny woman. "You can't give her to Maddy—she'll hurt Erie just to get back at Finn."

I don't know who this "Maddy" is, but if she hurts Finn, I'll kill her.

"As long as Iodine can perform, *I don't care*," Delmara says. "You have ten minutes to get out."

I lost Finn, and that was bad enough, but now I'm losing Jen, too? I thought Finn and Jen were awful half the time—how much worse will Sergio and this "Maddy" be?

"Jen?" I press my hands to the glass, and everyone looks at me like they forgot I was here. Delmara recovers first.

"The next time she speaks, shock her."

"Got it." The girl—Maddy—walks up the stairs to the platform.

"That's not fair," I say. "I haven't done any—"

The loop enters the water, and my entire body convulses with the shock, ripping the words from my throat. Distantly, Jen yells, but I can't think of anything except the pain of my muscles being ripped from my body. When it stops—I'm not floating at the top, so it must not have been long—I swim, muscles trembling, to Niku and put my hand over his scars. "I'm sorry," I say in ocean-speak.

The words have barely left my mouth when it happens again.

"Stop!" Jen screams, so loud I can hear her through the pain, and it does. It stops. "She was talking to the dolphin."

Maddy's voice comes from above. "She talked—doesn't matter who to. Rules are rules."

I can barely move, but I turn my head to find Jen. She can't leave. She's the only thing keeping my sanity intact now that Finn's gone. "Jen—" I reach my hand out, and this time, the pain doesn't stop until I'm floating belly-up on the surface. My body shudders, too weak to do anything but keep my gills underwater.

I don't hear Jen's voice anymore, but I do hear Maddy's. "I don't know how you got Finn, of all people, to turn his back on this place for you, but that's over now. Delmara has trusted me to fix this, so no more talking, not even to your dolphin. You'll behave like the other Mer, or you'll be shocked."

I can't reply. I can barely breathe, much less speak. Now I know how they broke Huron and Clair. Now I realize how much I was spared.

I'll end up just like them. I won't see the ocean again. Not as me.

The stats on the Save Erie page have skyrocketed since my news report last night. So many people have "liked" and shared the video that my mind boggles, but I know it isn't enough. Not nearly enough. I need to go *viral*.

Erie needs to go viral.

The door opens without so much as a knock, and I ignore it, thinking it's Sergio—because who the hell else would walk in without knocking? But at the first hitched breath, I know. Jen.

I stand and open my arms in one swift movement. With nothing more than another hitch, she walks into my embrace and sobs. There are no apologies this time. She must have been fired. Goddamn, that was fast.

Worse—it leaves Erie without an advocate at Oceanica.

"Shh." I smooth Jen's hair and press my lips to her temple. "Shh, you're okay." She doesn't try to speak, just cries into my shoulder for a good two minutes. That's a lot of tears from someone who said they didn't care about being fired yesterday.

When Jen finally pulls back and wipes her eyes, I lead her to the couch. Before I can ask what's wrong, she chokes out, "They gave her to Maddy."

The room shrinks around me, and I don't realize how hard I'm squeezing Jen's hand until she pulls away, cringing.

"Sorry." I stand and pace. This is bad. Maddy's as vindictive as a crazy ex-girlfriend—though we never dated, so she has no reason to be. Still, I know she's been pissed since I passed her over as my assistant. She wouldn't take it out on Erie, though, would she?

"It's okay," I say, trying to convince myself as much as Jen. "Serge won't let Maddy hurt her for no reason, and Maddy isn't stupid enough to foam the star performer. Erie will be okay—we'll just have to work a little faster to get her out."

"They shocked her three times before Serge dragged me out of the room. They won't let her speak anymore—not even to Niku."

My hands fold into fists, burning with the need to punch something. They'll turn Erie into another dead-eyed Mer, like the others, looking for a way out by any means necessary.

"Finn." Jen grabs my wrist. "Look."

She turns the volume up on the television. Erie's face from the video is plastered across *The Today Show*, and as the volume comes up, we hear the host say: "After the break." *What* after the break?

Jen pulls me to the couch as the commercials play. I swear they're longer than normal, but eventually, the screaming crowds return and the host is back, smiling.

"Welcome back. As we said before the break: we have an amazing video of a mermaid at the world's only Mer theme park, and her plea has captured the hearts of thousands overnight. Take a look."

They show the bit where Erie asks if I knew the ocean was there, and Jen's reply, all the way until Jen says we need help.

"You can see the rest of the video on our website," the host says, the website address posted in a banner across the bottom of the screen. Movement, thought, *everything* disappears as I stare at the freeze-frame of Erie's magenta eyes. Sure, *The Today Show* is just trying to drive traffic to their website, but that will, in turn, drive traffic to Erie's. Holy shit—I need to update the Save Erie page with this morning's events. People need to know she's in big trouble now.

I grab the laptop and type a new post about Jen being replaced by a trigger-happy trainer, mention the *Today Show* spot for those who haven't seen it, and at the very bottom, write a personal note: "Please, if you go to Oceanica and watch Erie's (Iodine's) show, tell her Finn loves her and is doing everything he can to get her out."

By the time I hit "publish," the number of likes have skyrocketed. Do the people on *The Today Show* even realize what they've done? How much they've helped with one thirty-second clip of video? Before I can wrap my head around it, the phone rings.

"Mr. Jarvis?" A woman's voice is on the other end. "This is Juliana Kaes from News 6 Miami."

"Um, yes, hello."

Jen raises her eyebrow at me, and I stick my finger in my ear to hear over the television.

"I see from your update that you were watching *The Today Show* this morning?"

"Yeah. I guess I have you to thank for that?"

"That's not why I'm calling. I'm wondering if you have time tomorrow morning for my crew to tape you again? *The Today Show* would like to interview you live."

I nearly drop the phone. "About Erie?"

"Their website exploded with so many hits after the video this morning that they'd like to speak with you live. The trainer who was just fired, as well."

A glance at Jen shows her eyes so wide, they're nearly falling out of her head. She must be able to hear Juliana's voice over the phone.

"That would be great." We make a plan to meet at Jen's place—because it's cleaner—at eight in the morning, two days from now. Juliana's crew will film because they're the closest NBC affiliate. The interview will be live at nine.

When I hang up, Jen jumps into my arms and kisses me. "Oh my god, I can't believe it." She says it so fast, it sounds like one word.

I can't make my mouth form even one word.

For the first time since I made my promise, I actually believe we might have a chance to save Erie.

Sergio returns while I'm still belly-up, as in control of my fins as a jellyfish. "Jesus Christ, Maddy. She has to perform in two hours."

Perform? I can't even move.

"Delmara told me to. Iodine will be fine." Every step of Maddy's feet on the metal stairs pounds in my head as she descends from the platform.

"She better be. This is my show now, and I don't care what your problem with Finn is—if you injure my star performer, I'll have you fired."

I can do nothing more than gaze at the ceiling, so I don't know how Maddy reacts to that, but it can't have been good, because Sergio sounds even more angry when he speaks again. "Go get them fish, and nothing rotten, Jesus. I won't let you sabotage this show just because you're pissed Finn doesn't want you anymore."

From the sound, Maddy slaps him. "Fuck you." Then her angry footsteps stomp off.

Sergio's weary voice travels through the water. "Are you okay, Io? Erie. Whatever."

Slowly, I turn to peer through the glass and make sure Maddy's gone. Can I answer? Will I be shocked again the moment I try? Everything changed so quickly, I'm not sure what's safe, so I swim to Niku and wrap my arms around him. I don't even trace his scars—I just hold him like the terrified minnow I am.

"It's okay, Princess," Niku says. I shake my head against his side because I'm too afraid to speak.

"Listen," Sergio says. "I won't shock you for answering a question or speaking nonsense words to your dolphin, okay? Just don't talk while Maddy's around. She's trying to get on Aunt D's good side."

I bury my face into Niku's side. I don't care what Sergio says—I can't trust him.

He taps on the glass. "Are you able to perform? I might be able to get you one more day, if not. We can tell the vet your forehead's still bleeding."

The dull ache hasn't left that wound in days, but it doesn't hurt as much as the rest of me right now. I stick my nail into the scab and rip it off, wincing as the water blooms red with blood.

Sergio nods. "Looks like the electroshocker reopened your wound. I'll tell the vet to cancel today's show."

He leaves, and I curl up around Niku's dorsal fin.

• • • •

I'VE MOVED BACK TO my old tank, with only the necklaces and the Ariel figurine for company. I told Niku the landfolk were making me move, but really, I asked Sergio to do it so Neek wouldn't be shocked because of me.

Sergio spends most of his time staring at his magic rectangle, ignoring us. He mutters to himself and taps at it constantly. I've even heard him say "Goddammit, Finn" a couple times. I can't ask what's wrong with Finn because Maddy hovers near the loop whenever we aren't performing or practicing.

"Holy shit," Sergio says after breakfast one day. "They closed the beaches."

Maddy picks at her nails. "Which ones?"

"All of them. Up to Miami."

She drops her hands. "What?"

He studies the rectangle, brows furrowed. "A kid was attacked this morning at Fort Zach. A local kid. In broad daylight."

Maddy clomps down the stairs, away from the shocker, and my breath comes a little easier.

"By a Mer?"

"Yep."

Sergio holds the rectangle out to her, the laughing voices turning to screams as she watches. Maddy's face pales, then pinches tight in anger. She grabs the phone from him, eyes moving back and forth across it as her hands begin to shake.

"That was my neighbor's son," she whispers. "They killed my neighbor's son." Her gaze darts to me, and her jaw clenches. "He was only eight!"

I don't know what she's talking about. One of the merfolk attacked a landfolk? That's ridiculous—none of the 'folk would come this close to land in the daylight. The threat of boats is too great. Unless the landfolk went hunting again, or the merfolk were so desperately hungry that they decided to hunt something other than fish.

I shudder at the thought of eating a landfolk and jump when Maddy slams the rectangle on the tank. "Explain this!" she screams. "Why are they doing this? Why are they killing kids?"

The laughter is back on the rectangle, but I see the movement below the water, just beyond the rocks. None of the landfolk seem to notice, until a little boy, as young as the children who watch us perform, throws his hands up and yells before disappearing beneath the surface. Blood—so red, you can see it from this distance—blooms in the water. A tail pierces through the blood, rising into the air. A tail that's green right to the tip.

Eaton.

My brother—Crown Prince of the Seadom—killed a landfolk child.

The breakfast I just finished comes back up.

"Why did they do it?" Maddy screams again as I heave. "Why are they killing kids?"

Sergio grabs her shoulders and yanks her from the tank, even as she screams, "I'm going to kill you all!"

He pulls her from the room, still screaming, and I wipe my mouth with the back of my hand. Breakfast and bile float past me to the hole that sucks everything up—Finn called it a "filter"—and I'm left alone, shaking like Maddy was, trying to figure out what happened to make Eaton kill an innocent child.

I wake before the alarm goes off, my body wrapped around Jen's. We're naked, and as I run my hand from her breast down her stomach, she sighs and rubs her ass against my cock, turning me on so hard, I can't fall back to sleep now. She turns with a sleepy "hmm" that I can't resist, and I kiss her as I slip a finger inside, then two. I love the half-asleep noises she makes. I kiss her bare shoulder and realize that I want to be the kind of guy she would call her boyfriend.

I kiss from her shoulder to her breast to her thigh, and she shudders and grabs my hair when I lick her. The first time she tries to pull me up, I ignore her and smirk as she squirms under my tongue. The second time, I let her pull my head to hers and kiss her so she can taste how sweet she is.

"Fuck me," she whispers and grabs a condom from the side table as I twist my fingers inside her. She moans and digs her nails into my shoulders.

By the time we finish, she's just as awake as I am. "Nerves?"

"You." I kiss her again before she pulls away, laughing. My gaze follows her as she gets out of bed and crosses to the bathroom, closing the door. I've never felt like this before. Am I in love?

When the shower starts, I climb out of bed and open the door. "Room for another?"

"Has the alarm gone off yet?"

"No."

"Then yes."

I love the feel of her soapy body beneath my hands. Everything's slippery and warm and wet. She presses her back against the tile and puts one foot on the edge of the tub as I get her off with my fingers, then gives me a soapy hand job that leaves me shuddering against her shoulder. Goddamn—I could do this forever and be happy.

We've showered and finished breakfast by the time Juliana Kaes and her crew arrives. They set up in the living room, while Juliana goes over a brief "this is what to expect" speech. Yeah, I know—the big spoiler is the question about being in love with Erie. Jen and I should probably have a quick chat about that; it wouldn't go over well if I said I was in love with a fish, but regularly fucking the human girl next to me.

Jen bobs her head when I whisper that in her ear, and then we're shuffled to the couch, miked up, and it's time to smile and put on a show for the nation. For Erie.

The host of *The Today Show* asks a few questions about Erie's background first, which I give brief answers to. It's very similar to the questions Ms. Kaes already asked. When the host says, "And there's a rumor you and Ms. Stevens are a couple?" Jen laughs. It's so convincing, I'm almost hurt.

"We were Erie's trainers," she says. "Yes, we're close, but we both love Erie and want to see her freed."

"That brings up an interesting point," the host says, and I know the "do you love her" question is coming. "We did some digging and found that you, Ms. Stevens, are the younger sister of one of the trainers who died at Oceanica—Mrs. Hannah Michaels?"

Hannah. My stomach clenches as a wave of adrenaline shoots through me. Hannah, who had Jen's eyes. Hannah, whose eyes were ripped out by Carbon. For a moment, my ears buzz with Jen's voice saying, "Erie will turn on you just like Carbon turned on Hannah." *That's* how Jen knew his name. *Fuck.*

"Mr. Jarvis?" The host pulls me from my thoughts.

"Yes, sorry. I was worrying about Erie—she's got new trainers who are more than willing to hurt her."

My attempt to change the subject is in vain; the host keeps speaking. "It must have been a surprise to find out that your co-trainer was the sister of someone who'd been killed by a Mer."

I press my lips together in a fake smile and nod, because *yes, it fucking is*. "I was speechless." A glance at Jen shows she's sitting with a frozen, deer-in-headlights smile, and all the warmth I'd felt for her this morning drains away, until all that's left is betrayed anger. Every part of me hardens. It's all I can do to keep my hands from folding into fists as I continue to speak to the cameras.

"Why would someone do that, after all?" I turn away from Jen as her eyes plead with me, begging me not to freak out. "But we're not here to talk about Hannah—we're here for Erie. She needs to be freed before she's turned into the same murderous beast as the rest of them. Because then, she'll be killed for sure."

"And you, Ms. Stevens?" the host says. "Are you here for Erie, or your sister?"

I'd like to know the answer to that, myself. I clench my jaw as I watch Jen, waiting for her answer.

"I'm here for them both," she says. "If my sister had treated the Mer better, it might be her here instead of me, but Erie had nothing to do with her death. We've treated Erie as well as possible, under the circumstances, but she deserves better.

She deserves to be free, not a slave to the whims of human entertainment."

My ears start to hum again as the anger builds. I don't know how I make it through the end of the interview without a complete freak out. When the red light on the camera winks out, Jen touches my arm. "Finn . . ."

I keep the fake smile plastered on my face and speak under my breath. "Don't say one fucking word to me until they're gone."

"But—"

"Don't."

The crew packs up, and we shake their hands and thank them for helping with the interview. I close the door behind them and watch them leave, my fingers folded into fists so hard, my knuckles hurt.

"Finn?" Jen says, tentative and small.

I squeeze my eyes shut. A few hours ago, I was willing to give up almost anything for her, and all she's done is manipulate me into betraying Oceanica. Now, I know how stupid I was.

Without a word, I brush past her to her bedroom, where my overnight bag sits on the bed—and glance at the overturned frame. Of course. When I flip the frame upright, Hannah stares back in an Orca World outfit, a brown-haired version of Jen smiling as she pets a dolphin. The necklace Erie ripped from Jen's neck sits around Hannah's, instead.

Goddammit. All that bullshit about wanting to train dolphins—it was Hannah's dream smacked sloppily onto Jen. I'm the stupidest man alive.

Jen's voice is soft behind me. "She never wanted to work with the Mer, but there was nothing else once Oceanica opened."

I throw the frame across the room and grab my bag, shoving through the doorway.

"Let me explain?"

"Fuck you." I turn on her. "I lost my job, my friends, my family . . . I gave up the rest of my life, and you couldn't even tell me the truth."

"When was I supposed to?" Tears fill her eyes. I hope she cries forever. I hope she drowns in her own misery. "What was I supposed to say?"

"I don't know, how about: 'Oh yeah, that girl Hannah you told me about—I know all about her because *she's my sister.*'"

Jen hugs her chest and looks away. "You kept talking over me when I tried to tell you, and I was trying not to cry. Even if I'd managed to get it out, you would have gone to Delmara, and I would have been fired, and Erie would be just like the rest of them."

"You're not Erie's savior!" I grab my bag again and head for the front door.

"I'm the one who taught her English."

"Disney taught her English." I grasp the doorknob, but Jen speaks before I can open it.

"And who do you think changed the channel?"

I tighten my hold on the metal, my hand shaking from the adrenaline pumping hot through my body. I asked Jen if she'd messed with the laptop, and she lied to my face. She lied about having experience with dolphins. She lied about Hannah. Her lies have cost me my relationship with Delmara, and Maddy, and probably Sergio once he sees the interview.

"Fuck you," I say again and yank the door open.

"Finn, wait—"

I slam the door behind me and hope to god she doesn't follow me out to continue this fight in the street. The last thing Erie needs right now is publicity of her former trainers screaming down the street at each other after an interview.

Maybe Jen realizes that, because she doesn't follow. She's probably curled up on the couch, crying into a cushion, her fake red hair hiding her lying eyes.

I can't believe I almost fell in love with her.

. . . .

I WAIT UNTIL I'M HOME to call Serge and tell him how utterly screwed we all are. When he answers, the first thing he says is, "She's fine. I didn't let Maddy hurt her."

"I'm not calling about Erie." I throw my bag on the couch and flop down next to it. "Jen is Hannah's sister."

Sergio pauses to processes that. "Hannah, as in *Hannah*? Dead Hannah?"

"Yes, dead Hannah. The reporter ambushed me with that tidbit this morning, on live fucking television. I had to act like I knew, but I swear to god, I didn't."

Shit—this is so bad. What was Jen even doing at Oceanica, if it wasn't to hurt us? How did I not figure it out sooner? All I had to do was flip that frame over, and I would have known. I'm such a dumbass, but so is Delmara for hiring her. How did she not know? Doesn't she do background checks? I know we needed another trainer to replace Craig, but this is just as much her fault as mine.

"Fuck," Sergio says, drawing out the word. "I thought you were calling about the kid."

"What kid?"

There's another pause. "You haven't heard?"

My skin prickles at the soft tone in his voice. "Heard what?"

"A kid was attacked at Fort Zach this morning. He was Maddy's neighbor."

Holy fuck. My mind reels, trying to find footing between Jen's lies and a Mer attack in daylight. "But . . . why?"

"Hell if I know," Serge says. "Maddy's ready to kill them all, so I sent her home for the day. Now . . . what the fuck is going on with Jen?"

I rub my face. "I don't know, man. I didn't stick around long enough for her to explain." Maybe I should have—at least I'd know what her plan is, then. It's not like I can call her up and ask.

"Jesus Christ," Serge says. I bet he's pulling his hair right now, face as red as Hannah's blood. "Jesus Christ," he repeats.

I'm speechless. This whole time, I've known there was something off about Jen, and I didn't bother to figure it out. And now, the Mer are attacking people in broad daylight? How am I supposed to make people sympathize with Erie when the Mer are attacking humans?

"Listen man, I gotta go. It's almost showtime."

"Yeah," I say. My brain is still reeling too much to form many complete thoughts. "Tell Aunt D I didn't know about Jen," I say before I hang up. "And tell Erie to smile." I have no idea how to save her now.

I haven't slept in days, and my fins are shredding. The first rip happened during a jump two days ago, and since then, every kick has torn them further. A live fish and a few days off would help, but all I get are dead fish and a daily show. The audience barely cheers for me anymore.

I'm checking the newest rip in my tail when Delmara strides in. I'd say she's angry, but I've never seen her look anything else, so maybe it's her normal face. She walks right to my tank and stares at me. I stare back.

"What's wrong with her?"

Sergio joins her at the glass. "Her fin rips every time she jumps. The vet says its stress."

"What the hell does a fish have to be stressed about?"

Maybe the fact that you took Finn away and shock me every time I talk? And feed me shit. And keep me prisoner.

Sergio shrugs. He may be nice enough, but he won't fight for me.

Delmara shakes her head. "She's not making enough money. I'm switching her to the three o'clock show. K and her boys will take the eleven back. I need her jumping again—do whatever you have to."

"I hate to say it, Aunt D, but the only way you'll get her performing like she was is to bring Finn back."

"Absolutely not." Delmara turns her angry gaze on Sergio. "He's trying to destroy this company. He'd see us all out on the street—him and that bitch girlfriend of his."

"He didn't know—" Sergio says, but Delmara cuts him off.

"Well, he does now, and I haven't heard an apology yet. If he wants to come crawling back on his knees and kiss my feet, maybe I'd let him work topside, but he's never going near the Mer again."

She storms away, but stops at the door. "You do whatever it takes to get her to jump, or I'll find someone who will."

Once she's gone, Sergio punches the glass. "Start fucking jumping, or she'll let Maddy shock you until you foam."

I glance up from my ruined tail. "Good."

Chapter 50: Finn

It doesn't take long for the backlash to begin. I'm drowning my anger in beer and checking the Save Erie page when I see the comment: "Fish Fucker!" It actually makes me snort. I don't know how the Mer mate, so how would I know how to fuck one?

Still, I'll have to keep my eye on the page, so no more vulgar messages appear. I'm deleting it when my phone rings. Jen. I take another long drink of beer as I hit "ignore." I really don't want to hear her bullshit excuses for lying to me. She went out of her way to deceive me and get me on her side, against Oceanica. What did she hope to accomplish?

You know what? I don't care. Jen's gone, and I need to focus on Erie. I also need something stronger than beer to make it through the rest of the day. I need to see Erie.

There's one public place on the island that you can see the shows from: Fort Zachary Taylor. If you climb to the top of the fort, you can see the highest jumps, even if the rest of the show is hidden.

On the bike ride over, my phone buzzes with texts. "Please, Finn, let me ex—" Delete. "We still need to work toge—" Delete. "I have a plan to save E—" Delete.

The show starts as I chain my bike to the rack next to a large "BEACH CLOSED" sign and walk up the path to the fort. Sergio's voice booms across this part of the island as he introduces Iodine and Cadmium. The crowd cheers, but it doesn't sound as loud as it used to. I climb the steps, gaze at the giant blue wall separating me from Erie, and wait for a flash of her hair.

I wish I could squeeze her hand and tell her how many people are in love with her. After Jen's betrayal, I'd be happy with Erie's cold fish lips forever. Let's be honest: if she became a human, like in the stories, I'd be all hers. Finn the fish fucker. That's me.

The music starts, and in my mind, I can see her routine. I crane my neck and strain my eyes, but I can't see her. No green scales. No magenta fins. The crowd still cheers when they're supposed to, but it sounds subdued. Whatever's happening in there, I can tell it's a bad show. Erie can jump so high, she should easily clear that wall. Something's wrong.

"You won't see her." My sister's voice travels across the fort to me, and I turn to find her at the top of the stairs. Her face is pink with sun, and her flip-flops slap against the stone as she joins me on the opposite end.

"I thought the beach was closed?"

"Just the water. You can still sunbathe. It's not like the Mer are coming onshore." Heather frowns at Oceanica. "There's a rumor Delmara will switch her to three o'clock."

My heart sinks. The three o'clock show is death to a Mer. Somehow, they know it's the least popular show—that they're no longer the favorites. Some of them snap and attack, but most of them stop eating, and you find them belly-up one morning, foam destroying their gills. No act has survived more than six months at three o'clock.

The music ends, and the crowd barely cheers. No one will rush the gift shop for stuffed Iodines. No one will excitedly tell their friends they "just have to see the show." Oceanica's no longer making a profit on her, which means Erie isn't worth keeping alive. They won't foam her—they aren't allowed to unless she attacks—but they'll neglect her until she gets herself killed, and they can go hunting for a new star performer.

"Finn?" Heather squeezes my shoulder. She knows as well as I what the three o'clock show means.

Before I can say anything, my phone rings. I'm so sick of it, I turn away from Heather and answer. "Stop fucking calling me."

"I have a plan," Jen says.

"I don't care."

"Would you listen to me for one minute? I know you're pissed, but I'm trying to save Erie. I talked to my lawyer, and we're creating the Save Erie Foundation. We need you on board, or no one will take us seriously."

I'm silent for a minute as I take that in. I don't want anything to do with Jen, but it's clear from the reaction post-interview that she's the media darling in this whole mess, not me. She's the one avenging her sister's death by taking down the giant corporation from the inside, while I'm the one who kisses fish.

"Finn?" she says when I don't reply.

Anger builds in my veins, and I use it to sharpen my words. "You know what, Jen? Because of your lies, my friends think I've betrayed them. I'm in the middle of a media war with a woman I considered my aunt two weeks ago. I've given up my entire career, and I might lose Erie, too. Your lies made all of this about your past and your sister, instead of Erie's future, so don't try to tell me you're helping."

I hang up on her and run my hand through my hair, pacing a circle on the top of the fort. I don't have time to deal with Jen's bullshit right now. I have a mermaid to save.

"Did I miss something?" Heather raises her eyebrows.

"*The Today Show* interview, apparently." I stop pacing and face her. "Jen is Hannah's sister. She's been lying to me all summer, and I found out on live television."

A small laugh escapes her. "So, you won't accept her help to save Erie?"

"Of course not—she doesn't care about saving Erie. She's been scheming against Oceanica all summer."

"And what, exactly, do you think you're currently doing?"

I scowl at her, then at Oceanica. "I'm not trying to bring down the whole business. I just want to get Erie out."

Heather picks at her nails. "Bullshit. You know humanizing one of them is going to kill the business model. And let's be honest, you're doing a shitty job of it so far. If I were you, I'd accept all the help I could get."

"Thanks, sis. You know, instead of selling Erie t-shirts, you could do something to help."

"What makes you think I haven't?" She digs in her beach bag, then pulls out an Oceanica business card and flips it over before handing it to me. On the back is the Save Erie Facebook address in her small handwriting. "Sam and I have been putting them in every bag we sell."

I glance at her, feeling like the world's biggest dick. "Thank you, Munchkin."

She squeezes my arm. "Don't mention it. You're my brother—if you care that much about saving a fish, I'll do whatever I can to help you."

• • • •

SERGE COMES HOME JUST after eight. "Stop what you're doing, we're going out," he announces.

As much as I appreciate that, I'm not in the mood. "I'm good, man. Have fun."

"The fact that you refused tells me you're not good at all. We're going out."

"Seriously, Serge, I don't feel like it."

"I don't care." He grabs the laptop and shuts it, then drops it on the coffee table with a *thud*. "We're going out, getting drunk, and finding you a mermaid groupie. We'll forget about Jen and Erie and be happy for a few minutes. So get up—and put a new shirt on, because no one's going to blow you in that ratty thing."

A blowjob won't make me forget about Jen and Erie, but I sure as hell wouldn't mind being drunk. Or eating something. "Fine." I stand. "But I'm not going down Duval."

"Schooner Wharf?"

"Deal."

Schooner Wharf is right on the harbor—a dive bar with good food, decent music, and plenty of drunk tourists. It's also not completely overrun with douchebags like Duval is. I'd probably get in a fight if we went down Duval tonight.

The upper deck is full, so we head straight to the bar instead. I'm two shots in when I notice Maddy and Nat sitting at a table on the opposite side of the room. *Bingo*. I don't need Jen's help to save Erie—I need the person who works with Erie to help save her. If I can get Maddy back on my side, I'll at least know Erie's safe while I come up with a plan.

I grab a beer from the bartender and make my way to their table. "Sick of the Porch already? Or are you stalking me?" I grin as I take the chair next to Maddy.

"Hello, traitor," she says, stone-faced.

"Come on, Mads, don't be like that. Jen used me."

"Doesn't feel so great to be used by someone, does it?" Maddy turns her back on me. Natalie shakes her head and does the same.

"Seriously? I'm trying to apologize here." I put my hands up in surrender. "None of this is my fault. Delmara should've done a background check before she hired Jen."

Maddy turns around and glares at me. "Nobody cares about Jen, you dick. Mer are attacking people, and we could all lose our jobs because you jumped in the tank."

"Whoa. Erie's not going to attack anyone once she's free. You can keep the rest of them. I just want to do right by Erie." And maybe Clair and Huron, but I won't tell them that.

"You're an idiot. You know what'll happen if APHIS and OSHA audit us because of what you did. Oceanica will be shut down, and it'll be your fault."

They turn their backs on me again. I put my arm around Maddy's shoulders and squeeze, even as she hunches them against my touch. "How 'bout this: I buy a round of drinks, we have a nice conversation, and when you go into work tomorrow, you let Erie talk to her dolphin without shocking her, okay? Can we agree on that?"

Maddy shoves my arm off her. "Actually, we can't. I'm not breaking the rules for your little fish girlfriend. I'm finally a trainer—no thanks to you—and I'm not sacrificing that just because you want to fuck a fish."

"Listen to yourself." I lean back in the chair and take a drink. "I don't want to fuck Erie, and it's not my fault that Jen lied about having experience with dolphins. That's the only reason I chose her as my assistant instead of you, you know that."

Maddy's chair squeals as she pushes it back and stands. "I'm done with you. If your fish girlfriend makes one fucking sound tomorrow, I'm shocking her until she foams." With that, she leaves. Natalie follows behind while giving me the finger.

The shots and beer threaten to come back up as I watch them walk away. I think I just fucked things up for Erie even worse.

The only thing I know about "three o'clock" is that there are fewer people in the audience. They fan themselves without cheering as Niku and I enter the arena, and when I pop my head out of the water to say hello, my eyes burn with the heat. At least it makes the water warmer.

With my tail ripped into ribbons, I can't swim as fast and I'm constantly behind. Niku helps by letting me hold his fins whenever we're close enough, but I know I'll be shocked for this later. If it wasn't for my desire to protect him, I'd quit swimming right now and curl up in the center of the tank until they foamed me.

I'm behind again. Niku's on the other side of the tank. I kick my tail hard to catch up and it splits all the way into the flesh. The pain is so jarring, I yelp and stop swimming. A thin ribbon of blood streams from the wound.

"Princess?" Niku swims to me. "Are you okay?"

The crowd makes noises of agitation—far be it for me to ruin their show. My shoulders sink as blood stains the water pink. "I'm fine," I lie. Niku can't do anything to help.

From the speakers surrounding us, I hear Sergio's voice. "Maddy, no. Not in front of the audience."

My head snaps up—Maddy sticks the loop in the water and anger rises in me so fast that I can't hold it back. I swim to the surface and point at the audience. "Go ahead, Maddy. Show them how you treat me when they aren't here."

She gapes as the audience grows silent. Sergio shakes his head, trying to get me to shut up, but I don't care. I'm a princess, and I'm not doing tricks for them anymore.

"That's right." I turn to the audience. "She electrocutes me whenever I make a noise, until my tailfin is in ribbons and I can't swim anymore. Well, guess what? I'm never swimming for you again!"

"You little—" Maddy says.

I spin to face her. "Do it! Shock me until I foam!"

Niku bumps me. "Princess, you shouldn't—"

"Maddy, stop!" Sergio shouts.

She doesn't listen. Before I can yell at her again, searing pain rips through my scales. My tail is being ripped in two—I'm being turned into a landfolk by the electroshocker. When the current finally releases, my entire body droops. The audience is utterly silent, except for a few young children sobbing into their parents' shoulders.

"Erie," Niku croaks.

Only half of my gills are underwater, and my eyesight's blurry. Foam eats my tail—soon, it will move all the way up, splitting it in two like a real Ariel.

Niku recovers first and pushes me underwater, swiping at my foaming tail with his chin. I want to tell him not to bother, but my vision clears and foam streams from the corners of my eyes.

"Neeky." Panic tinges my voice as I wipe at the foam, but it won't stop. "Neek!" My chest contracts in a sob, and then I'm crying—actually crying. Where water streams from landfolk eyes when they cry, seafoam streams from mine.

"It's okay, Princess," he says and wraps one flipper around me as well as he can. I give up and sob into the scars on his side.

By the time I've finished crying, the audience is gone. So is Maddy. Sergio stands at the side of the tank, arms crossed, a look of repentance on his face. He doesn't say anything as I swim to him and put a hand on the glass. It's a long moment before he covers my hand with his own. "Tag," I whisper.

His eyebrows pull together, and he pulls his hand away as the door behind him opens. I swim back to Niku, pain shooting through my tail at every kick, as Delmara walks in.

She joins Sergio at the glass. "I want her gone."

He glances at her in alarm. "We can't foam her—she hasn't attacked anyone. APHIS—"

"I'm not talking about foaming her—I'd never get the insurance money. Sell her. That ugly dolphin, too."

"Sell them?" It's a moment before Sergio says, "Finn would buy them."

Every part of me inflates with hope. I don't know what "sell" or "buy" means, but if Finn's involved, I want to be whatever they mean.

"No." Delmara's voice cuts through me like the foam through my tail. "Anyone but Finn. There are parks opening in Asia—sell them there."

Sergio's face pales. "The parks aren't finished."

"Yeah, well, the park being built in California won't buy a PR nightmare like her. Finn'll be all over today's footage, trying to convince the public he's in love with her." Delmara spits, as if even the words taste bad. "Sell her to China. Japan. I don't care. Just get her out of my park so I can find a new act."

A new act—that means they're going hunting again. They could catch anyone—my father, my brother and sisters, Grandmother.

"No," I say, voice rasping. "No hunting. No more acts." No more blackened shells.

Delmara's gaze snaps to me, and she sneers before turning it on Sergio. "I told you to do whatever you had to, or I'd find someone who would."

"Aunt," Sergio pleads.

"I will *not* be made a fool of again. No one believed in mermaids before me—I won't let this . . . *fish* undermine everything I've achieved. Do you understand?"

She stares him down until he presses his lips together. "I understand."

"Good. I need you online to help divert this. Madison can get her back in her tank, and then I'm suspending her until this dies down. Honestly, shocking a dolphin in front of all those children . . . it's a worse PR nightmare than Finn's become." Delmara turns on her heel and leaves.

Sergio faces me. "Don't worry—I'll call Finn. He'll figure something out." I swear he says "I hope" under his breath as he walks away.

I decide at that moment that I don't care what "sell" or "buy" means—I refuse to leave this tank until they foam me or Finn comes to get me.

My phone rings, but it's not Jen this time. It's Sergio. That's not good—he wouldn't call me while he's at work unless something's wrong. "Hey."

"They're selling Erie."

It's like a punch to the gut, and I almost drop the phone. When I can breathe again, I say, "What? To who?"

"Whoever will buy her. They're looking in Asia."

Oh god, if they send Erie across the world, I'll never be able to free her. "How much?"

"Two-point-five million."

"Two-point-five?"

"The point-five is for Niku."

At least they won't separate them, but damn, I thought I'd have more time to come up with a plan. "I . . . what . . . why?"

"She ripped her tail during the show and stopped swimming. When Maddy threatened to shock her, she freaked out and started screaming at the audience, telling them how Maddy treats her. Then she refused to perform. She won't leave the arena now, and Aunt D is sick of dealing with her."

I knew it was only a matter of time before Erie snapped. I kinda wish I'd been there to see it. "Two-point-five, huh? I can do that."

"She won't sell Erie to you, man."

"I'll figure something out. I gotta go." I hang up before Serge can reply and search YouTube for today's show.

When I see the footage, I nearly throw my laptop across the room. Trying to get Maddy on my side backfired—epically so. I have to do something, now, or Erie will die in that place, and it'll be my fault.

I peer at my phone for a long moment, trying to talk myself into making the call. I could come up with my own plan, but I've run out of time. Heather's right, I need as much help as I can get. I don't have to like Jen; I just have to work with her. I don't know if I can trust her, though. What other secrets might she be hiding?

It doesn't matter. All that matters now is buying Erie before a park in Asia can. I hit "Call," and almost hang up when I hear her voice on the other end of the line. "Finn?"

"They're selling Erie."

She gasps. "To who?"

"To us, if we're quick. Tell me about the foundation—have you already set it up?"

"I was waiting on you. I have all the paperwork, but it can take a while for the tax exempt status to go through."

"But we can raise money before then?"

"We can certainly try. The only problem will be the bill, if we can't secure the 501(c)(3)."

How does she know all this? How long has she been planning it? I pace the room, feeling like an idiot because all I've done is set up a stupid Facebook page. "Oceanica won't sell Erie to us. We need to fake who's buying her."

Jen's silent for a moment. "There are a couple of ways to get around that."

"Are they legal?"

"Some of them. Does it matter?"

"No."

"Good. I'll bring you the paperwork and call my lawyer to start figuring out the rest." She hangs up before I can say anything more, and I stare at my phone, wondering if I've done the right thing, or if I've played into her game again.

. . . .

JEN KNOCKS ON MY FRONT door, a giant stack of paperwork in her arms. Dark circles ring her eyes, like she's spent more time crying than sleeping, and despite the fact that I should be unendingly thankful for her quick work on the foundation, I can't help but think that this is some sort of trap.

When I finish signing, I toss the paperwork on the table. "Thanks for doing this. See you at the next Save Erie rally, or interview, or whatever." I brush past her to my laptop to update the page with the news that Erie's for sale, and we'll have a donation site up soon.

"Finn, we can't work together if you're like this."

"I don't plan to work with you unless we're in public or someone's got a camera."

Behind me, Jen sighs. "Listen, it's not what you think. I wasn't trying to take down Oceanica. I just had to know . . ."

"Know what?" I snap.

She swallows so hard I can hear it, and when she speaks, her voice is soft and thick with tears. "If it was Hannah's fault. If there was anything she could have done to keep it from happening. Maybe if she'd treated him better—"

My hands hover over the keyboard for a moment, remembering Hannah. Her smile, so like Jen's. Her gentle ribbing. Her knowledge . . .

The blood in the water.

I shudder and clamp my hands into fists.

Carbon's red-tipped claws when he finally released her.

With my back to Jen, I manage to say, "A sample size of one doesn't prove anything. Trust me, Carbon would've ripped Hannah's face off no matter what."

"Stop saying that!"

I finally face Jen, and just as I'd suspected, there are tears rolling down her cheeks. "Stop saying what? The truth? I know you have a problem with it."

"Stop saying he ripped her face off." Jen wipes her eyes and sniffs. "She drowned."

"People don't bleed that much when they drown."

Jen smacks me across the face with her tear-wet hand. I won't say I didn't deserve it, but I'm also not sorry for what I said. Her hands fold into fists, and she shoves them down at her sides. "I saw the video—"

"And I was *there*." I turn my back again and hear the unmistakable hitch of breath that means she's crying. I wish she'd leave—why's she crying in my living room? It's a few moments before she speaks, her voice soft but angry.

"I thought working with Erie had changed you, but you're exactly what Maddy said."

Now she's bringing Maddy into it? I stand so fast, Jen takes a step back. "You're right—I used you for sex, but you used me for so much worse. I fucking cared about you, Jen. I wanted to be your boyfriend. And then I find out on live fucking television that everything about you was a lie? That . . ." I swallow the rest, because I can't admit how much she hurt me. "Get out of my house. I have more important shit to do than listen to your lies."

"I'm not lying this time."

"That's the thing about lying to people, Jen. They stop trusting you."

I point to the door. She blinks rapidly and swallows hard before she leaves. I fold my hands into fists to stop their shaking.

I want to believe that this whole thing was some ill-conceived plan to prove that being nice to the Mer works, but it's honestly the stupidest thing I've ever heard.

I pace the arena as Maddy watches from the platform. Every flick of my broken tail sends pain shooting through my core, but I'm so angry I barely feel it. Right now, her arms are crossed, her foot tapping in annoyance, but I know, eventually, she'll grab the loop and shock me. I don't know why she's waiting.

Apparently, she's waiting for dark. As soon as the sun goes down, she grabs the loop and sticks it in the water.

"Princess." Niku's tone is warning, but I don't care anymore.

"Sorry, Neeky."

Before he can say anything else, Maddy does. "Get back to your tank, now."

I turn to her and bare my teeth. "No."

The first shock is quick—a reminder of how much it hurts. My tail throbs with my heartbeat.

"Get in your tank."

I lift my middle finger out of the water, and the second shock is long enough to leave me floating.

"Do you want to try again?" Maddy says. "Or do you want to continue this game until you're dead?"

Death is better than this life, and I'd rather die under the stars. I think one last time of my family—of Clair and Huron, stuck somewhere nearby. Tomorrow, they'll perform, and swim through whatever has become of me. They won't even know I'm gone.

Foam streams from my eyes again, and I imagine Finn wiping it away with his always warm fingers. I wish he had saved me in time, but I can't wait any longer.

"Just kill me." My voice rasps as I say it, and Maddy hits me with the loop until the world goes dark.

· · · ·

I FEEL BEFORE I CAN see, and it feels like someone stabbed me in the chest. I wipe the foam from my eyes and realize I'm back in the holding tank. I tear my nails down my face until I bleed.

Niku stares at me from his tank. Between us is the contraption they used to bring us in that first day, a net draped over the edge. For the Tides—they brought me back here with a net, and I didn't even realize it.

Sergio walks into the room, his magic rectangle lighting his face in the dimness. When he glances up from it and sees me, his shoulders slump in relief. "Thank god. I thought you were dead."

That was the plan. I rub the painful spot on my chest and find a dolphin-nose-sized bruise.

"Your dolphin punched you in the chest—I think he was trying to wake you up."

Waking me up wouldn't take so much force, but I remember once when my grandmother's heart stopped. Her guard punched her in the chest and she gasped and started to breathe again. He saved her life. I guess Niku saved mine, though I really wish he hadn't.

"Well then"—Sergio interrupts my thoughts—"since I'm fairly sure you won't foam in the middle of the night, I'm out of here. I'll tell Finn you're not dead."

There are so many other things I'd like him to tell Finn, but I can't say them to Sergio. Instead, I try to think of a way to kill myself. The loop almost worked—if it hadn't been for Niku, my heart might have stayed silent and I'd have turned to foam without ever waking up. Maybe I could jump out of the tank, or pull myself onto the platform and wait for the air to do its work. How painful would it be to dry out? How long would it take?

What would happen to Niku if I foamed? Would they kill him? Free him? Make him perform with someone else? One thing's certain—my death will mean they send another boat out hunting, which means another one of the 'folk will share my fate.

If I do that—if I kill myself and allow them to capture another of the merfolk—then I refuse to die alone. I'll take one of the landfolk with me.

The website is up and the donation page is ready to go live at eight a.m. tomorrow morning. Sergio comes home late, looking just about as beat down as I've ever seen him. He drops a plastic bag on the couch next to me and goes to the fridge for a beer.

"What's this?" I glance at the bag.

"Bunch of shit from Erie's tank. Thought you might want it."

I open it to find the necklaces and Ariel figurine. "Why the hell did you take these from her?" It was the only comfort she had.

"Aunt's rules—she told us to clear the tank. Maddy was about to toss it all, but I grabbed it for you."

"Thanks," I say, voice hoarse, though I have no idea what to do with all these necklaces. I guess I'll save them for Erie to take home when I free her.

Sergio grabs a slice of cold pizza and plops down on the couch next to me. "Your Mer is making my life a living hell."

"She'll be out soon. I'll raise the money, and find a way to make Aunt D sell her to me."

"What about the others?"

I grimace, thinking of Clair and Huron. I'd love to save them, too, if only so Erie won't have to go home alone, knowing their fate. Knowing they're broken. "I don't know, man. Let me worry about Erie first—I'll decide what to do about the others once she's safe."

He sulks, and an awkward silence falls between us. This is the worst part of this whole thing—I've lost my best friend. We may not hate each other, but our friendship will never be the same, because I chose Erie and he chose Oceanica.

Another video of today's show pops up on YouTube, and it very clearly shows Erie crying. Despair clutches at my heart as foam streams from her eyes and she sobs into Niku's side, the mics picking up the sound until the tech guy cuts them out. I add it to the website.

"Jesus Christ," Serge says as he watches his phone. "Would you stop posting that shit? You're making my job impossible."

I glance at his screen to find Oceanica's Facebook page, comments pouring in about today's show. "At least no one's calling you a fish fucker."

Sergio smirks. "Yeah, I thought you'd like that one."

The first real laugh in days punches out of my stomach. Of course it was my best friend who posted that. Maybe we'll be okay, after all.

• • • •

DONATIONS START POURING in as soon as the page goes live, and by noon, we've hit a hundred grand. That's a far cry from the two-point-five million plus transportation expenses and lawyer fees we need to raise, but it's a start. Jen's lawyer, Ed Hilley, also came through with an exclusive interview with NBC's *Nightly News*.

Which means, I need to play nice with Jen.

Our last fight replays over and over in my mind. Why would she continue stringing me along, even after I was fired? Was she worried I'd use her betrayal to get my job back? By the time I was fired, getting my job back was the least of my concerns. Didn't she know that?

Speak of the devil—my phone buzzes with a text. "I hear we have an interview tomorrow."

"Yep."

"Can I come over?"

"No."

It's a few minutes before she replies. "We can't act like this during the interview. We're supposed to be friends."

Friends. Not lovers. Friends. I have to force my hands to relax before I can type a message back. "I have faith in your acting skills."

That shuts her up for a while, but eventually, she texts again. "We have to talk before the interview."

The headache that's been forming for days finally sprouts, and I rub my temples before answering. "Are you scared they've discovered more of your secrets and lies?"

"Stop being a dick."

I don't bother replying and neither does Jen, so I'm only mildly surprised when a knock rattles my door. I crack it open, putting my foot behind it so she can't force it open. "I thought I said you couldn't come over?"

Her arms hug her chest as she studies her feet. When she speaks, her voice sounds empty.

"I'm moving back to South Carolina. I was going to leave tomorrow, but with the interview . . ." She lets it hang in the air for a moment, and when I don't say anything, she continues. "It's an exclusive, so it's not like I have to be around for another one."

She doesn't lift her head, and I don't know what she expects me to say. Does she want me to beg her not to go? "Good luck with the move."

I try to close the door, but she unwraps her arms and pushes it open. "Finn, please."

"Jesus Christ, what do you want from me?"

Jen finally lifts her gaze. "Forgiveness."

"Too bad." This time, when I shut the door, she doesn't resist and it slams in her face. From the other side, she speaks.

"Erie forgave you."

"Yeah, well, I don't have Stockholm Syndrome."

"And Erie's a fish."

Called out once again by the fish being more sympathetic than I am, but really, if Erie knew Jen lied about something important, she'd be pissed, too. Like when she was pissed at us for not telling her about the ocean . . .

Oh.

I lean my forehead against the door.

Jen says, "Hannah told me about you, you know. How you knew everything about the Mer, even though you were just a kid. How Delmara treated you like a son and gave you free rein over Oceanica. How you tried to flirt with all the girls—even the married ones. Even her."

Is she accusing me of hitting on her sister now?

"She said I'd like you—that we'd get along."

My hand folds into a fist. "So that's why you picked me as your mark? The perfect, unsuspecting target at Oceanica?"

"I didn't have a target—you're the one who chose me as your assistant."

"Because I thought you had experience with dolphins," I grind out.

Jen's silent for a minute and I feel stupid arguing through the door, but I know if I open it, I'll either feel pity for her tear-stained face or so much anger I'll punch something.

"Hannah was right." Jen's so quiet I almost can't hear her through the door. "I do like you—more than I should. I tried so hard not to, and you certainly made me want to hate you often enough, but I like you, Finn. I didn't want to hurt you then, and I don't want to lose you now."

I squeeze my eyes shut and press my forehead into the wood.

"I'm sorry I didn't tell you about Hannah sooner, but I was scared. First, I was scared that I'd be fired, and then, I was scared that I'd lose you. And I should have told you, because now I've been fired *and* I've lost you."

I knock my skull softly against the door as I think of the way Jen freaked out when I was attacked by Niku. Of her pale face and shaking hands when I made her get in the tank with Erie—the tank her sister died in. All the crass things I said about Hannah getting her face ripped off. My comment about the trainers who died.

I open the door and she stumbles forward, grabbing the handle so she won't fall. When she steadies herself, I search her face for the truth. I want what she said to be true.

She reaches for me. "Finn—"

"No more lies, Jen. No more secrets."

"I promise."

I press my lips together. I want to kiss her, but I don't want to fall down that rabbit hole again. Her apology doesn't change the fact that I'm going back to school next month and she's moving home. "I'll see you tomorrow, then."

She sucks in a surprised breath, then swallows. "I thought—"

"I forgive you for lying, but I have to focus on Erie, and you have to pack."

Her shoulders sink. "I understand. I just . . . do you want me to go? Home?"

My answer is immediate—I don't even think about it first. "No."

She swallows hard. "I'll see you tomorrow, then."

When she pulls the door shut behind her, I rest my forehead against the wood. All I can see is Jen's red hair spilling over her bare shoulder as she hovers over me in bed, a lazy smile on her lips, her eyes lidded. My hand tightens to turn the knob, and it takes all of my self-control not to run out the door after her.

I'm breaking. It starts in my mind with a tiny crack, then moves through my veins to my chest, where it lodges like the spine of a stingray. Finn isn't coming. I'll die in this gray tank, alone, while the landfolk watch with their dead eyes. I spend my days popping bubbles, but what I really want to pop is one of the landfolk.

Maddy's been replaced by a girl Sergio calls "Nat." She never comes near enough for me to kill. When she feeds us, she stands at the back of the platform near the loop and tosses the fish in. I'd have to jump clean out of the water to grab her, and I'm not sure I can do that with my broken tail.

The wound festers—foam simmers around the scales, no matter how much I wipe it away. Niku looks sick, too. His eyes are glassy and unfocused, and he barely moves, bobbing in the same place at the surface. He's breaking right along with me.

Without the structured days and my room of shells, I don't know how long it's been. Nat feeds us, but she doesn't stay, and I haven't seen Sergio in . . . days? They don't turn the lights off, so I can't tell if it's day or night. Nat could be about to walk through the door with her bucket of death, or she could never return. Eventually, I get hungry enough to swallow a bite of dead fish I've let sit too long, but as soon as it's down, I gag and it comes back up. I don't even curl up in my tail anymore—I just pass out when the pain and despair become too much.

A knock on the tank rouses me from blessed oblivion, and I curl against the noise as I glance at the glass. It's Delmara, moving her finger in a "come here" motion. I close my eyes and ignore her—she can't do anything more to hurt me.

"Shock the dolphin," she says, and I bolt upright, wincing at the pain in my tail. Maddy's on Niku's platform, loop in the water, a wicked smirk on her face as she hits the button. Neek's eyes sharpen, but otherwise, he shows no sign of having felt it.

"Now that I have your attention," Delmara says, "we're doing things differently. If you misbehave, if you make a noise, if you so much as glare at anyone, we're shocking him instead of you. Do you understand?"

The crack inside me grows as I glance at Niku. Niku, who purposefully swam under the net when he could have swam away to get help. He shouldn't be here, and he definitely shouldn't be shocked instead of me. I nod that I understand.

"Good. As soon as I find a buyer, we'll have to show you off, so smile."

Does she mean now, or when she "shows me off"? She must mean now, because she points at Maddy, who shocks Niku. Foam bubbles from the corners of my eyes as he begins to float.

"Let's try again. Smile."

With foam streaming from my eyes, I pull up the corners of my mouth and bare my teeth in what must be the most grotesque smile anyone's ever seen.

Delmara smirks. "We're getting somewhere. Now spin."

My broken tail sends pain shooting through my core, but I do as I'm told.

"Show me your tail."

I hold it in front of me, close to the glass, and she frowns as she studies it, then peers around the tank at the dead fish. "You need to eat."

I shake my head, and Delmara's eyes narrow.

"I don't get the insurance money if you foam from neglect. You'll eat, or I'll shock your dolphin again. Do you understand?"

I risk speaking in a whisper. "Mer don't eat dead fish."

She turns her head to Maddy. "Shock him."

A scream tries to rip out of my throat, but I choke it back, squeeze my eyes shut, and pierce my palms with my nails. I wish Niku would grab the shocker like he did with Finn.

"You'll eat the dead fish," Delmara says, "or I'll kill the dolphin. No"—her eyes light up—"I'll make him perform with someone else. Argon maybe . . ."

She means Huron. How does she know they dislike each other? What did Finn tell her? I have no idea what he's been doing all this time—what if he's abandoned me? What if he's gone back to her?

Delmara scrutinizes me even as she speaks to Maddy. "No one will pay two million for this—she can barely swim. Get them fresh fish, and clean this tank."

"Yes, ma'am." Maddy returns the loop to the wall and leaves.

When she's gone, Delmara speaks. "It's a real shame you and Jennifer turned Finnegan against me. He was my best employee—better even than my nephew. He had his father's enthusiasm for the ocean . . ." She gazes into the distance before her eyes harden. "His father was stupid, too."

So Finn hasn't gone back to her. That gives me a little hope—enough to play nice, at least. I don't know if she wants me to reply, but I can't either way. I've never met Finn's father.

"How old are you?" Delmara says. "How many years ago were you born?"

I wipe the foam from my eyes and risk speaking, since Maddy's gone. "What's 'years'?"

Delmara shakes her head. "Never mind. You must be just about the age I was when I met Cale Jarvis. I was a freshman at FKCC—a business major, but biology was a required credit."

This is stranger than before, and I hug my tail to myself. I don't know who Cale Jarvis is, nor what half of those words mean, but she keeps talking as though I asked her to.

"Usually, the professors of the low-level classes try to get through the semesters just as much as the students who aren't interested, but Cale was different. He was excited about teaching—passionate. He made it interesting. So much so that I took another of his classes, and then switched my major to biology."

Delmara stares at her fingertip as it draws mindless circles on the glass. "Cale was amazing. He was one of those professors who would talk for hours about anything he found interesting—biology or not. He'd hang out with his students. He really wanted to know them for who they were. If I ran into him on the island—which is easy to do; it's a small island—he'd tell me about some recent discovery he'd heard of. He wanted to discover something so badly, but he was stuck at the community college doing research on the effects of water acidification on the local reefs."

She finally looks at me. "Have you noticed that the reefs are dying?"

I nod, because I think that's what she wants from me. Grandmother said the reef wasn't what it used to be, but the landfolk have been hunting us for so long that I don't know the difference.

Delmara's eyes unfocus. "Yes, I thought so." She goes back to tracing circles on the glass.

"At the end of every semester—after finals—Cale would have a cookout at his house for his favorite students. That's where I first met Finnegan. I'm sure I'd seen him at Sergio's birthday parties, but I'd never paid attention before those cookouts. Finn must have been ten at the first one."

I guess from the way she says it that "ten" is young. I try to imagine Finn as young as the children at the shows, but can only see him as the Finn I know now. The crack in my chest breaks a little more as I realize how much longer Delmara has known him—how much it must hurt him to defy her.

"Finn would drag us around the house, showing off fish tanks and scuba gear, telling us about how he would be just like his dad when he grew up. He'd talk to us about whatever biology thing he'd learned—just like Cale." She flattens her hand against the glass as her shoulders sink. "He had so much promise. Once you're gone, he'll see reason again and come back to me."

I think Delmara might be finished talking, but she starts drawing circles on the tank again.

"The first Mer looked like you. I never saw it—Cale hauled it up in a net on accident while fishing for tarpon, and by the time he got back to the island, it was foam."

The crack breaks in two, and I sink to the dirty floor. She's talking about my mother. My mother, who disappeared first. If what Delmara says is true, Finn's dad killed my mother. Hauled her onto his boat and let her suffocate. That's how my mother died.

I want to scream, but Delmara will shock Niku, or force him to perform with Huron. I draw my nails against the bottom of the tank instead, letting the high-pitched screech scream for me.

"No one believed him, of course," Delmara continues, oblivious to the crack that's tearing me apart and the noise my nails are making. "Even I didn't, though I wanted to. Maybe Finn did—he was young enough at the time—but his mother certainly didn't. Cale went mad trying to find proof. Trying to prove it to *her*."

Delmara slams her fist on the glass, and I jump back, wincing at the pain in my tail.

"That stupid bitch ruined him. He wouldn't have gone out looking for Mer that day if he wasn't so desperate to prove it to her. I begged him not to go. The water was too choppy—no one was going out. But Cale went . . . and never came back."

She pets the glass. "Everything would be different if he'd stayed with me."

Maddy's heavy footsteps come through the door. "It took forever, but I found the freshest fish in the cooler."

Delmara straightens and holds her hand out for the bucket. She holds up one of the fish. "Are you ready to eat, Iodine?"

I glance at Niku. I've lost my appetite, but I can't say no.

Delmara walks to the platform and holds the fish out. When I surface, she doesn't appear nervous like all the other landfolk—she knows I won't hurt her, because then they'll hurt Niku.

"There you go, darlin'," she says as I take the fish. It turns my stomach to hear Finn's nickname for me in her mouth, but I take a bite and swallow.

She pats the side of the tank. "I'll get the vet to bring you some antibiotics." She leaves, then, and I'm stranded with Maddy, which is worse than being alone.

Chapter 56: Finn

We've raised half a million dollars by the time I need to meet Jen and her lawyer for the interview. I recognize Ed Hilley immediately—he represented the Stevens family in their suit against Oceanica after Hannah died. This guy grilled me on the stand four years ago. It's strange to think he's representing me now.

The news crew has set up in the Westin, in a suite that overlooks the harbor—and, in the distance, Oceanica. For the most part, the questions are the same, but we have more time to answer them.

"Tell me," the host says near the end. "If you could go back in time and stop the Mer from being discovered, would you?"

I almost say yes. If Dad had never found the first Mer, he wouldn't have gone mad trying to prove their existence. I wouldn't have stayed up late at night, unable to sleep because my parents were fighting about it. He wouldn't have gone out on that boat and never returned. All the trainers who have died would still be alive, working at Orca World. Serge and I would be working at the restaurant together. No one would have been attacked by the Mer.

And I would never have met Erie.

"No," I finally say, my voice rough. "Despite all that's happened, I'm glad I met Erie. When I look into her eyes and her whole face beams, it makes me whole. She's made me a better person, and I *will* get her back home, whatever it takes."

It's a selfish answer—and I'm sure Erie wouldn't agree—but it's true. Whatever happens, I'm glad that I met her. I'll never meet anyone like her again.

"What happens next?" the host says. "What happens after you free her?"

I haven't thought that far ahead yet, and I don't want to. I don't want to think about life going back to normal once Erie's gone. "I don't know. I go back to school, I guess, and she goes back to her family. I'll never see her again . . ." If she's lucky, I'll never see her again. That thought is almost as painful as the thought of not being able to save her at all.

• • • •

THERE ARE TWO EXTRA people standing with Ed Hilley by the time the interview is over. He introduces us as we walk to the elevator.

"Finnegan, Jennifer, I'd like you to meet Mr. Brian Goodwin, of Salty Slug Games, and Mr. Jason Cao, a friend from Hollywood," Hilley says.

The two of them couldn't be more different. Mr. Goodwin's in a dark suit, but looks like he would feel more at home in combat fatigues, while Mr. Cao is smaller than Jen and dressed in expensive clothes made to look relaxed and beachy. We shake their hands while I wonder why Hilley's brought a game company executive and an actor.

Mr. Goodwin speaks after the elevator doors close. "Nice to meet you both. I've been impressed by your story, and I'd like to help. I'm also a documentarian—or rather, I fund people who make documentaries."

"That's great," I say, "but we're not looking to make the mermaid version of *Free Willy*. We just need the money to buy Erie from Oceanica."

The corner of Mr. Cao's mouth turns up. "From what Ed says, you need more than money. You need a fake company based somewhere in Asia."

Jen gestures at his features. "I take it that's where you come in."

His smile widens, crinkling the crow's feet around his eyes. "Unless you plan to find an actual Asian businessman to help you, but I guarantee I'm cheaper."

"Especially since I'm paying him, so long as you let me record this endeavor," Goodwin says as the elevator dings.

We follow Hilley down the hall to the room he's staying in, and when he opens the door, a cameraman is there, recording my expression as I see the Save Erie headquarters Jen and Hilley have set up. There are fliers to pass out around town, pamphlets featuring "Undersea Land"—a fake marine park—with writing in both English and what I guess is Chinese, and a whiteboard with an updated amount of money we've raised.

I can't believe Jen put all of this together without me. She had no choice, since I wasn't speaking to her until yesterday, but I wish I'd have been part of it. I grab her hand and squeeze a silent thank you.

Hilley, Goodwin, and Cao brush past us into the room. Goodwin holds the door for us. "So, do we have a deal?"

I step into the room and pick up one of the brochures, studying it for a moment while my mind stops reeling. "Delmara has good lawyers."

"So do I," he says. "Trust me, I've dealt with the Chinese legal system to get *Draco: Urban Combat Armor* into overseas markets. They can wrap Oceanica in ink forever if she's difficult, and from what I hear, Ms. de la Cruz wants a quick sale. She'll be easy to manipulate."

The only thing I can think with my mind spinning is that I've played *Draco: UCA*. I hazard a glance at Jen, and she squeezes my arm. "Delmara's not a patient woman when she needs something. That's how I was able to get the job at Oceanica—she needed another trainer ASAP and didn't do a proper background check."

Hilley nods. "She's desperate to get rid of her PR problem—she'll push her legal team to approve the contracts as quickly as they can. They may not even bother translating the names if Cao is convincing."

I glance at Cao, who holds out his hand. "Better be fucking convincing," I say as I shake it, and grasp desperately to the hope that this will work.

I poke a bubble with my nail and it pops. Broken. Water rushes into the space it just occupied. There was nothing inside. I can't stand the bubbles.

All day, all night, ruthlessly popping bubbles, and they never stop forming. My tail has stopped creating them—so have my eyes—but the hole that pushes water into the tank makes new ones all the time. It's a constant battle between me and that endless hole. I will win. I have to win. There can be no empty spaces, except for me.

"Stop obsessing over the goddamn filter," Maddy says. Again. But I can't. I cannot tolerate the bubbles.

Every time they pop, the air goes free.

"Jesus Christ, Iodine. Delmara will be here any minute with a potential buyer. You need to eat."

I grab the fish that floats on the surface of my tank, but that creates more bubbles, and I have to pop them.

"Eat," Maddy commands. If I don't, she'll shock Niku, so I eat the fish I hold in one hand while I pop bubbles with the other. Niku is the only thing keeping me together now. I hold on to his name—*Niku, Niku, Niku*—because I can't remember my own. They call me Iodine. I've become Iodine. I am empty.

No. *Pop.* More. *Pop.* Bubbles. *Pop.*

Maddy growls and walks away.

I hear Delmara's footsteps before she enters the room. "And this is our holding area," she says to another set of footsteps. "These were our star performers: Iodine and Cadmium."

I continue to pop bubbles, refusing to acknowledge them until I have to.

A man's voice—with such a heavy accent I can barely understand him—speaks next. "If they were stars, why sell?"

"One of our former employees has been causing problems regarding this one. When she's gone, we can get on with business as usual."

She's talking about my landfolk boy. The one who promised to release me. The one who lied. I attack the bubbles with a new ferocity—it's safer to forget about him.

"Iodine," she coos, and I face her, popping the bubbles my tail stirs up. "Iodine, this is Mr. Cao, from China. Give him a smile, sweetheart."

I turn up the corners of my mouth, baring my teeth, then bite the bubbles that float in front of my face. Mr. Cao jumps back a little. He's almost as small as Delmara, with tiny eyes like I've never seen. He grimaces, and I huddle into my tail as a scowl spreads across Delmara's face. I've displeased her.

"Come now," she says and motions me closer. "Show yourself off. Mr. Cao has come all this way to see you."

I unwind my tail and swim closer to the glass, then spin a circle like she instructed me. Mr. Cao frowns, which means Delmara frowns.

"She look ill-used," he says. "Scarred."

"Just surface wounds." Delmara waves it away. "You'll never find a better-trained Mer. She eats on command, which can be a problem for some, and jumps higher than any Mer I've seen. We'll even give you the music, so you can keep the same routine."

"How much?"

"Two million for Iodine. Half a mil for the dolphin."

Mr. Cao's eyebrows shoot up, and he points at Niku. "Half a million? We can buy dolphin from Japan. Five grand."

"He's trained, and the secret to keeping her in line. Without that specific dolphin, you can shock her 'til she foams. She won't cooperate." She waves a hand in the air, as if I'm a lost cause. "He's worth half a million because he insures your investment."

They stop watching me, so I go back to eradicating bubbles—until he leans close to the glass and says, "Why you pop them?"

I watch him for a moment, wondering why he asked me a question. Delmara stands next to him, eyes sharp on my every move, and nods when I glance at her for permission to speak. When I do, my voice comes out hoarse. Misused.

"I pop them because they look like something, but they're nothing. They are lies."

A bubble floats between us, so I pop it.

I thought seeing Erie would be a good thing. Serge says she's eating and her tail is healing, so when Goodwin strapped a hidden camera on Cao before sending him into Oceanica as our negotiator, I was excited to see her. But from the moment she came into view, attacking bubbles with her claws, I knew that something was wrong.

This isn't my Erie.

"What's she doing?" Jen asks, leaning over my shoulder to get a better look.

I don't know—I've never seen any of the Mer do this. "I guess . . . I guess she's attacking the only thing that won't get her foamed?" It's the only explanation I can come up with, until she answers Cao.

They are lies.

Now I know what the bubbles are—they're my promise to free her.

I can't watch this. Without a word, I walk to the bedroom of Hilley's suite. I slam the door, grab an extra pillow, and scream into it. I don't know how long I sit on the edge of the bed, staring at the blue water that goes on forever. The water Erie should be in. Now, I *do* wish my dad had never discovered the Mer.

Eventually, Jen steps in, closing the door behind her. "Are you okay?"

Not a chance in hell, but I drop the pillow and squeeze my knees. "Yeah, I'm fine."

She sits next to me and grabs my hand. "Delmara agreed to the sale. We'll have Erie out next week."

I should be relieved—we won. But all I can think is that plenty could still go wrong. Delmara's lawyers could figure out who's really trying to buy Erie. Erie could attack someone and be foamed. We can get her back into the ocean, but she's too broken to survive.

"Finn, did you hear me?" Jen squeezes my hand.

"Yeah, I heard you."

"I thought you'd have some reaction to that. A smile or . . . something."

I gaze out the window. "I'll smile once I know Erie's safe and able to survive on her own."

"She won't be on her own—she'll be with her family."

What if she can't find them? What if they treat her like damaged goods? We know nothing about Mer society except for the little she's told us and the little we've noticed in the holding tanks. I don't want to burst Jen's bubble, though, so I force my face to relax. "Yeah. She'll be home soon."

"There," she says and pats my leg. "Keep thinking that and don't worry about the rest. Erie will be fine."

• • • •

WE'RE WALKING HOME from the hotel when my cell rings. It's Sergio, and though I really don't want to talk to him right now, I answer. "Hey."

He takes a deep breath. "I'm sorry, man. I have bad news." He actually sounds sorry as he says it, and I can hear him swallow. "They sold Erie to a Chinese marine park this morning. There was nothing I could do."

I don't know what to say. It takes crushing my jaw together to not tell Serge that I'm the one who bought her. I trust him with my life, but not Erie's, and I can't take any chances if I want to pull this off. Not to mention, he led me to believe that Erie was doing okay when she's very obviously not. He may have been protecting me, but I don't appreciate it.

When I don't reply, Serge speaks. "Dude, Finn, you okay?"

My voice actually breaks when I say, "Yeah," because I'm still not over what I saw. Serge must think it's because of his news.

"God, man, I wish there was something I could do. I told Aunt D you were raising the money, but she's gone mad over this whole thing."

The money is the other reason this could still fall through—we've raised enough to buy Erie, but not Niku, nor do we have enough for transportation yet. Now, we have to raise about a million dollars in a week. I can't breathe, and my hands tremble. I think I'm having a fucking panic attack.

"I gotta go," I say to Serge and hang up, shoving the phone back in my pocket while I take a deep breath. I can feel Jen's gaze on me, worried, but she doesn't say anything until we're outside her place.

"Do you want to come in?" Her hand grasps the doorknob. "We can have a celebratory drink."

It's been a couple of weeks since I've been to Jen's place, and I know that if I go in there now, I'll either end up in her bed or I'll see that picture of Hannah on her dresser and freak out.

"No." I watch her fingers wrap around the brass knob. If I look in her eyes, I'll fall right back into the place I was. "I . . . can't."

Her knuckles whiten. "Oh. Right. I'll, uh . . . I'll see you later, then?"

"Tomorrow." I leave so I won't see the hurt in her eyes. When I'm halfway down the street, I glance behind me, but she stands there, hand on the doorknob, watching me.

I go home and grab an overnight bag, then head to my mom's house. If I stay at mine, I'll end up telling Serge I'm the buyer.

Mom's car is in the drive, and she glances up from the kitchen table, surprised, when I walk in. "What are you doing here?"

"Staying away from Serge." I drop my bag on the floor and slide into a chair across the table.

She grabs her reading glasses from her face and studies me. I hate it when she does that. She looks more like a psychiatrist than a mom. "You want to talk about it?" she says.

"No, Dr. Jarvis, I don't."

A little smile pulls her lips up as she folds her glasses and sets them on the table. "Is it a girl coming between you? One with a tail?"

"Ha. Ha." I steal a potato chip from her plate, but my mouth is dry, and it sticks. I don't know what's wrong with me—I should be happy, giddy even. Instead, I imagine Erie popping bubbles, destroying what she thinks are my lies.

Mom folds her hands like she's sitting with a patient. "What's wrong?"

"Everything's fine. Delmara agreed to the sale. Erie will be free in a week."

The calculating psychiatrist disappears, leaving a shell-shocked mom in her place. "Delmara *agreed*?"

"Yeah . . . well, she thinks she sold Erie to a buyer in China." And if she finds out she didn't, I have no idea what I'll do. Probably break into Oceanica and end up in jail.

Mom sits back and taps her foot. It's a sure sign that I won't like what she has to say, but she's gonna say it, anyway. "Maybe this has gone too far."

"It hasn't gone far enough."

"Finn, listen to me. There's more to this than you trying to buy a fish—"

"Erie's not a fish!" I slam my fist on the table. "She's not another dead-eyed Mer. She's . . ." I swallow, throat tight, because, from what I saw today, she is another dead-eyed Mer, just like the rest of them. "She's broken," I whisper, "and it's my fault."

My breath hitches, and I clamp down on my jaw, not willing to dissolve into tears. I'm freeing Erie. There's nothing to worry about. She won't be broken for long.

Mom puts her hand over my fist. When I lift my head, she's all mom, no psychiatrist in sight. "It's not your fault, honey. This is all your father's doing. Every last drop of it."

"But—"

She squeezes my hand. "No. Trust me. What your father did . . ." She shakes her head and pats my fist. "Just trust me. It's for the best that you're no longer at Oceanica."

"Erie would never hurt me."

Mom stands and grabs her plate. "It was never the Mer I was worried about."

When she turns her back to take the plate to the sink, I snort. "You've gotta be kidding. Aunt D's harmless. I've known her my whole life."

"She's anything but harmless." Mom lets the plate clatter into the sink, not bothering to dump the chips in the trash or put it in the dishwasher like normal. "When your father disappeared, Delmara lost her mind, and I don't think she ever got it back."

I knew Aunt D had a hard time with Dad's disappearance—he'd been her mentor, after all. Serge said the family was worried she would commit suicide for a while, when she couldn't find another Mer to prove him right. She was desperate to restore his name, and she did. She found another Mer and opened Oceanica, and now, everyone knows my father was right.

Maybe it's "Dr. Jarvis" who lost something she never got back.

"Don't worry, Mom. Delmara won't hurt me—I'm practically her son."

The expression that crosses my mother's face is a blend of shocked agony . . . gone in an instant. "I have an appointment," she says as she grabs her purse from the table. She won't meet my eye as she walks out the door.

Guess Erie's not the only one who's broken.

I don't know how I get through the next week. I can't talk to Serge, or I'll tell him everything, so I spend my nights at Mom's place and let him think I've gone home with drunk tourists. He calls a couple times to make sure I'm doing okay with the news of Erie's imminent sale, and he never once mentions my biggest fear: that the lawyers have discovered the truth.

At six a.m. on the morning of the sale, Jen and I meet Ed Hilley at a side door to the hotel, so we can get in without the front desk staff seeing us. I'm sure they have cameras, but I don't want to run into anyone in the lobby who might recognize us and wonder what we're doing here so early.

The sale is set to take place at eight, outside, under a pavilion so the "Chinese media" can record the purchase of the country's first Mer with the ocean as a background. Really, it's so I don't have to sneak into Oceanica.

"Finnegan," Hilley says as he ushers us into the room. "This is the notary who'll witness the signatures. You'll sign everything except the last page here, then Delmara will sign in the pavilion, and then you show up for the last page—but not until she signs it. And voilà—Erie is yours."

"Why can't I sign the last page here?"

"You must both be present for the last page."

I groan. That throws a major wrench in my plan. "She won't sign it if she knows it's me she's signing them over to."

Hilley points to the contract—my name is spelled in Chinese characters under every line I'm meant to sign. "She won't know it's you, and since you're there to witness her sign the last page, she won't need to be told the other signee must be present."

Did I mention Hilley's worth every penny we'll eventually pay him? I start signing. When I'm finished, I call the captain of the boat we're taking Erie and Niku home in. I'm not letting them out in the harbor for anyone to follow.

Shaun, the bartender at the Porch—and captain of our ship—is wide awake and smiling, based on the sound of his voice. "Hey man, you ready?"

My fingers twitch. "As ready as I can be. Give me the parameters of the tank again?"

Shaun chuckles, and I can hear him clomping up the stairs of the makeshift platform. We bought a four-thousand gallon tank that Niku won't even be able to turn around in, threw it on top of a rather large shrimp boat, and built a platform for it. I didn't want to keep Erie in the hold because I didn't want to keep the ocean from her any longer.

"Okay," Shaun says. "Temperature is 75° Fahrenheit, salinity 36.25, dissolved oxygen 4.7mg/L, and pH is 8."

"That's a little warm."

"So's the ocean—it's the end of summer. I pulled from the deepest water I could overnight. This is what you're getting."

"I know, sorry." It should be close enough that Erie won't be shocked by the change, at least. I can't imagine what I'd do if I got her onto the boat, only to watch her foam from shock.

"Don't worry," Shaun says. "I'm ready and waiting. See you in a couple hours."

"Thanks again." We hang up, and I gaze out the window. The boat's docked behind Oceanica, ready to load Erie, so there's nothing more I can do. My only job now is to meet Sergio so he can sneak me onto the grounds. He doesn't know I'm the buyer, but he agreed to sneak me in so I could see Erie one last time before she left. He'll be pissed when he realizes I tricked him.

Before I can start pacing, Jen pushes me into a chair and rubs my shoulders. "Relax—everything's going the way we planned."

I'm glad she sounds sure, because I'm so anxious I feel like I'm on my way to pick up my first prom date. These nerves are worse than the ones I had before the first show. In no time at all, we have to leave for Oceanica, and the butterflies in my stomach wrench up a notch.

Sergio meets me on Whitehead Street with a blue Oceanica polo, and I throw a hat on so at least my hair won't give me away. If no one looks too close, they'll assume I'm just another employee, come to work early to see the first Mer sale in Oceanica's history.

To his credit, Serge looks fucking miserable. "You ready?"

"No," I say, completely honest, and he claps me on the shoulder as we turn down Southard Street to walk through the Truman Annex to Oceanica. I've walked this street so often—through the colorful, colonial-style row homes, past the perfectly manicured gardens. It's strange knowing this will be the final time.

The crowd gathered around the pavilion doesn't give us a second glance as we maneuver to stand behind Delmara, where she sits opposite Cao. All of Oceanica's employees ring the tent, including my sister, and I pray she doesn't give me away.

Cao speaks Chinese to the "media"—some local ex-pats who agreed to be our camera people. I catch Cao's eye, and his chin dips slightly before glancing at his phone.

"Forgive me," he says and bows to Delmara. "My boss run late. He says please begin, and he will arrive soon."

Delmara glances at the notary, annoyed, and I can't blame her—but she's also desperate to get Erie out of here. She grabs the pen and starts signing where the notary tells her.

It doesn't take long for her to reach the last page. I step forward, and Serge grabs my arm. "Dude, don't. You can't stop this."

Her pen scratches her final signature, and I shake Serge off. "Sorry, man."

At my voice, Delmara turns, her surprise turning to a gloating smirk. "You're too late, Finnegan. The sale is done."

I lean over the paperwork, hand shaking as I point to the line I need to sign. "You're missing a signature here."

"Mr. Cao assures me his boss is on his way."

Cao bows. "Indeed, he has arrived."

"Good." Delmara peers around the crowd, and I grab the pen from the table and sign my name. She spins back and grabs it from my hand. "What the fuck do you think you're doing?"

My heart hammers in my chest while the notary signs and stamps the contract, making Erie mine. "I'm completing the sale. Cao, the check?"

He removes the envelope with the cashier's check for two-point-five million dollars from his jacket pocket. Delmara's face turns red as she spins from me, to Cao, to the notary, and then back to me. "You . . . no. I'm selling her to China. To—"

"Undersea Land, care of one Mr. JiaWéiSī. That's Jarvis in Chinese."

"What the fuck?" Sergio says behind me.

Delmara's eyes widen for a moment before her hands close into fists, shaking. "I refuse the sale. No sale."

"You signed the paperwork."

Her nostrils flare as she presses her lips together, staring at me with such hatred I'm a little worried about what she might do. I've never seen her this mad, not even when she fired me. She lifts her hand, and I take a step back, but she grabs her walkie-talkie instead of hitting me. "Madison?"

"Yes, ma'am?" Maddy's static-laced voice comes through the speaker.

"Foam her."

"No!" I rip the badge from Delmara's shirt and run to the employee entrance as she screams for security. I have to get to Erie before Maddy does.

Maddy says I'm being "sold" today, although I'm still not sure what that means. From what I've gathered, it means Niku and I are leaving Oceanica, but that we're not going home. Maybe there'll be fewer bubbles in "China."

The long tank they put us into the first day sits between the holding tanks, as well as the net. I stare at the limp rope as I pop bubbles.

"Thank god, we're almost rid of you," Maddy says. I agree. China has to be better than this.

"Madison," Delmara's angry voice comes through the box Maddy holds. "Foam her."

"Gladly." The grin that crawls across Maddy's face is as suffocating as an octopus tentacle. She clomps up the stairs to my platform and unhooks the shocker. This is exactly what I've been waiting for. I'm ready to die, and I'm taking her with me.

I surface in front of the platform, smiling because she'll have to come close enough for me to grab if she wants to stick the shocker in the water. She hesitates. "Back up."

I stay where I am.

"I said back up, Iodine."

"Fuck that." The words come unbidden from a broken memory.

Maddy's eyes widen at my response, then slit into an angry glare as she finds the courage to step forward. She plunges the loop into the water, and I grab the pole, yanking hard. She teeters on those stupid human legs for a moment before falling. The water buzzes with electricity, and pain seers my hands, rips through my body as the shocker does its work. It cuts off with Maddy's giant splash.

Her gasp ripples through the water around me, and I turn to find her clawing toward the surface through the mass of bubbles she's formed. I reach her with one good kick, grab her brown hair, and yank her down. She screams, bubbles rushing from her mouth with the terrible sound, but I like these bubbles. These bubbles empty her. I sink my nails into her throat and rip. The air-scream stops abruptly.

Through the ribbons of blood spreading from her open neck, I see Niku. He smiles, too.

I swim to him, pressing my hands on the glass before I wince and pull them away. Foam fizzes from my palms and fingers where I gripped the shocker. Wisps of the webbing between my fingers floats free.

"Erie!" someone yells in the hallway, and I swim to the back of the tank, peering around Maddy's body as a man rushes into the room and stops abruptly. He has skin like everyone who works here, and cropped blue hair with a fin that sticks out of his forehead.

"Oh my god," he says. "What did you do?" His voice sounds familiar—echoing from one of my crushed memories—but I don't think I've seen a landfolk with blue hair, or an extra fin sticking out of their forehead.

He takes a step forward. "Erie? It's okay, darlin'. I won't hurt you."

Erie . . . that—that's my name. How does he know my name? I swim closer as he puts his hands on the tank, but I don't recognize him. His eyes are bloodshot, with dark circles around them, and worry lines cover his face, pinching it into a grimace.

This can't be my landfolk boy; he always had a ready smile and bright eyes. This man is broken.

"Are you from China?" I whisper.

Something deep inside his eyes shatters, and when he speaks, his voice breaks. "Erie, love, it's me. It's Finn."

"Finn." The name feels like a fish in my mouth. I know I've felt that before.

Without warning, he dashes up the steps, and I flinch at the shockwave as he jumps in the water. A curtain of bubbles envelops him, and his extra fin falls off, bobbing on the surface. When the bubbles dissolve, black hair floats in place of the blue, and I remember. His skin was black the first time he did this. This is my landfolk boy.

"Finn?"

He reaches a hand out to me, and I take it, wincing at my destroyed palm. I wrap my tail around him and he puts his lips over mine, blowing warm air into my mouth and through my gills. It's been so long since I was warm. These are the bubbles I've been missing—the ones from my landfolk boy. My Finn. I close my eyes and breathe him in.

When he tries to pull away, I squeeze tighter before I remember that Finn can't breathe underwater. I shove him to the surface, where he coughs, sucking in deep breaths of air.

"Maddy said you weren't coming. I'm supposed to go to China."

"No." He puts his warm hands on either side of my face and leans his forehead against mine. "Maddy lied—I was always coming. I'm sorry it took so long."

I want to stay like this forever—his warms hands on my face, my tail wrapped around his legs. "Are you taking me to China?"

"I'm taking you home, darlin'. Back to the ocean."

The ocean? Home? I can barely picture the Seadom now, barely remember the face of my grandmother and sisters. My sister—Clair. What about Clair? Before I can ask, Delmara runs into the room, Sergio behind her, and they freeze as they take in the scene. Finn holding me. Maddy's body floating face down on the other side of the tank, tinting the water pink.

"Finnegan Jarvis," Delmara barks, and I cringe away from him. "What have you done?"

His face pales as she walks across the room and up the steps, but his voice sounds strong when he replies. "This is what happens when you torture the Mer, Aunt D. They attack people."

"So now you plan to take this Mer—who has learned to attack people—and put her back in the ocean with Mer who are already attacking people? What about the people in the ocean? What about the kids at Fort Zach?"

"Erie wouldn't attack children. She drowned Maddy in self-defense because you *told* Maddy to foam her."

Delmara grabs the cord that's still attached to the loop and pulls it to her, dragging Maddy along with it. Her limp, lifeless hand is caught in the grip. With a good yank, Delmara gets the body halfway onto the platform. Maddy's open neck is exposed, the ragged edges white and puckering, the blood gone from them. Both Finn and Sergio gasp.

"Self-defense?" Delmara says.

Finn looks at me, and fear darkens his eyes. Fear of me.

Delmara doesn't give me time to explain—not that I could. "I wonder if Carbon was acting out of self-defense, too. Have you swallowed every lie that bitch girlfriend of yours spoon-fed to you? No wonder you never came back to me. You're just like your father."

She pulls Maddy's hand from the handle and shoves her back in the water. Finn moves away from the body—and me.

"Get out of the tank, Finnegan." Delmara sticks the loop back in the water, finger hovering over the button.

"So you can shock Erie 'til she foams? I don't think so."

"APHIS rules, not mine. She attacked someone—she has to be put down."

"She's not a fucking dog." Finn's fist pounds the surface.

"No, she's a fish." Delmara takes a step closer to the edge. "Get out of the tank."

Finn's eyes slit in determination. "No."

She raises an eyebrow in disbelief. "I thought you knew how painful the electroshocker is."

Finn's face pales again. "I do. That's why I won't let you use it on her."

Before Delmara can speak, Sergio steps forward. "Aunt D, you can't use the shocker with Finn in the tank."

She's about to shock Finn—my Finn. I watched her shock Niku to get to me, and now, she'll shock Finn. I don't know what to do. I can't attack Delmara. I sink to the bottom of the tank, wrapping in my tail.

Finn's voice travels, distorted, through the water. "You won't get the insurance money if you foam her."

"I don't need it. You just gave me a check for two and a half million."

"I didn't pay for foam!" He punches the surface again, and I cover my ears, but my hands hurt too much to press them against my head.

"It's a shame you fell in the tank when Maddy shocked her," Delmara says.

Sergio runs to the stairs. "Aunt D, no. You can't."

She clutches the shocker. "It really is too bad, but accidents happen all the time. You wouldn't be the first."

"Aunt D!" Sergio yells. "Stop it!"

I swim panicked circles around the bottom of the tank, waiting for the shock. Finn struggles to face Delmara against the whirlpool I create, but I can't stop. I can't do anything. She wants to hurt my landfolk boy, and I can't stop her.

"You should have listened to me, Finnegan," Delmara yells. "No one ever listens to me. Your father didn't listen, and look what happened to him. Lost at sea, looking for the fucking Mer."

"Aunt D—" Finn's voice pleads.

"He should have taken you with him and saved me this grief. You were all I had left. All I had of him, and you betrayed me for some other woman, just like your stupid father!"

I kick hard with my healing tail and take a deep breath before the top of my head crests the surface. All three of them scream.

I spin helplessly in the water as Delmara yells crazy bullshit about my father. Then I feel a pressure change, and see a magenta blur in the corner of my eye. "Erie, no!"

Delmara screams and tries to lift the shocker to block the mermaid coming at her, but Erie's already out of the water and slams her into the wall. They tumble sideways, roll down several steps, and slip through the railing, falling the rest of the way to the cement floor with a sickening thud.

"Aunt D!" Sergio yells.

"Erie!" I scream and pull myself from the tank. Erie rolls off Delmara, water seeping through her gills to mix with the growing puddle of blood on the ground.

I run down the stairs as Sergio presses one hand to the back of his aunt's head and the other to her neck. "She's still alive. Call an ambulance."

"Call your own ambulance—she tried to kill me." I'm more concerned about Erie right now. I kneel next to her and touch her face. She cracks her eyes open, but she can't speak because she's holding her breath.

"It's okay, darlin'. I've got you." I shove one arm under her shoulders and the other under her tail, and grunt as I try to stand. Holy fuck, is she heavy. There's no way I can climb the stairs with her.

"Hold on to me," I say. She digs her claws into my shoulders, which doesn't help, but does let me use one arm to grab on to the railing of the stairs and leverage her up. Her tail drags across the floor as I stumble toward the transport tank and dump her in. She claws my shoulders as she gasps water.

"Erie." I wrap my hands around her wrists. "You need to let go."

She releases me as if I've shocked her, and I turn to survey the scene. Sergio's on the walkie-talkie, calling for an ambulance. Maddy floats face down in the tank. Niku stares at us from the other tank, and I think he's finally smiling. Not for long—I don't have time to get him out now. Not with an ambulance on the way for Delmara—they'll euthanize Erie for sure.

"Serge, call Munchkin down. I need help with the tank."

"My aunt is fucking dying!"

"It's her own goddamn fault! Get Heather on the radio—now!"

He hunches his shoulders and grabs the radio again. I reach into the tank and run my hand over Erie's hair. "I'll be right back, okay, darlin'? I have to open the door so we can get you out of here."

She grabs my wrist and winces. "Don't leave me."

"Only for a second, love—I need help to move the tank. I promise I'll be right back. You believe me, don't you?"

Her wide eyes bore into mine for a moment before she nods. I brush my thumb over her cheek before I head to the "restricted area" door to let Heather in.

"Finn." The surprise in her voice is clear when she sees me. "You're soaking wet."

"I need you to help with the transport—and don't freak out at what you see."

Heather shoots me a suspicious glare that falls right off her face as she walks into the room. "Oh my god." She puts a hand over her mouth as her eyes widen. "What happened?"

She's about to freak out, so I grab her arms to make her focus on me. "Maddy tried to kill Erie, and Delmara tried to kill me, so Erie attacked both of them. It was self-defense, okay?"

She peers out of the corner of her eye at Sergio, who has his hand pressed to the back of Aunt D's head. "The ambulance is on the way," he says.

Heather leans back and gapes at Erie with wide eyes. "Is it safe to go near her?"

I drag her to the transport tank. "Munchkin, this is Erie. Erie, this is my sister, Heather."

Erie glances between us. "You never told me you had a sister."

"I thought it would upset you." I turn my back on her to show Heather how to power the transport. I steer; I have more experience trying to maneuver this thing around corners.

"Finn," Erie says as we get into the hallway. "What about Niku? He's supposed to come to China, too."

"You aren't going to China, remember? You're going home."

She grabs my hand, winces, then pulls away and waves it through the water. "But—is Niku going to China?"

We don't have time for this right now. "Niku's going home, too. I'll come back for him. Right now, I have to get you out of here before the cops show up."

"He's not coming with us?" A note of panic tinges her voice, but I can't console her right now. I'm trying to steer the transport around a corner.

"Erie, listen to me—they won't hurt Niku. I'll come back in two days and release him, but he has to stay here for now."

"No!" She thrashes in the tank, spilling water everywhere. "We have to go back. We have to save Neek. Niku!"

She starts yelling Mer words, and it breaks my heart. It's just like the first time we separated them, but we can't go back. By the time we reach the outside door, she's reduced to sobbing loudly, foam streaming from her eyes. I repeat over and over to myself that she'll be okay soon. We'll have them both home soon.

I open the door and nearly run into Jen and Hilley.

"What the hell is going on?" she says. "EMTs just rushed through the front door."

"No time to explain. Tell Shaun to start the boat." When she doesn't move right away, I yell. "Now!"

Jen runs to the boat, her backpack bumping against her side. We follow with the tank, faster now that we don't have corners and doorways to contend with.

"So," Hilley says as he follows us. "You want to tell your lawyer what the rush and emergency vehicles are for?"

I look him straight in the eye. "It was self-defense. I'll explain in two days."

We reach the dock, and I power on the crane. Luckily, the net's already draped over the bottom of the transport, so I don't have to try to get it under Erie. "Sorry, darlin'." I grab one edge, pulling it out of the water to hook up to the crane. "Heather, get the other side."

The blood drains from her face. "You mean, stick my hand in there with your murderous mermaid?"

"Just do it!"

Erie grabs at me as Heather sticks her hand in the water up to her shoulder. "Not the net, Finn. Please."

"We don't have time to get anything else." I bought a dolphin transport stretcher, but it's on the boat. Heather hands me the other side of the net to hook up, and once it's on, I kneel next to Erie.

"Hold your breath, love. Jen's up there waiting for you. I'll be there in a moment." I give her cheek a quick caress, then run to the controls. "Heather, make sure the net pulls up smooth," I yell as I hit the button to start the crane.

The extra netting slides from the tank, then goes taut. Erie whimpers before it pulls her from the water, raining drops as she moves higher and higher. Once she's high enough, Jen sticks her head over the side of the boat. "You're good!"

I move the net sideways—probably a little faster than I should—until she holds up her hand. Erie swings back and forth over the tank until Jen runs up the platform and grabs the net, almost falling into the tank as it swings back the other way. I hit the button to lower it, and once Erie's in the water, I release the rest of the net with a splash.

"Gotta go, Munchkin. Good luck."

"Be safe, Finn!" she yells as I run up the ramp to the boat.

I wave to her and yell at Shaun. "Go! Now!" We pull away from the dock as police run out of the employee entrance. They swarm Heather, pointing at the boat and yelling for us to stop. Fuck that—I'm not stopping until Erie's safe.

The net splashes around me, pushing me into the warm water, but it's not as heavy as the one I was caught in. The raw flesh on my hands screams as I grab it and force my way out, slithering my tail through the opening before I turn and see . . .

Ocean.

By the Tides, the ocean is so close. Blue water stretches away forever past the building we just came from. The front of the boat blocks it, but I can see water on the other side, too, though it ends in more ships and buildings.

"Finn!" I yell, and he rushes over, eyes wide and wild.

"What? What's wrong?"

I press my hands to the glass, ignoring the pain, and let the blue fill my sight. "It's the ocean."

His shoulders sag. "I know."

The boat moves past the building—past the land. Finn leans against the tank before sinking to the ground, his wet skin leaving a smear on the glass. Jen stands next to him and puts her hand on the tank, smiling. "Hello, Erie."

"Hello, Jen." It's been a long time since I've smiled, and it feels unnatural, but the corners of my mouth turn up. I put my hand over hers, and I can see the ocean between our fingers.

"What happened to your hands?" she asks.

"I grabbed the shocker." And then I grabbed Maddy's throat.

"Why did you do that?" she says. "Those wounds look brand new."

"They are."

Before I can say any more, Finn grabs Jen's hand. "Leave it for now, please." I can't see his face, but he sounds exhausted.

He runs his thumb over the back of her hand and the old, familiar jealousy grips my chest because I want to feel that warm touch so bad. "Finn?"

He tilts his head back so he can see me. "Yeah, darlin'?"

"Can we swim?"

A tired smile spreads over his face, warming me from the inside. "Absolutely."

"Your swim trunks are in my bag," Jen says, but Finn shakes his head as he stands.

"I'm already soaked."

He grabs the blue skin at his waist and yanks it over his head. I scream. I know he can change skins, but I've never actually seen him do it and didn't realize it would be so violent. I thought he just changed color, like a cuttlefish.

His eyes search the area, wide and fearful. "What the hell was that? What's wrong?"

I point a shaking hand at his blue skin. "You . . . you ripped your skin off!"

He gapes at me for a moment before laughter bubbles from his lips. "It's a shirt. It's not my skin." It ripples in the wind as he holds it up, his shoulders shaking with mirth. "It's fabric. Here, I'll show you."

Finn runs up the stairs to the platform and slips into the water, holding his blue skin out for me. It feels different than his palm or his black skin—rougher.

"See?" he says, as I inspect the holes that are impossibly devoid of blood. "It's a shirt. You put your head through this hole, and your arms through these. Come here."

He takes the "shirt" from me and scrunches it up so his hands are holding it through the top and bottom holes. When he lowers it over my head, I freeze. Finn's putting his skin on me.

"Give me your arm." He guides one of my arms through a hole on the side, then does the same for the other. He pulls the rest of the skin down until it rests just below my waist. Part of it sticks to my scales—the rest floats free in the water. I shudder. I'm wearing Finn's skin.

"See? Just a shirt."

I sink below the surface, but the bottom floats up to my armpits. Jen giggles on the other side of the glass. I bet she's never worn Finn's skin.

"Try swimming," he says, and when I do, the skin unfurls again to stick to my sides. I scream in glee and spin around the tank. When I surface, he runs a thumb over my cheek. "You can keep it."

"Really?" I suck in a breath and finger it, though the roughness hurts my raw hands. This is the first skin Finn wore with me.

"Really."

I sink below the surface again to study the skin, then glance at his chest—now the same color as his arms and face. I run a finger over his new skin. It's soft and smooth, and his stomach twitches as he laughs. I swim a circle around him, trailing my sore fingertips across the smooth skin. The skin on his legs is rougher, like the "shirt," and I follow it up one side of his leg to where it ends. I trace this strange, abrupt transition between "fabric" and skin until he grabs my wrist and pulls me to the surface.

He chuckles. "I'd like to keep my pants on for now."

A blush blooms across his cheeks, and my chest constricts. I don't want to leave him. Not even the beauty of the Seadom compares to Finn.

"Can we go back?" I whisper.

"Back?" The mirth drops from his face. "Back to Oceanica?"

I nod, and he runs a finger over my cheek. I don't want to lose this warm touch. I don't want to go home and forget about him.

"We can't go back. You killed Maddy, and probably Delmara—they'll kill you if we go back."

I swallow. "I don't want to leave you."

Finn pulls me to him, and his warmth seeps through the shirt. He wraps his arms around me, and I wind my tail around his legs, press my face into his chest. This is what I want the rest of my life to be—Finn and me, wound up so tight it's hard to tell where merfolk stops and landfolk begins.

He strokes my hair, whispering that everything will be okay. That I'll be home, with my family, and I don't have to perform anymore, but I would perform every day as long as he was there.

"Don't worry, love." He kisses the top of my head. "You've got me for the next twenty-four hours."

Twenty-four hours, and then I lose Finn forever.

I hug Erie until she finally pulls away. My fingers are prunes, my muscles too tired to tread water much longer, but this is the last day I'll see her, and I don't want to leave the tank.

Key West has disappeared over the horizon—we're in international waters now. Which means, we won. We saved Erie. And once we put her back in the ocean where we found her, I'll never see her again. Ever. I have twenty-four hours with the most beautiful creature on the planet, and, knowing that, I can't seem to pull myself away from her.

Erie doesn't move far—not that she could with the size of the tank. She keeps constant contact with either her fingers or her fins. I'd take her hand if it wasn't so obviously painful for her. Instead, I let her touch me, and run my hand through her hair whenever it's near.

Jen leans against the glass, sometimes staring at the water, sometimes at Erie. Whenever she catches my eye, she smiles. The knife of guilt in my stomach twists every time. I'm sending Erie home with no one. Not even Niku.

Eventually, my stomach makes a noise. I have no idea what time it is, but it must be late afternoon. "Are you hungry, darlin'?"

"Hungry . . ." The way she says it makes me think she hasn't felt anything—even hunger—in a long time. Her brows pull together as she concentrates, then shakes her head. "No. I don't think I'm hungry."

Of course—we've had her on an unnatural schedule all summer. She won't be hungry until the sun goes down. Again, guilt twists my stomach, and I pull her to me, kissing her hair. "I'm getting out for a bit, but I'll be back soon, okay?"

Her claws dig into me even as she nods. I kiss her hair again before I finally pull myself from the tank. My pants are heavy and water pours from me until I let them drop. At least Erie doesn't scream this time.

Jen hands me a towel, and I head to the cabin to change out of my soaking wet underwear and into my swim trunks. Even this feels like too much time away. I'm wasting minutes I don't have after tomorrow morning. I don't know how to let Erie go.

Jen wraps her fingers around my wrist when I come out. "You okay? Erie told me what happened."

I don't want to think of Maddy's body floating face down in the tank—of the horror I felt when I saw her neck, ripped into shreds. Of Delmara's crazy talk, or the fact that my "Aunt D" was willing to kill me. Of the sickening thud when she hit the cement floor. What the hell did my father do to make her snap like that? That thud will haunt my nightmares forever.

"Yeah, I'll be fine." I squeeze Jen's arm without realizing it, then release her and pat her arm instead. Maybe, once Erie's home, things will return to normal between Jen and me, but for now, I have one priority, and her deep magenta eyes are staring at me through the glass.

I spend half the day in the tank, half on the other side of the glass. As the sun goes down, all three of us watch the golden sky in silence. We'll reach the area where the fishermen caught Erie by sunrise, and then I have to let her go.

She curls up on the bottom of the tank, pressed against the glass, and I lay down on the other side, my hand over hers. "I love you, darlin'," I whisper when she closes her eyes.

The corners of her lips turn up, though she keeps her eyes closed tight. "I love you, too, Finn."

It's bright on the other side of my eyelids, and the constant hum of the tank is gone, replaced by . . . ocean. I open my eyes to morning sunlight and Finn's back pressed against the other side of the glass.

When I unwind, I see Jen, too. His arm is wrapped around her, and their legs are tangled together. My heart aches with the knowledge that they will go home together, and I will go home alone. I have no one, not even Niku.

"Finn," I whisper. He doesn't move. I want to wake him without waking Jen, so I can have him to myself for a little while, but with as tight as they're wound up, it'll probably be impossible. I swim to the surface. The ocean stretches out on all sides, waves lapping gently at the hull of the boat. We've stopped moving.

I hold my hand over the edge of the tank so water droplets fall on Finn's face, but he brushes them off and curls tighter around Jen. We might still have some time before "twenty-four hours" pass, but I've already lost him. I curl up as close to him as I can as foam leaks from my eyes.

Eventually, Finn turns over in his sleep and smacks his forehead on the glass. He jerks in surprise and rubs his face with a hand before his eyes focus on mine. "Erie," he breathes, turning my name into air. "Why are you crying?"

His thumb brushes across the glass, and the foam comes faster. I don't wipe it away, pretending instead that his hand is doing so on the other side of the glass. "The boat stopped moving."

Finn sits up and gazes at the water before turning back to me. "That means you're home."

"No." I shake my head, because where they caught me wasn't home. "I want to go home with you. Please don't leave me here. This isn't my home."

His throat moves as he swallows. "I'm sorry, sweet. This is where we have to say goodbye."

The sob that escapes me wakes Jen. "Morning, Erie," she says as she rubs her face. "Morning . . ."

Niku. She was about to say Niku, like normal, but Niku's back at Oceanica with the landfolk. Where I should be.

"Take me back." I push my hands into the glass despite the pain. "Take me back to Niku. Take me home!"

Finn puts his hands over mine, but the glass steals his warmth. "I'll let Niku go tomorrow—he'll be home in a few days."

"Please, Finn. Please don't leave me here alone."

"I already told you—"

"No!" I back up to the middle of the tank and cross my arms. "I'm not going. Take me home."

"Erie." Finn's voice breaks as tears glisten in his eyes. Jen touches his shoulder, but he shrugs her off and walks to the platform. He slips into the water, and I surface, but don't swim to him.

"Erie," he says again. "I promised I would get you out of Oceanica—back to the ocean. Back home. I *promised* you."

I remember when that promise was everything—before it turned into bubbles and was twisted by Delmara. I lived for that promise once, but now, I only want Finn.

His shirt clings to me as I swim close enough for his outstretched hand to run through my hair. I wrap my tail around him and pull him under. I run my nails over his face, over the smooth skin on his neck, his shoulders. When my nails dig into his skin, a few bubbles escape his nose, but he doesn't resist.

Foam seeps from my eyes, and he brushes it away with his warm thumbs. I release him and swim to the edge of the tank, staring at the water as I hear him surface and take a deep breath. He promised me the ocean. He's giving me the ocean. This is what I asked of him, and this is what I'm getting.

"Erie?"

I bury my face in his chest as he wraps his arms around me. He smooths my hair and kisses my forehead. "I'm sorry, darlin'. It's time."

I squeeze him tighter.

"Jen," he says. "Get the transport?"

With my face buried in his skin, I can't see Jen, but I hear the grinding motor of the crane and feel the change in the water as she lowers in the transport. My nails dig into his back as I hide from what's about to happen.

Finn holds me for a moment, his lips pressed to the top of my head. "It's time."

I swallow my tears, but I can't make myself let go. I take a deep breath, then another, and finally unwind my tail and slip away. He swims to the "transport" in the water and pulls it taut. It's not a net, but a solid piece of blue with two large holes in the sides.

"It's made for dolphins," he says as I inspect it. "They haven't made one for Mer, because no one's tried to transport a Mer yet."

"None of the others have returned." I swallow again as the realization sinks in. "I'll be the first."

I'll be the one who tells them what boats *mean*. What happens when the merfolk are caught. Why we never return. "My mother—she was the first to disappear. Delmara said . . . she said your father . . . he . . ."

Finn pulls me close. "I'm sorry, Erie. I'm sorry my father discovered the Mer. I'm sorry Delmara went looking to prove him right. I'm sorry for my part—"

I squeeze him. "I'm not. I wouldn't have met you."

The tears that have been turning his eyes to pools finally spill over, running down his cheeks to mix with the salty water of the tank. He puts his lips over mine and warm bubbles fizz in my gills, filling my mouth with Finn. I close my eyes, savor him until he pulls away.

"How . . . ?" I turn away from the anguish on his face and grab the transport. "How does it work?"

"Like the shirt," he says. "I'll hold it in the water, and you swim into it. You can put your arms through the holes on the sides. Then we'll lift you up and lower you into the ocean."

This is it, then. Time to do what no other merfolk has done. My voice shakes when I reply. "Just like that."

"Just like that," he echoes and holds the transport open. I swim into it like he said, put my arms through the holes, and wait. He runs a hand over my hair. "Hold your breath."

The transport jerks, and I almost scream like I did in the net. Instead, I close my eyes and take a deep breath as it cradles me. It doesn't hurt like the net did, but the feeling of being lifted into the air still makes the panic in my stomach peak. The entire thing swings to the side, and I squeeze my eyes shut harder. When I feel it lowering, I squint my eyes open.

The dark blue of the deep water kisses my fingertips as I reach for it, then whispers against the tip of my tail. The transport floats a bit as it hits the surface, but I wiggle out of it and slip into the ocean's embrace. It hums with life as I kick deeper, spinning in the water, reveling in the constant pressure of its hug.

Schools of fish flash in the distance—I can smell them. Their life. The blood pumping through their veins. The juicy flesh just beneath their scales. I run my tongue over my teeth at the thought of biting into a freshly caught fish.

A small splash sounds somewhere far behind me, at the surface. I've already gone deep enough that the surface is just a ripple of light over the waves, the boat a shadow.

I turn away from it and float in the depths, letting the ocean fill my senses. The smell of the fish, the popping of the shrimp, the rainbows of light refracting through the waves. I rip Finn's shirt off the way he did and spin so I can feel the warm water on every scale, over every scar. Even my hands hurt less than before. I close my eyes and take a deep breath—home. I'm home. And I'm never leaving the ocean again.

Chapter 65: Finn

As soon as the transport hits the water, Erie pulls herself free and dives. Jen and I watch her magenta hair disappear into the depths, and when she doesn't return, my knuckles go white on the railing. "Erie?"

Jen puts her hand over mine, but I find no comfort in her touch. "No," I whisper. "I wasn't ready yet."

"Finn, she's gone."

"No." I climb over the railing and jump in next to the transport. Erie will come back to say goodbye. She has to.

I stick my face in the water and open my eyes, but I can't see anything in the shadows. "Erie!" I scream into the depths. After a moment, something blue floats toward me. My heart jumps into my throat, but it's just my shirt. She took off my shirt and let it go.

"Finn?" Jen's worried voice travels down to me.

"It . . . it's my shirt." My voice breaks as I hold it up. "Erie's gone."

"I'm sorry," Jen says. "Get in the transport, and I'll bring you up."

I've already floated several feet from the boat. I start to swim toward the transport when a cold hand wraps around my ankle and yanks me under. Erie's face hovers before me as I cough and choke.

"Sorry," she says and pushes me to the surface. When she speaks again, it's in excited Mer words I don't understand. Her eyes are wider and brighter than I've ever seen them.

Releasing the shirt in my hand, I stop her chatter with a kiss. Not a breath of air through her gills, but a simple kiss. She stops gesturing and stares at me, her eyes dimming.

"You're going." It's not a question.

"I am." I caress her cheek with my thumb. "Do you know how to find your family from here?"

She closes her eyes and takes a deep breath, then turns her face to the north. "I do."

"Good." I turn her face back to me, and she opens her eyes. "Listen to me—this is very important. You're mine now—"

"I've always been yours," she says and runs her fingertips over my cheek.

I move my face into her hand and close my eyes—I don't want this touch to end. "I mean legally. If you're caught by another boat, you tell them who you are, tell them to call me." I open my eyes and focus on hers. "Finnegan Jarvis, can you remember that?"

"Finnegan Jarvis," she echoes, her fingers still tracing my cheek.

"That's right. Stay away from boats, but if you're caught, you tell them you belong to Finnegan Jarvis, and I'll come get you." The horrible, selfish part of me will forever hope it's a fisherman every time my phone rings.

She glances at the boat, and I turn her face back to me again. "Don't you go chasing boats just to see me. They'll have nets, and I may not be able to come get you right away. You understand?"

A small frown mars her face. "I understand. I won't go after boats."

"Good." I'm delaying the inevitable now, and I know it, but I'll never see her again. Never get lost in the depths of her eyes.

Now that she's back in the ocean, her eyes are endless. I brush my fingers over her face, touching every ridge, before I run my hands into her hair.

I can't do it. I can't leave her. My throat constricts and burns like I'm drowning—I can't get enough air. "Erie . . ." There's nothing left to say, though.

She pulls me into the water and hugs me. I hold her until I need air. When I surface, Jen and Shaun are peering over the railing—it's time to go.

"Niku will be home in a few days, okay?"

Her chin dips.

"And don't forget who to call if you're captured again."

"Finnegan Jarvis."

I put my hands on either side of her face and stare deep into her eyes. "Don't forget who loves you more than anything else in this world."

Erie smiles, albeit sadly, and whispers, "Finnegan Jarvis."

"That's right, beautiful. Don't ever forget that." I kiss her forehead once more, softly, before I release her. She unwinds her tail from my legs and kicks back, but not far. I could grab her again if I wanted to, but I keep my hands to myself and turn my back on her. She stays where she is while I climb into the transport.

It moves, and I hold on tight, staring at Erie the whole time. When it's even with the ship, I grab Jen and Shaun's hands and let them pull me on board. Erie's still in the same place—frozen like a statue.

"Goodbye, Erie," I say as I grip the railing to keep myself from jumping back in, from being lost at sea like my father.

She speaks the ocean back to me, and I imagine it's goodbye in Mer words.

As the boat motor starts, she dives below the surface, and as we pull away, she jumps, then jumps again.

Jen squeezes my hand. "She's doing her routine."

I swallow because I already know. Erie sends us off with her routine, and at the moment I should have jumped in, I squeeze Jen's hand hard and my tears start to fall. I don't think I'll ever be dry-eyed again.

I swim and jump and dance until I can't hear the motor anymore and the boat is just a speck in the distance. Then I float in the bubbles I created while foam streams from my eyes. Finn is gone. The only thing left to do is go home.

I turn north, feeling the pull of the current to find my way. I follow that pull, keeping an eye out for sharks who may have heard me splashing. My stomach rumbles, but between the boat and my routine, the fish have scattered, and I don't feel like expending the energy to hunt. I'm not even sure I could catch a fish with my burned hands and split tail.

The journey back takes all day, and the trip is lonely. By the time I see the long shadows of the petrified forest, I feel empty. I don't know if the Seadom survived. What if they weren't able to hunt? What if they starved? All day, I've tortured myself with these thoughts.

Before I reach the forest, though, I hear the first "Halt!" I stop and wait for the guard to swim to me.

"It can't be," he says as he nears. "Princess Erie?"

Princess—I haven't heard that since I left Niku's tank for the last time. My heart contracts at the thought and foam bubbles from my eyes.

He gasps. "Princess, you're dying! What can I do?"

I wipe at the foam, and his eyes widen. "I'm fine," I say, "just *crying*." Then I realize that he won't know what *crying* is. "I'm not dying. I just want to go home."

He still seems suspicious, though the foam has stopped. His training to never question a royal wins out, and he dips his nose. "Of course. I'll see you safely home."

The gray of the forest isn't as foreboding as I once thought it was. It's a natural gray, the last rays of the sun combing through its branches. It's not the sterile, doom-filled gray of the holding tanks where Niku waits. He'll be home soon. Finn promised.

When the forest clears, I get my first view of the Seadom since the hunt. The dazzling colors hurt my eyes, even in the dusk, and my breath catches in my throat. I stop swimming, wishing desperately that Finn could see this. The stunning beauty of my home.

The guard turns when he realizes I'm not following. "Princess?"

I swallow. "Forgive me. It's been so long." I'm not sure how long—Finn spoke in hours and months, but I never learned how to count those.

"Too long. Please, let me get you safe inside." He swims again, slowly, until I catch up. It's almost full dark when we reach the castle, and the guards at the door gape as we enter.

"Is that really the princess?" one asks the other as we swim past. I don't hear the reply.

The guard stops at my door, where Niku should be waiting. "I'll get your father."

"And my grandmother, please."

He leaves to find my family as I swim into the room lit by phosphorescent organisms. It's nearly the same size as the tank. I sweep my fingertips over the button polyps in the window that are the same color as one of the necklaces Finn gave me. Maddy took the necklaces, but I have Finn's skin. I grabbed it from the surface before I swam home.

I lay it on the bed, then sit next to it and sigh at the softness beneath me. It's been too long since I've felt something soft. I want to curl up on it and bury my face in Finn's shirt, but the pressure changes, and a silver ghost appears in my doorway.

"Erie?" Grandmother's voice is whispery compared to the last time we spoke, almost air.

I swim to her as she enters the room and holds her arms out. Her voice may be weak, but her grip is strong.

"Oh, my sweet minnow." She pets my hair, then holds me away from her and looks me over with growing unease. One of her nails follows the scar around my neck. "My dear, what did they do to you?"

I touch the scar, and my grandmother gasps and grabs my hand, making me wince. "Erie," she breathes, "your hands."

They're red and raw on the palms, with bloody lines where the webbing foamed away. My lip quivers. I have landfolk fingers.

My father's voice travels down the hallway. "Erie?" He rushes into the room, and Grandmother folds my hands in hers so they're not visible. Father stops short, the wave of pressure making me close my eyes for a moment.

"By all the Tides," he says. "You . . . look at you."

The way he says it makes me want to hide my scars, every last one of them. I tuck my split tail behind me, and Grandmother keeps my hands tucked out of view between hers, but the scars around my neck and on my forehead are still fully visible. Father doesn't look much better, though. The imposing king is gone—he's as tired and broken as Finn was.

"Hello, Father." I bow my head.

In one kick, he crosses the room and gathers me in his arms. I freeze for a moment, surprised, then throw my arms around him, too. Foam streams from my eyes.

"Oh, my sweet princess," he says, smoothing his giant hand over my hair. "I thought I'd lost you forever."

This is the first time my father has said anything kind to me since my mother disappeared, and I curl into his embrace. Eventually, he pulls away and cups my face in his hands. His eyes hold the storm I remember. "I will tear the land apart to find who did this to you, and I will destroy them."

I put my hands over his. "It's okay, Father. I already killed them."

The storm dims, and his hands drop to my shoulders. "You? You killed the landfolk?"

"Two of them." I glance at my grandmother, whose silver eyes are as shocked as my father's. "The two who hurt me the most."

Father releases me and glances around the room in disbelief. "And what of Niku? Reports said he was captured with you."

My heart constricts, making it hard to speak. "Niku will be home in a few days. Finn didn't have time to get him out because of the landfolk I killed, but he promised he'd free Niku tomorrow."

"Finn?" Grandmother says. My heart lurches again.

"The landfolk man who saved me."

Grandmother pulls me to the bed and makes me sit. "Tell us everything," she says and runs her nails through my hair.

The only part I leave out is how much I love Finn.

Chapter 67: Finn

I watch Erie jump until I can't see her anymore, then watch the horizon, feeling dead inside. No amount of comfort will heal this wound. Jen must realize it; she squeezes my hand and goes into the cabin, leaving me with the water.

The coast guard is waiting when we reach American waters, and they escort us back to the harbor. A police car waits in the parking lot.

"Finnegan Jarvis?" the officer says.

"That's me." I jump onto the dock. I went through all that trouble to free Erie legally and she undid it with one rake of her claws.

"I need you to come to the station for questioning."

"Am I under arrest?"

"Not at this point. We just want to make sure we have all the facts straight."

I turn to Shaun. "Thanks for your help, man." I shake his hand before turning to Jen. "I'll call you after."

"Good luck."

She squeezes my arm, and I get into the cop's car. At the station, he takes me into a questioning room and grabs a cheap paper cup full of coffee.

"Thanks," I say. "I haven't slept much lately." My hands are jittery as I lift the cup to my mouth. He waits for me to take a sip before he sits and opens a notebook.

"We've watched the security footage, but there's no sound. I'd like to know what happened in your own words."

I tell him everything I can remember, and he starts writing, occasionally questioning me for clarity. By the time I'm done, I've had two cups of coffee and need to pee.

"Well," he says at the end. "Your story matches Mr. de la Cruz's, and it's clear you didn't have a hand in Mrs. de la Cruz's death—"

"Aunt D's dead?" A whole fistful of emotions punch me in the chest. *Aunt D.* She was my mentor, my "aunt," my . . . my everything, until Erie. Everything I've done for the past six years has been for her and my father. I mean, yeah, she was about to shock and drown me, but . . . I still can't believe she would have actually done it.

"Are you okay, Mr. Jarvis?"

"No." I rub my face, wishing the coffee had been spiked. "I just . . . I haven't had time to process what happened yet, and now . . ."

"I understand."

I can't believe Erie killed Aunt D. Corporate. Who'll take over Oceanica? "What . . . what does this mean for the rest of the Mer?"

He taps his pen on the notebook. "I have no information about that."

Fuck. I'll have to ask Sergio, and I really don't want to. "Are we done, then? I could use a beer and a good night's sleep."

"Of course." He stands and opens the door behind him. "We'll call you if we have any other questions."

I shake his hand and call Jen. When she arrives, the bag of necklaces is sitting on the passenger seat. I had no time to give them to Erie.

• • • •

JEN STOPS THE CAR IN front of my house. "You want me to come in?"

"I need to talk to Serge," I say, though really, I just need some time to myself. I haven't told her about Delmara yet. "You want to help me get Niku tomorrow?"

"Of course."

The TV is on when I walk in. Serge sits on the couch next to the door, beer in hand, but I don't think he's actually watching it because the local news is on. We never watch the news.

"Hey, man." I shut the door behind me and stand awkwardly next to the couch. "The cops told me about Aunt D. I'm so sorry."

Sergio sets his beer on the coffee table and stands. His eyes are red-rimmed, his face blotchy from crying. His fists are clenched like he wants to punch me.

"Serge, I—"

Before I can apologize again, he does punch me. Pain flares through my jaw and my head snaps to the side.

"Fuck!" I throw my arm up to block any further threats, but his fists are back at his sides as he yells.

"This is all your fault! My aunt is dead because of you!"

"She was going to kill me!"

"You fucking deserved it!"

I step back, the door handle digging into my spine. "You don't mean that."

He's shaking with rage, and I think, at this moment, maybe he does mean it.

"Do you know how many lives you've ruined to save a fucking fish? How many you're about to ruin when you shut down Oceanica?"

"Whoa." I hold my hands up in surrender, the bag of necklaces still dangling from one. "I just wanted to get Erie out. It's over, dude. I'm done with Oceanica."

He stares at me, chest heaving, before he leans back and shakes his head. "You stupid motherfucker. You don't even know, do you?"

I slowly lower my hands. "Know what?"

"Fuck." He sighs and drops onto the couch like all his muscles gave out at once. "I figured you knew." He grabs the beer and chugs it.

"Knew *what*?"

Sergio stares at the empty beer bottle, shaking his head. "Aunt D never changed her will after she fired you. Oceanica is yours." The bag of necklaces slips from my slack fingers. Holy shit—I had no idea I was even in Aunt D's will, much less the recipient of her half of Oceanica. No wonder she was so pissed I chose Erie over her. Guilt squeezes my chest until it's hard to breathe. "I . . . I didn't know."

We're both silent for a long moment before I collect the bag from the floor, deposit it on the kitchen counter, and grab a beer from the fridge. I take a swig, then grab another and take it to Serge before dropping onto the other side of the couch.

"You didn't actually think I'd kill Aunt D to get control of Oceanica, did you?"

"No." Sergio's shoulders sag. "There's no way you could have set that all up. I'm still pissed you didn't tell me you were the buyer, though. I would've stayed inside with Erie."

"I wouldn't have made it past the guards without you."

"Then I would've put someone else in the room."

"Which would have been suspicious." I take another sip. "I'm sorry, man. I had to play this one close."

Serge faces me, hands gripping his knees so hard his knuckles are white. "At the very least, I would have grabbed Aunt D's radio so she couldn't tell Maddy to foam Erie. Then no one would be dead."

I swallow hard, because he's got me there. "I'm sorry. I should have told you. I was just . . . too worried someone would find out. Erie means everything to me. I couldn't let it spill."

He watches me a moment, jaw clenched, then makes a physical effort to release his hands. His face is still red, but I bet mine is, too.

"Well." He takes a deep breath. "I hope Erie's safe, at least."

Even just hearing her name makes my heart break all over again. "Home by now, I hope."

There's another long, awkward silence as we both drink our beer and stare into space, mulling over what happened. Sergio is the one who breaks it.

"So, now that Oceanica belongs to you, what are you going to do, *boss*?"

What *am* I going to do? I now own the controlling stake of Oceanica, which means the other shareholders can't outvote me. They can sue the shit out of me, but ultimately, Oceanica's fate is in my hands.

"You know what I'm going to do."

Serge sighs and drinks the rest of his beer.

"Clair, Huron, and Niku first."

He slaps his forehead. "Fuck! Niku."

"What do you mean, 'Fuck. Niku?'"

"With everything that happened, I forgot about him. I don't think he's been fed in two days."

Dealing with a grumpy, ill-fed Niku isn't going to be fun. I drink the rest of my beer and stand. "We'll get him tomorrow." I take the bag of necklaces to my room and try my best to keep worried thoughts of Erie at bay while I fall asleep.

Chapter 68: Finn

We don't free Niku or the Mer the next day. Instead, Hilley accompanies me to the lawyer's office, where I sign the paperwork to take over Oceanica. It's a mountain—even more than the stack I had to sign for the foundation—and after that, there wasn't time to take the boat out. Instead, I call Serge to meet Jen and me at Oceanica.

I expect to see Maddy, like usual, but Maddy's dead, and everyone else looks at me as if I'm as dangerous as the Mer. But when we enter the door to the holding tanks and the dank humidity greets me, it feels like home. The tanks look so much smaller now that I haven't been here every day, and I place my hand on the glass of Erie's tank for a moment as memories course through me.

Next, I go to Niku. He looks a bit more alert than the last time I saw him, and he swims to the edge of the tank. "Hey, buddy. We're getting you out of here tomorrow, 'kay? Erie's already back home."

Neek nods that he understands, since I can't hear him if I'm not in the water.

"Let's go see who's left."

As we walk into Clair's room, the first thing I see is her bright red hair. Her red eyes narrow when she sees me. "Hello, Clair," I say to her, then turn to the blue-haired Mer in the tank with her. "Huron."

Huron looks like shit—he's so thin, I can't believe he's still alive. His expression is . . . well, expressionless. There's no life in his eyes. I can't believe he hasn't foamed yet.

They don't know English, but I speak to them anyway. "You're going home tomorrow. Erie's already there waiting for you, so just hang on for one more day, okay?"

At Erie's name, Clair's eyes narrow further, but Huron doesn't react at all. I'm not sure he's going to make it back to the Seadom, but if the shock of switching tanks doesn't kill him, at least he'll die in the ocean, and not in this gray room.

"Where's Radon?" Jen asks. I was so focused on Clair and Huron, I didn't even realize the orange-haired merman was gone.

"K killed him," Sergio says. "He became aggressive to Argon when they stopped performing, and she ripped his gills out."

"Damn," Jen says, but I'm not surprised. To be honest, releasing Clair is probably a horrible idea, but hopefully, Erie will be able to temper her aggressiveness.

"We'll be back for you tomorrow," I say to the pair and turn away. "Let's go see the others."

No one else has died since Oceanica shut down, which leaves us with seven Mer to release. Three days of trips, and it'll be done. We head upstairs to Delmara's office—my office now—and I grab my old badge so I can get into Oceanica without Serge's help. I give Jen her old badge, too.

"All right, I'm going to take the boat out to fill up. I'll need the transport tank and the cranes ready in the morning."

Serge looks at Jen, who shakes her head. "I'm not an employee—I'm going with Finn."

"Ugh, fine," Sergio says. "You really suck as a boss, you know that?"

I laugh. "Yeah, I'm not manager material. But hey, if you want a promotion after this, I'd be happy to let you fire everyone."

"Gee, thanks. That sure would boost my resume, though."

"Done. Congratulations on the promotion to manager. Now, make sure my shit is ready in the morning. We're getting Niku and K out first."

Serge frowns. "You really think that's a good idea? She's not exactly . . . forgiving."

"She's a fucking princess, dude. You want to stop the attacks? Giving back the rest of the royal family will do that."

"Okay, okay." He holds his hands up in surrender. "Good point. God, I wish you hadn't discovered quite so much about them."

Me, too.

• • • •

I SPEND THE EVENING pouring over my dad's Gulf maps, finding a good place to drop them off. I need something far enough away from humans that Clair and Huron will be safe, but close enough that we don't have to spend a night on the ocean again.

I settle on a spot just west of the Dry Tortugas—north of where we dropped Erie, and only three hours out. From what Erie said, it should be closer to the Seadom than where we left her, and people don't usually go that far out. Perfect.

We wake up early and get the transport tank into Niku's room. I explain how it works, and he dips his nose in a nod.

"How are we going to explain it to Clair and Huron?" Jen says.

That's a really good question. I was planning to show them by getting into it myself, but it would be a hundred times easier to use their own language. "We could let Niku explain it. Open the tube to the practice tank—we'll get all three from there."

I explain the new plan to Niku before moving the transport tank and crane to the practice room. When all three are together, Clair looks from Niku to the platform, where the electroshocker hangs on the wall.

"No one's going to shock you for speaking now, Clair. I promise."

She looks at Niku again—he must be translating—and her eyes narrow before she finally speaks in a whisper, then glances at the electroshocker again. When no one moves toward it, they have a short conversation. From there, it's fairly smooth. Clair and Huron get into the transport just fine, and don't try to attack us at any point. I can't believe that, in the end, it's going to be this easy to free the rest of the Mer.

"Time to head out?" Jen says.

"Actually, I'm going to take Serge on the first trip. We still have some things to work out, and I think, when he sees the reaction of the Mer to the open ocean, he'll realize that this is the right thing to do."

Jen smiles, then kisses me. "You're a good person, Finnegan Jarvis."

"You're the only one who thinks so."

Her smile softens. "Erie thinks so, too."

I finally smile, because that's true. She did.

Jen gives me another brief kiss. "Be careful, okay?"

I chuckle a little and push a piece of red hair behind her ear. "I'm not getting into the water with Clair. I'll be fine."

• • • •

ONCE WE'RE CLEAR OF the island, Serge crosses his arms, leaning against the helm. "You and Jen getting back together?"

Are we? I think Jen wants to, but I'm heading into my senior year of college. Do I want to be dating someone who lied to me? Do I want to be dating anyone at all right now? At least Jen understands my relationship with Erie, and doesn't think it's weird or gross.

"I don't know," I answer honestly. "I don't know what the fuck I want right now. My life was so perfectly planned out before Erie . . ."

The mangrove islands disappear behind us before either of us speaks again.

"I hope she was worth it." Serge's voice is soft. Not accusatory, just . . . sad.

"You met her."

"Yeah, but I wouldn't have traded Erie's freedom for my aunt's life."

I look at him, but he's staring at the water. I stare at the water, too, and I know that I wouldn't bring Aunt D back if it meant that Erie wasted away and foamed in that gray tank. Sergio and I will never agree on this.

Apparently, our friendship is another thing I'm willing to lose for Erie's freedom.

Miraculously, Huron survives the three-hour trip to the drop site. We release Niku first, so he can make sure it's safe, then Clair, then Huron. There's a bit of life in his eyes as he gets himself into the transport to leave the boat, and I honestly hope he makes it home from here.

Serge is impatient to get off the ocean, so he takes over the crane controls while I watch for Huron to pull himself free from the transport.

"All right!" I call, once he's out. "Bring it up."

Niku surfaces to breathe, and I remember the bag of necklaces. "Niku!" I yell. "I have something for Erie!"

I grab the bag, duck under the transport, and lean over the edge to drop it for him. The transport drips water on my head as it swings back to its position above the tank. Below, the bag of necklaces splashes and spreads out before the plastic fills with water and starts to sink. Even if the necklaces fall out, Niku can show Erie where they are.

"Shit!" Sergio says, and I turn just in time to see his surprised face as the transport swings back at me. It slams into my chest, and my foot slips on a puddle, sending me tumbling headlong over the side of the boat.

"Finn!" he yells.

I manage to take a breath before I hit the water, and I kick for the surface as both Niku and Huron yell, "Clair!"

Fuck.

Clair.

Pain lances through my back as her claws sink in and yank me down. I can feel them scrape against my ribs, and—horrifyingly clear—one slides between two ribs. There's a *pop* as it punctures my lung.

It takes everything I have not to scream and lose the air that's still in my lungs. Clair's behind me, so I can't grab for her gills like I did with Chlorine. No shocker. No wetsuit. No coworkers. I'm helpless.

She grunts in pain, and her claws tear from my skin. I whimper as her nails slice me, so sharp they're soft until the saltwater hits the wounds and pain flairs through me like a bristle worm sting. The surface is so far away, and my back is on fire with pain. I can *feel* the cold seawater seeping into my lung.

I'm going to die. I'm actually going to die this time—there's no way for Sergio or Erie to save me.

With a surge of adrenaline, I kick toward the surface, but my head buzzes with the need for oxygen, and my back is screaming in pain, and I'm so far away. I try to reach with my hands, but the pain in my back overwhelms me, overriding everything until I feel the familiar, smooth surface of Niku's dorsal fin against my palm. My muscles recognize this and react from memory, and Niku—who once tried to drown me himself—pulls me to the surface. I gasp air, coughing up blood and seawater, and look for the boat.

Where's the boat?

Clair must have dragged me farther than I thought.

Where's Clair?

Where's the fucking boat?

My heart speeds up even faster, and I cough again—all blood and foamy seawater. I'm turning into foam just like a damn Mer.

"Niku," I gasp. "Where's Clair?"

He dips his nose underwater a couple times. Right, his voice isn't audible in air. I let myself sink so my ears are under.

"Don't worry about Clair."

That sounds ominous, but if he's not worried about her, I won't be either. "Where's the boat?"

"Too far away for me to detect."

Fuck.

Okay, no time to panic. Serge saw me go overboard—he'll call the coast guard to look for me. They can bring an emergency helicopter.

Even a copter will take over an hour to get here—and then they have to find tiny me in this vast expanse of water. A shark will find me before they do. Does Serge even know *how* to call the coast guard? Can he pilot the boat? I didn't show him the controls . . . why didn't I show him the controls?

Another foamy, bloody coughing fit interrupts my panic with its sharp pain.

Niku nudges me, and I dunk my ears underwater. "What can I do?"

Nothing. There's nothing Niku can do. Tears begin to run down my face, dripping into the ocean, because this is it. I'm really going to die.

"Just . . ." I take a deep breath and cough up bloody foam. "Just tell Erie I'm sorry I couldn't get them all out."

He taps me under again. "Fuck that. Hold on."

Niku maneuvers so his fin is in my palm again, and the pain is horrible, but I hold on. When he dives just under the waves, I do my best to hold my breath, though I can still feel the cold seawater seeping into my punctured lung.

He swims until I can't hold on anymore. When my arm muscles finally give out, I float on my back instead.

He swims an agitated circle around me. "No sharks," he says. "We're close. I'll be back. Don't die."

Don't die. Ha. "Try my best," I say, and then cough, the foam more red than white now.

Niku leaves me alone in the middle of the damn ocean, turning to bloody foam. And, to be honest, I deserve this for all the Mer I foamed on land. No one will ever know what happened to me or find my body. Just like the Mer we stole from the Seadom.

Just like my father.

Chapter 70: Erie

Just as I predicted, my room of shells has been moved to a larger space, my mother's blackened shell still within the swirling pattern. There's a new blackened shell, too. The one that represents my abduction. I count the shells between that and the larger, bright white conch shell that celebrates my return to see how long I was gone. Finn spoke in hours, weeks, and months, but I never learned those measurements of time. This is my calendar, and there are one hundred and two shells between the abduction and the return.

One hundred and two days in that gray tank with the threat of "Corporate" hanging over my head. One hundred and two days as a prisoner instead of a princess.

My nails bite into my palms, still sore from the electroshocker burns. Clair's been there for double that time. I hope she's still alive. She was gone one hundred and thirty days before I was captured. It took them less than one hundred and two days to break me—no wonder they broke her before I arrived.

I remind myself again that Finn promised he'd get her out. And Huron. And Niku. My chest constricts at the thought of Niku, and it's almost as if I can hear his voice saying, "Princess."

"Erie."

That *was* Niku's voice. I spin.

He floats just inside the doorway, and I launch myself at him, spinning him upside-down before squeezing him so tight, I'm worried my tail will snap in half. Foam streams from my eyes as I bury my face in his familiar scars, then kiss him on the nose.

"Neek." The name is a strangled sound in my throat.

"Erie." He says it with force, but so low that no one else will hear. My name, just for me, because I forgot it for so long. "Princess," he says, louder, the echo of it etching into my scales. I *am* Erie, not Iodine. I'm a princess, and I belong here, in this castle under the sea.

"Finn's dying."

The words snap me out of my joyful reverie. "What? How? How do you know?"

"He fell off the boat, and Clair attacked him. I stopped her, but . . ." Neek looks at the shells on the floor. "He's not going to make it back to land. I brought him here, instead."

"Here?" My heart lurches in my chest. "He's in the Seadom?"

"Just a short swim away."

"Take me." I turn and swim out the door—

Right into a merman.

He grabs my arms to steady me, then releases me with a gasp, as if I've burned him. "Princess, forgive me." He bows so deep, the only thing I can see is his inky-black hair floating around his ear-fins.

Black hair and ear-fins. For the Tides. All the breath rushes out of me at once, and he looks up, concern in his brown eyes.

"Finn?" It's no more than a whisper of hope.

A shadow crosses his face. "Cale, my lady. You saved me from the boat."

Of course it isn't Finn—it can't be Finn. Niku just said Finn is dying. This is the same merman that I pushed out of the way at the hunt. The one with the strange nose. I never realized before that it's a landfolk nose. I reach my hand out to touch it before I remember myself and pull back, a warm flush covering my chest and cheeks. "Forgive me, I thought . . . never mind."

"You thought I was your landfolk boy—the one who rescued you?"

It's more a statement than a question, and the slight accent in his voice reminds me that Finn can't speak the ocean. This merman may have the same hair and eyes, and even a landfolk nose, but he's not my Finn. Niku nudges me hard. Finn's dying. I need to get to him.

"I . . . yes. I can see now that you aren't. I apologize." I almost bow, so used to being a prisoner instead of a princess.

"I'm glad he returned you safe. Please, don't let me keep you." He bows again.

I follow Niku down the hall, turning once more to glance at the strange features of the advisor.

"It's rude to stare," Niku says.

"He has a landfolk nose," I whisper.

"And you have landfolk hands," Neek says.

I fold my hands into fists, so the burns and missing webbing aren't noticeable. A nagging familiarity follows me through the halls; the sense that I'm forgetting something, something buried in my memory beneath layers of bubbles. When we get outside, I grab Niku's dorsal fin; my tail is still healing and will only slow us down. Thoughts of the advisor's disfigurement sloughs from my scales as we race through the water to get to Finn.

• • • •

IT'S A GOOD THING SHARKS are wary of getting too close to the Seadom, because as soon as we clear the safety of the petrified forest, I can taste the blood in the water. Finn floats at the surface, breathing shallowly, and every time his chest expands with air, bubbles leak from his back, along with a thin, constant stream of blood. His back is torn, and when I say his name, it chokes out of me on a strangled breath.

"Finn."

He moves to right himself, and groans. I wrap my tail around his legs, careful not to touch his back or squeeze too tight.

"Erie." He rests his cheek on the top of my head as I press mine into his chest. "I'm sorry, darlin'. I'm not going to be able to free the rest."

"Shh." I press my face harder into his chest. "You're going to be okay. Niku can get help."

Finn shakes his head. "No time." He pulls away to cough, and red foam floats away from us. I stare at it, heart burning with a desperate need to help him. There has to be something I can do.

"He can find a boat. Or . . . something. We'll think of something."

Finn wipes away the foam streaming from my eyes. "Just . . . take me back to the island. After. My dad disappeared in the ocean, and I want my mom to have a body to bury this time."

A shiver runs through him, head to toe, over and over. He's dying. It makes me think of one of the movies I watched—the one where the woman cried a tear and brought the monster back to life. I finally learned to cry, and I still can't save Finn.

He cups my cheek and smiles sadly. "I'm so glad I met you, love. You transformed me—everything about me. I'm going to die a better person than I lived."

I smile through the foam in my eyes. "I guess that story was true, after all," I choke out. "Merfolk can transform landfolk."

Finn chuckles and bows his head toward me, his hair shifting to reveal his ears.

His ears.

Just like the landfolk advisor.

His ears. His nose. His black hair—Merfolk don't have black hair.

Or noses.

Or ears.

A broken memory bubbles up. Delmara, "Corporate," ranting about something I didn't understand—a man named Cale . . . who disappeared, who left her to find the Mer.

The advisor's name was Cale.

By the Tides, it *is* true. I can transform Finn.

He grunts in pain, and I realize I'm squeezing him.

"Finn, it's true!" Desperation pierces me again, a different kind of warmth blossoming in my chest. "I can transform you!"

He chuckles again. "Usually, the person dying is the one who suffers from delusions."

I don't know the word, but I understand the meaning. "No *delusions*. I met a landfolk transformation in the Seadom. He had a nose and ears."

Niku interrupts, his voice completely stunned. "The advisor."

I turn to him, all excitement. "Yes!"

"For the Tides," Neek says. "I think you're right."

"What the fuck are you talking about?" Finn says.

"The advisor." I grin, hope growing. "I thought he was deformed, but he looks like a human with scales. He *is* a human with scales! The stories are true—I can transform you!"

"Erie," Finn says softly, as if I'm a child. "I'm drowning. There's a hole in my lung."

"Yes!" I sound a bit too excited about that, but I can't help it. "That's how it works. The stories say the human must drown first."

"And then what?"

I glance at Niku, who shrugs. "Instinct?"

"Instinct?" Finn barks out a laugh, then groans in pain and coughs up more bloody foam. "You want me to trust that you can transform me on *instinct*?"

"You're dying, anyway," Niku points out. "At this rate, you'll die from blood loss before you drown. And then, it probably won't work."

"It won't." I'm sure of it. Somehow, instinct has already taken over, and I know that if Finn bleeds to death, or dies in some way other than drowning, this won't work. "We have to fill your lungs with water."

He studies my face, takes a rattling breath, and coughs up more bloody foam. "You're asking me to die even faster. Immediately. What if it doesn't work?"

I grab his hand and place it over the scar on my chest, hoping he can feel the buzzing warmth that's growing there. "Trust me. It will work. I know it will."

At his unsure look, a bolt of fear goes through me, but Finn will die in my arms no matter what happens. Whether I can transform him or not.

"Please," I whisper. "Let me save *you* this time."

Tears run down his face to mix with the salt water. After an excruciatingly long time, he nods. "Okay." His voice is hoarse, and shakes with his fear. Or pain. Or both. "I trust you."

Every part of me fills with warmth at his words. I'm going to do this. I'm going to transform Finn into a merfolk.

"Okay," I say, breathless. "You have to drown."

"Erie." He studies my face again, terror in his eyes, and for a moment, I don't want to try this at all. "If this doesn't work, take me back to the island, okay?"

I nod. "I promise."

"Good." He smiles, but his lip quivers, and his eyes flood with tears again. "You'll have to hold me under. I'll try to surface otherwise." He runs his warm fingers down my face. "I love you, darlin.'"

"I love you, Finnegan Jarvis."

He closes his eyes and presses his forehead to mine. Then he dips his head into the water and presses his lips against my own. I pull him down so he's fully submerged and accept his breath for the last time. Even the air tastes like blood. I hope this works, and it's not already too late.

With his first gasp of water, Finn jerks hard in my grasp. His eyes fly open, panicked, and his fingers dig into my arms. The pain brings me back to reality.

I'm killing Finn.

All those times I wanted to steal his air, and now, I finally have and . . . I can't do this.

Bubbles burst from his mouth and nose, from the hole in his back. I unwind to push him to the surface, but Niku lunges forward and rips him from my grasp. He dives, dragging Finn with him while I scream.

By the time I reach them, there's no more bubbles or blood. No more foam. No light in Finn's eyes or life in his limbs, and I feel like the heat in my chest is going to rip me apart from the inside.

Now! Instinct screams through me. *Do it now!*

I press my lips to his again as warm water rushes from my mouth to his, filling any space inside him that still had air. When I pull away, Finn is pale, silent and still. All the heat that was inside of me turns to ice as I wait for something to happen. For it to work.

I press my hand to his chest, but Finn is cold. As cold as the tanks at Oceanica.

No.

It didn't work. Finn floats in the current because I finally stole his air.

"No," I whisper as foam streams from my eyes. "No, please."

I kiss him one last time, and a final bubble pops from the hole in his back.

Warm lips press against mine, but I have no air to give. Warm water rushes into my mouth, my throat, my lungs. It tingles with pinpricks of pain, like muscles waking after they've gone numb. The pain spreads through my chest to my legs and neck. From the crown of my head to my toes and fingers. Everything tingles and hurts.

Warmth spreads from the pricks, and a sharp pain in my lungs makes my back arch. It feels like Clair's ripped fresh wounds in my skin. The hairs on my arms and legs thicken. My legs seal together from the groin down, restricting my thrashing. I press my palms into my eyes—they feel like they're popping out of their sockets.

Scratches on my throat rip open.

Every muscle strains against my form and the pressure of the water around me. The sounds of the ocean have become one loud, high-pitched hum, and as my muscles give out, I realize that it's not the ocean I hear. I'm screaming.

I collapse in on myself all at once as the pain fades, and fall through the thick water until I tap the ocean floor and sediment plumes around me. I lay where I landed, unmoving.

A shadow swims closer, tentative, until it speaks in a soft voice that electrifies every piece of me. "Finn?"

I blink slowly as Erie comes into focus. More focus than I've ever seen her. Even in the dim light this far down, colors I can't describe flow across her body, like bioluminescence in every color of the rainbow, pulsing with her heartbeat. I try to touch the colors, but I'm distracted by the translucent webbing between my fingers. All of my tiny hairs have turned to scales, as alive with the dancing colors as Erie's own. I glance at my hand, then flip it over and wiggle my webbed fingers.

The scales extend up my arms, across my chest, and down my sides to my . . . tail. Everything below my waist has disappeared into a large tail, like hers, tipped in iridescent black. There's a slight divot between my legs, but other than that, it's Mer. *I'm* Mer.

I breathe out, but nothing leaves my mouth except the sound of my sigh. Water flows through my neck. I try to touch my gills, but Erie grabs my hands. "Be careful."

Her voice has so much depth now—it sounds like a song. Like a brook trickling over pebbles on its way to the crashing ocean. If she screamed at me, it would be a storm pounding the rocks on the shore.

I run my fingertips from the top of my neck to my shoulders, wincing at the pain in my newly ripped flesh. I have gills. Like a fish.

Erie gently takes my hands in hers, and now she's the one with human fingers. I gaze into her eyes—I thought they were endless before, but now I know the true meaning of infinity. I can see every bit of her. The flush of worry and excitement across her shoulders, the depth of concern in her eyes, even the way she holds her fins, closing me off from the world. Protecting me. I've only ever glimpsed the surface of her emotions before.

"Are you okay?" she breathes.

I run my fingers over her lips. They feel soft now, not like shark-skin at all. She's always been the most beautiful creature, but now, I no longer see her as a creature—a fish. How could a human ever compare to this? How did Erie ever see anything in me?

"You . . ." I pull her close and kiss her. A proper kiss, no water or air in the way. I kiss her long and deep, and she melts into me. When she wraps her tail around mine, it feels natural, though my legs could never have bent in such a way.

I understand now why my father went out in the storm, desperate to find the Mer. Why he was so enamored—obsessed enough to give his life for just one more glimpse. Like him, I've always felt like I belonged to the ocean, and now, with Erie's help, I do.

Corporate said the mermaids weren't dangerous, but it only took one of them to bring Oceanica down. And to give me a new life.

· · · ·

CONTINUE READING FOR a sneak peek at See The Depths, book two in the Speak The Ocean trilogy.

Don't want to miss a new release? Sign up for the newsletter at https://rebeccaenzor.com/

Chapter 1: Finn

The old stories say humans can become mermaids, but everyone knows that's a lie. I knew, even as cold water seeped into my lungs and blood seeped out. As Niku the dolphin grabbed my ankle and dragged me to the bottom of the Gulf of Mexico. As Erie pressed her lips to mine and breathed warm water into my lungs, expelling all the air inside.

I knew I couldn't become a Mer, even as the scratches on my neck ripped open, becoming gills, and all the hair on my body fused into scales, and my legs sealed together into a long, green tail tipped in a black so dark I could get lost in it.

And when I opened my new, large eyes and saw the mermaid before me, alive with colors humans can't even perceive, I knew everyone was wrong and the old stories were true. I've become a merman.

Erie's magenta-tipped tail wraps around mine, her eyes shining like the moon, and as she leans in for a kiss, her hand travels down my newly scaled stomach. I've never seen a sex organ on a male Mer, but as her fingers move with determined confidence, my now-hidden dick makes itself known.

"Whoa, darlin.'" I grab her hand and pull away, not yet used to the water that streams through my mouth as I speak. "Maybe let me get used to being a fish first, huh?"

The flush that covers her scales disappears as she frowns. "I'm not a fish."

"A sea-human then." I brush a quick kiss over her lips—soft now that I'm also a fish. "Let me get used to my tail, at least."

The flush returns as she brushes the magenta tip of her fin against me before unwinding her tail from mine.

Without thinking, I lift my arms like I'm treading water, although all it takes is a few flicks of my black-tipped tail fin and the dorsal fin that runs the length of my green-scaled back to stay afloat. Niku—Erie's dolphin bodyguard—snorts, and Erie giggles at my awkwardness.

"Ha ha." I lower my arms. "You grow legs and see if you're any better on land."

Erie gives a wistful little sigh and glances at the surface. "I would give anything . . ."

I know what she means. I gave up everything to become a Mer. My family, my friends, my future . . . all of it is lost to me. All of it except Erie, and the whole expanse of the Gulf of Mexico around us. All the fish, all the reefs, all the . . .

"That's a boat," Niku interrupts my thoughts. "We need to go."

My new senses are overwhelming, but after a moment I pick out the low rumbling of the motor. Is it my boat? Did my best friend, Sergio, figure out how to drive it after I tumbled into the water and was attacked by Erie's sister, Clair? What if I swim up to the surface—what would Sergio do? He'd freak out, of course, but . . . no. I can't let him know that humans can transform into Mer. If word got out about that, all sorts of stupid tourists would throw themselves into the water and get killed trying.

As it is, they'll all think I'm dead, and everyone will find it ironic that the man who saved a mermaid was then killed by her. Who knows what they'll do now. Close more beaches, hunt the Mer to their home, maybe get the Navy involved . . .

"Finn." This time it's Erie's voice that snaps me out of my thoughts. "Come on."

With one last look in the direction of the boat, I turn away to the deep, dark water. I'm a strong swimmer, but when I try to kick my former legs separately, I end up flopping in the water with an undignified squawk.

"Shut up," I say before either of them can laugh again.

Erie motions to Niku. "Let Finn grab your dorsal fin until we're away."

I hold on while Niku's powerful tail shoots us through the water. This was part of our routine at Oceanica Marine Park where Niku and Erie performed, so I'm used to the difficulty of holding on, and he's used to the extra weight, but now I can breathe while we glide through the water.

Niku slows once the sounds of the boat fade. This is Mer existence since humans discovered them—constantly on alert for boats. Oceanica paid a hundred thousand for each of their Mer, and with many of them dying from starvation or shock—or attacking a human and needing to be put down—the park was always happy to buy any Mer anyone could catch.

It wouldn't make financial sense, except they sold out every Mer show at max capacity. When you're the only mermaid marine park in existence, you can charge as much as you want for tickets—people will pay.

"We're close," Niku says as a shadow looms in the distance.

Erie grabs my hand. "I can't wait for you to see the Seadom." A rainbow of excited colors plays over her scales.

"I can't either, darlin.'" It's true—I've been curious about the Seadom ever since she accidentally mentioned it in Oceanica. She never talked much about home, and I didn't push her to since I wasn't sure she'd ever see it again. All I know is that it's west of Key West, somewhere in the Gulf of Mexico, and it's hidden well enough that humans haven't found it yet.

While we swim, I imagine the Seadom in some dark underwater cave, the only light coming down in weak shafts from holes in the ceiling. So when we reach the first dolphin guard, I'm not prepared for the *trees* that soar toward the surface in the distance. It looks like a winter forest—all dark branches with no leaves.

The guard dips his snout and "speaks the ocean," as Erie would say, which I can't understand, other than Niku's name.

"Finn," Erie says, pointing to me. "Finnegan Jarvis."

After months working with Niku, I've learned the nuances of dolphin body language, and this guard's says he's skeptical, but he's not going to question her. He says something in ocean-speak, ending with "Finnegan Jarvis."

The guard dips his snout at me, and I return the nod. I'm going to have to learn to speak the ocean quickly or this will be a difficult life.

We leave the guard to his duties and swim to the trees. When we get to the first one, I touch it, and it flakes. The trees were petrified—perhaps by a volcano long ago—and now the leafless branches reach toward a watery sun. The science-geek part of my brain clicks into overdrive as I try to figure out how this happened. "This is amazing! You live in a petrified forest?"

Erie giggles and grabs my hand again. "Not quite." She tugs me away from the coolest discovery since the Mer, but I continue to stare in awe at the trees as we pass through.

Until the forest thins and I stop swimming at the sight of the actual Seadom. My new, larger eyes are bombarded with colors—reds and purples and yellows and greens. A . . . field, I guess . . . of soft mushroom corals spreads out from the forest, ending at a reef, the likes of which I've never seen. It honest to god looks like a city—like the cover of *The Little Mermaid*—with limestone towers covered in polyps and bridges—bridges!—over what must be colder water currents. And everywhere there are Mer.

I'm struck dumb by the sight. The colors. The activity. The *size*. How the fuck haven't humans discovered this yet? It's probably big enough to see from a plane.

Erie grins as wide as I've ever seen her when she swims in front of me. "I knew you'd like it."

"Holy shit, darlin', this is . . ." I don't have the words to express how amazing this is. And then the guilt stabs me in the heart when I realize again that we ripped Erie away from *this* and trapped her in a tiny, gray tank for four months.

She spins around me, and I pull her close, hugging her tight. She spins us both through the water, laughing because she doesn't know where my mind's gone. Then she unwinds and tugs me forward. "Come on. There's so much to show you."

· · · ·

ERIE TAKES ME TO HER favorite spot in a garden of mushroom corals that are the same magenta as her hair and fins, then to the castle, where I once again get sidetracked looking at the walls. There are fish here that I've never seen, and I thought I knew all the reef fish in the Gulf and Atlantic.

"What was that?" I peer into a crevice where an unknown fish darted into the limestone.

Niku shakes his head. "Of everything in the Seadom, you're most curious about the dead trees and a common scaleglass angelfish."

"Humans don't even know that type of fish exists. It's amazing."

Erie pulls me along, ignoring the wide eyes of the merfolk who see me, until we reach a doorway on the right. She swims inside and spins. "This is my room."

It's almost the same size as the tank she lived in at Oceanica, with a couple openings to provide light, a limestone shelf where the shirt I gave her rests, and what looks like a giant jellyfish comb that she falls back onto with a sigh.

"Is that . . . your bed?" I didn't think Mer had beds. Or shelves. Or castles. My mind is working overtime trying to rearrange my preconceptions to fit all of this.

Niku pokes me with his nose. "Don't get any ideas."

I hold my hands up in surrender. "I'm still learning how to swim. I'm pretty sure any of those 'ideas' are beyond my capabilities right now."

The look Erie shoots me says she'll compensate for my inadequacies as soon as possible, and I feel a bit like prey. I'm not sure I'm ever going to be up for fish sex, but we'll cross that bridge when we get to it . . . hopefully never.

As Erie swims past me back into the hallway, her fins caress mine, and my stomach twists. I'm pretty sure that bridge is coming a hell of a lot sooner than I'd like.

I follow her down the hall until she turns through another doorway to the left. The room is massive, easily as big or bigger than the million-gallon arena where the Mer shows were held. Spreading across the floor in whorls and spirals are hundreds—maybe thousands—of shells. Clam shells, snail shells, even a few small conch shells. Some of them are unnaturally black. What sort of Mer weirdness is this?

I swim slowly above the patterns, tail moving as little as possible so I won't disturb them. I pluck a black shell from the floor and rub my finger over it—a smudge of black comes off on my hand. Ink? The black shells have somehow been dyed.

Erie joins me and says, very softly, "Huron. That's Huron's shell."

I drop it back into place. Huron was Erie's boyfriend before humans caught them and separated the two of them into isolated tanks in Oceanica. I freed him this morning with Clair. What happened to him? What happened to Clair? Niku told me not to worry about Clair, but what did that mean? A shard of ice runs through me at the thought of her nails piercing my lung, then being ripped away, and I glance at the dolphin before my attention is pulled back to Erie.

Her gaze sweeps the room. "You spoke of weeks and months, but this is how we tell time." She points to a small spiral. "Ten days," she says, then, pointing to a larger whorl made up of several spirals, "The rainy season." Then another. "The lobsters mate in the deep water." And one more. "Algae bloom in the north and drive the fish closer to the Seadom."

There are a few black shells in that swirl, and she picks one up, turning it in her fingers. When she arrived at Oceanica, her fingertips were blackened just like the shells. "When a merfolk is taken by a boat."

She sets it back down as I begin to count the other blackened shells. I don't need to—I know exactly how many Mer have passed through Oceanica, and, before that, through the tanks at the community college, KWCC, where Oceanica's owner, Delmara de la Cruz, did her research. If you count the first Mer my dad found and accidentally killed, that's eighty-four Mer we've captured in six years. I'm a monster.

Erie grabs a conch shell near the center of the room and wraps my hands around it. She looks into my eyes as she says, "The day I returned."

So far, Erie's the first Mer to return after being captured, and I almost didn't get to her in time. I place the conch shell back in its place while Erie swims to the back of the room where piles of shells sit, waiting to be used. She grabs another small conch shell and swims back, placing it in the very middle of the room's spiral design.

"The day you became a Mer." The smile on her face is large and bright.

I return her smile, although my insides churn with guilt. "I guess I'm official now."

Niku snorts. "You aren't official until you've met the king. Who won't be very happy about this, I might add."

"The . . . king?" I guess it's time to meet Daddy.

ACKNOWLEDGEMENTS

First, thank you to Laura Lamb, who's been my first reader and cheerleader from the start. I wouldn't have started on this publishing adventure without you, and I wouldn't have continued it either. And a huge thank you to M.A. Tyrskyluoto, who kept me writing even when I felt like giving up. I would still be writing pony fanfic without you pushing me to expand my creativity.

To Lev Mirov, who started me writing and was so patient, although I was *so* bad. And to everyone at DV, BTSR, C03 (and the Sisters), Other Worlds, Panacea, and the rest: you were all a part of this journey.

To my best friends and critique partners: Juliana Brandt, Courtney Moulton, and Michael Mammay. You helped me go from "aspiring author" to "published author," and have patiently listened to every rant and rave and always pushed me to do better. I would not be here without you.

To Cait Greer, who made the most amazing cover! I can't believe you took my "just no mermaid tails" and made such a gorgeous cover out of it.

To my first readers: Cameron Bearden, Erin Haubert, and Diana Beebe, who cheered for every chapter and pointed out early plot holes. You kept me writing that messy first draft even when I didn't want to. And to my Ream supporters, Liv and Reverie, who leave supportive comments and voted on which cover of the book to use (I agree with you!).

Thank you to Jenny Woods for answering my questions about a silly mermaid book (I'm sure that email came as a surprise). And thank you to Shaun Griffin, the actual Captain Shaun from the book, for answering my Key West questions.

A huge thank you to everyone who's read all or part of the book, in various stages: Amy Ravenel, Aly Mierzejewski, Brian Crawford, Lazarus Avery, Roselle Lim, Kurt Hartwig, Ryan Goodwin, Edward Branley, John Hilley, Lauren Spieller, Angela Perry, Jamie Howard, Melissa Barlow, Laura Weymouth, Kati Gardner, Samira Ahmed, Samantha Ervin, Eric Smith, and Kisa Whipkey.

To my coworkers, who listened endlessly about this book and the publishing process. You are all saints.

Thank you forever to my family, for always believing in me and supporting my dreams, no matter how wild they seem.

And to Jordan, who cooks me amazing food, and takes care of the animals, and teaches me to do scary things (but not mountain biking, sorry), and makes me leave the notebook at home to go out and enjoy life. I love you.

• • • •

About the Author

Rebecca Enzor is an environmental chemist in Oak Harbor, WA, where she lives with her husband, a cat, three dogs, and sometimes chickens. Obsessed with everything ocean, she studied fisheries biology in college and electrocuted herself collecting fish in a river, which inspired several key scenes in her debut novel, Speak The Ocean.

Her articles on writing science in science fiction can be found in Writer's Digest "Putting the Science in Fiction".

For more about Rebecca's work, please visit rebeccaenzor.com

Read more at rebeccaenzor.com.